Adrian Grafe

The Ravens of Vienna

Addison & Highsmith

Addison & Highsmith Publishers

Las Vegas ◊ Chicago ◊ Palm Beach

Published in the United States of America by
Histria Books
7181 N. Hualapai Way, Ste. 130-86
Las Vegas, NV 89166 USA
HistriaBooks.com

Addison & Highsmith is an imprint of Histria Books. Titles published under the imprints of Histria Books are distributed worldwide.

Library of Congress Control Number: 2022932285

ISBN 978-1-59211-138-1 (hardcover)
ISBN 978-1-59211-287-6 (softbound)
ISBN 978-1-59211-291-3 (eBook)

One

Stretching out from the chestnut and lime trees, shadows invaded his office overlooking Schwarzenberg Platz that late afternoon.

'I'm just on my way out,' he called.

As he turned toward the window, the street lamps came on as though sparked into life by his glance. He gazed at the monument, finding Karl Philipp's triumphalism and his hat a little silly in these days, although perhaps they had always been silly. Motorists in a hurry sounded their horns, sirens blared. A nightjar took flight. He started as he recognized the man's voice telling the secretary in the lobby: 'I'm here to see Lichtblau.'

He got up from his desk and walked over to the pegs on the wall to pick up his coat and hat. He had his back to the door and, as it opened, he paid no attention.

He felt a hand on his arm.

'Not so fast, Lichtblau. Inspiration hurrying you?'

'Hellroth, I've already told you. The bank can't let you have any more. This is people's money we're talking about. Everybody's money. Not just Jewish money.' Felix Lichtblau glanced with revulsion at the swastika on the German's armband.

'I don't care whose money it is. My life's on the line if I don't come up with the goods.'

'Your problem, not mine. Anyway, you haven't balked at putting my own life on the line and the lives of hundreds of our employees,' replied Lichtblau, slipping into his coat.

'Cigarette?' said Hellroth.

'How much?' asked Lichtblau, refusing the offer with a wave of his hand.

Hellroth named his figure. He had known Lichtblau for some time and had always liked his fearlessness combined with a kind of innocence, if not naivety. This made Lichtblau reckless at times, so little store did he seem to set by his own life and person.

'I can get two-thirds of that for you. But this is the last time. The other third you will have to find elsewhere.'

Lichtblau drew a key from his coat pocket and unlocked a cabinet door. He took out a checkbook and put it on his desk. He sat down on the chair behind his desk and looked as though he was about to write the check when the German snatched the checkbook away from him and then spat on the floor.

'I should have spat in your face. Maybe I will, one day.'

'Maybe you will,' said Lichtblau, 'for all the good it'll do you.'

'I don't believe in good or bad,' said Hellroth, writing the figure he had just told Lichtblau on a check and flinging the checkbook back at him. 'Sign.'

'I've told you. Two-thirds of that is all I can let you have.'

'Sign,' repeated Hellroth, taking out a pistol stuck in his belt, previously hidden from Lichtblau behind his jacket. 'Whether you do or not, I'm sure we'll be seeing each other again soon enough at Morzinplatz.'

'Shoot me dead right now if you like, race fanatic. Take me to Morzinplatz. You may think you're living in one of those *Flaktürme* of yours. History and your enemies will prove you wrong.' He stared the Nazi down. 'That's all the bank can give you. That's all you'll get from anyone in Vienna at this time. Take it or leave it.'

Hellroth flipped the pistol round in his hand so that he was holding it by the barrel. He made as if to strike Lichtblau over the head with it. Lichtblau caught the German's arm.

'What point is there in harming me? It won't bring you an inch closer to the money you want. And I'm sure your superiors would be interested to know about the two Jewesses. Perhaps they are not as discreet as you would like them to be.'

'Leave them out of it, Lichtblau.' Hellroth hardly blinked now at how much Lichtblau knew. 'If I find out they've given away anything about me, I'll kill them or have them killed. Sooner or later, they'll be done for anyway.'

'I wouldn't be so sure about that if I were you. Maybe some other SS officer is interrogating them right at this minute. And learning lots of juicy facts about you.'

'Where are they?' said Hellroth. 'Where have they disappeared to?'

'You'll have to find that out for yourself. I'm not your informant.'

'You mentioned them first.' Hellroth tried to keep calm.

'You haven't seen them for a few weeks, have you?' Lichtblau said. 'You must have been wondering where they'd got to.'

'That's enough, Lichtblau', replied Hellroth, 'you may have the money —'

'I do have the money,' said Lichtblau.

Hellroth studied Lichtblau's face. He felt outwitted. 'Two thirds, then.'

'You have the power, and you can kill us at will, Hellroth,' Lichtblau said, picking up the checkbook, ripping out and tearing up the page on which Hellroth had written his desired amount, wrote out a tenth of that sum on the next page, signed the check and tore it off down the perforated line. He tendered it to Hellroth, but when Hellroth took it between his fingers, Lichtblau did not let go of it.

'You can kill us all, I say, but you won't have the last word.'

'I'll be the judge of that, Lichtblau', replied Hellroth, pulling the check out from Lichtblau's hand and turning on his heel, 'You'll be hearing from me. I always knew there was something weird about those two Jewesses. When I see them again —'

'If you see them again,' said Lichtblau.

'One of them's got a kid,' said Hellroth, 'and we're holding him.'

'What did you intend to do with the boy?' asked Lichtblau.

'Use him. Extort information from him. Torture him. Kill him. He was already being most —'

'Cooperative? I'm sure he was, the way you were treating him.'

But Lichtblau kept his ear to the ground and knew more than even Hellroth did. While the young man had been held at the Metropole, some kind of squabble had broken out, with some of the guards fighting over loose women who had entered the building and brought drink with them. Then, they had started propositioning the men, including the officers and the guards at the door. The boy managed to slip out during the commotion. The front door was left unlocked. The guards were too busy to bother with him and just let him go.

'I'll treat you a thousand times worse,' Hellroth felt that.

'You've got as much money as I can give you. Even that amount is more than we can spare here at the bank. As for the boy, he's out of here.'

It was a strength of Hellroth's — his only one — to have realized he was possessed of, at best, average intelligence and a weakness to be unduly impressed by the intelligence of others. But Lichtblau really did always seem to be one step ahead of him. Hellroth lit his cigarette and pondered a while.

'I'll have all the kid's classmates brought in for questioning. I'll have them — and you — tortured until you beg to tell us everything you know.'

'Go ahead,' replied Lichtblau, 'I can guarantee it won't get you anywhere. Anyway, I'm sure your father would be interested to learn exactly what you get up to here in Vienna. Still hero-worshipping his little boy, is he? Still has all those photos of you in uniform all over his living room, has he?'

Hellroth gaped at him, so amazed that the cigarette between his lips fell to the floor.

Lichtblau had gathered from previous conversations with Hellroth that his father was something of a sensitive spot with Hellroth. At the mere mention of his father, his behavior would become unstable: he'd either get violent or break into tears. Lichtblau glanced at Hellroth as he puffed on his cigarette and tried to assess the impact of his words on his enemy. Hellroth's mouth was twitching, seemingly uncontrollably. Finally, Lichtblau tried pushing his luck a little further:

'So how are things then... at 9, Friedrichstrasse in Munich?'

Hellroth had come to suspect Lichtblau of leading a double life. He had had him followed once or twice but had never been able to pin anything specific on the man. Lichtblau did not ask him what he wanted or needed, the money for, and Hellroth had come to accept Lichtblau — and this was his main problem with him — as someone you could always threaten with torturing or killing, but whom you could not manipulate. He did not answer Lichtblau's question, which, in this conversation at least, was the latter's victory. He simply smiled at him haughtily in an attempt to save face. He, the German invader, needing to save face in front of a slimy Jewish Austrian banker, the irony of it! He walked out of Lichtblau's office, still holding the check in his hand.

When Hellroth had gone, Lichtblau waited a few moments to let the officer lose himself in the streets among the rare strollers and the night shadows assaulting the city. He wrote a note telling his colleagues in the check payment department to put a block on the check he had just written for Hellroth (he always told them to block such checks, and they did), then delivered the note to their office himself. He would have to get to the two Jewish women before Hellroth found out he had been lying and made them all pay for his lie with their lives. He then finally put his hat and coat on and walked out of his office building. As he wended his way home through the streets, he occasionally nodded either to passers-by or to soldiers patrolling. Two or three he had managed to bribe into informing him of Nazi plans and movements or helping him in other ways (what was money for, after all?). As he crossed Heldenplatz, he spat on the ground and urinated on the plinth of the statue of the Archduke — a futile but, to his mind, symbolic gesture of resistance to annexation and the whole nightmare that followed. The corona shining around a street lamp dazzled him for a second and then faltered. He wondered if he, and if they all, would get out on the other side of this war, this nightmare, which they had neither caused nor deserved. He became lost in musing as he thought of his wife and children.

A few blocks away from his apartment building in the Favoriten, someone hissed to him — 'Pssst!'— from inside the darkness of a doorway. When he approached, he saw the face of a boy of perhaps about seventeen, looking out at him.

'Sir, we've never met, but I know all about you, and you know all about me, too.'

Lichtblau realized at once who it was. 'You must be Thedel. Where's your mother at present, and why aren't you with her?'

'She said we had to split up if we wanted to survive. She said I had a good chance of surviving as I have never been circumcised, and with my light brown hair and fair skin, I'm told I don't look Jewish. The soldiers took me away to the Metropole for questioning. They said they wanted to know everything about me and where my mother and her girlfriend were. But I got away from them quite rapidly. I knew you lived near here. And my mother has since disappeared, along with her friend. Maybe my mother's dead.'

'What do you want me to do for you?'

'Mother said you would take me in. She said if I asked you to help me, you would feel I were trying to help you.'

Lichtblau knew that was true: all his life, he had felt that every request he had ever received came from people who were really trying to help him. He had felt it was so, even as a member of the executive board of his bank, when he had to deal with the problems of the war, with people, good people, sometimes poor people, who needed loans fast and had no immediate prospect of paying them back.

'Hellroth and his men will probably be looking for you.'

'Hellroth won't think to look for me at your place. He needs you, or thinks he does, so I don't think he'll bother you at your home. I won't stay long. In two or three days, I'll be going. My mother said to keep moving on.'

In this world grown so threatening, where reason and hope had all but vanished, Lichtblau felt there was something determined about the young man that forced his respect and, in the circumstances, aroused his sympathy.

'I'll tell the children you've come to give them a little tuition.'

Two

'A couple of days will be fine,' Thedel said. 'And don't worry, I'm not expecting you to turn your home into a hostel for refugees on the run from the police and the Wehrmacht; in fact, I think we may be able to help each other.'

Lichtblau felt that with each new day the Nazis were tightening their stranglehold on the city and the country. Many of his friends had left for England, the United States or, like his novelist friend Stefan, Brazil. A few had bought safe conduct out of the country, either with money or information. Kristina Lichtblau's brother had managed to get to New York and was able to keep them informed about the Allies' progress. But it might only be a matter of time before he and his family were deported or killed where they were. He could hear it with his inner ear: the noise of time. The Nazis — wrongly — considered him useful to them because of his connections to money in Austria and abroad, and for some reason unknown to himself, he seemed to have managed to stave off Hellroth, but that could only be short-lived. Both money and safety were in ever-shorter supply in Vienna. He felt he would not be surprised if the knock at the door did come.

And come it did. He and Kristina were asleep when they heard footsteps and voices — drunken voices — on the wooden staircase leading to their flat. A cat squealed, and a man's voice laughed. 'Kick it to the bottom of the stairs!' Then there were two thumps: one on the staircase and another against the front door of the Lichtblaus' flat.

'Open up this second, or we'll shoot the lock, and then it'll be your turn! Open up!'

The whole incident took place in the most utter confusion. Kristina shrieked, pulling at the soldiers' lapels, begging them to leave her family alone. But the soldiers, whose breath smelt of drink, had clearly heard similar pleas countless times before: they just wanted to expedite their routine duty and return to their bacchanalia. However, Kristina's shrieking did have one positive impact on the situation: in the heat of the moment, the soldiers took only the couple and seemed to have been unaware of, or forgotten, the existence of the two Lichtblau children. The two boys had been so happy at Thedel's presence that they had taken to sleeping in the spare room under the eaves, which was currently Thedel's room. Thedel motioned to them not to make a sound. They bit on their pillows as their tears flowed. Once their parents had left with the soldiers, Thedel again signaled to them to keep quiet. They fell asleep after a while. But Thedel lay awake in his bed until dawn, thinking. Then he fell into a fitful sleep.

In the morning light, over a silent breakfast with the boys, he wondered whether the Nazis would come back for them. It fell, then, to Thedel, who was barely an adult himself, to take charge of the Lichtblau boys in war-torn Vienna. He felt himself now at even greater risk than before but could not abandon the family who had so uncomplainingly taken him in. From being protected, he had turned protector, as circumstances demanded. He considered it impossible for the two boys, Heinrich and Johannes, to go back to school. He decided their best course of action, if not their only one, was to try and get to the friends of his mother with whom he intended to stay after leaving the Lichtblaus. He did not know how to move around the city without being recognized, if only by the guards and soldiers to whom he had given the slip while at the Metropole. But he would learn quickly — he had no choice, and, besides, he was tall for his age. Heinrich, the more imaginative of the two Lichtblau boys, suggested that Thedel get hold of a pair of horn-rimmed spectacles. He would be able to wear some of Lichtblau's clothes, and along with the spectacles, plus the fact that he would be accompanying two smaller boys, he would look quite unlike the boy he had seemed to be at the Metropole.

Either by coincidence or sensing that he might not be with them long, Lichtblau had happened to give each of his sons a considerable amount of cash on the evening he and his wife were taken away. When they told Thedel they had money, he began to work out a scheme for them to get to his mother's friends by taxi, and after that, use the money to escape from the country. First, though, they had to negotiate with the taxi driver. Thedel took the precaution of giving him a vague address some minutes' walk from his mother's friends'. But after a couple of minutes, the driver suddenly grew bemused or curious.

'So, where are you running away to?'

The boys were silent for a second. Then Heinrich found the courage to speak. 'We're not running away. We're just going to see some friends.'

'I recognize your complexions. I can smell your smell. You're Jew-boys, aren't you?' The taxi driver seemed to be getting more unpleasant by the second. 'I could turn you straight in to the authorities now. And doubtless get handsomely rewarded for doing so.'

'You could do, but you won't,' said Thedel.

'I will,' smiled the taxi driver.

'Not for now, you won't.' Thedel pressed the barrel of a pistol against the side of the man's neck and pulled the trigger back with a click. 'Pull over here.'

The taxi driver did as bidden. Thedel told the boys to get out of the taxi.

Thedel said to Heinrich, 'Write down the taxi's registration number and number plate.'

Then he turned to the taxi driver. 'I'm not in the business of killing, but if you carry on trying to hand over your passengers to the Nazis, you won't live much longer.'

'Shoot me or let me go,' said the taxi driver, glancing at his watch and shrugging as though this sort of thing were nothing new to him and his very life worthless.

'Great free ride,' said Thedel getting out of the car, 'or rather not so great.' He was tempted to shoot the glass out of one of the car windows, just for the pleasure of riling the man, but thought better of it. The spirit of vengeance and hatred plagued the air they breathed quite enough as it was. He grabbed Heinrich and Johannes by their jacket sleeves, and together they ran into an alleyway out of sight of the taxi driver. Within a few minutes, they reached the friends' address his mother had given him. He had never met those friends. They opened the door to him and looked surprised when not one but three boys walked into their flat.

The surprise proved mutual. Three people greeted the boys: two men and a woman. Thedel's mother had led him to expect only a man named Markus Jäger and his wife, Ursula. Jäger introduced the other man as his brother. He said he and his wife had been friends of his mother for some time and were delighted to meet her son, about whom they had heard so much. Markus Jäger, his wife, and his brother Josef at once recognized the two Lichtblau boys. Thedel wondered whether he could trust any of the three, especially the brother.

Thedel, in fact, recognized Markus Jäger's brother, though he — the brother — did not seem to recognize Thedel. Thedel had seen him on several occasions when he had gone to the Café Central or coffee-houses on the Kärntner Ring with his mother for hot chocolate. He had even been introduced to him once or twice. Every time Thedel had seen him, he had been in the company of a different woman. One of those women, he now realized, had been Kristina Lichtblau, not yet married at the time.

Jäger and his wife decided the three boys would sleep in the same room. The Jägers did not question Thedel in any detail about his presence or about the Lichtblau boys, seeming to take it as part of the unsettled nature of life in wartime Vienna, where every day brought some new event, and people would appear, disappear and reappear — or not — almost as a matter of routine. Thedel told them he had taken the boys under his wing while his own mother and the boys' parents had urgent business to attend to. He kept the fact that he had once seen the brother with Kristina Lichtblau to himself. But he wondered whether Josef Jäger, the brother, remembered him at all. He did not seem to. It was true that Thedel would look unrecognizable now to anyone who had known him as a child but had not

seen him for a few years. He remembered Josef Jäger had a shadow of a scar beneath his right ear and, at the breakfast table the next morning, Thedel inspected
the side of the man's face to see whether he still had his scar. He had.

'What are you looking at?' Josef Jäger asked him.

'I was just thinking...' replied Thedel.

Josef Jäger yelled in irritation. 'You were looking at my scar but won't admit
it!' His brother, their host, told him to calm down.

'We've met before,' Thedel went on. 'When I was a child, I sometimes used to
go to the Café Central with my mother. I think I saw you there. That's all.'

Josef Jäger looked perturbed at the mention of his past, especially at the name
of the Central. 'Halcyon days...' he murmured. No-one spoke for fear of interrupt-
ing his reverie, but Thedel again sensed that Josef Jäger was not to be trusted
(though who could be trusted in Vienna in 1940 with the city overrun with Nazi
soldiers and spies, and so many trying to profit from the war any way they could?).
Thedel tried to convey with his eyes his feeling about the man to Heinrich and
Johannes.

Heinrich broke the silence:

'And just how did you get your scar?'

Josef Jäger exchanged looks with his brother and sister-in-law. He got up and
walked over to the window. He looked out, lit a cigarette and drew on it. Then he
went back to the table and sat down again. There was a carving knife in front of
him. He picked it up and fiddled with it as he spoke, sometimes running his thumb
along the blade. He looked at Heinrich.

'Thedel is right. I often used to go the Central. And I still do. I'm a freelance
journalist. When I had nothing else to do, I used to go and sit in the Central and
watch the customers. I often used to see the same faces. They also came to know
my face, and sometimes we would get into a conversation. My various employers
used to give me money to buy people drinks. I would talk with spies, foreign

correspondents, psychoanalysts, all people who were privy to secrets they would sometimes allude to under the influence of drink and like-minded company.

'There was one man I never did to talk to, at least not until later. But I couldn't help noticing him. He dressed smartly but soberly, not flashily. He was elegant but without looking as though he wanted to impress. Besides, he didn't seem to care what anyone might think of him. I noticed that people would often go and speak to him when he was sitting alone. He himself would sometimes pass from table to table exchanging a few words here and there. He inspired trust. That was the impression I got of him. People confided in him and seemed to sense that he would not betray their secrets. There seemed to be something discreet, priest-like even, about him. He did not appear to notice me, and I had no reason to speak to him. But one day, things changed. He started coming to the Central accompanied by a woman. I was already intrigued by this man but grew even more so now because of seeing him with this woman. She at once struck me as quite different from most of the other women I was used to seeing at the Central. She differed, in fact, from almost all other women I had ever seen. She looked as though she were, in a way, the female counterpart to the man, so that, despite my having grown used to seeing the man on his own, I was not at all surprised to see him with this particular woman. She had long blonde hair, wide-open blue eyes I wanted to drown in, and fine, delicate features. Her eyes were not only wide-open; they rarely left his. She sought out his gaze constantly and held it.

'After seeing them together a few times, I began to grow envious of him, of his so effortlessly having won the heart of this woman who seemed as near to perfection as it is possible to be. I already begrudged him his popularity, but this was too much for me. I asked one or two people I knew a little and whom I had seen talking to the man, 'Who is the lady?' They did not answer by telling me her identity: they merely confirmed what was already all too obvious. She was his fiancée, and they were shortly to be married.

'Once, the lady came to the Central on her own. She looked happy. She arrived with a light song on her lips. I heard it. She scoured the café for her fiancé, I

presumed. Then, not finding him, went and sat at a table. I went over to her and asked her whether I could have a word with her. She agreed. I invited her to my table, but she declined. I then asked her if I could sit at hers. She refused, too, politely but firmly. She showed no interest as to why I should want to speak to her. She remained silent, waiting for me to have my say. I simply told her I loved and adored her. She looked at me for a second, narrowing her blue eyes, and asked me to leave her alone. But I couldn't. I just couldn't. There I was, rooted to the spot. A man at the next table overheard the lady telling me to leave her alone. He stood up. 'You heard what the lady said. Now go back to your own table, and there won't be any trouble.'

'Who's causing any trouble?' I said, 'This is none of your business.' A waiter came over to the man and whispered a few words in his ear. Then the man said to me, 'They want us both to leave. We'll settle this outside.'

'Yes, we will,' I replied.

'When we got outside, the man said to me, 'I hate men who bother women.'

'I wasn't bothering her,' I replied.

'Then why did she tell you to leave her alone?'

'Not your business,' I replied, at which he lunged forward and punched me in the stomach. I reeled backwards, and he held me down with his knee across my chest and one hand on my throat.

'She's spoken for,' he said, 'leave her alone. Understand?'

At this, I spat in his eye. He drew a knife and, still holding me down, made as if to slit my throat but at the last second nicked me beneath the ear.

'Stop,' I heard a woman's voice say.

The man and I were equally astonished. The beautiful woman from the café was standing over us. There was a glint in her eye, and she looked half-amused. 'Get up, both of you. Hand me the knife.' We got up, and my adversary gave her his knife. Then addressing me, she said: 'Now let me see to this wound.' But if her air had been one of amusement, it soon departed. 'How dare you use violence of this kind?' She took a vial of antiseptic lotion from her handbag, poured a little on her handkerchief, and dabbed the cut behind my ear. I had lost some blood.

'That's how I got my scar,' Josef Jäger concluded, looking at Heinrich. He and Johannes did not realize, as Thedel did, that Jäger had been talking about the boys' mother.

Josef Jäger turned to Thedel. 'The Central is still there. But to me, it seems to belong to another lifetime, another era. I can't say I remember meeting you there.'

'I was smaller then.'

'Who is your mother?'

Josef Jäger studied the adolescent's face. Thedel again sensed he could not trust Josef Jäger and did not know whether or not to trust Markus Jäger, despite his mother's friendship with him and his wife. Markus Jäger knew his mother and might well find it strange if he lied. Nevertheless, he decided to lie. If Markus Jäger considered his reply unsatisfactory or provocative, he would surely let him know. Thedel decided to make up a name at random and uttered it.

Neither Markus Jäger nor Josef Jäger showed any response. Josef Jäger just looked at him closely again, then glanced at his brother before looking away. His brother said:

'I think it's time for you boys to go and do some work. Thedel will help the boys do their schoolwork.'

Thedel and the brothers returned to their bedroom, where Thedel once again spent hours awake, troubled by Josef Jäger and his story and feeling unsafe with him and his brother and sister-in-law.

Three

The SS had been interrogating the Lichtblau couple in separate cells for hours on end. They kept up the pressure on them, trying to spot discrepancies between their respective stories. They suspected Lichtblau of working against them. At the same time, they thought that he was supplying Hellroth with large sums of money that they assumed Hellroth used to serve the Führer's cause. They went easy on Lichtblau for this reason, telling him that the kind of interrogation they were putting him through was routine, and they welcomed his helpful attitude towards Hellroth. However, they also insinuated that if he did not confess to taking part in resistance activities against the Führer and the Reich, and tell them who else was involved, they might have no alternative but to put pressure on his wife. What surprised them was that when they put this to Lichtblau, he did not even wince. Even when they brought him a note from his wife, in her handwriting and purportedly in her own words, begging him to tell them what they wanted to know, he still showed no reaction.

The chief interrogator in charge of the Lichtblaus was Hermann Georg. Several of his underlings came to him and told him they would be delighted to go to work on Kristina Lichtblau and then take her to Lichtblau to show him the results of their work. They were prepared to torture her in front of her husband if Georg gave the word. Georg told them to go and tell Lichtblau that if he did not reveal everything he knew about anti-Reich activities in Vienna, his men would torture his wife in front of him. Again, Lichtblau kept perfectly calm. He said that he was unable to help them with their inquiries and that they could torture and kill his wife or anyone else, but that that would not enable him in the slightest to further their investigations. He told them to their faces that they were stupid and wasting their time, and that if the Führer or even Hellroth were to find out that they had mistreated him or his wife — especially his wife — they would be risking their own lives for nothing. Georg's men suggested they torture Frau Lichtblau anyway since there was every likelihood that Lichtblau was bluffing. Georg told them that the Reich needed the Lichtblaus and that she, in particular, was not to be harmed.

Georg went to see Lichtblau a few days into his captivity. 'I have received a telegram ordering us to harm Kristina.'

'I don't know why that is,' Lichtblau replied. 'And I don't need to know why. Your telegram is your own affair. Just tell me whether or not we are free to go.' It was true that all Georg's attempts at interrogating and unsettling Lichtblau had proved fruitless. Georg let them go the following day.

As Lichtblau and his wife were walking away from the Metropole, once they were out of earshot and eyeshot, Lichtblau turned to his wife and said:

'I knew you had contacts, but I did not know they ran quite that high.'

'Will we ever know everything about each other?'

'We must get to the boys,' he said, 'and decide on our next move. Perhaps we and the boys will not be so lucky next time if these barbarians send men less stupid next time, or soberer.'

'The boys could join up with Thedel for a while. I know a man — or, rather, I used to know a man — who may be able to help us.'

'You and your men,' replied Lichtblau. 'Who's the man?'

'His name is Alfred Nubik. He's someone I used to see at the Central. Perhaps he even still goes there. If he's still alive, of course. I think he will agree to help us if only I can find him.'

'Shall we go to the Central now?' asked her husband.

'I'll go,' she replied, 'you must get back to your office. The bank will be falling apart without you.'

'I'm leaving the bank.' His wife stopped dead in her tracks. Lichtblau carried on walking for a split second, and then he halted too and turned to her. 'I've handed in my notice. I've had another offer. I'll have a good salary and won't be handling other people's money anymore.'

'So, what will you be doing? Why didn't you tell me about this?'

She stopped accusing, and they fell silent. They carried on walking till they were quite near the city center. They passed a man who looked like a businessman. He wore a dark suit and tie, had a short-cropped beard and mustache, and carried a briefcase. The man had black hair. The Lichtblaus both knew him by sight and nodded to him as they passed him. Suddenly Lichtblau felt a hand on his shoulder. He turned round. It was the businessman-type fellow. Kristina turned round, too.

'Who are you?' Lichtblau said to him.

'I know your wife,' replied the man, 'and she knows me.'

'What's your name?' said Lichtblau.

'I used to speak with your wife sometimes at the Central,' he replied, looking at Kristina again.

'Nubik!' she said, 'I've often felt there was something familiar about you.'

The man spat on the ground. 'The life I had, the life we all had, is long over. Now we may be tortured or killed from one day to the next.'

'You look perfect, Alfred!' laughed Kristina. 'Haven't the Nazis tried to find where or who the real Alfred Nubik is?'

'They probably have, but I'm not too bothered about the real one at the moment. I'm too busy playing Wilhelm the businessman. As soon as the Nazis arrived, I went undercover for a few weeks. When I surfaced again, it was like this. I once ran into a group of Nazi soldiers on the street who didn't know me. They asked me where I lived in Vienna. I took so long telling them that they grew fed up with listening. Finally, one of them rammed his machine-gun butt into my stomach, and I started screaming and moaning. One of them wanted to shoot me dead right on the spot because he found the noise I was making too abhorrent.

But one of the others mentioned the name of a tavern quite nearby, and they all lost interest in me and walked off.

'A few days later, I happened to spot the same group of five soldiers out on patrol. I went into an empty disused building I could see they would be walking past. I fired a pistol with a silencer on it at them through an open window and killed three of the five of them instantly. The other two ran off. They didn't know where the shots had come from. I left the building I was in by a back door. I then took a circuitous way round, putting my pistol in a safe place where I knew I would find it again, and went back to where the three soldiers had fallen to see if the bodies were still there. They weren't. Some of the soldiers and policemen who were there noticed my interest in the scene and asked if I had seen a gunman running away. I said I hadn't, and they did not detain me.'

'Well, well,' said Kristina, 'I never thought I'd live to see Alfred Nubik turn killer.'

'This is war, and we're all fighting for our lives.'

'And each other's. And our freedom,' said Kristina.

'Ah yes, each other's, and our freedom,' Nubik assented.

'We need your help, Alfred.' Kristina's face had darkened.

'Anything!'

'We're looking for somewhere to place the boys for a while, out of harm's way. We gather they're staying with some friends of ours for the time being, along with an older boy, a lad named Thedel —'

'I know Thedel. Tall boy, looks older than his years. Quite mature. Quick thinker.'

'How do you know him?' asked Lichtblau.

'Same way as I first met your wife: from the Central. His mother used to take him there. He kept in touch with me till a little before —'

'Before you became a businessman?' said Kristina.

Nubik nodded.

'That makes things easier for us. We'll tell him we've asked you to help him and the boys.'

'I don't want him to know it's me, or at least not yet. You're practically the only ones in Vienna who know. My life is in danger, or will be if anyone identifies me as responsible for the three soldiers' deaths. Some of the Reich boys at the top may already suspect me of being not quite the businessman I seem, although I do what I can to allay their suspicions with my —'

'With your supplies?' Lichtblau said. Nubik nodded.

'What can you do for Thedel and our sons?' Lichtblau asked.

'I can help get them out of the country, to England, say. They would be safe there and might even prove an asset to Churchill in the fight against the Führer.'

'How do you propose to get them out?'

'I need time to think. I'll need money — not for myself but to help smooth their way and solve any hitches they may encounter. They'll need passports. Will one or both of you be going with them?'

'I will stay here,' Lichtblau said, 'I must fight the Reich and fight it from within the country. Kristina will, I hope, go with them. I think I can find someone in England the boys can go to.'

'Your contacts will be useful. I'm sure the boys will be well taken care of in England, as long as they survive the journey and nobody stops or betrays them to the Reich on the way. Meet me here in a week's time, and I'll tell you then whether or not I can help you.'

'A week from today?' Lichtblau said.

'That's right,' said Nubik, 'as long as we're all still alive.'

They agreed to meet at the same time and place a week later. The Lichtblaus went one way and Nubik the other. Kristina looked over to the other side of the road and saw Josef Jäger walking the same way as her and her husband, and looking at them. She realized at once he had seen everything. Lichtblau looked back and forth from one to the other.

Jäger walked over to them and said, 'That's funny. I've just come from my brother's. Your sons and the boy Thedel are with him and his wife. I was just telling them how I got my scar.' He smirked and looked Kristina in the eye.

'Kristina, you haven't changed. What were you discussing with Alfred?'

After the Anschluss, Lichtblau had distrusted all journalists, this one above all. He answered before his wife could say a word:

'If it's any of your business, we happen to know he's very much alone. We were asking him how we could help him.' Lichtblau loathed himself for lying and for justifying himself to this journalist. 'Herr Jäger, if you have something to say to us, say it. Otherwise, we'll be on our way.'

'Hmmm,' said Jäger. 'Consorting with Nubik. A smooth talker. But is he quite as trustworthy as he seems?'

'We'll decide for ourselves who is trustworthy and who is not,' Lichtblau said.

'As you will.' Jäger nodded to Lichtblau and bowed low to Frau Lichtblau, blushing as he did so. Then he left them.

When they got to Jäger's brother's, they found that the three boys had gone out. Jäger's brother was at home, though, and he looked worried.

'My brother Josef was here when the three boys arrived. There was no way I could have hidden them from him. He may denounce us all. I cannot kill my own brother or have him killed.'

'Do you mean he would not kill you or have you killed?' Lichtblau said.

'He would,' replied Markus Jäger. 'But I am not to be blamed for that. My father was displeased with him at the time he made his will, and wrote Josef out of it. He is a freelance journalist, and his work is intermittent, made even more so by the war. He will do almost anything for money. He will work for the Nazis if necessary, or if the price is right.'

'Maybe he already is working for them,' Lichtblau said.

'We must get the boys away,' Kristina broke in, 'Away from here, somewhere your brother and our enemies can't get to them, out of Vienna, out of Austria.'

'They've gone to see a friend of Thedel's.'

'I don't want Josef to harm Nubik,' Frau Lichtblau said, 'or anyone else for that matter.'

'My brother is unpredictable and self-seeking,' said Markus Jäger.

A bottle of wine stood on the table in the middle of the room. Markus Jäger asked whether anyone would like wine and, when Lichtblau said he would, Jäger went over to the sideboard to get a corkscrew. He opened a drawer, and Lichtblau saw at once that there was a pistol in the drawer along with some identity papers. Jäger took out the corkscrew and shut the drawer. He had had his back to the Lichtblaus and did not know that they had seen the contents of the drawer nor that they had exchanged glances over them. Jäger was a long-time friend of the Lichtblaus, who hoped he could be counted on. Lichtblau wanted to believe his boys and Thedel were safe in his hands. He felt especially uneasy about Jäger's brother, who, he was sure, was capable of manipulating the situation for his own ends. His uneasiness about Josef Jäger was compounded by the sight of the pistol and identity papers in the drawer. Lichtblau wondered whether these objects had something to do with Josef Jäger. He also wondered whether Josef Jäger was not trying to involve his brother in his schemes or whether Markus had some schemes of his own. He supposed the identity papers in the drawer were those of someone whom Josef Jäger, or even perhaps Markus Jäger, was trying to prevent from leaving Vienna or Austria. Lichtblau was afraid of being indiscreet or appearing so: it was not his home, after all, and Markus Jäger had taken in his children at his own request, a request that he was, in any case, more and more having second thoughts about.

The boys returned. Their parents kissed their sons and told them one or both of them would be back in a day or two. They asked the boys where Thedel was. They replied that Thedel had run into an acquaintance of his a few yards from the Jägers' apartment block. They were talking, so the boys had decided to come back to the flat alone and leave Thedel to speak with his acquaintance.

Just as the Lichtblaus were walking out of the building, they met Thedel walking in. 'Thedel, we need you to do something for us.'

'Name it,' replied the young man.

'There is a sideboard in the dining-room,' Lichtblau continued, 'and in the top left-hand drawer is —'

'A gun.' Thedel smiled. 'Along with some identity papers. The funny thing is Herr Jäger doesn't seem to make any great secret of these things. You've seen them, I've seen them; any passing visitor can see them as soon as anyone opens the drawer. It's almost as though he were defying nosey parkers or as though he wants people to know what he has in his drawer.'

'I don't know the reasons for his behavior,' Lichtblau said, 'and, by the way, we're not asking you to take these things from the drawer. He'd know at once it was you boys, and anyway, it would be wrong.' *Or in peacetime, it would be wrong,* he thought to himself.

'So, what do you want me to do?' Thedel asked.

'We're going to try and get the boys out of the country. You can go with them if you want to. We need to know whose identity papers are in the drawer. We thought maybe — we don't know how or why yet — the rightful owner of those papers, or the papers themselves, could be useful to us for the boys' journey. It even occurred to me that maybe they are the papers of someone who has died or been killed and that on that basis they might be useful to us.'

'You realize all this is risky,' broke in Kristina. 'If Markus Jäger senses you're trying to trick him in any way or using Thedel to find out his secrets or poke about in his belongings, it could spell havoc for us all. It could put the boys' lives in danger. You've never trusted Josef, and I have an uneasy feeling about Markus, too.'

Her husband turned to Thedel:

'Thedel, if you can get the name on the ID papers, so much the better.'

Four

Thedel and the boys said goodnight to Jäger and his wife. The three boys were all sleeping in the same room adjoining the living room where the sideboard stood. They shut the door and waited for the Jägers to retire. Then they began to whisper. It was decided that Johannes, as the smallest and lightest of the three, would creep into the living room when everything had fallen silent. He would be wearing his gloves to muffle the sound of his opening and closing the drawer. He was to open the drawer, read the name on the ID papers, close the drawer and return to the bedroom.

When the time was right, Johannes picked up a torch and got out of bed. He went into the living room. He had the torch on, and Thedel and Heinrich were watching him from their room. He opened the drawer as gently as he could. But when he did so, he had a shock: there were no papers at all in the drawer. He started rummaging in it and made a bit of noise as he did so. But he was unsuccessful in his task. He went back to the bedroom, but just as he was about to tell the others what he had discovered, they heard footsteps approaching their room, and Markus Jäger came in.

He said: 'What was that noise? You all seem to be wide awake. This is no time to be messing about. Do you realize that?'

'We're sorry, sir,' said Thedel, 'It's true I've been having trouble getting to sleep lately. We're sorry if we disturbed you.'

Jäger nodded and smiled. 'Go to sleep properly. Good night again.'

'Good night,' said the boys as one.

Jäger walked away but turned round after a few seconds and stood in the door-frame. 'I've removed the papers from the drawer, as you've seen. Too much of a temptation. There was also a pistol in it which I've taken, too.'

Thedel was worried he would have to disappoint the Lichtblaus.

A few days later, Lichtblau came home to his wife and told her he had run into Hellroth in the street.

'He said he knew we were trying to get the boys out of the country. I didn't react to this. He insisted I would be endangering their lives. If they were caught within Austria or even beyond our borders, it would almost certainly mean death for them, and perhaps for us, too. I told him if it was money he wanted, I was afraid I couldn't help. I told him I wasn't in that line any more. 'Kill us all,' I said to him, 'but I can't stump up any more checks.''

'He wants to see me, doesn't he?' asked Kristina.

'I'm afraid he does,' replied Lichtblau, who had long ago ceased being surprised at his wife's intuitions. 'He's expecting you tomorrow at ten in the morning at his office.'

'Don't worry,' said his wife.

'How could I not worry? Your life and the boys' lives mean far more to me than my own.'

'But you won't travel with us if we go.'

'It's not that I won't. I can't,' Lichtblau replied.

The next morning, Kristina Lichtblau sat face to face with Hellroth. Wolfgang Hellroth's mother had died in childbirth, leaving him in the care of a father who had little time for a nursling and even less interest. The boy had been left to his own devices as he grew up. His father had had a succession of mistresses, some of whom had temporarily mothered Wolfgang, more out of pity than love. His father moved to Vienna after the First War to try and make a fresh start in life. As an old man, he had moved back to his home town of Munich, to the house in Frie- drichstrasse, which he had never sold but never kept up. The old man lived in a house that was falling more and more apart with each passing day. His son joined the Party and the army when the Führer rose to power. The old man suddenly began to take an interest in his son, praising him to anyone who would listen (which was hardly anyone except the son himself, since his father had no social contacts to speak of) and surrounding himself with photos of his son in the uni- form of an officer in the Abwehr. His son's position in the army was the only thing he had ever had to be proud of in his life.

In the nineteen-thirties, Hellroth had got into the habit of frequenting the Central, and it was there that he had first set eyes on Kristina Lichtblau. He was the man who had defended her from Josef Jäger when Jäger had forcibly tried to get into conversation with her at the Central. It was he who had given Josef Jäger the scar beneath his right ear. Kristina Lichtblau had never been the slightest bit curious about Josef Jäger's opponent and considered Josef Jäger himself as nothing more than the brother — albeit the wayward brother — of a friend of her hus- band's.

A secretary who did not pay Kristina Lichtblau any attention nodded towards Hellroth's office and let her knock and enter without announcing her. He smiled on seeing her. He stood up and held out his hand, signifying that he wanted to take her hand in his and kiss it. But she did not hold out her hand.

'I've seen you —'

'At the Central,' she replied.

'Quite. You want to get your boys out of the country and perhaps your husband and yourself, too.'

'It's true we want to get the boys out,' said Kristina, 'This is not their war.'

'It's everybody's war, Frau Lichtblau,' said Hellroth.

'What do you want?'

He looked at her intently. 'I see you haven't forgotten that afternoon at the Central,' he said, 'I know I haven't.'

'You haven't answered me, Hellroth,' she said, 'Either tell me what you want, or I'll leave.'

'Don't try telling me what to do, Frau Lichtblau. Beauty doesn't mean everything is permitted. Anyway,' he went on, lighting a cigar, 'I don't want you to leave.'

'What then?'

'Sleep with me.'

She made as though to slap his face, but he forced her hand down.

'I could have you all shot like dogs right this minute.'

'Why don't you, then?'

'Damn you. It's been like this ever since that afternoon at the Central. I had noticed you often, before then, of course. I knew I never stood a chance with you any more than Jäger did.'

She felt only revulsion for him. 'You always were a fake. You only defended me at the Central to try and impress me so I would sleep with you, the mighty officer in the shiny Abwehr uniform. But you're nothing but a Nazi puppet. They can have you. No one else wants you. They're your mummy and daddy now.' It was his turn to try and slap her, but her words stopped him:

'You realize I'm pointing a gun at you? I wouldn't have come without one.'

'Security's not up to scratch downstairs,' he murmured.

'I rather think not,' she said, 'What those dullard bully boys downstairs will do for a pretty face. They let me through as though I were Marlene Dietrich.'

'If you sleep with me, I'll provide safe passage for your boys to the country of your choice.'

'No deal.' She turned towards the door. 'And anyway, I don't believe you have sufficient authority for that.'

'So why come?' he said.

'I didn't have any choice, did I? My husband for money, me for...'

'I'll see how I can use the boys, too,' he said.

'You won't get them,' she replied.

'Think about my offer. Talk it over with your husband. He's not the jealous type. This is war, Kristina. And you've told me yourself I have no standards of decency or honor. Those things don't win wars. And anyway, they don't count any more, if they ever did.'

'Maybe they don't,' she said, 'at least, not to you and your ilk.'

Hellroth shrugged and blew smoke rings from his cigar into the air.

'I'll be in touch.'

Hellroth wished his smoke rings would hang in the air and harden; but they just spiraled up, coiled into each other and dissolved.

Five

Tom Oliver looked out over his college garden and its white rose bushes, chill in the damp autumn air. He saw shrubs shrouded in mist to each side of the lawn bled of all color at this time of year. An owl — a visitor, he thought, from the Botanical Gardens — looked down at him from a beech branch; he noticed a swift nesting in the eaves. His scout brought him a letter on a silver tray and withdrew as soundlessly as he had entered. Hardy was the only person authorized to enter and exit, if not at will, at least as necessary: Hardy and one other person. The letter was from Herr Lichtblau:

Your name has been passed on to my wife and me as that of someone who might be willing to help us. Would you agree to take in our two teenage boys Heinrich and Johannes, possibly with our friend Thedel, who is a little older but still a teenager? By the way, Thedel's mother, Dagmar, and her friend Ilse seem to have disappeared. Perhaps you have heard of them. We understand you are in touch with local headmasters and that you would be able to place these boys in appropriate schools. We would like the boys to go to the same school, if possible. All three speak excellent English. They are impeccably well-mannered and more than capable of holding their own in conversation. Here in Vienna, more and more of us Jews, including children, are being taken away. We feel we need to take swift action to protect our boys and Thedel. I have decided to stay in Vienna for the time being since I believe I can be useful to the Resistance here, what little resistance there is, at any rate. My wife may travel with the boys. Viennese society grows worse every day, more and more dangerous and corrupt. Hence the more outward-looking we are, the more ties we can form with the Allies and the outside world, the better. We know you understand our situation and have most likely heard of us from the Pastor. We also have mutual friends in Geneva (Lichtblau gave their names). *If you write to me c/o them, they will pass on your reply.*

Oliver slipped the letter into his inside jacket pocket. Later, in the evening, he walked up the High to Carfax, turned right into Cornmarket, and went on to St Giles. He stopped at the Eagle and Child. There he met his friend Reuel, as he did most evenings after dinner.

'I've been asked to take in some foreign boys, Reuel,' said Oliver. 'We've got some room at Wadham. They sound bright, too. Maybe a bit young for university, but later we might even be able to get them in a year or two early.'

'That's a lot of diplomacy and paperwork for you,' replied Reuel.

'That's beside the point. Do we want to help innocent victims of other people's wars? Or do we want to curl up in front of our log fire, fondling our brandies and our fellow pleasure-seekers?'

'Speak for yourself,' said Reuel.

'Well,' asked Oliver, 'are you in or out?'

'You win as ever, Tom. Count me in. I'll coach them if need be to get them ready for university.'

Tom Oliver's instinctive hatred of convention made him a natural friend of refugees and a natural enemy of the enemies of freedom, be they Nazis or anyone else. Walking back to his rooms, he wondered how the boys would get out of Vienna, then out of Austria, then to England. But others had done it before them. He got into bed and tried to sleep but could not. He turned on the light and wrote to Herr Lichtblau, telling him he agreed to help the boys in any way he could. He wanted to tell Herr Lichtblau that if his wards were captured or killed, he could in no way take responsibility. But he decided that that was understood. He wished him and his wife well with their plans and looked forward to meeting him after the war. Later that day, he sent the letter to the address in Switzerland given by Lichtblau. Oliver had no doubt it would be smuggled from Geneva to Herr Lichtblau in Vienna. He did know the Pastor's circle, and they him.

Kristina Lichtblau went into her husband's study. He was sitting at his desk, as always, with his back to the door. He did not appear to hear her when she came in. She stood behind him, waiting. After a brief silence, he looked up and said, without turning round:

'You, in return for safe passage?'

'That's what it looks like,' replied his wife, who knew her husband's intuitive gifts as well as he knew hers.

'We'll have to get the boys out without his help, then,' said Lichtblau.

'What if his protection could save their lives?'

'What if this, what if that? What if they die tonight? What if we all die tonight? We don't even know whether he'd keep his word, assuming you decided to go through with it. If his superiors knew he was prepared to help the children of a Jewess get out of the country unscathed in return for sleeping with that Jewess, I don't think they'd be best pleased. It would be a kind of collaboration and draw down on him the wrath of the Reich while making the Allies all the keener to capture or kill him.'

Kristina was quiet for a moment. 'He hates Jews with a vengeance. But he has a weakness for women and seems to be in love with me. I believe he won't harm the boys if I ask him not to.'

'Only if you agree to sleep with him. And even then, I think you're being naïve. These people don't care about love. They just want power and the death of all Jews and anyone who resists them,' said Lichtblau. 'I have received a reply from England,' he went on. 'They are prepared to have the three boys.'

'So, it's decided. We must try to get them to England, then,' said Kristina.

Josef Jäger rose from his seat in Hellroth's office.

'If I hand the three boys over to you, what's in it for me?'

'A thousand dollars,' said Hellroth, smoke rising from his Havana cigar.

'Five thousand,' said Jäger. 'But why would I trust you?'

'Neither of us trusts the other.'

'But I can scrape by as I am,' said Jäger. 'You, my boy, need results.'

Hellroth decided not to dwell on the slight. 'Yes, I can't quite get the results they're asking me for. And there's that bitch Jewess. I wish I'd never set eyes on her. But I have. That was your fault. I should have let you have her at the time. I thought I was just a cog in the killing machine. And I am. But I can't get her out of my mind. And I've been slacking.'

'I've got the scar you gave me to show for your stupidity,' Jäger said.

'I think I should try and capture all five of them together: the Lichtblaus, the two boys and the other boy,' said Hellroth. His patience with Jäger was running out; he had never in his life much enjoyed talking and was sick now of talking to Jäger. Besides, several of his recent operations had failed. Lichtblau was no longer a source of financing he could rely on, if he had ever been.

'You realize that if my brother hears about any of this, he will not only cut me off but go straight to your superiors, too. The boys are uncircumcised, and their identity as Jews is not evident. Your reason for wanting to bring them in and perhaps kill them is not clear, either, and you might easily be accused of wasting time and resources on people of no importance to the Reich.'

'I know nothing about love, Jäger, but it seems to me that war is like love: it is not always reasonable, and sometimes it is savage and vindictive.'

'You're a proud man, Hellroth,' Josef Jäger retorted. 'You have obtained Austrian money to finance your operations, and while they succeeded, or seemed to, your superiors left you in peace. Then the money dried up. You went to Lichtblau. You begged. That, to you, was a worse humiliation than death. You found out rather late that his checks were fakes. You're currently down on your knees to both the Lichtblaus. They're too strong for you. You can torture them, even have them put to death. But they believe you can't kill them. That's what bothers you.

'Anyway, enough philosophy. Your superiors will be on to you about all this, if they aren't already. Now you are trying to blackmail his wife. It is risky for you and all very —'

'Unsavory?' mooted Hellroth.

'Quite. Punish Lichtblau if you must, but leave his wife and children out of it.'

'A beautiful Jewish widow, still young, and not poor either, would suit you, wouldn't she, Jäger? Admit it; you're as keen as I am to get her husband out of the way or to get your hands on her.'

'The things you say are like yourself: beneath contempt. I will not stoop to respond.'

'Ah, but you will for a few thousand.'

'I'm a poor journalist, made even poorer by this war you've inflicted on us. I am in no position to refuse an offer of money. But you haven't got the kind of money I want. Lichtblau has left his bank. Your fountain, if that's what it was, has run dry.'

'Bring me the boys in a week's time. I'll have the money for you by then.'

'I want to see the money first. Then we'll discuss the boys.'

Hellroth shrugged. 'You're not the only one who's noticed those blue eyes, those fine nostrils, who's imagined —'

'Enough!' Again, Jäger was adamant. 'I'll see the money here in cash a week from today.' He walked out of the room, leaving the door open, and left the building.

A little way away, on the opposite pavement, Alfred Nubik was standing around. He seemed abstracted, and nobody looking at him would think he noticed anyone or anything. But the opposite was true. His one thought now was to find the Lichtblaus and tell them he had seen Josef Jäger coming out of Hellroth's official building. The staircase in the building had a window at every landing that looked out onto the street. He knew Hellroth's office was on the fourth floor and had seen Josef Jäger pass in front of the staircase windows from the fourth floor down to the ground floor and out. Nubik walked for over an hour until he came to the block of flats where the Lichtblaus lived. Although he knew that he could try and gain access to their building and that they would welcome him, he still preferred to wait outside. He did not stay still but walked up and down the street to avoid casting suspicion on either himself or them, trying to look thoughtful and distracted but really watching out for someone entering or leaving the building whose help he might enlist to get one of the Lichtblaus to come out. He prevailed upon an old woman who showed no curiosity about him to ring at the Lichtblaus' door and tell them Alfred wanted a word with them outside. She nodded, walked into the building and within minutes, both the Lichtblaus had come out. He merely told them he had seen Josef Jäger leaving Hellroth's office building and presumed, because he had come down from the floor where Hellroth had his office, that the two of them were up to something. The Lichtblaus thanked him and went back to their flat. They decided they had to get their boys and Thedel away from Markus Jäger and his family, but without letting Markus and his wife, or the boys themselves, sense there was anything amiss, or at least that there was any connection between the move and Josef Jäger.

The Lichtblaus went straight to Markus Jäger's place, intending to remove the three boys and put them as far out of harm's way as was possible in the Vienna of 1941. They found the three boys safe and sound. But once they had entered the flat and the front door was shut behind them, Markus Jäger put his forefinger to his lips. They fell silent. Jäger and his wife looked worried. Kristina Lichtblau noticed that Jäger's hands had started to shake. Jäger pointed to the ceiling. The Lichtblaus then realized why the Jägers looked concerned. Boots were stamping around down on the floor above them. Lichtblau walked over to a table, sat down at it, drew a notebook from his jacket pocket and wrote: *How long has this been going on?* He motioned to Jäger to come and read his words. The latter did so and replied in the same way: *Since yesterday afternoon.*

All the time?

Yes, including overnight. Has not stopped once.

How many of them are there?

I don't know.

Have you seen any of them?

No.

Who lives in the flat above you?

No one now. The Jewish family who lived there vanished a few months ago. To my knowledge, they have not been back.

Didn't you see or hear them coming in?

No. But there's a fire escape, and they may have come up that way and then broken in from outside.

The Lichtblaus decided to take the three boys to the home of another friend of Lichtblau's, Karl. Lichtblau wrote articles for Karl's journal, *The Flame,* which had — or had once had — a wide readership in Austria and Germany. Karl himself was something of a loose cannon. The Nazis were disinclined to arrest Karl, for the moment at least, since they wanted to keep as much of the population on their side as was humanly possible, which was hardly at all. However, Lichtblau knew that despite having many enemies, Karl also had many sympathetic contacts and would help get the boys out of Austria if he could. But first, they wanted to take the boys back to their own flat to enable them to get a change of clothing.

Once they were inside their own flat, however, they heard a strange sound — strange because it was so immediately familiar. It was the sound of boots tramping back and forth on the floor above them. There were similarities between this new situation and the one they had just come from at Markus Jäger's building. An old Jewish man used to live above them but had gone missing several months before. A few nights before his disappearance, he had come down and spent some time with Lichtblau, whom the older man had always held in the greatest affection. The man, Max Nate, always ate little, and whenever he did, it was the simplest things one could buy: bread, potatoes, and occasionally cheese. His flat was bare: no pictures on the walls and a minimum of furniture. You felt he would have happily slept on the floor if necessary. He had one set of clothes that varied not at all from one season to the next. He had owned a tobacconist's, which he had sold when he retired two years previously. His favorite client had lived a few streets away in Berggasse, a man who always took an interest in him when he came to buy his pipe tobacco, a man with a stern manner but extremely gentle eyes. He had got out. He had been fortunate to know an ambassador and a princess. Nate had gathered that the man's sisters, elderly like Nate himself, were not going with their brother.

Nate had confided to Lichtblau that he sensed the Nazis would be coming for him soon and handed Lichtblau a check made out to him. 'As you know, Lichtblau, I have no children, no living relatives either. You and your family have been my only family these past years. I have lived a thrifty life. I want you to have this.' The check he handed Lichtblau was for a colossal sum.

'Take this before they rob the bank or force me to hand over my money. Cash it at once if you like. I know you'll know what to do with it to keep it safe. I know, too, that you'll use it wisely. I have heard boots tramping in the building. But one day, those boots will be burned as fuel for flames.'

The next day Lichtblau transited the check through his bank to a Swiss one. He destroyed all traces of the operation at his bank but held back a small portion of the money. Lichtblau felt he would have to rebuild his life outside Austria if he and his family survived the war. He told his wife about the existence of the money and the fact that he had placed it in a Swiss bank for safekeeping. Nate had certainly considered him and his wife as his children, and their sons as his grandsons. He intended the money for them all.

Now he was gone, and the enemy was stomping up and down in his flat. Their presence there, Lichtblau thought, was meaningless: there was nothing in it worth taking, and he and his family would try not to let themselves be intimidated by the din. The street itself was hushed, and there was nothing and no one to spy on — except perhaps him and his family. The enemy was pressuring him; it had been the same at Markus Jäger's flat. That alone explained their presence. Invisible marching boots were hounding him and his family. Perhaps Hellroth was telling him: cooperate with us, do as we tell you, or you'll suffer the same fate as the old man.

The boys grabbed their change of clothes. The five of them — Lichtblau, Kristina, Johannes, Heinrich and Thedel — went back out onto the street. All locking eyes, they tacitly agreed to split up: Lichtblau with Johannes and Thedel, Kristina Lichtblau with Heinrich. Lichtblau and his wife conferred in whispers. They would not go to Karl's: Karl was likely under close Nazi surveillance, and it would be even more dangerous at his place than it had been at Markus Jäger's. Three hours later, they all managed to meet up near the place where Alfred Nubik lived.

Nubik lived in a hut by the North Bridge on the outskirts of the district of Döbling. Here, when he felt truly alone and unwatched, he slipped off his businessman's mask. He was a young-looking thirty-four, with a mobile face and a gift for mimicry, so that he could look or act older or younger at will. He was not Jewish. He was well-spoken. His family lived in the Tyrol. The Nazis had never seen him for what he really was. He had not been called up by the Reich and had no military activities. He always smiled at the Nazis whenever he saw them. Such was his chameleon talent that those Nazis who recognized him treated him as an insider.

Nubik explained his position to Lichtblau and his wife. 'It might be hard for me to get your boys out of the city or the country. But I could distract the Nazis at a checkpoint while you or someone else drives through and tries to make a break for it to the border. I can smuggle letters or other objects around since I know how to get about in this nightmare. I can hide weapons in my businessman's briefcase: I've got special pockets in it which are undetectable.'

'Could you kill Hellroth?' asked Lichtblau

'Do we want him killed?' rejoined Kristina, 'Or do we want to enlist his help in getting the boys out?'

'Not at any price,' said her husband, giving her a look that Nubik noticed. He said, 'I think Hellroth is bluffing. There's a world of difference between what he says he wants and what he really wants. He's afraid. He wants to save his own skin. He's a coward. He has to be diverted, distracted, like the soldiers I was talking about at the checkpoints. Offer him whatever he wants. Call his bluff.'

'Hellroth won't be duped by that. He's in love with me,' said Kristina. 'He wants to break my husband and me apart and prove his virility to himself into the bargain.'

'To himself, and his friends and his superiors,' said Lichtblau.

'Hellroth has no friends,' said Nubik, 'and his superiors are hardly going to pretend to be impressed by one of their gofer's conquests. However beautiful,' he added, with a wink and a smile to her husband.

'Well, Kristina,' said Hellroth, 'have you talked my offer over with your husband? Take a seat.'

Kristina, standing in front of Hellroth in his office, declined. 'And don't call me Kristina. I have, in fact, talked it over with my husband. It seems we are not being allowed to forget you. Your officers enjoy breaking into innocent people's homes. And rarely take their boots off.'

'Nor their gun-belts. A little persuasion can work wonders.'

'Not with us. If you will help us get the boys safely abroad, my husband is prepared to look around for some money for you. You have never refused money in the past.'

'You've never been in greater need of me,' said Hellroth.

'There are kinds and degrees of need. You're setting out to destroy a family. My family.'

'Everything will be destroyed!' Hellroth bellowed, fleetingly revealing his savage temper. 'And better things rebuilt in their place!'

'Your policy of extermination, killing and division will not avail you in the end.'

'How much money can he get?' asked Hellroth.

'That remains to be seen.' Kristina felt her stomach lurch with the disgust she felt for the man. 'We need guarantees first.'

Hellroth got up from behind his desk and walked up to Kristina as though to provoke her in her disgust. 'I could call my guards in now and have them hold you down while I raped you. And then let them have their turn.'

'Why don't you, then?' Unperturbed, Kristina returned his gaze. 'I know why. You want me to come to you of my own volition. But that I will never do.'

Hellroth turned away from her, walked to his office door and opened it. 'Perhaps you never will. But we'll see.'

Then he went back behind his desk and settled down to his paperwork again without a further glance at Kristina Lichtblau.

Six

After breakfast in Hall, Tom Oliver walked back across the quad, up the staircase that led to his rooms, and into his study. His eyes scanned today's papers. Front-page headline: *Allies joined by USA*. He had a tutorial to teach in half an hour. To that end, he picked out the books he would need from the bookshelves and his notes from a file in his filing cabinet. He sat down in his usual armchair and perused books and notes till the three students he was expecting arrived. They all sat down in armchairs too. Oliver asked one of the students to read aloud his weekly essay. Hardly had the student got to the bottom of his first page — he was particularly conscientious and had written twenty pages, hoping, with length if not quality, to impress the famous don and Master of the college — than there was a muffled, barely audible knock at the door and Hardy, his scout, entered. He whispered a few brief words in Oliver's ear. 'Can't they wait!' Oliver seemed cross. Hardy again whispered in his ear, but there was hardly any point in doing so since the three students, all with their heads buried in their books and notes as though they were concentrating on them in preparation for discussion, could not fail to make out every word the scout said: 'They are most insistent. They have come from Vienna and just arrived in Oxford. They have not eaten or slept for some days. They say they cannot rest or eat till they have spoken to you.'

'Gentlemen, I regret to inform you that I shall have to call a halt to this tutorial. The circumstances in which we are currently living mean that we must be even more ready than before to offer assistance to those needing it — assistance and refuge, especially to the displaced. We here at Oxford are not cut off from the world, as some philistines would have it. On the contrary, wherever humanity and humanist values are attacked, we must do everything we can, in the privileged position which is ours, to defend and protect the victims of such attacks. This is what I am at this minute called upon to do. We will reconvene tomorrow afternoon, as soon as I have had time to deal with the pressing matters of which I have just been advised.'

The students got up as one man and walked down the stairs and out into the December air. To prevent Oliver's visitors — there were two of them — from being objects of curiosity, Hardy had kept them out of sight of the students. In a few minutes, he again knocked at the Master's door and showed the two visitors in. Tom Oliver shook hands with them both and, extending his hand, invited them to sit down. He asked them to explain their purpose.

'My name is Ilse König and this is Dagmar Windmoden. We are friends of the Lichtblaus. We discovered that, each unbeknownst to the other, we were both being used by the same man, a Nazi named Hellroth. We found out that we both hoped that if we slept with Hellroth, as he forced us to do, he would protect us and spare us the fate of other Jews. After a while, he seemed to get nastier and even more threatening, while his demands became —'

'Indescribable?' said Tom Oliver.

'That's it. Through a mutual friend, who put us in touch with each other, we discovered we had been tricked every way possible by Hellroth. We decided we had no choice but to flee. Herr Lichtblau told us that if we made it to England, you might be able to help us.'

'And I have a son,' broke in Dagmar Windmoden, 'who is still in Vienna.'

'How old is he?'

'He's eighteen.'

'I wonder where his father is.'

'He's out of the picture. He abandoned us both when my son was three, and we've never seen him since. He may be alive or dead for all I know.'

'Why didn't you bring your son with you?'

'I left Vienna in a great hurry. It was almost literally a matter of minutes. I hardly had time to pack a few things. Thedel, my son was staying with friends. I left him a brief note in our flat telling him I'd had to leave, but otherwise telling him very little in case the Nazis broke in and saw the note. I told him to stay with his friends and left him money. I know it probably seems wrong to you that I didn't bring him with us. I feel unbearably guilty about leaving him behind. But he has good friends in Vienna and knows how to live in hiding.'

'What are you expecting from me?'

'We don't know yet, Professor Oliver,' replied Ilse, 'Any help you can provide. Advice on how we are to manage over here. And on what we're going to do. We have some money, but our resources are not infinite.'

Oliver turned to Dagmar. 'If you stay here, I can put you in touch with other German-speaking refugees, Jewish and otherwise. I can introduce you to friends of mine and help you become accustomed to life in England.'

'Many people in Vienna want to leave or feel they have no choice but to leave, especially if they are Jewish,' said Ilse. 'Among the people I know, only Herr Lichtblau seems intent on staying. He has his beliefs, his principles and his activities. They seem to be worth more to him than his own life.'

'I am glad to tell you he hopes his sons will be coming here with Thedel,' said Tom Oliver.

'How will I ever be able to thank you?'

'It seems a bit early for that.'

'Thedel has a job working a few hours a week at a coffee-house.'

'The Central,' said Oliver.

'He is well-liked and discreet. He keeps his eyes and ears open. Many Nazi officers frequent the Central. Thedel sometimes waits at table. He helps certain people in the Resistance: keeps them up to date.'

'I will write to Herr Lichtblau telling him that he will have to decide how to get the three of them to England. And perhaps Frau Lichtblau will travel with them.'

Seven

The two ladies have arrived safely in Oxford, so you'll no longer have to worry about them. Thedel's mother wants you to send him to Oxford with your boys.

Lichtblau looked up from the letter from Tom Oliver he was reading, dated January 1942. There was another missive on his desk.

Come to my office on receipt of this letter, Hellroth had written.

Lichtblau did not know why Hellroth wanted to see him. and did not consider going to Hellroth's office a priority. The boys had to be expatriated — exfiltrated — as soon as possible. He wondered what Kristina would do. He closed his eyes: pictures came into his mind of Kristina in her air-blue gown the first time he had laid eyes on her at the Central when she had seemed something like the best side of Vienna, contemplative and forward-looking...their wedding-day, when at his request she had worn the same gown...coming home from the maternity clinic carrying their first child in a basket. He had been the envy of every man in Vienna. Perhaps he still was. *She's as beautiful as ever,* he thought, *and the stress of war, even as it takes its toll on her face, is making her even more beautiful. She can't stay with me. She'll have to go with the boys.* He could see no other alternative.

Kristina had taken the boys and moved to some friends of hers two nights previously. Lichtblau had not seen them since then. They were due to return briefly to the flat this evening. He waited for them. He heard the key turn in the lock and the door open, and then Heinrich and Johannes walked in, shepherded by Thedel.

'Where's my wife?' he asked Thedel.

'She accompanied us to your front door and whispered to us to go in to you, saying she had to go out again. She was away before any of us could say anything.'

Thedel slipped away. Lichtblau decided he could not leave his sons alone. He would have liked to contact Nubik to ask him to keep tabs on Kristina, but Nubik had no phone. Kristina Lichtblau had many friends in the city and many contacts. She was her own woman, and he had no doubt that if she left the boys and went off so abruptly in the late evening without saying where she was going, she must have her reasons for doing so: to his mind, she could only be working for the good of them all. And yet the figure of Hellroth suddenly arose in his mind.

On the following afternoon, he received an official envelope. He knew at once it was from Hellroth. It contained this from him: *This note cancels my last. Do not come and see me yet. I will summon you as and when I need to.* He remembered the conversation he had had with Kristina about Hellroth and wondered whether the timing of Kristina's disappearance and Hellroth's note was pure coincidence.

On the same afternoon, Thedel was in St Rupert's Church in the city center, not far from the Café Central. He was sitting in a pew in the middle of the nave, lost in thought, when the sound of a woman sobbing struck his ear. She was kneeling on the opposite side of the nave from him, a few pews behind him. He walked over to her and sat down near her in the same pew.

'I've left your sons with your husband.'

'Thedel! It's good you're here. Hellroth wants me to go to him tonight at nine and stay with him till tomorrow morning. If I refuse, he says he will kill us all. But, if I agree, he claims he will help get the boys out of Austria.'

'Why not kill him first?' They exchanged a brief smile, given the place they were in.

'Even if I could, what good would it do? They would only replace him with someone just like him, or worse. I want you to do something for me.'

Thedel smiled, always glad to help, especially when someone like Kristina Lichtblau wanted his help. 'I'll try.'

'My husband's bound to be worried. Go and tell him you've seen me. Tell him I'm fine. He's not to worry about me. I'll be back by mid-day tomorrow. He's not to look for me or to send anyone to look for me.'

'Why don't you go home now?'

'If I went home now, my husband would not want me to go out again. I've agreed to go and see Hellroth tonight because the boys' lives and safety mean more to me than anything else in the world.'

'What if he doesn't keep his word? These Nazis —'

'I have no choice. Brute force rules our lives nowadays.'

'I'll give your husband your message.'

Thedel walked out of the church and started in the direction of the street where the Lichtblaus lived. As he was walking past the Central, a young man sitting just behind the front windows got up and, hailing Thedel, came out to the street. Thedel halted and waited for the young man.

'Who are you?'

'My name is Werner. I come from Oxford. I'm a student there. My tutor is a man called Tom Oliver.'

'So my mother and her friend have arrived safely?'

'Yes. I know you by sight because she showed me several photos of you. She said you might be in or near the Central at some point.'

'Tom Oliver is keen to help you get out of Austria and be reunited with your mother. He thought it would serve no purpose sending an Englishman who, even were he to speak excellent German, as Tom Oliver does, would be bound to give himself away by his accent.'

'So he asked you,' said Thedel, hearing that the young man spoke native German with a Viennese accent.

'No, I offered to come. When your mother and her friend first came to see Tom Oliver, I was having a tutorial with him. Hardy, his scout, led me and the other two students who were taking the tutorial out of Oliver's study by a side door and down a back staircase, telling us the professor had urgent business to attend to. All this aroused my curiosity. Once the three of us had walked out of the college, I pretended I had forgotten something at Tom Oliver's, told the others to carry on without me, and crept back up the back staircase that led to the professor's study. I stood on the landing and listened in on the conversation. I went away and wrote a note to Tom Oliver confessing I had heard his conversation with the two visitors and telling him I would be the ideal person to come and get you. No one in Vienna would think my presence here anything out of the ordinary. I am Viennese born and bred. You must come back to Oxford with me.

'There's one more thing I need to tell you. Tom Oliver is in touch with a Viennese family, the Lichtblaus. He will be glad to welcome them to Oxford if they can make it safely to England.'

'I know the Lichtblaus. Their boys are moving around Vienna a lot at the moment. I don't know whether the parents intend to leave Vienna straight away. The mother may be in order to stay with the boys. I'm not sure about Herr Lichtblau.'

'Put your handbag and coat down.'

Kristina did as ordered.

'Now, I will frisk you. Raise your arms.' Hellroth made as if to touch Kristina. She shuddered and backed off. 'I have no gun on me.'

'And I have no reason to trust you.'

'I have come as you ordered.'

'Requested.'

'I have come.'

'You have threatened me once with a gun, Kristina. Why would you not do so again?'

'You say you will help the boys get out of the country?'

'Champagne?' He produced a bottle and two glasses.

'No.'

Hellroth walked over to the door. Holding the bottle with both hands, he raised it to head height and then brought it down hard on the metal handle, breaking off the neck of the bottle. He spun round and sprayed the foaming drink all over Kristina. She shrugged and, with a look of repulsion, turned away from him. He poured the remainder of the champagne down his gullet, straight from the now jagged-edged neck of the bottle.

'Time to take your dress off. That's why you came, isn't it?'

She obeyed.

'And the rest.'

She obeyed again. He took an object from a drawer in his desk that Kristina could not quite see. She felt ready to throw up. Hellroth took a camera from its case.

'A little souvenir to show my superiors. And your husband, of course. He needs to know what kind of woman he married.'

A camera flash dazzled her. He opened the door to his bedroom. She saw a picture of the Führer hung above the bedhead.

'Go in. Lie down on the bed. Don't get into bed till I've taken a few more photos.'

She again complied. He followed after her. He put the camera down and took off his clothes. He picked the camera back up and prepared to take another photo of her. But, in a second, he started at a pounding on the front door of the flat. The front door burst open with a crash, and three men walked in, one in front and two behind. The one in front bawled, 'Hellroth!' And, sensing Hellroth was in the bedroom, went straight in, followed by the other two men. Hellroth was pulling his clothes back on as though he was a character in a fast-motion sequence of a film. Kristina had got under the covers. She had done so out of modesty: she was not hiding, and her face and shoulders were visible.

'Hellroth! You're needed at headquarters. Why haven't you been in to work? Think you're a real stud, don't you, you randy old dog.'

Though all the men were aware of Kristina Lichtblau in the bed, none of them looked at her or paid her the slightest attention.

'I was just about to, sir. I'll come with you now.'

Evidently a high-ranking officer, the spokesman of the three was holding a pistol and looked as though he might point it at Hellroth any moment. He seemed not to respect Hellroth at all. It was as though Hellroth was barely an underling to him. He sounded as though he were weary of doing menial tasks like chasing up lower-grade officers and gave the impression that the Reich would be better off if people like Hellroth were dead.

The officer signaled to Hellroth to lead the way out. The officer followed him, with the other two coming up behind. As the men were walking out of the bedroom, one of the two soldiers at the back turned round and looked at Kristina. He smiled at her. He unsheathed his pistol. He winked at her and then pretended to aim at her. She screamed. He shot at the bed, taking care not to hit her. She screamed again, and all was silent. She waited till the men were out of earshot, not bothering to lock the door behind them. Then she got up and put her clothes back on.

The previously clean white sheets were not red. They were now wet and dirty. A present for Hellroth and his Führer. *His, not mine.*

Kristina Lichtblau could not be accused of lacking presence of mind. She thought for a second before leaving Hellroth's flat: there might be things potentially useful to her and her husband in it. She rifled through a pile of papers, some of which were lists of names. A couple of the documents had her surname and those of some of her and her husband's friends on them. These she folded up tightly and put in her handbag. She found a passport in a name she did not know and took that with her too. Then she headed toward the hall and out of the front door.

Rather than going home straight away, she decided to go and see Nubik first. By doing so, she hoped to put any Nazis who might be intending to follow her back to her place off the scent and lose them altogether. She hailed the first taxi she saw. It turned out to be a man she knew. She needed to get out of the area fast and without being followed. At one point, the taxi driver jerked sharply right, doubled back the way they had come, and then resumed their original course to Döbling, where Nubik lived.

On arrival, the taxi driver would take no payment from her.

'We all need money at this time.' She tried to press his fee on him.

'Money's worthless here these days.'

'Unless you want to leave the country.'

'All right, but where would I go? I may have to die, but if I have to die before my time, I'd rather die here than anywhere else. Rotten life, rotten town.'

The man was kind, but how would they overcome all that evil if everyone was as resigned as he was? Kristina looked around to make sure she had not been followed and saw no one watching her. She walked until she came to the North Bridge and then descended the steps that led to the bank of the Danube. It was mid-afternoon. She looked up to the sky. A squall was scudding across it. When the storm came, she would take shelter under this bridge or another. She knew this riverbank as a place where people used to go on sunny Sunday afternoons. It had been *Un dimanche après-midi à l'Île de la Grande Jatte*, pure Seurat. Apart from the moorhens swimming on the water, oblivious to human upheaval, places like this were now deserted or had become the haunts of men who were waiting to be rounded up. Or so she thought. She had not been here since the start of the war. Nubik had told her he lived here, near this bridge or under it. But here, the river had grown grey and dark; there was no grass or trees. The dogs in the foreground no longer played and had grown mangy, scowling and cringing, half-dead. She soon spotted Nubik, who was deep in conversation with another man. He signaled to her to come and join them. The man bowed briefly to her and left them.

When the man had walked away, Nubik said to Kristina Lichtblau: 'He is...helping us.'

'You're all helping each other, including Felix.'

'There is no pressure from us,' replied Nubik, 'to keep Felix here. His decisions are all his own. If anyone knows that, you do.'

'Too true!' said Kristina, laughing and sighing at the same time over her husband's stubbornness.

Hellroth stood before his superior, Michael Lucht. Lucht was sitting behind his desk with his boots up on it, scrutinizing Hellroth as though he were some weird and unpleasant animal. A pistol lay on his desk.

'You don't seem to be getting great results at the moment, Hellroth. Fallen under the spell of a little Jewish witch, eh? You're missing a lot of opportunities and letting a lot of people slip through the net. Perhaps you'd like to be Gauleiter in the back of beyond. Perhaps you'd like to be nobody in the back of beyond. You might be more use to the Reich. We're all expendable.'

The three men who had brought Hellroth in were standing behind him. The two low-ranking soldiers were smirking to themselves and each other. Lucht stood up, picked the pistol up from his desk and went over to Hellroth. He stroked Hellroth's cheek with the weapon.

'What can you do to persuade us to let you live? Or to keep you in Vienna? I doubt that little Jew-girl will miss you. Though you might miss her. Mother you never had, eh? Poor little boy. I have my superiors to report to. If your results are no good, I have to take the rap for it.'

Hellroth preferred to come clean: 'I admit I have been distracted lately.' He was smiling, trying in vain to get the others to smile with him: all men together for alcohol, cigars and skirt-chasing, all men against Lucht. Lucht did smile, or pretended to:

'Kill her next time. And bring me her dead body. Naked, of course. And we'll let my men — how to put it — experiment with her body. Now get out.' He gestured with his chin to the other men to leave him, too: 'Keep an eye on him.' As they were on their way out, one of them turned round to Lucht:

'I shot her as we were leaving. I don't know whether she's dead or alive.'

'You missed a great opportunity. Why didn't you kill her outright?'

'I wanted to leave that pleasure to you or Herr Hellroth, sir.'

Once outside, Hellroth laughed loud and long. It was all he could do to try and, once again, save face. Whether it be Lichtblau or his own superiors, others were finding it too easy to humiliate him. He offered his three escorts champagne. Of the three, the two privates agreed at once. The third man balked at first but soon fell under the influence of Hellroth's and the two underlings' glee. At the Central, Hellroth ordered four bottles of champagne, a bottle for each of them, and told the waiter to take away the glasses he brought with the bottles. He pretended to drink out of the bottle. The others took after him, though they really did drink from their bottles. After they had had three more bottles each, Hellroth still pretending to drink, 'Schnapps all round!' he called out. The three escorts each had several glasses of the liquor, Hellroth getting the rounds but protesting that he could not drink anything else on top of champagne.

'I know a man who can give us a real rush of pleasure,' the officer said.

'Take us to him!' said one of the underlings.

'Where can we find him?' said Hellroth.

'At this hour of the night, he deals with his clients by the river, in Döbling, near the North Bridge.'

'Can you take us?' asked the same underling.

'I can't drive in the state I'm in,' said the officer.

'I'll drive, of course,' said Hellroth, 'I didn't have any schnapps, and I know the way.'

The officer said: 'We'll have the time of our lives. This man really knows his job.'

The officer handed Hellroth his car keys, and the four of them got into the officer's car. Twenty minutes later, he parked the vehicle some yards from the bridge he had mentioned, down by the riverbank. A fire shone under the bridge, and a few men could be seen gathered around it.

'Here's the place,' said the officer. Then sleep overcame him.

All three of Hellroth's passengers had by now fallen asleep. He eased a gun belonging to one of the two underlings, who were sitting in the back seat, out of its holster. He did the same with the pistols of the other two men. They carried on snoring.

Hellroth knew what he wanted to do and knew he would have to work fast. If the men woke up, they would expect to find what the officer had promised. They trusted Hellroth and assumed he would wake them up. He carried a pistol silencer in his inside jacket pocket. He put it on one of the pistols. He checked the pistol was loaded, held it to the heart of one of the two soldiers in the back of the car and fired it. The man jerked forward and then fell back against his seat. The private next to him half-opened his eyes momentarily but closed them again straight away. Hellroth gave him the same treatment as his colleague. He opened his car door as softly as he could and went to pick up a brick a few yards from the car. He carried it back to the car and wedged it against the accelerator. He turned the ignition back on, then gently shut the car door. The car was facing the river. The officer was still asleep in the passenger seat. Hellroth wondered whether to shoot him before he let the car go. He decided not to. He made sure the car doors were locked. He put the car into gear, took off the handbrake and, with a grin of satisfaction, watched it drive itself into the river, where it nosedived into the water. In a few seconds, all trace of it was gone.

Hellroth turned away from the water's edge and looked towards the fire with the group of men around it. By this time, one of them, a young-looking, bearded man, had walked a few steps away from the group and was staring full-on at Hellroth. Hellroth wondered how much he had seen. Should he kill him on the spot? But if he did so, he would have trouble with the other men around the fire. He wasn't sure that, even with the guns he had, he could master them all. So he decided he would scare them, or the bearded man at least. He walked towards him, pointing his gun at him:

'Your name?'

'Wilhelm.'

'Papers.'

'I have none with me. I have none.'

'Occupation.'

'None.'

'If you tell anyone what you saw just now, I'll have you flayed alive, you and all your friends. You realize your days and those of your ilk are numbered as it is.'

'You can count on us.'

Hellroth fired his gun, which he was still pointing at the man. The bullet from it just grazed the outer edge of the man's right hand.

Eight

Recounting her experience with Hellroth, omitting no detail, Kristina Lichtblau was walking with her husband when they met Nubik, his right hand in a bandage. He told them what had happened the previous night just by 'his' bridge.

Lichtblau pondered. 'The three soldiers deprived him of his prey. He felt humiliated, even more so as his commanding officer must have given him a good dressing-down in front of the three. His pride has been hurt. He's going to be searching for you now, Kristina. This incident won't have deflected him from his course; it'll only have made him even more determined.'

Kristina, strong as she was, seemed to be on the verge of tears.

Nubik had a suggestion to make. 'Frau Lichtblau can come with me for a couple of days if you like, while you make arrangements for her and the boys to leave. Hellroth is unlikely to come back, or not straight away at any rate. Just in case he does, though, I have an idea.'

Nubik stayed in a hut near the bridge in Döbling where he and his fellows congregated. Kristina Lichtblau stayed inside while Nubik stood outside. He had explained his idea to her, and she had agreed at once. She stepped out of the hut. Nubik inspected her. She had cut off her long hair and put on a pair of Nubik's old trousers, ragged and soiled, as was the shirt of his she had put on. She was also wearing a false beard of his and a pair of his shoes with holes in them.

That night, a Nazi patrol car pulled up near the bridge. Two soldiers got out. There were seven men around the fire. Hellroth had not counted the men who had been around the fire the previous night and who had witnessed at least some of his deeds there.

Nubik had told his comrades they would be joined that night by a relative of his from the provinces. As they had started off as three, before themselves being joined by others, they just accepted the newcomer as he was. Their one concern was to survive and help each other survive as best they could until the end of the war. They generally kept to themselves and spoke to few people other than each other. They did not suspect that Nubik was not who he claimed to be nor that he had a certain number of social connections in Vienna and beyond. Nor would it ever have occurred to them that the newcomer whom Nubik had introduced to them as Herbert was a woman.

Hellroth had decided it would be too compromising for him to return to the scene of his crime of the previous night. But he wanted to make sure that the bearded witness to that crime with whom he had spoken would not reveal anything of what he had seen. He had described Nubik, 'Wilhelm,' to the two soldiers and told them to isolate the bearded man, scare him a bit, and remind him of what he had been told by the officer who had spoken to him the night before. But when the soldiers had drawn close to the men and their fire, they realized they had a problem. They were all bearded, all dressed in the same way. Without killing the whole lot of them on the spot, it would be impossible to carry out Hellroth's orders. Besides, the two soldiers happened to know that Hellroth had recently suffered humiliation at the hands of his superiors and felt disinclined to make any special effort for an officer who seemed likely to be demoted – or worse – before long. They aimed their guns at the men around the fire. One of the soldiers called out:

'Which one of you is Wilhelm?'

'I am,' Nubik said.

'Come with us,' they said, motioning to him to leave the fireside.

A few yards away from the others, the soldiers began to question Nubik:

'What did you see last night? How many of them were there? What happened to the car?'

Nubik did not reply to any of these questions.

'Yes, there was some kind of incident,' he said. 'I told the officer who was here I would not disclose anything of what I saw.'

The two soldiers seemed satisfied with this reply and started walking back to their car. But just before they reached it, they started conferring frantically and, as one man, turned round and headed back to the group huddled at the fire.

'You others must have seen the incident,' one of them said.

They both turned to Nubik. 'What makes you think these others won't spill the beans?'

Nubik answered, 'These others and I, sir, are like you. We don't want any trouble. They won't say anything, I assure you. You can tell your commanding officer he has nothing to worry about.'

'We will interrogate them individually.'

'You're wasting your time. You won't learn any more from them than you have from me.'

The silent one of the two slapped Nubik on the face with his gloved hand. 'Don't speak to us like that. You're coming with us.'

The same soldier turned to his partner: 'This way we can prove to Hellroth we've done our job properly. He'll be pleased with us, and we can get something out of it.'

They started walking back to their car again, this time with Nubik walking between them. Suddenly a voice sounded: 'Stop! Put up your hands now, or I'll shoot you both in the back! Wilhelm, take their guns from them!' Nubik obeyed.

'Now turn round!' They did so, finding themselves face to face with one of the men who had been sitting at the fire. He was pointing a gun at them. He — in fact, it was Kristina Lichtblau — handed her gun over to Nubik, and stepped away.

'Now I'll walk you to the river,' Nubik said to the two men.

He gesticulated to them to start walking to the water's edge. He said to them, 'Turn and face me.'

They now had their backs to the water. He strode up close to them and shot them once each through the heart. They both toppled over into the water.

'War is war,' he murmured. But he knew he would have to move on. He could not stay by that bridge any longer. Just as Hellroth would have to answer for the disappearance of the officer and two underlings he had killed when the men did not return, Hellroth would be sure to look for the two soldiers — and 'Wilhelm'.

A few days later, Hellroth was in his office interrogating a man.

'I've told you all I know. Kill me or let me go.'

'Tell me again,' said Hellroth.

The man under interrogation was one of those who had sat around the fire. All the others had taken up quarters elsewhere. That had also been this man's plan. But he had decided to hang around a day or two, not realizing or wanting to realize the danger he was in and believing the others had over-reacted. Hellroth had himself driven back to the scene after his two men had not returned, and Nubik had done the same to the two men's car as Hellroth had to the car he had arrived in a couple of nights before and had it drive itself into the river. Hellroth had found only this one man there. Under torture, the man had told him about their strange companion – strange because he looked like a man but sounded a little like a woman when she spoke – who had had a gun and threatened the two soldiers with it, and about his other companion who had shot the soldiers by the water's edge, so that they had fallen, dead, into the water. Hellroth did not suspect that the man with the woman's voice was Kristina Lichtblau in disguise.

In reality, Hellroth was listening with half an ear. He had been trying to trace Kristina Lichtblau since his abortive afternoon with her, but his search had proved fruitless. He had been unable to find her husband or sons either. He was growing more and more obsessed. The dressing-down he had received from Michael Lucht had signaled, he felt, the end of his career in the army and put paid to any hope of

advancement. He had started carrying a hip flask around with him and had recently been seeing the world and the war through a permanent alcoholic haze. He
would have to win back Michael Lucht's trust or kill him in secret or on some
invented pretext, then hope to be appointed in his stead. He decided to go to the
Central to see whether he could pick up some information as to the whereabouts
of the Lichtblaus. On his way, he spotted an object lying on the pavement and
bent down to see what it was. Someone behind him forced him to the ground and
pulled his hands at once behind his back. A gun barrel was held to his back.

'Who are you? What do you want?' he cried.

All he got in reply was: 'Don't try and get near that Jewess, or any Jewess, again,
do you hear?'

Hellroth said: 'I hear,' failing to recognize Nubik's voice.

'Now on your way, and don't look back, or I'll shoot,' said the voice. Nubik
eased up the pressure of his gun on Hellroth's back to let him get to his feet and
walk away. When Hellroth was some way down the road from his assailant, he
turned round and saw the man's face. He was too far away for the man to get an
accurate aim on him. Hellroth had good enough eyesight, but Nubik was currently
unrecognizable to him without his false beard.

Neither man lingered. Somewhat shaken, Hellroth carried on towards the Central. In a few minutes, though, he found himself face to face with Michael Lucht
and two henchmen.

'I've been looking for you, Hellroth. Where are the three men I sent to get you
a few days ago? They haven't been seen since they left my office with you.'

'How should I know?' replied Hellroth. 'They agreed to drink with me, so we
all went to various *Gastwirtschaften*. I bought them some rounds they willingly
accepted. Then the officer asked us if we wanted some thrills, so I drove them to
a place the officer knew. I left on foot. They were rather... busy. I haven't seen
them since.'

'You're lying,' said Lucht.

'I haven't seen the Jewess since last time, either.'

'Yes, that's tricky.' One of the two henchmen took both Hellroth and Lucht by surprise.

'Who asked you?' Hellroth again felt the sting of humiliation at the hands of an underling.

'No, no, let him speak,' Michael Lucht insisted. 'Maybe he knows something we don't. What can you tell us?'

'I shouldn't have spoken. It was nothing.' The soldier was red-faced, surprised at his own temerity. 'I spoke out of turn.'

'You're excused,' said Lucht. 'Now, what about the Jewess?'

'If you mean Frau Lichtblau, the word is out she has taken to dressing as a man and wearing a false beard. Only her voice might distinguish her from dozens of men who look like that.'

'That's going to make finding her rather tricky, as you say.' Lucht turned to Hellroth. 'Your little Jewess is turning out to be a more complicated proposition than we thought. And as for you, Hellroth, are you good for anything at all?'

At that, Hellroth disregarded Lucht's gun and punched Lucht on the jaw. He reeled backwards. Hellroth fell on him, continuing to beat him.

'Get him off me!' shouted Lucht to the two henchmen.

The one who had spoken pressed a gun to Hellroth's temple: 'Get off him.'

Hellroth was bearing down hard on Lucht's nose, mouth and throat, almost suffocating him. But when Lucht and Hellroth were both back up on their feet, the soldier carried on pointing his gun, this time at Lucht.

Hellroth smiled at Lucht: 'Your judgments of people are too hastily formed, or too rashly spoken,' he said to Lucht.

'You wouldn't dare,' said Lucht, simultaneously addressing Hellroth and the soldier pointing his gun. 'The Führer will have you tortured and strung up on display as a warning to all would-be traitors to the Reich.'

'You won't be around to see that, I'm pretty sure,' said Hellroth, removing Lucht's pistol from his belt and tipping all the bullets from it. He placed the weapon in Lucht's right hand:

'It'll look as though you were about to fire first.'

Lucht was about to throw his pistol to the ground when Hellroth ordered the soldier: 'Fire!'

'Don't!' cried a voice from behind Hellroth and the two soldiers. 'Michael Lucht has insulted the name of Frau Kristina Lichtblau. He deserves stronger punishment than a bullet through the heart.' On both these counts, the speaker was sure to touch Hellroth.

'Who are you?' said Hellroth, turning round. By now, the soldier had let his firing hand drop, having also been distracted by the voice, as had his fellow. Lucht took advantage of the distraction to fall on Hellroth. The two men again wrestled on the ground. Their fight was vicious and personal. Hellroth cried out, 'Kill him!' But the two soldiers were in such a state of confusion that they no longer trusted either man, if they ever had, or knew whom to obey. Hellroth, at length, managed to press his own pistol against Lucht's heart.

'Enough,' Lucht said. 'I surrender.'

'On my terms, of course,' Hellroth said. Both men got up. They could just make out a figure running into the distance. The figure had a beard.

'What are your terms?' asked Lucht.

'Promotion. And no further talk of Kristina Lichtblau from you. It is in your gift to promote me. I take it as read that you consider us both henceforth to be of equal rank. Both lieutenant colonels.'

'Agreed,' replied Lucht, though they all knew he would have agreed to anything to save his skin. Hellroth fell silent. From now on, lieutenant colonel or not, he would have to be watchful every minute of the day. And he had to find the bearded figure with the strange voice he almost recognized.

Nine

Tom Oliver had indicated to Lichtblau in a letter that he should take his two boys and Thedel to a monument in the city, the Pestsaüle. The letter had not come straight from Tom Oliver: Werner, the Viennese youth currently studying with him in Oxford, handed it to Lichtblau at the street address Lichtblau had given Tom Oliver. This youth was due to be at the place indicated, along with Thedel, the son of Dagmar who was under Tom Oliver's protection in Oxford.

The three boys — Heinrich, Johannes, and Thedel — along with Werner and Lichtblau, had now gathered together to plan an escape from the country. They were all standing by the Pestsäule. Their discussion had to be brief, or it was bound to look suspicious to any passing soldier, policeman or spy. Lichtblau was far from being unknown in the city, whether to his fellow citizens or the Nazis. They all agreed they had to think fast and that Lichtblau should be the first to leave the gathering. He would slip away on his own without any prolonged goodbyes. Being used to traveling between Austria and England, Werner would take charge of Heinrich and Johannes, leaving Thedel to travel separately. Werner and the two boys would leave in a day or so, and at any rate as soon as possible: for most civilians, Jew and non-Jew alike, the city was all but uninhabitable. Werner had all the required documents — though that in itself was no guarantee of successful passage — but what about the boys? Werner had noticed that their passports were out of date, but the Nazis did not always look rigorously at such documents. They sometimes seemed just to flick through them and wave travelers on. At other times, though, they would pick on people whose documents were in order and even arrest them in a ploy to keep the population fearful, and their superiors satisfied that they were doing their jobs.

'*If anyone can help provide convincing travel documents for the boys,*' thought Lichtblau, '*it is Nubik.*'

He explained to Werner and Thedel where Nubik's bridge was and told them and the others to meet him there at nightfall, as Nubik's movements were unpredictable during the day when he was, besides, seldom at his hut.

At nightfall, they reconvened at Nubik's bridge as planned. But Lichtblau did not know that Nubik had upped sticks so that there was no one there but themselves. Suddenly, in the penumbral haze settling over the river and beyond, a car drove towards them, dazzling them with its headlights. The car stopped. A Nazi officer got out, pointing his gun at them.

'What are you doing here?'

'Walking, taking the air, sir. These are my sons and these others friends of ours. We aren't doing anything wrong.'

'I'll decide that. Your papers.'

Lichtblau handed his over. The officer scrutinized the papers with some apparent care.

'So, you are Lichtblau,' he said at last. 'You have a wife, I think.'

'The mother of my sons here, yes.'

'Where is she now?'

'I haven't seen her for some days. I don't know where she is.'

Johannes, the younger and more sensitive of the Lichtblau boys, began to cry.

'Be quiet, you sniveling puppy, or I'll shoot your father and brother dead right before your eyes. And then I'll shoot you.'

'Why don't you leave that pleasure to me, Lucht?' said a man's voice. A silhouette stepped out of the darkness behind one of the pillars under the bridge.

'Hellroth, go away from this place at once, or I will kill your friends now.'

'They are not my friends,' said Hellroth, 'And I, not you, will decide whether they are to live or die.'

Michael Lucht turned his gun away from Lichtblau and the others and towards Hellroth. Hellroth began walking in Lucht's direction. They both looked oblivious to the presence of anyone else.

'Drop your gun, Lucht. Are you sure you are in any position to serve the Reich? Only two days ago, I was your inferior. Now we are equals.'

'Then stop giving me orders,' said Lucht.

'Besides, it is not correct of me to say we are equals,' replied Hellroth. 'You don't seem to have heard the news.'

'What news?'

'I have just received a second promotion. I am a full colonel now. You are henceforth my inferior.'

'We'll see about that,' said Lucht, 'I'll go and make inquiries.'

'I have the official confirmation here, signed by the Führer himself,' said Hellroth, taking an envelope out of his inside jacket pocket. 'And you may not leave until I dismiss you.'

'Let me see your paper,' said Lucht. Hellroth handed him his envelope. Lucht examined the document and found that it was as Hellroth had said. He put the paper back in the envelope and handed it back to Hellroth.

'You have always envied me, haven't you, Hellroth? And now you taste your victory and think it is my defeat.'

'I taste my victory and drink it to the dregs,' said Hellroth, 'You are dismissed, Lucht. Out of my sight, before I report you for loitering with strange men. And boys.'

'You wouldn't.'

'Try me.'

Michael Lucht walked away, and this time Hellroth did not detain him. Instead, he turned to the assembled company.

'Lichtblau, you are wondering why I did not kill him, perhaps. There's no love lost between us. I could have claimed self-defense.'

'Hellroth, what goes on between you and your colleagues is no concern of mine. I am just trying to protect my loved ones.'

Hellroth said, 'I could have killed him just now. He won't kill me. He has an exaggerated respect for rank and authority — our German disease. I'll probably kill him sooner or later. I'd like to hear him squealing like a piglet at slaughter. He probably expects me to try to kill him. He is dull, mediocre. He can't really give orders. He can only carry them out. Where is she?'

'She's vanished,' replied Lichtblau.

'Rumor has it she's taken to disguising herself as a man and wearing a false beard.'

Lichtblau realized at once that his wife had been in touch with Nubik and most likely got her disguise from him. He knew Nubik to be resourceful. He and his family and friends certainly needed Nubik's inventive streak now.

'You will all follow me now,' said Hellroth, 'I'm taking you to the Metropole for questioning.'

'What about?' asked one of the boys. Hellroth took off one of his leather gloves and slapped the boy across the face with it. 'Conspiracy. Anything you like. Anything I like. Jewishness.' They walked a couple of minutes before coming to an army van. Hellroth waved them all in. Then he went to the driver's seat and drove the van off. But the van halted abruptly after a few minutes. A partition stood between the front and back of the van. Those in the back could hear, but not see, Hellroth shouting to another man. The front door on the driver's side opened, and Hellroth got out. Both he and the other man were shouting at the tops of their voices. Other voices soon joined theirs, and an even worse clamor arose. Those in the back of the van heard shots being fired. By sleight of hand, Thedel managed to open the back door of the van from the inside. He pushed it open a millimeter at a time. He, Werner, Heinrich, Johannes, and Lichtblau slipped out of the van one by one. Lichtblau told them to walk away casually, slowly, silently, with their hands in their pockets. The shooting and altercation between Hellroth and the men who were his adversaries went on unabated. Lichtblau had shut the back door of the van. The whole back of the van, including the door, was windowless. About half an hour after he had got out of the van, Hellroth got back into it. A group of men who, he thought, must have been sent by Lucht, had roughed him up and brought him within an inch of his life. He started to wonder whether his interest in the Lichtblau family had not made his position fragile, even though he had just been promoted.

He drove on but, after a while, could not help sensing that something about the van had changed. It felt lighter. He pulled up and got out to check. Even before he had opened the back door, he realized the prisoners had escaped. He cursed himself for his foolishness. He decided to put out alerts to various checkpoints at the city's outer limits and beyond to prevent the Lichtblau group from getting away. He decided he would see to Lucht himself, separately. But when he got back into the van, he became aware of a pain in his left thigh. He rubbed his hand over it: it was covered in blood. He decided to go back to his quarters to disinfect the wound. A bullet from the gun of one of Lucht's men – if that was who they were – had grazed his thigh. He parked the van outside the building where his quarters were, but as soon as he stepped out of the van, he collapsed in a faint on the ground.

Werner, Heinrich and Johannes took shelter at Werner's parents' flat. Werner's parents were proud of their son's entrance to Oxford University. Proud, too, of their son's willingness to make his way from Oxford back to Vienna in extreme circumstances to help the Lichtblau family and their friends. But they were uneasy about the presence of Heinrich and Johannes in their flat. If the Gestapo found out that they were there or that their son was helping them, they would be imprisoned at once.

'The boys may stay for two nights,' Werner's father told him. 'Any longer would be too dangerous for us all.'

Werner replied, 'I have to provide them with the necessary papers to get out of the city and the country. As soon as I have them, the three of us will leave for England.'

Werner tried to enlist his father's help. He said he would think it over.

When the boys came into the dining room for breakfast, Heinrich and Johannes found Werner's father looking down onto the street. Werner's father turned to the boys:

'Werner, I don't need my passport. I'm not planning to leave Vienna for the time being, nor is your mother. I'll take our passports to a friend of mine this morning. He will exchange the data and the photos with those of Heinrich and Johannes.'

'We have photos of ourselves,' said Johannes, 'but they're at home. Our father doesn't want us to go back there. He says it's too dangerous.'

'You can't leave the country, or even the city, without identity papers, including your photos.'

'There's a man in a suit hovering about outside,' said Werner's father, 'I've never seen him before. Is he anything to do with you?'

Johannes and Heinrich went to look out of the window.

'I think so,' said Johannes, 'He looks like Nubik, a family friend of ours. He may be able to help us.'

Johannes pulled the curtain back an inch. Nubik at once looked up as though he had been expecting some such movement. Johannes and Nubik nodded to each other. Then Johannes went down to speak to Nubik on the street. Heinrich, Werner and Werner's father watched from the window. They saw them confer and gesticulate vigorously before Nubik walked off, and Johannes came back up.

Nubik's plan was to walk over to the Lichtblaus' flat. If the coast was clear that way, he would go up and get the photos.

'How will he get into the building and the flat?' said Werner.

'He will know how to do so if my father isn't there. That's the sort of trick Nubik always has up his sleeve,' said Heinrich.

Thedel had decided to walk to his mother's flat in order to think things over and plan his next move. On the way, a bearded man dressed in a businessman's suit and tie stopped him politely and asked for directions to a certain place. Thedel obliged. The man replied, 'Thank you, Thedel.' They looked at each other.

'I know who you are,' said Thedel, 'you are Frau Lichtblau.'

'Thedel, you know your mother has been involved with —'

'An officer of the Gestapo,' said Thedel. 'She and her friend got trapped into illicit relations with him.'

'He's tried to do the same thing to me,' said Kristina, 'I can no longer appear in Vienna as myself. Our friend Nubik has helped me to disguise myself. The Nazis are stupid. To them, a businessman with a beard could never be a woman. The officer led me to believe he could and would help my sons escape from the country if I slept with him. I had no choice but to agree. But at the last minute, some soldiers broke into the officer's lodgings and marched him away. One of the soldiers fired at me as he was leaving, pretending to wound or kill me. After they had all left, I went through the officer's papers and found a safe-conduct pass amongst them. If it could somehow be duplicated, it would be useful to us all.'

'No, no, Frau Lichtblau,' said Thedel, 'keep it for yourself and your husband.'

'Whatever I have is yours, Thedel. Your mother has helped me many times. If I ever get to Oxford, I'll be happy to see her again. But the main thing is for you to see her again.'

'Frau Lichtblau, we must, then, try and get your pass duplicated. Our lives may depend on it.'

While they were talking, a Nazi soldier came into sight and walked up to the two of them.

'What were you talking about?'

Thedel replied, 'I was just giving this man'— he pointed with his chin at Frau Lichtblau — 'directions.'

The soldier said, 'Why would you want to help him? I could shoot him dead right now, and no one would miss him. Scum of the earth.'

Thedel replied, 'He says he has been feeling dizzy and having amnesia spells.'

Kristina began coughing and turned her back to the soldier and the young man.

'He also has some kind of sickness,' said Thedel. 'Whether you shoot him or not, by the sound of him, he hasn't got long to live.'

The soldier said: 'When the glorious Reich is established once and for all, people like him won't exist anymore.'

Kristina turned back round to face them. Suddenly she crouched down, brought low by the apparent violence of her cough. Then she grabbed the soldier's booted calf with both hands and clung on hard. He tried to shake her off, but she would not budge. Thedel edged slightly behind the soldier. He could just see Kristina's face. She flashed him the briefest of glances. Thedel went to where he could see the soldier's face and threw up his arm as though to give the Nazi salute. The soldier did the same quasi-mechanically. Kristina grabbed the soldier's other calf and, in a single wrench, managed to unbalance him so that he tottered over backward. As he did so, Thedel managed to snatch the soldier's pistol from its holster. He held the man's right arm away from his body, and Kristina was holding both his feet down. Thedel sat down hard on the man's neck. He was now lying on his back on the ground, pinned down by his two assailants. Thedel pressed the soldier's pistol to his heart.

'Papers, wallet, money, the works,' said Thedel. He had an empty beer bottle in his jacket's outer pocket, which he whipped out and struck the soldier over the head with. The blow stunned him unconscious at once.

'We have to move from here,' Thedel said. 'Frau Lichtblau, you mustn't be seen with us in public again. You are already a suspect, and they are probably out searching for you.'

'You now have enough identity papers — the ones I've given you, and this soldier's — to get through checkpoints and out of the country,' said Kristina. 'We need to change the names on them and the photos. As soon as the soldier comes round, he will inform his hierarchy, and the army will comb the city for the two of us. My husband has a friend who may be able to help you with getting the papers in shape.'

Thedel handed her a slip of paper and a pencil, and she wrote down the friend's particulars.

'You mustn't tell him anything about my new circumstances, or my disguise, or what we've done, or where you think I might be. If he asks, tell him my husband and I are all right. Tell him it is we who have suggested you contact him. If you do so, he will do anything he can to help you.'

'Frau Lichtblau,' said Thedel, 'you should take this soldier's pistol for yourself. You need it more than we do. With God's help, we will be gone in a couple of days.' She took the gun and put it in her right-hand trouser pocket.

They were just about to take leave of each other when a police car drew up. The driver, who was the only one in it, got out.

'What happened to this man?'

'We were wondering the same thing, sir,' replied Thedel, 'We came across him lying here. He has lost consciousness. Shall we help you put him in your car?'

The policeman spotted the empty beer bottle Thedel had used to cosh the soldier lying on the ground. 'He seems to have had a drink too many,' he said.

'Looks that way,' said Thedel. Then, to try and put an end to the conversation before the man started asking them awkward questions or requesting their papers, Thedel approached the unconscious soldier and picked him up off the ground. The policeman opened the back door of his car, and together they laid the unconscious man on the back seat.

'He'll be fine,' said Thedel, 'he'll probably have a headache when he wakes up.' Kristina and Thedel smiled at the policeman, vaguely nodding, and made as if to leave in the hope that he would take the hint and be on his way, too. The policeman sat down in the driver's seat and turned the engine on. He wound his window down. 'How did he get the bump on his head?'

'We don't know,' replied Thedel, 'we found him lying on the ground where he was when you stopped.'

Kristina and Thedel nodded again in unison.

'Where can I contact you if need be?' said the policeman.

Thedel dictated an address to him.

'Let me check this against your papers.'

'There's no point in your looking at my papers. I've moved since my papers were issued to me.'

'Let me see them anyway,' said the policeman.

'All right,' said Thedel, looking down and fishing around in his pockets, 'here —' He looked up, and as he did so, he spat hard in the policeman's eye: a thick gob of spit which made the policeman touch his eye at once, while Thedel took aim and spat in the man's other eye. His eyes were drenched in phlegm and spit. At this point, Kristina and Thedel ran off. They headed into the first side-street they came to.

The policeman wiped his eyes on his sleeves and got out of his car, peering around him to try and make out which way the pair had gone. He saw no clues as to their whereabouts but walked a few hundred yards. At the entrance to the first side street he came to, he noticed a false beard on the ground and picked it up. He did not associate it with the two people who had just escaped him. He walked back to his car and took the concussed soldier to a hospital. The doctors examined the soldier. He had probably been struck on the head by someone using a bottle. Nevertheless, he could be expected to be all right, apart from a headache, when he came round. The policeman said he would return later to see how the soldier was getting on and drove back to his headquarters. He had pocketed the false beard, and being something of a joker — a phenomenon unheard of in the Gestapo — he attached the beard to his face just before entering the building.

In the hallway, he happened to pass Michael Lucht. The two men knew each other. The policeman saluted Lucht, but Lucht did not return his salute. He was too astounded.

'Where did you get the false beard?'

'I found it on the ground somewhere on the outskirts of the city.' He explained precisely where. The policeman was supposed to have been patrolling the streets by car.

'What made you stop your car and get out?' The policeman explained the sequence of events that had led up to his finding the false beard on the ground. He described to Lucht the physical appearance of the two people who had been close to the soldier lying on the ground when he first drew up in his car. One of them had been a businessman-type with quite a long beard like the false one he found on the ground.

'The one you have is not *like* that of the person you saw: it *is* that person's,' said Lucht. 'And that person is a woman. We must try and find the two of them. I know who she is. It will be hard for her to hide without her beard.'

The concussed soldier later confirmed that he had been knocked out by the two people he had approached. And one of them did have a beard exactly like the false one the policeman showed him. They had been wary of showing him their identity papers, as the policeman had also found in his turn. Lucht wanted to get to them before Hellroth did.

Thedel sat with Markus Jäger in his flat, Jäger telling him they would all have to act fast before his flat was raided or —

'Or what?' asked Thedel.

'Or my brother turns up,' replied Jäger. His brother had been seen going in and out of various Nazi offices. They gave him the freedom to come and go as he pleased, flattered, according to Jäger's brother, that a journalist should take such an interest in them. His brother, said Jäger, had in fact made life rather difficult for himself. Now he seemed to be making other people's lives more difficult than they already were.

'Have you thought —' Thedel began.

'Of killing him?' replied Markus Jäger. He had often thought of it. It sickened him that people like his brother thought they were making history and that their deeds would be considered valorous by future generations. His brother claimed to be reporting on history to pass on testimony to future generations. At one time, when his brother had been young and idealistic, he had wanted to be a writer, a real one. In the previous decade, he had fallen in with a group of reporters who used to meet at the Central. The immediacy of reporting and instantly seeing your name in print made the hours he had been spending alone in a small rented room, racking his brains to come up with a few paltry paragraphs of fiction per day, seem tedious and arid. He found that, when he was reporting, he could write quickly and fluently. Josef Jäger was reserved, or pretended to be, but apparently friendly. People opened up to him, confided in him. But he was also, at times, an uneasy, jittery sort of character.

'He stifles his conscience. He hides from himself. And other people. Why the Nazis accept him is a secret he keeps to himself. Maybe it's his respectable appearance. Or he's doing secret deals with them.' There were even times when Markus Jäger envied his brother, whom the Nazis never bothered and even supported. Thedel sensed this in Markus Jäger. It made Thedel wary of him.

Thedel started wondering whether Markus Jäger would ever get around to helping him. Perhaps he did not really want to. Was Herr Lichtblau too trusting, too unsuspecting?

Jäger went over to the phone and made a call in muffled tones which Thedel did not understand. He put the phone down and then made another call. This time Thedel heard him mention the name 'Josef Jäger.' He was asking whether Josef Jäger was there. He was not. Did the other person know where he was? It was his brother Markus Jäger speaking. The young man gathered that Josef Jäger would be busy all day and was possibly out of town. But you could not be sure of anything. Nobody's word was to be trusted. Markus Jäger turned to face the young man. Sweat was dripping down his forehead. He would take the papers they had with them to a friend of his who would doctor them to make them appear to be the young man's. Thedel had an identity photo that he handed him.

'What are you going to do while I am away at my friend's? It is too dangerous for you to stay here on your own.'

Thedel said, 'Dangerous for you or for me? Everything is dangerous for everybody these days.'

'True,' said Markus Jäger, 'but with luck, you will be on your way out of the city and heading to England by tomorrow evening.'

'Is your brother a danger to us?' asked Thedel.

'He would sell you for next to nothing.'

'I gather he is in thrall to Frau Lichtblau,' said Thedel somewhat daringly.

'Maybe he is. But you will have understood from what I said before that he has gone over to the Nazis, and they would like to destroy the Lichtblaus. They are biding their time a little. I must go to my friend now.'

Markus Jäger and Thedel then both made to leave when there was a knock at the door. Markus Jäger heard his brother's voice calling, 'Markus?'

'That's Josef, my brother,' said Markus Jäger to the young man. 'I'll hide you in the bedroom.'

'No,' said Thedel, 'I'm not scared of anyone. I'm no hero, but I won't run away from your brother.'

'Yes,' replied Markus Jäger, 'but still, my brother may use your presence here to try and incriminate me with the Nazis.'

Markus Jäger went as far as the door but without opening it. 'Josef, I'm busy. You can't come in now.'

'Is that bitch with you?'

'I always knew you were cut out to be a poet,' replied Markus Jäger. He constantly mocked his brother for having abandoned his literary ambitions for a gutter journalist's life. 'Say that kind of thing again, and you won't say it a third time.'

'Ever the hard man, Markus,' said Josef Jäger, 'Can't you take a little brotherly teasing?'

As he was talking with his brother, Markus Jäger was gesticulating to Thedel to leave his flat by a door at the back, which he signaled led outside so that the teenager could get out the back way without Josef Jäger seeing him. He and Markus Jäger glanced at each other, and, despite what Thedel had said a minute before, they nodded in agreement that this was no time to argue. Thedel stole to the back of the flat and ran down the outside stairs and into the streets behind the block of flats. He had no idea why Markus Jäger was helping him in this way, especially as he had caught him snooping among his possessions in his own home. Was it all part of some kind of rivalry with his brother? Was he privately undecided about throwing in his lot with the Nazis, which would make him no better than his brother, an idea he could not stand, or siding with people like the Lichtblaus and himself? He seemed to want to help him escape to England, almost as though he was going to England and not someone else. Thedel felt this Markus Jäger had something of a split personality: he was attracted to the Nazis but, for the moment, held the uprightness of the Lichtblau group in high esteem.

'She's either with you or she isn't, or she's going out the back way,' said Josef Jäger. 'If you don't let me in, I'm going to break down the door.'

'I have three locks on this door,' said Markus Jäger, 'and like you, I have a gun. I've told you I'm busy. Now run along, little brother.'

'Don't worry, big brother. I'll be back with a few friends of mine. And sooner or later, I'll even bring you her head on a silver platter.'

Markus did not respond. He waited for his brother to go away. But he did not.

'Can you hear me, Markus?'

Markus Jäger was now sure the teenager was some distance away. He wondered how he would get the faked identity papers to him, assuming his friend agreed to do the job and do it fast.

'Listen, Josef, isn't it time you returned to your friends? You were made for each other — if you know what I mean.'

'You'll pay for this, Markus. But above all, so will she.' Then Markus Jäger heard his brother walking away from his front door.

Kristina had an agreement with her husband that if circumstances should ever prevent them from meeting up at their flat, as was the case at present, they would do so at Markus Jäger's. It was the latter who had suggested this arrangement to them. She was at this moment heading towards Markus Jäger's flat. She did not realize that Josef Jäger was now a menace to her and that the Nazis had bribed Josef Jäger to work for them. He wanted to use his situation to hurt the Lichtblaus. But, among her many other talents, Kristina had the gift of elusiveness, a useful one at such a treacherous time.

Markus Jäger left his flat in the same way as the teenager had and set off through the backstreets of Vienna. About a mile from his flat, as he was approaching his friend's, the document forger's, he heard a woman's voice whisper his name. He stopped and looked around. Kristina stood on the other side of the street from him. She seemed pleased to see him, and the distraught look on her face vanished.

'Markus, I was just on my way to your place. Have you seen Thedel?'

'He's been to my place but left before I did. It's no longer safe there. My brother is on the rampage. He's declared war on me. The Nazis have quite easily managed to bring him over to their side. He will do us all as much harm as he can, especially you and your family.'

'He's lost his ideals and grown disillusioned.'

'You used to be his ideal, Kristina. But he's a Nazi now, all but officially.' Markus Jäger thought to himself: 'Josef has all the power, and I have none. Perhaps I will one day become like him.'

'Where's Thedel going?'

'My brother turned up at my front door. I had Thedel leave by the back way. I don't know where he is now. I have the identity papers I told him I'd take to a friend to see whether he can and will prepare them for the young man's departure. I'm on my way to his place.'

'How will he find you, or you him?' asked Kristina.

'I'll think of that later. First, I'll go to my friend's to ask him to work on the papers.'

'Thedel knows Vienna well. He will also be looking out for you, but not near your place. I think he'll go to the Central and wait for you around there. He knows how not to attract attention.'

'Where will you go, Kristina? Where will you sleep tonight?'

'Thedel's mother Dagmar is a very good friend of mine. She's in Oxford. She's left me the keys to her flat. My husband knows I have them, so I'm all right for accommodation. But I can't stay much longer in Vienna. Nubik will help me to leave and will leave himself.'

'Won't Thedel go back to his mother's flat if he doesn't find me, or someone to give him his papers, at the Central?'

'He probably will if he doesn't get arrested at or near the Central. Go to your friend's, get the papers done, and go to the Central. If you find Thedel there, bring him to his mother's flat. If he is not, come to her flat anyway. We may find he's there already. Whatever happens, we must hope that Thedel will be on his way to Oxford by tomorrow evening.'

So Markus Jäger made his way to the Central. He did not find Thedel there and was about to step outside the front door of the café and head to Dagmar's flat when two men barred his way, one in Nazi uniform: his brother Josef and Hellroth.

'Fancy seeing you two together! Whatever next!' said Markus Jäger.

'Where's Frau Lichtblau?' replied Hellroth.

'Search me, little boys,' said Markus Jäger, who knew that what his brother, Hellroth and probably all Nazis abhorred most was levity, especially at their expense.

'You insolent dog! Tell me where she is!' shouted Hellroth, shaking Markus Jäger by the shoulders and then making as if to throttle him.

'Aren't you the dog who's been deprived of his bone and looks around bewildered, wondering where it has gone or who took it from him?' replied Markus Jäger, quite unfazed, looking Hellroth straight in the eye, 'Don't ask me where she is. Ask your friend Lucht. Hasn't he gone up in the world? Perhaps a little too high up for your liking, Hellroth. But don't worry, what goes up, must come down.'

Hellroth turned to Josef Jäger. 'Your brother's a little caustic. What shall we do with him?'

'Do with him whatever the Führer would do with him.'

'Well, I'm sure the Führer would like to see him in Mauthausen. But perhaps it isn't quite time yet. What were you doing in the Central, Jäger? You seemed to be looking for someone.'

'Everybody seems to be doing that these days,' replied Markus.

'You're a little too clever for your own good, Jäger.'

'Josef,' said Markus Jäger, keeping his eyes off Hellroth throughout the whole conversation, 'either go inside and have a drink or be on your way. I'm off now. I have nothing to add to what I've already said. Aren't you tempted by the prospect of a little schnapps?'

'Or something more toxic, you mean?' replied his brother.

'You said it, not I,' replied Markus Jäger.

The conversation could have gone on indefinitely, except that a car drew up just then, out of which stepped Michael Lucht. He seemed surprised to see Hellroth talking with two civilians just outside the Central.

'Talk of the devil,' said Hellroth, who no longer bothered disguising his hatred of his rival.

'What were you saying about me,' replied Lucht, 'that was so complimentary?'

'This gentleman'— Hellroth pointed at Markus Jäger with his chin — 'said you would know where Kristina was.'

'I did not say you would know,' broke in Markus Jäger, 'I said that if Hellroth and my brother Josef wanted to know Frau Lichtblau's whereabouts, they had better turn to someone like yourself better placed in the hierarchy. I was using your name to needle my brother and Hellroth.'

'What if I did know where she was? What's it to you?' demanded Lucht.

'I want to talk to her,' said Hellroth, 'I suspect her of aiding and abetting escapees from the Reich. I suspect her of betraying the Reich. It is my duty — our duty — to find her and make sure she does not offend again.'

'You mean you'd like to imprison her in your bed, you loathsome provincial slob,' said Lucht.

'You mean you wouldn't, Lucht?' said Hellroth.

'I knew you would be here,' said Lucht. 'And I've come because I've been doing a little research.' He looked at the Jäger brothers.

'Lucht, you're asking for trouble,' said Hellroth. He began walking away, mumbling threats, oaths and vile obscenities. Lucht called after him:

'I wrote the Führer a full report on my findings and sent it to him by express motorbike courier. If I were you, I wouldn't hang around Vienna too long.'

Hellroth turned round: 'You're lying.'

'Say what you like. He'll be reading it by now.'

Markus Jäger inwardly breathed a sigh of relief: he had managed to flatter Lucht, or at least stay on the right side of him. He did not care what he said to Hellroth, who was dangerous because he was cowardly but afraid of displeasing his hierarchy. One day he might join Lucht, join even Hellroth, subscribe to their aims, and doubtless pay the price not only in permanent, nervous uneasiness but above all in self-loathing, a self-loathing he already felt crawling over his skin like a disease that itched and scratched.

Ten

'I'm uneasy. Werner's been in Vienna for three weeks now, and I haven't heard a word from him. He told me he'd phone if he could, which means he hasn't been able to.'

Dagmar and Ilse looked from Tom Oliver to each other. 'Maybe he hasn't met up with Thedel after all.' Dagmar's voice trembled.

'Idle speculation will only make you feel worse. All we can do is wait to hear from Werner or Thedel.' Tom Oliver put a comforting hand on her shoulder.

It was after two in the morning when there was a knock at the door of Tom Oliver's bedroom. His scout had instructions never to bother him at night except in case of extreme emergency. Oliver pushed his companion away from him and went to the door.

'Yes?'

'Sorry to be a nuisance at this time of night, sir. There's a gentleman on the phone what says he wants to speak to you, sir. Says it's urgent-like.'

'I'll come right away.'

'Hello. Is that Professor Oliver?'

'Speaking.'

'My name is Alfred Nubik. I'm a friend of the Lichtblaus. They are having some trouble at the moment but so are most people in Vienna. Your number has been passed on to me by Werner, your student. He wants you to know he's all right. He has met up with Thedel, who's in good shape, too. Werner is with the two Lichtblau boys, Heinrich and Johannes. They're expecting to leave Vienna any day now. The hold is tightening on the Lichtblaus. They have some complicated business with an SS officer. The same officer also managed to draw Dagmar, Thedel's mother, and her friend Ilse into his web. Are they safe and well with you?'

'They are. Safe and well, but worried out of their minds about Thedel, the Lichtblaus, and their other friends in Vienna. What kind of dealings?'

Beads of sweat had started to form and glisten on Tom Oliver's already shiny bald pate.

'As you may have gathered, the officer, Hellroth, tried to pressure Herr Lichtblau into giving him large sums of money. Herr Lichtblau worked in a bank until recently. The officer claimed he did so at the behest of his hierarchy. He also made false promises to the two women in return for having illicit, forced relations with him. They managed to give him the slip. Perhaps you know this already or know the rest. I doubt they will return to Vienna as long as the war lasts. But I'm phoning to tell you that Werner and the Lichtblau boys should be leaving Vienna very shortly now and on their way to you. Frau Lichtblau will think things over.'

'What about Thedel?' asked Tom Oliver.

'I gather he's trying to put together the necessary travel documents to flee the country and get to Oxford, too, where he wants to join his mother.'

'I'll start preparing for Werner's return with the two boys.'

'You do understand about Dagmar and Ilse, don't you? I gather from your tone that they've told you about their trouble with the officer. They simply had no choice.'

'I quite understand,' murmured Tom Oliver. 'Perhaps I should come myself and help Werner. My academic credentials mean the Nazis would think twice before laying a hand on me.'

'Sir, I assure you,' said Nubik, 'the Nazis don't give a damn about anyone's credentials. They are not interested in credibility, their own or anyone else's. The time for propaganda is over. Their only stock in trade is brute force. Brute force and lies. Power, money, betrayal, especially betraying their own; and keeping their leader's extermination process in full swing.'

Tom Oliver's companion was signaling to him to return to bed. Tom Oliver scowled and looked away. 'Let's hope they all get out alive.'

'Let's hope,' said Nubik.

'But what about you?'

'The whole Austrian population cannot expect to flee. I'll go on doing what I can where I —'

'Hello, what's up, can you hear me?' The line had gone dead. Tom Oliver was left holding the receiver in mid-air.

'You lost him?' called out his companion.

Tom Oliver did not go back to bed. Instead, he stood staring into the dark. All his life, he had been excessively academic, excessively sociable. Now all his communicativeness seemed somehow to be bearing fruit. He saw how he could make use of all the contacts with colleagues, writers and others he had built up over the years, to save lives, especially young lives, the lives of people like those to whom he had always been most devoted. People now depended on him and the use he made of his position, intelligence, diplomatic skills and network of friends and acquaintances.

He got dressed and went outside into Wadham Quad, leaving his companion to wonder where he'd gone, and why. When not indulging in the pleasures of the flesh, being the 'immoral front' as he called it, he had lived most of his life in and for books and words and thought. He had made a living and a career out of them. But the political situation in Europe in the nineteen-thirties and then the war had made him feel he was being called upon to act, or to act in a different kind of way than before, and beyond his usual scholarly activities. The languages he had learned – to impress his teachers, understand obscure texts, get ahead in his career – he could now use to communicate with people in different parts of Europe and further afield. He felt as though his whole life had been preparation for this.

Dagmar and Ilse had found their way to him. But Thedel was still in Vienna. Dagmar had told him Thedel had not been circumcised. That would be helpful if he ran into trouble. But, circumcised or not, he was known as the son of a Jewess, and that put him at risk.

Lichtblau was certainly active in the Viennese Resistance, though he was so wily it was hard to pin anything on him. The Nazi officer had drawn Frau Lichtblau into his game, but she was surviving and helping those around her survive or get away. He wanted to make arrangements in Oxford for the two Lichtblau boys, if only they managed to get there. The Nazis were massacring people, and in doing so, the humanist ideals to which he had devoted his life. He was no saint, not even a priest or turbulent bishop like his friend Bell or that friend of Bell's, the quiet but steadfast German pastor whose writings he admired and who was trying with ruthless dedication to overthrow the Reich. But even Falstaff had times when he tried to be good.

He peered at the stars as though they held an answer to all his questions or could assuage the turmoil of his feelings. But they had no solutions to offer him. Truly, man was a fallen creature, fallen from Eden, fallen from Olympus, from the heights of the music and poetry whose servant he had always sought to be. He thought of Iris and Lydia, two friends, one or other of whom might take the boys in.

As for Werner, what would he do when he got back from Vienna — if he got back? Would he finish the thesis he was working on under his supervision? Or would he be too traumatized by his experience of war-torn Europe? Werner himself did not mind being sometimes nicknamed 'the Oliverista from Vienna.' In fact, he took it as a compliment. Tom Oliver had high hopes for him. Werner was his only student he saw as having the ability to get an Oxbridge job and perhaps succeed him one day. One day. For some reason, Tom's mind reverted to his many visits to the brothels of Paris, Vienna and Berlin. They seemed a long way behind him. His all-consuming need for pleasure had often led him astray. He had taken part in orgies demeaning for some of the people present, who were clearly

dependent on such gatherings for their livelihood; they let the paying clients treat
them worse than beasts of burden. He had enjoyed a culture of hedonism as strong
as, if not stronger than, the humanism which, as he often told anyone who would
listen, including the university authorities, was his priority and his guiding light.
Was that hedonistic culture which he had, like his friend Christopher, lapped up
in Berlin and Vienna, itself partly responsible for the war? The paroxysm of indul-
gence had given way to absolute horror: were they not somehow connected? It did
not bear thinking about.

The night seemed to be retreating, blowing away in the dawn breeze as though
it were a dove's feather. What was prompting him now to help these oppressed
people, these Jews threatened with extinction? Nothing in his earlier life could
have presaged it. Why not? In fact, when he was a young teenager, he had either
been trying to survive psychologically in a public-school environment that did not
tolerate people who were different or indulging his love of pleasure in all its forms.

He had been blinded at school by a version of history that always told stories
in terms of the reigns of monarchs. Even if it recounted their wars, too, it never
even hinted at the sufferings of what was wrongly called 'ordinary people,' let alone
the soldiers fighting the wars decided by the aristocrats. But then, he had received
the call to active service in France. Public-school life had taught him to toughen
up, on the outside at least. He knew his carapace was less hard than he tried to
make it seem, but on the battlefields of France, he learned that he was not tough
at all. The First War both broke and remade Tom Oliver. It re-educated him,
giving him direct insight into the best and worst sides of human nature. The public
image of the war, he would say, was far kinder and more idealistic than the reality.
From then on, he had started to become aware of other people's existence, of their
suffering. He witnessed the onset of the Second War with distress, but he was now
prepared for it, though he was still unable to conceive of a war more cruel than the
First. He would soon be put right on that score.

His companion would be waking soon and then pestering Tom Oliver to go
down to London or Brighton for the day or to go boating on the Cherwell. He did

not have the heart to go to another city today. But a punt on the Cherwell, a dip at Parson's Pleasure, were things he could never resist. Oxford was idyllic. Yet he obscurely felt it was too idyllic for him at this time unless he could do his part to reduce the misery in the new dark and perverse world. He walked over to the entrance to his staircase and back up to his rooms. When he went into his bedroom, he saw that his bed was empty. There was a note on his pillow. It read: *Your love is strictly universal. There is only one person in the world you really love.*

'Myself,' he said out loud, 'Myself.'

That was, he knew, what his companion's note meant. Yet, at least he tried to put his 'universal' love into action. He lay down on his bed, wiping a tear from his jowl. And then he thought of the Bohemian poet's words: *Du musst dein Leben ändern! You must change your life!* He would try and do that, too.

Eleven

'What did he do to you?'

They were lying in bed.

'Nothing.'

'So, how did you get this long cut?'

Kristina did, in fact, have a horizontal cut along her back below her left shoulder blade. 'Oh, that? That's nothing.'

'You keep saying nothing. Why don't you answer? How did you get it, my love?' Lichtblau tried not to get angry.

'He tried to embrace me. He pulled a knife on me. He held me to him with the knife behind my back. He cut me once with the blade. He said he didn't mean to do it. He said he was just using the knife to threaten me.'

'You know as well as I do,' her husband replied, 'that these people say and do whatever they like.'

'He wanted me to give myself freely to him. I was going to. But I got cold feet at the last moment. It was then he drew his knife.'

Her husband was incredulous. 'Were you really going to give yourself to him?'

'It was for the benefit of the boys. He said he would help them leave the country and me with them.'

'You can't trust a word these people say, and anyway, even supposing he had helped the boys flee, he would hardly have let a prize like you slip through his hands.'

'I'm not a prize, more a liability.' They both laughed. Many men in Vienna had desired Kristina Lichtblau and loved her from afar. Many men in Vienna still desired her, including several Gestapo officers who, though they wouldn't admit it for the world, would pay a high price for a mere glance from her (she would not give them even that trivial satisfaction).

'I was prepared to let him use me since he had led me to believe he would help us, that's all. But I wasn't going to give myself to him. Give him anything of myself, I mean.'

'I know you weren't.'

Their bed was in the cellar of the building in which Kristina's friend Dagmar had her flat. Dagmar had told her years before about the existence of the cellar, any access to which was invisible to the naked eye. The entrance was not a door through which just anyone in the building could pass. A trap-door leading down into the cellar from Dagmar's flat was the only way to get to it. Dagmar's flat was on the ground floor, and the trap-door was in Dagmar's living room. Her living room had a fitted carpet which, in reality, was not stuck or nailed down and which, when lifted up, allowed the trap-door to open and close. Thus it was that the Lichtblaus had the run of both the flat — in which they had rarely spent any time, for fear of compromising Thedel or Dagmar, even though the latter was out of the country and Thedel, they hoped, shortly to be — and the cellar. The only problem was that to get to the flat, and therefore the cellar, they had to go through the front door of the building and out of it when they wanted to leave. Anyone seeing them going into Dagmar's flat would, if they rang at the door ten minutes later, be surprised not to get any response. So the cellar was as safe as possible but not entirely safe from a suspicious or collaborationist neighbor who, once inside the flat, would doubtless seek the Lichtblaus high and low in order to discover where and how they had vanished. Still, they decided it was the best place for them and would serve at least until Kristina had left for England.

'Nubik needs to know where we are,' mused Kristina, 'he's the one keeping us all together.'

'Not true, my darling. You're the thread running through all our lives.'

'Including those of some undesirable people.' They both smiled.

A few days afterward, in the cellar again, they heard the front door of Dagmar's flat blown open by a bullet and boots stamping around on the floor. They supposed that one of their neighbors had denounced them since they were not tenants, and Dagmar was known to have fled the country. Hellroth already knew the flat because of his dealings with Dagmar, and Lichtblau and Kristina thought they could make out his voice. He and his henchmen sounded as though they were overturning the furniture, emptying crockery and silverware onto the floor so that it came crashing down. Lichtblau looked at his wife and rubbed his hands gleefully. She could see what he was thinking. The more those oafs upturn and spill things on the floor, the less likely they are even to think of taking up the carpet. Even if they did take it up, they would have to do so at the exact spot where the trapdoor was, and the trapdoor was anyway so well blended into the wooden floor that it looked almost identical to the other floorboards.

Around twenty minutes later, they heard the soldiers stomping out of the flat. They heard Hellroth shouting that he'd been had, just as he'd been had by those two little Jewesses. He and the soldiers were furious now. The Lichtblaus heard them knocking at the flat on the ground floor opposite Dagmar's. They knew there was a couple, a young man and woman, who lived there. Was it they who had tipped off the Nazis — even if involuntarily — as to the mysterious comings and goings in the flat opposite theirs? Was it the young woman, since the man was out during the day while she seemed to stay at home and had exchanged brief greetings with the Lichtblaus several times? They heard knocking at the neighbors' door. Then silence. Lichtblau, always hopeful, mimed drinking his wife's health with an imaginary glass in his hand. Then a gun-butt rapped upon the front door of the flat across the hallway. It opened, and a heated discussion began between the men and the young woman. Hellroth's voice prevailed over his men's and the young woman's. He wanted action. He wanted blood. He wanted the Lichtblau couple or the young woman and her husband would pay with their lives. The woman started screaming.

The Lichtblaus heard Hellroth's voice: 'Stop, you dogs. Not now. We have nothing to show. We must get the Lichtblaus. If we don't find them soon, don't worry. We'll come back for this bitch.' The group of Nazis left the building. The young woman broke into sobs and shut her front door.

But shortly afterward, they heard her come out of her flat and walk across the hall to Dagmar's. The Nazis had left Dagmar's flat open, and the young woman walked in. Lichtblau looked at his wife and put his forefinger vertically to his lips. Then he climbed the cellar steps to the top. He heard the young woman walking around Dagmar's living room. She was saying, 'My God, my God.'

Finally, she went near the spot where the trapdoor was. Lichtblau suddenly pushed it open. The young woman fell over and screamed from fright. Lichtblau crawled out of the trapdoor and put his hand over the young woman's mouth.

'Please be quiet. You have to come with me down to the cellar. You go first.'

The young woman nodded and obeyed. Lichtblau pulled the carpet back into place, climbed down the trapdoor, shut it, and went down after the young woman. Kristina stared at her for a second.

'Did you betray us?' Lichtblau asked. 'What harm have we done you? And now you have done yourself and your husband much harm. If they don't find us, they will come back for you.'

'My husband will be home this evening. What will happen when he discovers I've gone?'

'You'll stay here while I go and speak to your husband,' said Lichtblau.

'He doesn't know anything about this, so leave him out of it,' she replied.

'You're hardly in a position to tell us what to do,' said Kristina. 'Your husband will obey us, and so will you. Yesterday your life was as safe as it could be in this city at this time. Now it is no safer than those of our Jews, though you're not

Jewish. You tried to betray us to the enemy to shore up your own safety. Rather a mistake, don't you think?'

'Look. I want to help you, and I want to help us all. I paid for my mistake when they came for me the first time.'

'And it will be far worse next time,' said Kristina, 'They could have gang-raped and killed you this afternoon.'

'They nearly did,' said the young woman.

'You'll stay indefinitely now. I'll bring your husband down this evening.'

'You say you want to help us all,' said Kristina, 'but — how can we trust you after what I've done?' The young woman was distraught. 'I made a wrong move, but this is war.'

'We know that.' Kristina gave her a doubtful look.

'I'm asking you to trust me, however hard it may be for you, however unworthy of such trust I've shown myself to be. My husband will help you, too, I'm sure. I'm your prisoner here, and any punishment you mete out to me, I would deserve. But you're also, I know, protecting me.'

She turned more particularly to Kristina: 'I know you don't want to hurt me. We can help you. We're freer than you. We have no children. Dagmar told me all about you. The Nazis never did us any harm till Dagmar disappeared. Hellroth went mad after that.'

'But they've harmed and killed so many others.' Lichtblau watched her intently.

'I wanted to save my husband and myself. I was wrong. Nothing is normal or predictable now. Since the war started, I've seen people I thought were bad do good things. I used to think I was good, but that was arrogant of me, and now I've done a bad thing.'

Kristina stood up and backed away from the young woman. 'You seem to know Hellroth.'

'He had been coming here for Dagmar. Sometimes I was at her place when he arrived. The three of us used to talk. Or rather, since he imposed himself on her, she decided that whenever he came, she would ply him with champagne and cigars to get him to talk, see what he'd disclose. He told us how he was involved in money matters with your husband. And he never hid the fact that he had feelings for you, Frau Lichtblau.'

Lichtblau looked doubtful: 'If they really were what are usually called feelings.'

'Dagmar grew more and more scared of him. He always told her to trust him, but he didn't realize she saw through him. He was exploiting her, but she was using him as protection until she could get out of the country. She started to panic. She had to get out before the situation with Hellroth got even more out of hand.'

The three of them suddenly fell silent. Voices resonated in the hallway; boots shuffled. The young woman made out her husband's voice along with what all three of them realized was Hellroth's. They could hear the whole group, including the husband, going into the couple's flat. They didn't bother to shut the front door, and the three in the cellar could hear the husband: 'I don't know where my wife is, but I don't think she can have gone far. She'll probably be back soon.'

They heard Hellroth's slothful, languid tone of voice: 'We'll wait, then. Always supposing you're telling the truth. Beware if you're not.'

Then they heard nothing for a few minutes. Now the sound of glass tinkling. The husband must have given the soldiers drinks. Then, after about forty-five minutes, there was silence again. The three in the cellar started to pick up the sound of snoring. The young woman wrote something on a scrap of paper and handed it to Frau Lichtblau: *My husband keeps high-alcohol-volume vodka in the drinks cabinet. I'm sure he's given them vodka and lime.* The three in the cellar now felt able to whisper to each other. They gathered that under the influence of drink

Hellroth and the soldiers had fallen asleep, while the young neighbor's husband was still awake.

'I'll go and see him.' Lichtblau got up.

'No. You stay here. You'll be safer. I want to make sure my husband's all right.'

'You must understand I don't feel you're quite trustworthy despite your protestations of regret about denouncing my wife and me. I'll go and try and see your husband, and I must hurry before the soldiers come round. I'll tell him I know where you are and to go to a certain place —'

'Where?' pleaded the young wife.

'I won't tell you now. You're our prisoner. What's to say that if I let you join your husband, you won't just try and buy your freedom from the Nazis by telling them you really do know, finally, where my wife and I are?'

Within the minute, Lichtblau had climbed the steps to the trap-door and was standing just in front of the neighbors' flat. He breathed and reflected for a moment. He had no weapon to defend himself or threaten anyone. The young husband might not be awake after all, but rather one of the Nazis who had abstained from drinking — or drinking too much — in order to protect his group if necessary. Lichtblau changed his mind about going into the neighbors' flat and retraced his steps back to the trap-door in Dagmar's living room.

Just about to go back down the steps, Lichtblau sensed he had been followed. He turned round to see a young man.

'You must be Dagmar's neighbor. I take it you have the key to this place.' The young man nodded.

'Have you pulled the door of your flat shut?' Again, the young man nodded.

'What about the door to this flat?'

The young man shook his head.

'You must go back and lock it.' The young man did so and returned to Lichtblau.

'Now, we can talk quietly but freely. Your wife and mine are down in the cellar. You must go and join them. I have business to attend to in town. I'll bring back food for the three of you tomorrow.'

'Why can't we all get out of here now?'

'We've spent some time wandering from place to place, and for now, we have nowhere else, or at least nowhere better, to go. I'll try and devise some plans. If I come up with something, I'll tell you about it when I get back. You know your wife tried to betray us?'

'I can't excuse her and must share the blame with her. We've been under pressure from the Nazis ever since Dagmar disappeared. I say the Nazis: I mean Hellroth and his men.'

'So you tried to save your skins by selling my wife and me to Hellroth?'

'Look, Herr Lichtblau. We made a mistake. I'm grateful to you, and I'm keen to join my wife. The Nazi soldiers will be waking up before long. When they do wake up, they'll see that I, too, have vanished.'

The young man started walking down the steps to the cellar. Lichtblau closed the trapdoor, covered it with the carpet, and slipped out of Dagmar's flat, double-locking it behind him, and out of the building. A plan did take shape in his mind. First, he would go and see Michael Lucht and tell him the truth: Hellroth had let some people he hoped would be informants vanish; he and his men had got drunk in these people's flat and were at that precise moment snoring their heads off. Then, to avoid any awkward questions from Lucht, he would tell him he would only give him specifics on condition Lucht agreed not to ask where he came by such knowledge.

'You'll have to go there now,' he said to Lucht, 'if you want to catch Hellroth. When he sobers up, or even before, you might ask him what he thinks he's doing. The people he harassed know nothing of any use, are not guilty of anything, nor are they Jews.'

Lichtblau gave Lucht the couple's address, insisting again he should go straight away. Lucht buckled on his pistol, saying he would take four men with him. He turned his back to Lichtblau as he belted on his gun, and when he turned back again, Lichtblau had gone. Lichtblau's one thought now was to find Nubik. Lichtblau felt that if he were to walk around the area of the Central, he would run into him sooner or later. It was Nubik, in fact, who spotted Lichtblau first.

'You mustn't stay in this area. The Nazis are tightening their grip on the city center a bit more every day. People are being escorted to Praterstern or the Metropole, never to be seen again. Why are you still here? You should have got out by now.'

'My wife and a couple are holed up in the cellar of our friend Dagmar's flat, while in the flat opposite Dagmar's, a group of Nazis led by Hellroth are asleep in a drunken stupor. Hellroth has caused us all more than enough damage. I've just told his enemy Lucht that Hellroth has slipped up.'

'So you're saying you're hoping Lucht will kill Hellroth? Or, better, that they'll kill each other?'

'I could hardly be expected to mourn Hellroth after the way he's treated my wife.'

'I know Dagmar's building,' Nubik said. 'There's an empty flat in the building across the road. We'll go and see how Lucht deals with Hellroth, and when they've gone, you'll be able to get back to Kristina and the couple. It's about time you got Kristina out of the country.'

'That's true. Let's go to this flat you're talking about.'

The two friends went their separate ways and met up an hour later in the hall of the building which Nubik had described. The two kept a look-out on the building opposite. Presently they witnessed a sight they had not expected to see: Hellroth, blindfolded, was being escorted out of the building, half supported, half dragged along by a soldier on either side of him. His colleagues had left him his boots: otherwise, he was totally naked. A second later, the rest of Hellroth's party

— three soldiers — came out with Lucht and a henchman of his own, walking behind the three soldiers. Lucht's henchman had a gun trained on them. The middle one was wearing a pair of men's underpants over his head. Nubik and Lichtblau presumed they were Hellroth's.

Was Lucht going to make up a firing squad and have his old enemy executed forthwith – or do it himself? Lucht indicated to the two soldiers supporting Hellroth to let go of him. He staggered about, looking as though he were about to topple over but never quite doing so. Lichtblau very slightly opened the window of the flat. Lucht said something to Hellroth, and Nubik and Lichtblau distinctly heard and saw him reply: 'I've already told you. I don't know where she is. I don't know where they are. I haven't seen them. I only saw the husband. He gave us the drink. That's all I know.'

If Lucht lets Hellroth go after such humiliation, Lichtblau thought, *Hellroth will never rest till he gets his revenge.* The only way Hellroth could improve his standing would be to bring in the Lichtblaus and the young couple, even though Lucht and everyone else knew, or at least assumed, that the young couple was not involved in the war, or not until that day, at least.

'What assurance do I have that if I let you go, you'll bring them in? What assurance do I have that you won't come after me if I let you go? I'm not mad, after all.' Lucht wore the look of a school prefect growing tired of some junior boy's antics.

'None and none.' Hellroth sounded equally weary.

Lucht took a pistol from the holster around his waist and pressed it against Hellroth's temple. 'The joke's over. I could kill you now.'

'As for me,' Hellroth said, always willing, on any occasion, like all tyrants, to talk about himself, 'I saw the Führer two days ago. I restored his confidence in me. I'm sure he'll be interested when I tell him about this incident.'

Lucht smiled. 'If you tell him. Quite frankly, just at this minute, you don't look like you're in any position to tell anybody anything.'

Hellroth suddenly shouted: 'I'll bring you her and her money-grubbing hus-band and the other two. Just give me back my clothes.'

'You'll bring her to me...' Lucht was thoughtful. But he still held the pistol to Hellroth's temple.

'She'll be yours for the taking,' Hellroth said, unable to disguise the note of pleading in his voice. Hellroth and Lucht both knew Hellroth was fighting for his life.

Nubik glanced at Lichtblau. Lichtblau was looking down but not at the scene taking place outside. Instead, he held a dead leaf in his hands and was taking it apart from the veins. Nubik watched the soldiers hand Hellroth back his clothes.

'Won't I ever be rid of that oafish killer? Won't Kristina? Won't Vienna?' Lichtblau had reached his limit. 'Why doesn't Lucht just kill him now and have done? Or is he worse than Hellroth?'

'Lucht needs Hellroth,' Nubik said. 'Hellroth is a source of information. High-level stuff. He does the evil jobs in this city the Führer tells him to do. And then some. And anyway, Lucht enjoys looking down on Hellroth and watching him make all the mistakes he makes. Hellroth makes Lucht feel good about himself.'

'Lucht is bad enough. But he hasn't got Hellroth's rage to do evil. So, to the Führer, he's a person of little account.'

'But in his way, he's even worse,' said Nubik, 'Hellroth's a mindless fool. But Lucht's a machine.'

'Comes to the same thing, pretty much, doesn't it? And they both want —'

'Kristina.' Nubik could not understand why her husband had not made her leave Vienna for her own safety a long time before.

By now, Hellroth had put his clothes back on. The whole group was walking away. Lichtblau and Nubik heaved a sigh of relief.

'You must be getting back to Kristina.'

Lichtblau nodded in agreement.

'What about you?'

'I'll go and pray a while.'

So Nubik walked towards the city center and into the area of the Central. He looked into the café as he went past it and saw Lucht with two or three cronies, laughing heartily. He wondered if they were laughing about what they'd just done to Hellroth. He went into St Stephen's Cathedral and got down on his knees. He shut his eyes and silently began to pray. After how long he did not know, voices behind him interrupted his orison. He made out Hellroth's voice, talking to a fellow soldier.

'Did you see him earlier?'

'I did. He was at the Central with two or three soldiers. They were laughing.'

'I'll kill him,' said Hellroth, for it was he, 'before he kills me.'

'Why didn't he kill you when he could?'

'Fear. He knows I know the Führer, who knows about our feud. Lucht's hoping for more promotion. If I disappear, even if he isn't responsible, the Führer will think Lucht killed me. So he bides his time, humiliating me and playing his little games of one-upmanship. He prefers playing his schoolboy pranks to working for the Führer. He humiliated me this afternoon.'

'What did he do?' Hellroth described to his friend the scene he and Lichtblau had witnessed that afternoon. When he had finished his story, the friend did not speak. He breathed heavily as though to sympathize with the emotion Hellroth had expressed at being humiliated, especially with soldiers of lower rank involved. Hellroth's pride was his greatest weak spot.

The canon walked up to them. 'Gentlemen, the cathedral is closing for the night. And this is no place for conspiracy.'

The soldier stood up, as did Nubik some way behind them. Hellroth stayed sitting and looked as if he hadn't heard the priest. But then he sprang up and pulled his pistol from his holster. With his left hand, he grabbed the priest's hair and jerked his head back. With his right, he pointed the gun at him.

'Remember, you have lost all authority here, you dog.'

He pushed the priest down to the floor. Then, as Hellroth, the other soldier and Nubik headed for the door, Nubik glanced back at the priest. He was standing back on his feet and looking after the two men. Nubik gave the priest a wink, just visible to the priest as a single glimmer in the near-darkness of the cathedral: no candle, but just a human eye. An eye not to receive light but to give out light. The priest winked back, light-house flashing to ship and back again.

Hellroth turned to the soldier. The curfewed streets were almost pitch black. 'Bring her to me. Bring me them both. I'll show Lucht the precious booty and then shoot him dead.'

'How do I know you won't shoot them all?' asked the soldier. 'You've done far worse things. I need guarantees.'

'Bring me them, or I'll kill you.'

'You could, if it pleases you. Nevertheless, I can try and deliver the Lichtblaus and the other couple to you. But what have they done?'

'The Lichtblaus I consider as traitors to the state. The new state.'

'Again, I ask you: what guarantees?'

'I'll get the Lichtblaus with or without your help. You're not indispensable.'

'But then, nor are you. You're just one tiny cog in the Nazi death machine. And proud of it.'

Hellroth made as if to strike him but held back as the soldier said: 'What's in it for me?'

'A hundred thousand Reichsmarks,' replied Hellroth.

The soldier reflected. 'Two hundred thousand.'

'You may be a praying man, but you're not so otherworldly after all.' The soldier could hear the smile in Hellroth's voice.

'One more thing: I'll need a Beretta 38/44.'

'The shepherd needs a crook to drive the sheep into the fold?'

'Mmm,' said the soldier, audibly growing tired of the oaf. 'I'll bring them to you as soon as I can.'

'And when is that?'

'You realize that maneuvering them where I want them is not going to be easy?'

'A week from today.'

'That's not long enough. I'll need a month. And the machine-gun. If your superiors find out how you use the resources they put at your disposal —'

'Three weeks' time at my office. No more speaking — I'll have the weapon you want sent to you.'

Twelve

Dagmar was speaking to Tom Oliver over the strains of Harry Parry's clarinet in the bar of the Randolph. 'I know they're planning something big.'

'I've heard so from Thedel. Hellroth seems to have used the Lichtblaus all he can, and now he thinks he has milked them dry. Nubik has told them to start preparing to get out.'

'I haven't heard from Werner for some time.'

Tom Oliver's teaching had become uneven in recent months. How could he keep his mind on Bohemian, Russian, or Aztec poetry when the world he had always known and loved was falling apart? How could the center not but collapse? And he doing nothing to stop it. But another voice seemed to speak within him: *You may not be on active army service this time around, but you are fighting for civilization in your own way.*

He must carry on not only teaching but networking in his different languages with refugee organizations and would-be refugees and members of Resistance movements like the recently-executed German pastor with whom Eden had so shamefully refused to work.

'Perhaps Werner is in trouble,' Dagmar said.

Ilse, Dagmar's friend, rushed into the bar. 'Thedel has phoned for you, Dagmar. He's on the road. Werner is traveling separately from him with the Lichtblau boys. It was thought best they split up in order to try and reduce suspicion. Thedel doesn't know where Kristina, Werner, Johannes and Heinrich are at this time. He may join forces with Heinrich. They don't expect to meet again till they are all in Oxford.'

Tom Oliver was due to dine at High Table and wanted to wash and dress. At dinner, there were a few foreign scholars he did not know, invited by his colleagues.

'Now that the Vichy government holds sway in France, what with Austria, Poland and Czechoslovakia overrun with Nazis, it is only a matter of time before Britain is invaded.'

Oliver looked at the fellow who had just spoken. He was some way from him down the long banquet table.

'If that's your position, why don't you get out of the country while the going's good?'

The man seemed stumped for a reply.

'What about South America?' Oliver went on taunting him. 'How do you come to be at this dinner? Who invited you?'

'I did,' said David Lyne, the college's French lecturer, blushing and looking down into his plate.

Oliver left his seat and walked up the table to the guest. 'Vous êtes pétainiste, n'est-ce pas ? Vous êtes méprisable, espèce de collabo! Now get out!'

The man stood up and left the dining hall at once. 'Why on earth did you invite that man, David? Don't you know there's a war on?'

'Look, Tom, he's a distinguished expert in his field. I had no idea about his politics and no reason to question it.'

Another of the diners spoke: 'What's his name, anyway?'

Lyne was looking more and more uneasy. 'His name is Jacques Soubrenie. And don't worry, I won't be inviting him again.'

But Oliver would not let it go at that. 'I'll have you thrown out of this college and, if I can help it, this university.' With that, he pushed his plate away, thrust his chair back and walked out of the dining hall.

A few nights later, in the bar of the Randolph, Tom Oliver spotted Ilse engrossed in conversation with a man he could only see from behind. He and Ilse exchanged smiles, and he went over to where she and the man were sitting. When he saw the man's face, he recognized him as the Frenchman who had dined at his college's High Table.

'What the hell are you doing talking with this traitor, Ilse? Dismiss him at once, or I will!' Oliver shouted.

'You cannot have me dismissed me from a public place like this, Professor Oliver,' said Soubrenie calmly.

'How do you come to be talking to him?' Oliver's hands were shaking.

'I was sitting in here on my own. He walked in and offered to buy me a drink. That's not a crime, is it, even in wartime?'

'Be careful who you talk to, Ilse, and what you say. This man has the gall to say he is on the side of the Occupation in France.'

'Professor Oliver.' Soubrenie looked wryly amused. 'Do you think we could meet on another occasion? But for now, I would like to entertain the lady, if it's all right with you.'

'Ilse, the college closes at eleven. Please make sure you are back by then.'

At five past eleven, Oliver's bedroom door, which he never kept locked, opened.

'You want to know what he said to me — if he told me anything useful. He told me he was a genuine academic, which is why Lyne had invited him to Oxford. He said what had happened at your High Table had been an unfortunate incident. He had handled the situation clumsily. Your interruption naturally changed the tenor of our conversation, and he felt obliged to tell me things he would not have done otherwise.'

'Whatever else he may be, he's no Pétainist. No Pétainist in England would admit to being so, what with de Gaulle being so close at hand.'

'You're right, as always.' She approached him where he lay on his bed and ran her hand down his face from his forehead to his chin.

'What you mean,' said Oliver, taking her hand in his, 'is that he's a romantic Frenchman, and by the end of the evening, he had you hooked.'

'I can't say any more about him except that yes, I find him charming. And have agreed to see him again.'

'He asked you to give me a message, didn't he?'

'For your meeting? Seven at the Randolph tomorrow for drinks and dinner on him.'

'On him?' Oliver turned down the corners of his mouth. 'Not on your life. Nor dinner at all. Drinks I can see no way to get out of.'

Ilse smiled and shut her eyes. 'Frenchmen may be charming but English charm is… incomparable.'

'English charm may be incomparable. But still, you would prefer French.'

Ilse smiled again and, this time, did not reply.

Soubrenie was waiting for Oliver with a glass of champagne as the don walked into the bar. He thrust the glass into Oliver's hand. 'Peace offering from France.'

'Peace? Not much of that around at the moment. Although there may be glimmers.' Oliver tossed his drink back in a single gulp. 'What did you want to see me about?'

'I think I might be able to help you.'

Soubrenie went on to explain. He had been in some confusion when he praised the Vichy regime at table. He was new to what he called 'this lark.'

Lark? Résistance. He was going back to France shortly and had contacts in different parts of Europe. He took orders from de Gaulle. Pétain thought he was in his employ, and Soubrenie was sure no one in Vichy suspected any different. He could help his friends in Vienna get to England via France.

'I'm not sure France is on their way,' said Oliver, realizing Ilse must have told him about the Lichtblau group. 'You seem to know a lot about my friends and me. Why are you so keen to help anyway? Haven't you got enough trouble on your hands in France?'

Soubrenie got up and made as if to leave: 'If you don't want my help, you'll get no complaints from me.'

'Sit back down for a second. As far as I know, my friends have no plans for traveling by way of France.'

'It might even be better for them if they did travel that way. The people I know in the Résistance networks could assist them. They could even turn the fact that they are native German speakers to good account. If they came across any German military in the occupied territories, they would be able to talk their way out of trouble. We could even arrange to have fake German passports made up for them.'

'Look. One minute you're proclaiming your undying devotion to the likes of Pétain and Laval, the next, you say you're a member of the Résistance and prepared to go out of your way to help my friends. If I thought you were in earnest about Vichy, I would have turned you over to the British army by now.'

'You're right. I'm asking you to trust me.'

'That's not all. I'm wondering whether you don't want a reward for services rendered.'

'Well,' replied Soubrenie, 'for one thing, I can't guarantee my services as you call them will be successful. I can only do my best. For another —'

'Ilse.'

'Ilse,' confirmed Soubrenie. 'I have to leave Oxford shortly and return to France via de Gaulle in London. The Résistance needs me in France. But I want Ilse. She could even be useful to us in France.'

'First, I won't let you take Ilse with you or try to send for her later. Her journey here was risky enough. She's staying put here for the remainder of the war. Second —'

'Second, you're still not convinced that I'm to be trusted or that I won't be leading you and your friends into some kind of trap.'

'And third —' Here, Oliver really did hesitate.

'Third,' said Soubrenie, 'you have feelings of your own for Ilse. Am I not right?'

'I'll mull all this over,' said Oliver. 'Perhaps we could adjourn to somewhere less —'

'Public?' the Frenchman said, 'Quite. I'll relate my train of thought more freely to you.'

Thirteen

In their carriage smelling of anxiety and moldy leather, the train carrying Kristina, Heinrich, Johannes, and Werner, hurtled across Austria. They had not boarded it at Praterstern, where the Nazis controlled all arrivals and departures. Instead, Nubik had managed to get hold of a Daimler and chauffeured the group out of the city to a less well-guarded station. He had also acquired a Nazi officer's uniform. He had pulled his cap low over his forehead and at checkpoints along the way, he either did not stop at all but waved his way through or, if he saw that he had to stop, barked at the soldiers manning them: he and his passengers were in a hurry, he had papers from high up commanding him to take these people to their destination, and if they tried to hold them up, he would be reporting them to Commandant Hoepner in Berlin. The soldier on duty would gasp at the name, even though Nubik had made it up and there was no such person.

Such men were trigger-happy but respectful of hierarchy and used to obeying orders, so Nubik's spiel usually worked. Once, a soldier refused to open the checkpoint to Nubik. While he went inside the roadside hut to call his office, as if to make inquiries, two of his colleagues stood one on each side of the car with machine guns in their hands. It was night, and thanks to the light in the hut, they could see him through the hut window talking to someone on the phone. He hung up and disappeared from view. Letting them stew, he didn't reappear for quite some time. Then he went back to Nubik, who was smoking a cigar and staring straight ahead of him as though the irksome soldier was no more important than a fly.

'I shall make a note of your number plate, and then you may pass.'

Nubik gave a vague wave of his hand as if to say, it's all the same to me.

'And I shall make a note of your name and rank. I'll transmit it to the Berghof along with a note informing them you kept us hanging about here for no good reason when I have an urgent mission to perform handed me by Commandant Hoepner. And you know from whom he gets his orders.'

The barrier went up, and Nubik could now drive off. Yet he sat there, not moving, just drumming his fingers on the steering wheel. The soldier stared into Nubik's face.

'And I'm sure,' said Nubik, returning his gaze, 'that the officers at the Metropole will enjoy meeting you. Once I've told them all about you, that is.' Nubik blew out a smoke ring.

'All right,' said the soldier, 'I'll phone through to my colleague at the next checkpoint to tell him to let you drive straight through. Apologies for the delay.'

Kristina had been observing all this from her seat in the back of the Daimler, half-terrified that the soldier would hold them up, half-marveling at Nubik's acting talent. She realized she had never known who Nubik really was. She only knew he had always been there when she needed him. She trusted him instinctively. Soon he would be dropping them off. There would be another car waiting for them, and Nubik would return to Vienna. She thought it unlikely they would ever meet again.

For the moment, they drove on into the early hours. They occasionally passed or overtook cars and army trucks. Nothing hindered them. Kristina felt a sadness welling within her. Nubik sensed as much.

'I'll try and get to your husband as soon as I'm back in Vienna. I'll arrange for you to receive news of him, and he of you and the boys, as soon as possible.'

It was dawn when the Daimler drew to a halt. Kristina, Werner and the boys had all fallen asleep. Becoming aware that they had stopped moving and the engine had gone silent, Kristina opened her eyes. She looked out of the window and saw Nubik engrossed in conversation with a young soldier. Kristina took advantage of what seemed to be a lull in their conversation to get out of the car and walk over to them. Only when she was up close to them did Kristina realize the soldier Nubik was talking to was a young woman. Nubik introduced Kristina Lichtblau to her by her full name. But when it came to introducing the young woman to Kristina, he became tongue-tied: 'This is… This is…' Nubik looked from one woman to the other, then momentarily turned his gaze from both.

'Anna.' It was the young woman who spoke.

'Anna,' echoed Nubik. Kristina noticed a tear running down the young woman's cheek. She stepped forward, kissed her and wiped away the tear.

'Thank you.'

'We'll be as safe with you as we have been with Nubik,' said Kristina. 'But why are you dressed as a soldier?'

'For the same reason as Alfred. As cover. I've been disguised like this for two years — though not all the time — and no one has noticed anything strange.'

Kristina withdrew from Nubik and the young woman and went back to the Daimler to wake Werner, Heinrich and Johannes. She turned around and saw Nubik and the young woman conferring heatedly. Then, finally, he beckoned to her to go and join them.

'We thought Anna could drive you on in the Daimler, and I'll return to Vienna in the Volkswagen.' He pointed to the car in which Anna had arrived.

Nubik said, 'To tell you the truth, I'm not sure you're well-advised to continue your journey by car. You can get stopped and searched at any time, shot at or blown up along the road. I think your best bet is to take the train. If your papers are in order, you'll be less likely to be bothered. Anna will, I'm sure, be happy to take you to a train station. You won't stand out from the thousands of people currently crisscrossing Europe.'

'Where's the nearest rail station?' asked Kristina.

A voice called out from the Daimler:

'What if the train gets blown up or bombed? Or redirected? What if someone blows up a bridge just as our train is crossing it? What if the SS get on board and kill everyone, or carry out random or selective killings?'

'No means of transport is completely safe at this time, Johannes,' replied Nubik. 'You'll just have to accept that. Things will stay like this till the war's over.'

'But are we safer away from Vienna?' called out Werner.

'And will we be when we're out of Austria?' Heinrich added his own doubt.

'Infinitely safer,' replied Nubik. 'To stay in Vienna would be suicidal.'

'So why is Papa still there?' said Johannes.

'And why are you going back?' Heinrich chimed in.

They all realized these questions struck to the heart of the matter.

'Your father works with the Resistance in Vienna. He appears to the Nazis to have collaborated with them so much that they mainly don't suspect him. Plus, he's a good talker. The Nazis may —' At this, Heinrich and Johannes burst out sobbing almost simultaneously.

'I don't want to hear any more,' said Johannes. 'I know he's in danger all the time. If he makes a mistake or is seen talking to the wrong people —'

'What about my question?' said Heinrich.

'I'm returning to Vienna for the same reason your father is staying there. To play my part in the Resistance. To help your father. And, besides, I have nowhere else to go.'

'You could come with me,' said Anna.

'We've been through this already, Anna. I know where I belong.'

'You belong with me.' Anna was exasperated. 'But you're bloody-minded. Come with me if I take these friends of yours. Then we'll be safe, and our worries will be over.'

'No, they won't. And anyway, I can't rest while Lichtblau is still in Vienna. If I didn't go back, I'd be betraying and deserting him and, in a manner of speaking, even his wife and children.'

'It's no good trying to reason with such men as Alfred Nubik and my husband. They put other people's lives above their own.' Kristina looked resigned.

'Alfred, look at you,' broke in Anna, 'you're not a hero. You're a drug dealer to the Nazis, dressed as a businessman, plying your goods from one end of Vienna to the other.'

'That's how I survive in this hell,' said Nubik. 'And I'm not a drug dealer to the Nazis. They think I'm their dealer. But I'm not. There's nothing, or just bad stuff, in what I sell them. And I use the money I make off them for the Resistance. It's true I'm no hero, and I don't want to be. There are no heroes in this war. Heroes are just for books and films. But I've managed to bring these four as far as you. That's a start, isn't it? Anyway, such considerations won't help us. You should be on by now.' He bowed low before Kristina and kissed her hand. He shook hands with Werner and the two brothers. He and Anna embraced fleetingly, and then he got back into the Daimler.

Anna called out to him: 'We'll be together again.'

As he drove off, he put his hand out of the driver's seat window and waved. They all waved back except Anna, who had turned away. The people war left alive, it separated from each other, and destroyed what should have been a shared future. Still, he hoped Anna was right.

Fourteen

A man seated in the corner of their compartment was writing in a notebook. He would at times look up and appear to be ruminating, though he darted a glance at the group whenever he did so. The train passed some mountains. Kristina Lichtblau did not know which ones they were, nor even which country they were in. Two men in uniform slid open the compartment doors. The man in the corner laid his things down and stood up at once. He looked over to Kristina to bid her do the same and to get Werner and the boys to do so, too. They all followed suit.

'Destination?'

The man replied: 'Stuttgart.'

'Stuttgart,' repeated Kristina.

'What for?'

'To stay with friends,' said the man.

'Same here,' said Kristina.

'Are you Jews?'

The writing man said neither he nor the others in the compartment were. The other officer seemed annoyed.

'Stop trying to defend the passengers.'

He told him to take down his trousers to prove whether or not he was telling the truth.

'Would you have me do that in front of a lady?'

The two officers withdrew from the compartment and conferred. Then they went back in: 'The lady will wait outside.'

Werner and the boys got up as though to follow her, but the men gestured for them to sit back down. They let Kristina pass, telling her to wait just outside the compartment. They slid the compartment door shut and closed the curtain over the door. Kristina tried to overhear. The man had done as he had been ordered to do, and the officers had found no evidence to show he was Jewish. Her sons had not been circumcised, but she did not trust the officers not to harm them. As for Werner, she did not know whether he was Jewish or not. If he were Jewish, he would most likely have stayed in Oxford rather than venturing on a perilous journey back to his homeland.

Voices were suddenly raised in the compartment, and she heard Heinrich screaming: 'No! No! Please! No! Please stop!'

She took out two Lugers from inside the top of her skirt, slid the door back, pressed one pistol each into the backs of the two officers and pumped bullets into both men at once. The bodies dropped to the floor.

'Good work,' the writing man said. 'Now, we will open up one of the train doors and throw out the corpses. Later, if you wish, we'll toss your guns out of the window.'

Heinrich and Johannes huddled in each other's arms in the corner of the compartment. The writing man and Werner dragged the bodies out of the compartment and down the corridor to the carriage door.

Just before they opened the door, Kristina said: 'Their pulses! Let's make sure they're dead.' They found the bodies were lifeless and threw them out.

'Do you have any bullets left?' the writing man asked Kristina. Then, as she had not, he advised her to throw her pistols away. They would all be above suspicion now.

A while later, a ticket inspector opened the door and checked their tickets. He asked the five passengers whether two soldiers had been through. They had looked in, the writing man told him. They had asked where they were going and what their business was. Then they left them alone.

The inspector said nobody on the train had seen them for some time. Where could they have got to? The writing man threw up his hands in a gesture of helpless ignorance: he had no idea where they had got to nor even where they had been going.

'Munich,' said the inspector. But the train was not due to stop in Munich for another hour, and there had been no stop since the train had left its departure point. It was a mystery. The writing man said that if he saw them, he'd report at once to the inspector.

The inspector nodded and left the compartment. A few minutes later, Kristina began to cry. Johannes and Heinrich had never seen their mother cry before and, in turn, burst into tears again. Kristina glanced over at the writing man. She had never killed anyone before. She had promised herself — and God — she would never do so. How would she ever forgive herself?

The man replied, 'Everyone who is caught up in this war, everyone who, like you, is fleeing their home, everyone who in their heart is praying for the return of peace and justice and the end to this nightmare —'

'Enough, please.'

'I beg your pardon. What is your name?'

'My name does not matter. These are my sons. This is our friend.'

'You have killed two men who might well have tortured and killed your sons and all of us in this compartment. You've killed them. But you haven't murdered them. Your act was necessary and, in these circumstances, right. You must protect yourself and these young men at all costs. The men you killed would have killed everyone on this train without the slightest qualm.'

'You're right. And yet I feel it is wrong to kill.'

'Such feelings do you credit, but here they are wrong. These young men's lives are worth more than your scruples. You had no choice. You must put this behind you now and look to the future.'

'My name is Kristina Lichtblau. You haven't told us yours.'

'Richard Bauer. I'm from Innsbruck. The place is overrun with Nazis. I have a friend in the Wehrmacht — which in reality he hates and which he scams and betrays as much as he can get away with — who drove me out of Innsbruck in the boot of his car. They waved him through the checkpoints. He dropped me in the countryside. I walked for a few days until I caught this train.'

Johannes spoke up: 'If he's your friend and hates the Wehrmacht, why didn't he come with you?'

'The Wehrmacht people think he's working for them, but he isn't. In fact, he's trying to undermine it from the inside. Another thing is that he was expected back to work shortly. Suspicions would be easily aroused if he didn't show up.' He looked at Kristina, 'What about your —'

'My husband? He's like your friend. He's decided to stay and work for the Resistance. So far, he's managed to survive. He was a banker until recently. Whenever he has to deal with the Nazis, and never by his own choice, he uses fake money and checks. They're either too stupid to notice they're fake, or they fob them off onto someone else.'

'Maybe I can help your husband get out of Vienna.'

'I've just told you. He doesn't want to get out. Or rather, he feels he can't leave. It would be worse than desertion and betrayal combined.'

Bauer now held his tongue briefly. Then:

'Can you get a message through to your husband? I have friends in Vienna who could help him get out.'

The man was obstinate, if nothing else.

'It's kind of you, but my husband has his own friends and contacts in Vienna. He's also a proud man, to those who don't know him, at least. Not proud, but dignified. An artist. A poet. To be an artist and a poet meant something in Austria before this war.'

'It still does,' said the man. 'In fact, it means much more now than it did before.'

Just then, a Nazi soldier burst into the compartment, pointing his FG42 at the assembled company: 'Where are the two soldiers who were on this train at its departure point?'

Everyone in the compartment except Bauer stood up and put their hands in the air. He remained as calm as if the soldier had not been there and hardly bothered to glance up at him.

'No idea,' he yawned.

Kristina refrained from looking at him and kept her eyes fixed on the soldier, as did Werner, Johannes and Heinrich.

'You there,' said the soldier pointing his machine gun at Bauer, 'stand up when you're in the presence of a soldier.'

Bauer appeared to feel in his pockets, perhaps for a cigarette.

'Leave your pockets alone, stand up, and put your hands up!'

'I am Colonel Bohnhorst. I report to General Guderian. You are only doing your job, and I will not report you for this, as long as you let matters rest there.'

To Bauer's surprise, though he did not show it, the soldier maintained his aggressive stance. 'It is also my job to check identities as and when I decide.'

'You're quite right. And it's true I'm not in uniform. May I reach into my pocket and hand you my papers?'

'You may.'

As he was doing so, the soldier asked him, 'Who are these people?'

'They are friends of mine and of the Reich. They are traveling with me, under my authority and General Guderian's.'

Bauer handed him some papers bearing what looked like the letterhead of the Wehrmacht. The soldier took his eyes off Bauer and began inspecting the papers.

Almost imperceptibly, Bauer shot a glance at Kristina and then booted the soldier in the groin with all his might. The soldier stumbled forward, placing his hands over his genitals so that his FG42 fell to the floor. Bauer snatched it up, put the barrel to the soldier's head and fired a brief round. Kristina looked away.

'There was nothing else to do,' said Bauer, 'These men will kill anyone who dares so much as to breathe the same air as them.' As previously, the group now dragged the corpse to a train door and threw it off the train along with the man's machine gun.

'We're not far from Stuttgart now. The soldier may well have had comrades or superiors waiting for him there. We will have to leave the train and the station as speedily and as discreetly as possible. They'll probably want to take in passengers for questioning when they find out the soldier is not on the train.'

'But we have nowhere to go in Stuttgart,' replied Kristina, 'I've told you. We are trying to get to England. We just want to get another train from Stuttgart station.'

'The schedules are so disrupted you might be hanging around the station for hours, easy prey for all kinds of trouble. So I suggest you come to my friends in Stuttgart. Then we'll take stock of the situation and see what your best move is from there.' Bauer's papers were strewn on the floor. He gathered them up.

'Are those army papers?' said Johannes.

'They're fake army papers. I use them to get about. They've served me well so far.'

'Have you killed before?' said Heinrich.

'I'm not a soldier, but, yes, I've killed since the start of the war, either in self-defense or to protect others who like you, like us, were being threatened.'

As the train pulled into Stuttgart, the group filed into the corridor and towards the nearest door. Bauer's plan turned out to be harder to carry out than he had envisaged. At least one Nazi soldier stood in front of each of the train doors. These soldiers were checking passengers' papers one by one as they got off the train. Gunshots reverberated, and screams could be heard some doors down from Bauer and the others. Bauer led the way as they got off the train. He was holding his own — fake — papers in his hand along with those of the four others. As soon as the soldier standing in front of the door had seen Bauer's papers, he looked at him and gave the Nazi salute. Bauer responded in kind, nodding to Kristina and the others to do the same. The soldier then engaged Bauer in a discussion, Bauer responding in low tones; by instinctive mimicry, the officer also lowered his voice. After a few minutes, the conversation visibly drawing to an end, Bauer brought his heels together and again gave the Nazi salute. He gently took the papers from the soldier's hand and, at the same time, slipped a wad of banknotes into his hand. With a show of gallantry, Bauer waved the four on before following them.

Once they were away from the station, Kristina asked him about his discussion with the soldier.

'I showed him my papers and told him I was escorting the four of you because you were relatives of a close friend of the Führer's. I told him I reported to the friend: it was in the soldier's interest not to hold us up in any way but rather to smooth our way. Otherwise, he might land in trouble. That was how we got away unscathed from the station. He asked me about the missing soldiers, and I just shrugged and told him we had not noticed anything unusual on the train.'

'You're a rather convincing liar,' said Kristina.

'I live dangerously,' agreed Bauer.

'What you said about us and the Führer' — Kristina suddenly whipped a handkerchief out of her bag and blew into it — 'was dishonoring to us. But I see there was no help for it.'

'Your husband is a lucky fellow,' said Bauer.

'That's what they tell him,' Kristina said with a smile. 'The situation in Vienna is getting worse by the week, if not the day.'

'So you would, after all, like me to help your husband get out? Perhaps he's torn between two kinds of moral duty. One to his family, the other to the cause of freedom in Vienna. A difficult dilemma. Don't think he loves all of you less for choosing to stay where he is.'

'I don't doubt his love for us, but I'd just feel more reassured if I knew he was out of harm's way.'

'Your husband's wishes must be respected. I may be able to help you, however, to get to England if you are prepared to go via France. I myself am on my way to France. I have Résistance friends there who will help us. I have another Résistance friend who is, I think, in Oxford at present.'

The five of them had been walking all this time through the streets of Stuttgart. Finally, Bauer stopped outside a grey stone townhouse in a leafy residential neighborhood.

'My friends live in this house. Please wait for a few minutes here while I go and talk to them.' Bauer drew a key from his pocket and let himself in, vanishing behind the front door, which he shut behind him at once. There were few Nazis to be seen, and if one or two in uniform did occasionally walk past the Vienna group, they paid them scant attention.

After three-quarters of an hour standing outside the house, Johannes and Heinrich started to express their impatience, stamping their feet and raising their voices. A soldier passing by in a car pulled up beside them: 'You know loitering in the streets is forbidden. What are you doing here?' Kristina gave him a big smile: 'Waiting for a friend, sir.'

She nodded towards the house, trying to say as little as possible so that the soldier would not detect her Viennese accent.

What's your friend's name?' Kristina replied, 'It's Arthur Kaufmann.'

The four of them were staring at the soldier. A beetle was crawling very close to the man's left ear. Johannes and Heinrich were fascinated, almost mesmerized by it, especially as the soldier himself did not appear to feel it. The stares of the boys gradually became smirks. Finally, Johannes could no longer control himself and burst out laughing. The soldier leveled his machine gun at Johannes. Kristina interposed herself between her son and the soldier.

'Drop your gun,' said a voice from behind the soldier. The soldier was unfazed and did not budge.

'Who are you?' he shouted without turning around.

'If you value your life, drop your machine gun.'

The soldier called out, 'I agree to lower it as long as you show yourself to me face to face.'

The voice responded, 'How many people have you shot in the back since the war began?'

The soldier said, 'Why, you cur, it's not because —'

Suddenly the soldier howled and dropped his weapon, clasping his left ear with both hands. The beetle had climbed inside and was causing the soldier acute pain. Werner rushed forward and picked up the soldier's machine gun, pointing it at the soldier.

'Now you can see me,' Richard Bauer muttered to the soldier who had managed to stop howling but was still clasping his ear and hunched over with pain.

'We can take him with us, use him as a hostage,' exclaimed Heinrich gleefully.

'You fools!' said the soldier. 'Do you think the Wehrmacht cares what happens to one of its foot-soldiers?'

'Stop speaking! Stand up straight!' ordered Bauer. The soldier obeyed.

As he did so, a van came into view and drew up beside the group. Five Nazi soldiers leaped out of the van, pointing their guns at Bauer, who said to them: 'This man — this soldier — threatened these people for no reason. I have been asked to escort them. They are relatives of a close friend of the Führer's.'

The group of soldiers and the prisoner all made the Nazi salute. 'I'm a Nazi officer. I will kill this man if you don't all leave now.'

'Don't kill him!' one of the soldiers suddenly called out.

'Why shouldn't I kill him?' replied Bauer. 'He was quite prepared a second ago to kill me, this woman and these young men.'

'He's my brother,' said the soldier who had called out.

'Do you think the Jews have no brothers?' broke in Kristina quite unexpectedly. 'Have they no sisters, relatives or friends? Your brother himself said before you came that no one cared whether he lived or died.'

'I care,' replied the soldier who claimed to be his brother.

'I'll make a deal with you,' Bauer said to the group of soldiers. 'I let this man go, you all go away together, and we forget this incident. I could have killed this man before you arrived.'

'Hand over my brother, and we'll go, just as you said,' said the soldier who had spoken before.

'No!' cried one of his fellow soldiers. 'We can take the lot of them prisoner and get a lot of kudos from the Wehrmacht for bringing them in.'

'But what if this man is telling the truth about his ties to the Führer?'

A young woman in SS uniform came out of the house behind them, the one Bauer had been into, where he said he had friends. She ambled up to Bauer and kissed him on the lips. Turning to the group of soldiers, she commanded, 'Drop your guns to the ground.' They did so. 'Now get out of here and don't come back.'

'What about my brother?' said the soldier who had spoken earlier. 'You don't need him.'

'He threatened us,' said Bauer, 'we're not going to let him off lightly.'

'Do as I say,' said the woman in SS uniform.

'My brother has a wife and family; if you want to keep one of us, take me instead of him. I have no wife or family.'

Bauer looked towards the woman, who shook her head. 'Swap refused.'

Then the soldiers got into their van and drove off. Kristina and the others all walked towards the house and went into it, with Bauer leading the way and the soldier in front of him. The woman in SS uniform locked the prisoner in an alcove at the top of the house, then came back down and joined the others.

'How was I?' she said to Bauer.

'Wonderful!'

'What shall we do with the prisoner? He can't stay here indefinitely. Either let him go or take him with you.'

They heard a rumbling coming from upstairs. Bauer took out his pistol and went up to the alcove in which the soldier was imprisoned. He unlocked the door. The woman in the SS uniform had tied the soldier to a chair, and he had been jumping up and down to attract attention. He was gagged, too, so he could not speak. Bauer loosened his gag. 'What do you want?'

'Let me join the woman and the youths. I'll help you take them where they want to go, or can go, at this time. So far, I haven't killed anyone in this war, nor has my brother. As for you, despite your papers and swagger, I don't believe you're in the army. The woman in the SS uniform is not a member of the SS either. You're both either renegades or have acquired papers and uniforms falsely. I'm sick of this war. I was a math teacher before, and I led a quiet life. I can't tell a Jew from a non-Jew. I'd like to desert, as maybe you have done. You need to make up your minds. My brother and the group of soldiers may be back any minute with reinforcements. They are unlikely to be lenient. And then the war and everything else will be over for you and your friends.'

Fifteen

Lichtblau was having trouble sleeping, rolling over and over in his bed, when he had a bed to sleep in. He had not heard from his wife and sons for some time now. He was going through a phase of despondency. Doubts as to how worthwhile his presence was in Vienna had begun to assail him. He had found work as an office clerk at a printer's, run by a couple named Willy and Ada Schwartz, in Hütteldorf on the western outskirts of Vienna. They only required him for a couple of hours a day. They printed mainly for a publisher of children's books. That was all the work he could get because of the war. The rest of the time, Lichtblau stayed away from the city center and his old bank. He wrote. He and his friends would meet up every other day, at the flats of different friends. They would explore various means of resistance and what they would do if and when their side won the war. Some of them were men who, like him, had sent their wives and children out of the city, out of the country. Alfred Nubik sometimes joined these meetings. They all thought of Nubik as a law unto himself. Two or three of them — though not Lichtblau — could not help secretly wondering whether he was not a double agent who would sooner or later sell them to the Nazis. Yet — they also told themselves — he had already had plenty of opportunities to do so, and nothing had happened to suggest he had betrayed them or that he would betray them. He knew the whereabouts of various Nazi officers at any given moment, and when asked how he knew, he replied that he sold them certain substances they seemed to enjoy, alhough those substances were not what they thought they were.

Nubik and the others discussed Hellroth with Lichtblau.

'He saw Kristina once and has wanted her ever since. He's made having her his one channeled aspiration in this war. Apart from acquiring as much power as possible.'

'But he didn't get her. And now she's gone.'

'If he knows, he must be in a blind rage about it,' Lichtblau said, 'he always said she'd give in to him, come to him.'

Nubik tutted. 'His twisted mind.'

Norbert Klauss, a friend of Lichtblau's from the printer's, said: 'Maybe we can cause Hellroth a little trouble. Set up a trap. Kill him. We could use —'

'My wife's name to draw him into a trap?'

'How can we do that,' interrupted Willy Schwartz, the printer, 'if he thinks she's left the country?'

'But that's just what we have to do!' Nubik, natural strategist that he was, clapped his hands in glee. 'Lead him to think she's left the city so that he decides to send people after her and bring her back. In a while, we inform him that his henchmen have caught her. They will bring her in and arrange to meet at a certain time and place with her. Except neither the henchmen nor Kristina turns up. Only Hellroth does.'

'Hellroth and we do,' said Schwartz.

'As for the henchmen, we'll think of ways to throw them off the scent.'

'Another thing,' said Lichtblau, 'we need to get —'

'We need to get Michael Lucht involved,' Nubik interrupted.

'How do you always know what everyone's going to say?' said Willy Schwartz.

'For the same reason the Nazis seem to trust me. I appear to know, but I don't. I pay attention. Take calculated guesses. I listen a lot. Or overhear. On the street. In cafés. Under the bridges. In any group, I'm usually the silent one. I learn a lot. It helps me survive. People think I know things. Sometimes I do, often I don't. It's calculated bluff. I left school early, lived on and off the streets. People have always liked my face and confided in me.'

'Like my wife,' said Lichtblau.

'Like your wife. But don't worry — she's told me lots of secrets about you but never anything good.'

'That's all right, then.'

'Any news?' said Nubik.

'None.'

'So, what are we going to do?' Willy Schwartz was getting impatient. 'Or are we just going to wait for the Nazis to kill off all the Viennese?'

'Here's a different idea. We'll send word to Hellroth that a certain lady has information to communicate to him which could gain him high-level promotion – you know, more stripes, more responsibility, higher pay, more access to big money, more access to big Jewish money, more access to women, more access to Jewesses, more opportunity to exterminate Jews. All the usual stuff,' said Nubik.

'Why would he trust such information, Nubik? He'll see right through it,' said Willy Schwartz.

'We could either send it to him anonymously, and he could take it or leave it. He'd most likely take it since he's gullible and liable to assume automatically that the 'certain lady' is Frau Lichtblau. Or it could come from me. He knows me.'

'So, what you're saying,' said Schwartz, 'is two birds, one stone.'

'Right,' said Nubik. 'We'll find a way of drawing Lucht into the trap. This way, we don't kill anyone. Instead, we let them kill each other — which is what they've always wanted anyway.'

'What about our writing, our publications?' asked Norbert Klauss.

'We'll carry on doing them,' said Lichtblau. 'Nazi ideas, if one can call them that, are strategies of domination and terror. No one gives any credence to such ideas, least of all them. They just bow down before them as they would to gods of wood or stone and cower before the little fellow. We must keep on attacking the Nazis, intellectually or any other way we can, till the end of the war.'

Sixteen

'Until the war ends, at least, my place is in France,' Jacques Soubrenie said to Ilse. 'You can join me there after the war, or I'll come to you in Oxford.'

'Will there be an 'after the war'? What life will there be then, and for whom?'

'Maybe Thedel, Werner and the others will be passing through France on their way to England — more absurd things have happened — and I'll have the chance to help them.'

'Maybe this, maybe that,' responded Ilse, 'Maybe nothing.'

'We won't be any use to anyone, let alone win the war in that sort of spirit.'

'You're right,' said Ilse, 'I'm sorry. As soon as I get word about Thedel's and the others' whereabouts, if they're planning on coming via France, I'll let you know.'

Tom Oliver lay back on his bed in the darkness of his room in Wadham.

'Why are you doing all this? To placate your conscience about not being in the army?'

Oliver struck his pillow. 'Is it worse than waiting tables? Worse than grinning like a fool at customers to scrape up a few meager tips?'

Oliver's companion got up from the bed and walked across the room. 'You help Jewish refugees because it's good for your image, while you despise the people close to you.'

'I don't despise them, or you,' replied Oliver. 'It's my contribution to the war effort. And I enjoy doing it. Life is or should be sweet as honey. I try and make it so not only for myself but for those whose lives are threatened or have —'

'Grown bitter?' his companion said.

'I like life bittersweet at times, and that's the way it often is.'

By eight in the morning, Tom Oliver had gone down to the porter's lodge and picked up his post. He examined an envelope postmarked Vienna. Rather than go into Hall for breakfast, he headed towards St Aldate's and the coffee-shop opposite Christchurch. He needed to be alone and free to think lucidly in order to take in whatever Herr Lichtblau had to tell him. He took his cup of coffee to a quiet corner on the first floor of the coffee shop, sat down and opened the letter from Vienna. He read as follows:

Lichtblau thinks our policy regarding the Jews is successful. I am delighted. It is the only thing we agree on, in spite of my efforts to convert him. I caught Lichtblau writing you this letter. He will cease all communication with abroad from now on, including with his family. I caution you not to try and make contact with Jews, anyone connected to Jews or members of Resistance groups in Vienna or elsewhere in Austria. Lichtblau himself means nothing to me. His wife married the wrong man. One day she will realize her mistake.

Colonel Hellroth

Oliver did not know what was true and what was not in these lines, though they seemed genuine enough. He turned the page. After the opening greetings, he read:

I have no idea where my wife and children are. There are fewer and fewer inventors left in Vienna. How was your trip to Helsinki? My health's rotten — this is the third time I have had a cold this year. I remember you telling us about the French artist who painted almost nothing but nudes: has she been able to sell much of her work? I recently met a hunter I happen to know. He has been moving toward

The message stopped there. Tom Oliver mulled over the contents of this paragraph. But his thoughts drifted. Should he have gone, like Wystan, to America? In idle moments he caught himself envying what must be the ease of Wystan's life cocooned in the largesse, friendliness and wealth of America, cut off from the terrors of Europe. He and Herr Lichtblau had a while before agreed that if Herr Lichtblau ever used the word 'Helsinki,' it would mean he was in grave danger since he was in some kind of hellish situation and at risk of sinking. It was the third time Lichtblau had 'had a cold:' he had tried and failed to get letters through to him twice already. 'Inventors' meant Jews. Oliver looked again at the phrase 'My health's rotten': this was a clear allusion to Hellroth. Oliver sensed that Herr Lichtblau was both telling him to beware of Hellroth and hinting that some kind of plan was afoot to put Hellroth out of action. The main thing, in Tom Oliver's eyes, as far as he could grasp the situation, was to kill Hellroth. The reference to the French artist was Herr Lichtblau asking Oliver whether the French Résistance would be able to help his wife and the others get to England if called upon to do so. 'Hunter' most likely pointed to Josef Jäger, of whom Tom Oliver was already aware and whose behavior was probably what had led to Herr Lichtblau's being captured while writing his letter. The Nazis were clearly trying to use Jäger and his journalistic and spying skills and people like him to wear down any remaining resistance in Vienna. Oliver knew, though, that Josef had a brother, Markus, and the surname alone might apply to either brother or even both.

The Nazis might well be torturing Herr Lichtblau to gain a maximum of information as well as to put pressure on his Resistance friends — supposing they could prove he had any — to throw in the towel. Oliver had once read a poem in German which began, *Nur die Liebe allein schafft das Leben*. Love alone creates life. It was by his favorite German-speaking poet, another Bohemian, Felix Lichtblau. The second he read it, Tom Oliver had known he would, if ever given the chance, do whatever he could for the man who had written that poem, as well as anyone connected to him. And it was true that the statement and its three terms would hardly make its author congenial to the Nazis.

Oliver wanted to get a message to Werner, Kristina Lichtblau and her boys to tell them that the Nazis were probably on their trail and that they would be wise to split up since Hellroth and his people would, he thought, expect to find them together. Werner had promised to phone Oliver at least once a fortnight from wherever he happened to be. It was now fourteen days to the day since Oliver had last heard from him. He decided to cancel his tutorials and arrangements for the day and sit by his phone. He wondered whether Werner and the others had not been captured or killed. It was as though Oliver were somehow paralyzed. His attachment to helping Jewish refugees mattered more to him than his academic activities. This was his life's work, as much as if not more than his teaching, writing and translating. Yet they were inseparable since the one enabled the other: thanks to his gift for languages, he had won the sympathy of people across Europe. And his academic reputation had been useful in making diplomatic contacts in the Foreign Office and overseas.

A knock at the door. It was a coded knock. Each of Oliver's close friends and companions had a special coded knock so he would know who it was. If he did not answer the door after this coded knock, it was agreed that Oliver would not open the door, and the visitor would leave straight away. After two coded knocks, Oliver had not opened the door. He was so intent on the phone he had hardly heard the knocks. He finally went to open the door. Ilse was already walking away. Hearing Oliver open the door, she turned round to see him beckon to her to come in with an inclination of the head.

'I thought you loved Soubrenie.'

'How could I not love you?' she replied. 'Love and be ever grateful to you?'

'I'm waiting to hear from Werner. Meanwhile, his parents may phone.'

'I'll wait with you,' said Ilse.

His mind wandered back and forth between Ilse's kindness to him and his concern over Werner's plight. Werner's agreement to participate in Tom Oliver's contribution to saving Jews had arisen thanks to Oliver's personal and academic charisma, which had fired Werner's enthusiasm not only for the German language but more particularly for Viennese art and literature. He had made Werner feel useful by sending him on this mission. But he had likely sent him to his death. Werner had said he would be happy to die for such a cause. He had not told his parents about his trip to Vienna. When Werner's parents found themselves no longer able to contact him at Oxford, they had started phoning the Master of Wadham. At first, Oliver had bluffed his way through these conversations with Werner's parents, who had always been wary of Oliver because of the whiff of scandal and hedonism that clung to him. The phone rang: it was Werner's father. Oliver felt that the gravity of the situation required him to come clean. The equanimity with which Werner's parents accepted their son's foray into the war effort surprised him: 'His mother and I are proud of him. Even prouder, I should say. Still, we're worried. Do you have children, Professor Oliver?'

'No. But I, too, am proud of Werner.'

'When can you expect him home in England?'

'By and by. You'll have seen him in Vienna. He's now somewhere between Vienna and England. I wish I could tell you more than that.'

The phone rang two hours later. The time was just after one in the morning. Tom Oliver said to Ilse, as he picked up the phone, 'I just hope —'

'Tom Oliver. Who's calling?'

The line went dead. Ilse looked into Oliver's eyes quizzically. A few seconds later, the phone rang again. 'Hello, is that Werner?'

'This is not Werner. We are holding Werner along with two boys and their mother at SS headquarters here in Nuremberg. Werner told me he was due to phone you tonight. As you can hear, I have taken that duty upon myself. I am commander-in-chief of this station. I expect to send the four of them to work camps, together or separately. There they can expect to be exhausted, tortured and put to death.'

'There must be a reason for your phoning. You could have just dealt with them forthwith.'

'True, I could have. But I might have an offer to make you. If you send someone to take Werner's place, I'll let him and the others go.'

'Someone to take his place? Is that all?'

'I need money,' said the voice. 'Someone to take his place, and money.'

'How long can you give me to think it over and get some money together?'

'I need an acceptance or a refusal right now. If your answer is positive, we'll discuss the rest.'

'I agree,' said Oliver. 'How much money are you asking for?'

The voice named a sum. Oliver found it much too large for his own resources but decided not to reveal any reaction. 'How do I know you have Werner and the others? This call could be a hoax.'

Then Oliver heard the voice saying: 'Thorsten, bring the prisoners over here. Not the woman.' At that point, the line went dead. Suddenly it was as though Oliver had become unaware of Ilse's presence. She started to walk to the door. Just as she was opening it, Oliver called out: 'No, don't go. Looks like it's going to be a hard night for me.'

'You don't really want me. You don't need me.'

'I need you for tonight, at least. And I'll need someone to help me. Not help me. Help them. They're in trouble, caught by the SS, or so a man claiming to be SS says. He says he'll let them go for money and a substitute.'

'I'll be the substitute,' said Ilse, 'Dagmar saved my life by bringing me here with her. I have no children. I can substitute for her son and the others if it will enable this SS man to free them. And I'll take him the money.'

'He says he's holding four people: Werner, Frau Lichtblau and her two sons. Yet it's strange: he only wants one substitute in exchange for four people.'

'Plus money,' replied Ilse, 'How much does he want?'

Oliver told her the figure. 'But I'm not worried about the money for the time being. I'm worried about the four of them being held by the SS, if that really is the case.'

The phone rang again. When Oliver picked it up, the voice at the other end said, 'This is Werner. It was I who gave the Herr Commandant your number. He stopped us at a checkpoint in Germany. Our papers are in order, but he won't let us go. When we told him we were on our way to England, he assumed we had money. He will have us tortured and executed if you do not provide a substitute and money. I'm with Frau — with the lady — and the two boys. I —'

'I will tell you an address in Germany to come to in two weeks' time.' The Commandant had snatched the phone from Werner. 'I will bring these prisoners to that address. If your substitute is there with the money, your friends will leave the place unharmed. I won't, by the way, guarantee their safe passage thereafter. If your substitute is not there or comes without the money, I will have the prisoners tortured and killed, as Werner told you. I'm not convinced their papers are not fakes. I will contact the SS in Vienna, and we will check their identities. Maybe these prisoners are wanted there, especially the lady.' Then he dictated the address in question to Oliver.

'Why is this money so important to you?'

'That can be no concern of yours,' replied the officer.

'You're in some kind of trouble, aren't you?' said Tom Oliver. 'Otherwise, you wouldn't be selling prisoners in this way.'

'Do not provoke me, Professor Oliver. I could kill your friends on the spot without needing to justify my actions to my hierarchy. On the contrary, they'd give me credit for it.'

'Why don't you, then? Why all this talk of money and substitutes?'

'I'm looking for bigger fish than these. They mean nothing to me and everything to you. If I can use them as bargaining chips —'

'You speak of a substitute, Herr Commandant. Why do you want one? Why not just take the money?'

'Maybe I will,' said the officer. 'The substitute will remain until I've counted the money and made sure it isn't fake. Then I'll decide what to do with the substitute. If the substitute can be useful to me, I'll use them.'

'You have the advantage and the weapons,' said Oliver. 'How can I be sure you won't keep the prisoners, the substitute, and the money?'

'This is war, Professor Oliver. You can be sure of nothing, and you're right to say I have the advantage. Let your substitute be at the address I've dictated to you, two weeks from today at noon. If the substitute fails to show up, your friends will die. I'll call you back in forty-eight hours to find out what you've decided.'

'I am sure of one thing. You're in trouble, whoever you are. You're embattled and trying to buy your way out.' The phone clicked. Tom Oliver sat staring into space.

'You were direct with him, provocative even,' said Ilse.

'He's not your average Nazi killing machine. If he were, he would have done away with the prisoners by now without bothering to phone me. Or, if he really is a Nazi killing machine, he's also scared and under threat. We'll have to find some way of —'

'Working on him?' suggested Ilse.

'Right,' said Tom Oliver.

Two nights later, Tom Oliver's phone rang again. It was Werner.

'He wants to know what your decision is. He has separated the two boys from their mother though I've seen them occasionally, and they are apparently being held in the same building as us. The officer has not otherwise mistreated us. He wants the receiver now. I'm handing it over to him.'

'What have you decided, Oliver?'

'Professor Oliver,' replied the interested party. 'I haven't yet made a decision. I need more reassurance as to the safety of my friends and the fact that you will let them go on to the completion of any deal. In any case, I don't have the kind of money you talked about.'

'What about the substitute?' said the man.

'I'm not even sure I can find one. I can't see the point in your asking me for one. If the money isn't enough for you, I don't know what will be.'

'For one thing, I need money. And for another, I can't go to my superiors empty-handed once the prisoners have been registered, which they have been. If I tell them I've set them free because I've reached an advantageous deal for them, I must have something — or someone — to show for it. Your friends' papers seem to be in order, but they may not be real. If they turn out to be fakes....'

'All right, all right,' said Oliver, 'your prisoners are not my immediate family. If I never see them again, I'll live.'

'Ah, but Werner is your student, I gather,' said the man. 'His parents wouldn't like to lose him, and nor, I dare say, would you.'

'Well, as you rightly say, this is war. War entails loss.'

The man sighed. 'You're being tiresome, Professor. I can torture them until they say who they really are and what their plans are. They may well have interesting information about the Resistance, especially in Vienna. Soon there will be no escape from the Wehrmacht. The whole of Europe will be the Reich, not only Germany, Austria and Central Europe.'

'That remains to be seen,' said Oliver.

'Do we have a deal, or don't we?'

Oliver replied: 'Do you know Hellroth?'

'Why?'

'I believe he has a gift for offending everybody and threatening them.'

'I can't comment on a fellow officer, especially with someone on the enemy side.'

'Maybe Hellroth isn't your best friend. A lot of people would like to see him incapacitated. Maybe you are one of those people. What I'm telling you now is worth more than what you're asking from me.'

Oliver was left with the sound of breathing for a couple of minutes, and then the connection was cut off.

A few nights later, at about three in the morning, Oliver's phone rang once more. It was Werner. 'Professor Oliver, you need to make sure you keep the deal. To send someone sooner than the deadline stated, if possible.'

'Why is that, Werner?'

'The officer is sitting next to me. He wants information. He's putting pressure on us.'

Ilse was with Oliver, following the conversation. She nodded.

'Ilse will go. She'll bring a small sum with her; all I can rustle up for the time being.'

Ilse said to Tom Oliver: 'Pass me the phone. I want to speak to the officer. Tell Werner.'

Oliver, surprised at her unusually bossy manner, acquiesced. The officer agreed to speak to Ilse, who said to Tom Oliver, 'I want to speak to the officer in private. Please withdraw.' Oliver shook his head. 'No, Tom, I'm determined to speak to the officer alone.'

Seventeen

Sitting cross-legged under a bridge, alone with his early-hours thoughts, Alfred Nubik gazed at the skyline shading from black to blue. He thought constantly about the Lichtblaus. Where was she? Was she in England yet? Why had there been no news from her since she left Vienna? As for her husband, he had changed: though active as ever, he had grown quiet and withdrawn. At the same time, Nubik detected in him something steadfast and resolute that he had not noticed before. Though Lichtblau had told his wife and sons they would all be reunited, he had admitted to Nubik that, in reality, he doubted this. He had to defy the Nazis. Since the Anschluss and before he had already been defying them with his culture and poetry: he affirmed the soul's serenity amid the storms of personal life and history, expressed in regular, rhymed stanzas of stark simplicity. Love alone creates life. The Nazis had been too blind to realize he had been fighting them this way for years. Perhaps he himself had been only half-aware of it.

When he got up, he saw an envelope on the ground a few feet away from him. It bore his name. He picked it up, and began walking towards the Ringstrasse. He was due to be meeting Lichtblau and his Resistance friends later that day. They were his mortal danger and his lifeline. He drew motivation from them while feeling that, for many of them, their days were numbered. He could try and flee the city but had no idea where to go. He was like Lichtblau: not the kind to run away. If he left the city to save his own life but no one else's, the weight on his conscience would be too much to bear.

As soon as the sun had risen, Nubik opened the envelope. He drew out the following message: *TELL LICHTBLAU HIS WIFE AND SONS ARE IN DANGER. SOMEONE MAY HAVE TO GO TO GERMANY.* The note was unsigned. He could not tell who it was from or even whether the message was true. He wondered how it had reached him and who it was who knew how to find him. The link between the two sentences he also found puzzling. The thing posed a dilemma: if it were a hoax, it would unsettle Lichtblau for no good reason, but if it was real, swift action must be taken.

He knew Lichtblau had stopped sleeping at his own place and moved around the city and suburbs from one friend to another. This early in the morning, he did not know where to start looking for him. He expected to see Lichtblau that evening with the Resistance group. But Frau Lichtblau's situation was urgent if the note was to be believed. Why hadn't the people behind the message gone straight to Lichtblau? That was just it: Lichtblau had become elusive, whereas everyone knew where to find Nubik, and everyone knew he knew everyone. He decided to make his way across the city to Hütteldorf, where Willy Schwartz the printer had his office. Standing some way off from it, he waited for the printer, who lived in the building, to open his curtains. When he came into view, Nubik hailed him and explained he needed to tell Lichtblau urgently that his family was in danger. The printer invited him into his office. He dialed a number and told whoever answered to get Lichtblau to come to the phone. The printer passed the receiver to Nubik, who told Lichtblau the message. 'Of course, the note may be meant to confuse us all.'

'I think,' said Lichtblau, 'I'll try and contact our friend Tom. My hunch is that he may be able to tell us more.'

Oliver confirmed that Herr Lichtblau's family was in Germany and under threat. He had been asked to put someone up as surety for the Lichtblau family, and Ilse had agreed to go. She was currently on her way to them, at risk to her own life. He did not understand why someone from Vienna was being required to go to them, too. In fact, the tone of the note was far from imperious: 'someone may have to go.'

What was the purpose of the note? wondered Oliver to himself. *To try and capture more of the Lichtblau circle and weaken the Viennese Resistance?*

Herr Lichtblau later related the conversation to Nubik. 'Someone from here should go, if only to keep you informed.'

Lichtblau replied, 'We don't even know who put that note in your way.'

'As Tom Oliver didn't know who it was,' replied Nubik, 'I wonder whether Ilse did not get a message through to someone here. Then they passed on this information to me, not knowing how to find you. So, it's likely to be someone both Ilse and I know.'

Both men were quiet for a second, then Nubik went on: 'I think this has something to do with that young couple who lived opposite Dagmar's flat. They escaped, and we never heard of them again. Dagmar may be in touch with them. Perhaps they're trying to help us, as far as they're able to. I wish we could find them.'

He thought of the young husband and wife, ordinary people, confused, seemingly prepared to compromise to save their own lives and yet wanting to help others.

Eighteen

Kristina, Johannes, Heinrich and Werner were walking through a copper-beech wood that Kristina wished her husband could share, he who so loved field and forest. Ilse had not gone far from Oxford when she received a message from Tom Oliver telling her she need not go to Germany after all: the prisoners had got away. She decided to keep going and try and make her way to Paris.

It had rained during the night and, now that the sun had risen, steam wafted from the ground. Kristina inhaled the scent of leaf mold as she walked, casting occasional sidelong glances at the boys. The Nazi officer — the one who had spoken to Tom Oliver and Ilse — had held them at a makeshift police-station-cum-prison. The three policemen at the station had hated the Nazi officer, whom a sub-lieutenant always accompanied, more bodyguard and minder than a real soldier. Before long, the policemen got wind of the officer's plan to sell the prisoners. There was, they felt, no certainty his plan would work, and they considered him as something of a coward. The policemen decided to throw a party for the officer and the sub-lieutenant to congratulate him on his haul of prisoners. They slipped a drug into his schnapps while he was dancing with a local girl in league with the policemen. The drug knocked him out. They then opened his mouth and poured lye down his throat. He never came round. They had him buried and told his superiors he had had too much to drink, fainted, and proved impossible to revive, despite their best efforts. The superiors made no further inquiries. However, the officer had informed them about the prisoners from Vienna: they had naturally wanted to know what had become of them. The policemen told them that the prisoners had persuaded the sub-lieutenant to let them out of their cells for an hour on condition they stayed on the premises. Once they were out of the cells, letting a little time elapse, Werner pretended to have a fainting fit and, gasping for fresh air, begged to be allowed to go outside. The others insisted he could not be left alone and told the sub-lieutenant he could accompany them if he did not trust them. At that very moment, the Nazi officer called him to go and join him. From where he was standing, the sub-lieutenant tried to explain that he had let the prisoners out. But the officer was now too drunk to take much notice of this and threatened to sanction the sub-lieutenant if he did not come to the party straight away.

When the sub-lieutenant later went outside to check up on the prisoners, they were gone. How could he go and tell the officer, in the middle of a party specially organized to celebrate his capture of the prisoners, that those same prisoners had now escaped? The officer was completely drunk by now. He was also succumbing to the charms of the local girl. The sub-lieutenant tried to tell him what had happened but got no response. He then told the policemen, but they refused to believe him, or pretended to refuse to do so. They were attending the party at the officer's gracious invitation, and — although they did not say it in so many words — if the prisoners had got away, it was the sub-lieutenant's fault. The latter rounded on the policemen. Things were getting out of hand: the prisoners had escaped, and the Nazi officer, whose second he was, appeared to have lost consciousness, as, in fact, he had. He ordered two of the three policemen to stay with the officer and the third to search the area with him. He took two dogs along with the policeman.

The situation proceeded to worsen even more for the sub-lieutenant. He told the policeman to take one of the dogs while he took the other. They were each to describe a semi-circle as they walked and to meet halfway. But when the sub-lieutenant got to what he thought was the mid-point, the policeman was not there. The sub-lieutenant had let his dog off the leash, and taking advantage of a moment's distraction on the man's part, the dog had run away. The sub-lieutenant panicked: he had lost the prisoners, the policeman, the dog, and the Nazi officer. He stumbled around for another hour or two, periodically calling out to the policeman or the dog, but neither reappeared. Finally, he trudged back to the scene of the party he had left a while earlier. By this time, the two remaining policemen had poisoned the Nazi officer. All the guests had left: he found only the two policemen seemingly trying to revive the officer.

'His pulse has stopped beating,' said one of the policemen. The sub-lieutenant did mouth-to-mouth on the officer, but he did not respond. 'He had too much to drink and could not handle the excitement of the party. His heart just gave way.'

The sub-lieutenant let fall a tear: 'He represented my only hope of promotion, he and his prisoners. When my superiors find out about this, they'll likely kill me.'

'Why don't you go back out and look for the prisoners again? One or both of us can go with you.'

'You can go to bed now. Deal with the body in the morning. I'll take a dog and have a last look for the prisoners.'

He walked out into the night. About half-past four in the morning, the two policemen were woken by the sound of a gunshot followed by a dog barking. The policemen got up and, guided by the dog's barks, went into the forest. When they finally found the dog, it was standing over the sub-lieutenant who lay dead on the ground with a bullet through his temple. He had shot himself.

'So, he was right — he won't get his promotion.'

'We need to report all this to the SS. That'll at least reduce suspicion on our account.'

Gerhardt Schmidt, the policeman who, of the three, had contacts in Vienna, decided he needed to inform them of the same events. He also knew a cousin of Lichtblau's. Schmidt, his two policemen colleagues, and Lichtblau's cousin all stood against the Nazi regime.

The forest into which the Lichtblau party had walked a few hours before seemed to Kristina to go on forever. Snow had begun to fall. As dawn broke, she looked out over a world covered in white as far as the eye could see. For some, she knew that summer was false and winter the only truth in the world. But to her, this white winter world was a beautiful lie. As if to confirm it, a gust of wind swept a salvo of snowflakes into her face, where they turned to water on her cheeks. She wiped them away and gazed at Werner and her two sons, still fast asleep. They were lucky to be so: it was the innocence within them that enabled them to sleep so soundly even after all they had been through on the train and in the cell, and without forecasting what the future might hold in store for them. No sun shone in the sky, which was white but not like the snow, for it was paler and almost dirty.

The Nazi hierarchy told the policemen to bring the prisoners back at all costs. This was precisely what Gerhard Schmidt and his two colleagues had been hoping to hear. Schmidt felt he had to go and warn the Lichtblau group that the Nazis wanted them, especially now the latter had lost one of their officers in suspicious circumstances. They could not understand why things had gone so wrong when there were five members of the Wehrmacht all stationed at the same place. Was there a traitor in their midst? Schmidt replied that he had known his two colleagues for years, during which time he had worked with them on a daily basis, and if either of them were traitors or had anything to hide, he himself had never seen any sign of it. They replied that they would be sure to reward him if he reported anything untoward. As for the prisoners, even though they were undoubtedly some way away by then, one woman and three young men, all with Viennese accents, could not indefinitely travel through Germany at a time when everyone's identity was being constantly checked.

So, Schmidt set off in a police car in search of the Lichtblau group. He could not drive into the forest – assuming that was where they had gone – and decided to skirt around it to its farthermost tip. He parked on the northern edge of the forest and switched off his headlights. Leaning forward, he slumped over the wheel and began to doze when a tapping at the window jolted him awake. Kristina and Johannes were looking in on him. He unlocked the car doors and beckoned to them to climb in.

'The Nazis will be looking for you wherever you go. The Nazi officer who took you in is dead.'

'So is the sub-lieutenant. He found us walking through the forest and threatened to kill us all on the spot. He lined us up and was about to shoot when Johannes started crying.

'Stop sobbing,' the sub-lieutenant shouted to him.

Heinrich muttered to me, 'Has he no children of his own?'

Pointing his gun at us all the while, the sub-lieutenant said, 'What did you say, boy?'

'Do you have no children of your own?' Heinrich said, perfectly calm.

'I have two boys.'

Heinrich said, 'Do you want them to die?'

His eyes widened, and he shook his head as though the thought of his sons' dying was too much to bear. Just then, I heard a slight crackle in the snow somewhere on the ground behind us. Someone fired at the sub-lieutenant's head, sending a bullet through his temple. He fell to the ground. Whoever killed him ran away at once, leaving the four of us to make of the incident what we would. So, we waited till all was quiet and arranged the body to make it look like suicide.'

Schmidt told her, 'I can't spend too long with you. I'll take you to a train station. I'm supposed to report back to the Nazis. When they find I haven't brought you in, I'll be in trouble. So, I have to have time to think, to work out what to do.'

Out of the blue, Johannes said: 'Did you know if ever this war ends, I'd like to be a policeman?'

'Would you like to try my uniform on?'

Schmidt pulled up and took off his uniform, while Johannes, who, like his brother, was tall and looked older than his years, passed his own clothes to Schmidt.

'Johannes can keep my uniform on. I can get another easily enough. I'll leave you my pistol, too. I'll tell the Nazis that after an extensive search, I failed to find you but heard first-hand reports that you were now trying to make your way back to Austria. That should throw them off your scent.'

They drove along back-roads, occasionally passing military vehicles. The Lichtblau group expressed their anxiety over possible checkpoints. Schmidt reassured them there were none between where they were and the town they were aiming for. Don't worry. A few moments later, they saw ahead of them on the road two military cars parked sideways on, stopping all the cars going in both directions one by one.

'Johannes and I will handle this,' smiled Schmidt as he braked and they took their place in the queue of traffic that had formed on their side of the road. There were two policemen questioning motorists but not telling them to get out of their cars. When it was Schmidt's car's turn, the policeman walked round to Johannes's side. The policeman saluted to Johannes, who saluted back. Johannes had Schmidt's policeman's cap pulled low over his brow.

'Where are you headed?'

Johannes told him, 'Cologne.'

'Where are you stationed?'

Johannes replied, 'At a small station in the suburbs of Stuttgart.'

The policeman explained, 'We're looking for the killer of an army officer. He was found dead in a forest south of here about twenty-four hours ago. That's why we're stopping all traffic.'

Johannes nodded.

'Why aren't you driving, colleague?'

Johannes replied that he wasn't feeling well.

'Who are these lady and gentlemen?'

Schmidt, in the driver's seat, replied: 'The lady is my wife, and the younger boy is our son. The other young man (he meant Werner) is a friend of ours. Your colleague is the son of a very good friend of mine. He offered to drive us to our destination, but as he felt unwell, he prompted me to drive — under his authority, naturally.'

A look of doubt flashed across the policeman's face, and he beckoned his colleague, a lean man with a long, straight mustache, to join him. He relayed to him what Johannes and Schmidt had just told him. They conferred.

Then: 'I must ask you all to get out of the car. We need to go through your story again and run it by our colleagues at your station.'

Schmidt, Werner, Heinrich and Kristina got out of the car. Johannes opened his door and started to get out of the car, but just as he was half in and half out, he slid to the ground clutching his chest.

Schmidt said to the policemen: 'Look. You can see your colleague's ill. He has to see a doctor as soon as possible. He might even be useful to you in the hunt for the soldier's killer. He's loyal to the Reich and can prove it. And I'm telling you, if he dies before he sees a doctor, the Nazis will blame you for it.'

Schmidt gave the Nazi salute, thus obliging the two policemen to do the same. The lines of cars at their roadblock stretching in both directions were growing longer by the minute. Some of the vehicles were police or military. Some motorists were holding their horns down and shouting. The policemen conferred again. 'We'll let you and the sick colleague drive on. The lady stays here with us along with the two boys till you come back. We'll check out your story later.'

'The lady's wanted elsewhere, sir. It is my task to take the lady to her destination. Please help us instead of slowing us down.'

'Who is this lady, who seems so important to you?' asked the mustachioed policeman.

Kristina spoke, 'I'm on a mission for the Reich. I'm not authorized to reveal details of my identity. I only mention this to you because this policeman is sick and because of the urgency of my own mission. I work for the services of General Globocnic. I have a safe-conduct pass here in my handbag if you want to see it.'

Even on his side, especially on his own side, some considered Globocnic as bad as the Führer – and as frightening.

'That will not be necessary,' said the first policeman, overriding his mustachioed colleague who looked angry and seemed on the point of objecting. 'You may proceed.'

Kristina, whose hand had remained on the outside handle of her door ever since she had got out of the car, now pressed the handle and got back into the car, where she sat looking straight ahead all the while. Schmidt, Heinrich and Johannes likewise got back into their respective seats. Schmidt started the car and pulled away. He and Johannes saluted the two policemen as they went past them. None of them spoke till they were out of sight of the roadblock.

Johannes started laughing and reached to take off his — Schmidt's — cap. 'Keep the uniform on, and don't relax too much. We have all the makings of an unlikely group, and they are right to be suspicious. Grit your teeth and prepare for other nasty surprises. You and your mother acted beautifully; you may have to do a repeat performance.'

'What will you do, Herr Schmidt?' asked Kristina. 'If your superiors find out all about your latest doings….'

'Don't worry about me,' replied Schmidt. 'We're doing our best to make things that bit harder for the Reich. We'll go on doing so as long as we're able to. We're not afraid to die, and we'll fight tyranny to the death. Kill us. Try to turn us into ghosts or memories. We'll still resist.'

'What you're doing for us could spell your execution.'

Schmidt made as if he hadn't heard her.

'I didn't care for the policeman with the mustache. He was taking notes as his colleague was talking to us, inspecting us, the car, everything to do with us.'

'He's only doing his job. He's entitled to be suspicious.'

Schmidt slowed down as they drew near a town. 'I'll drop you here. Just follow the signs to the station. Johannes, you can take off my uniform and put your own clothes back on; I have a spare shirt and trousers in my bag. You can put my uniform in your suitcase. You never know; it might come in handy. It could also be a liability. But if you've done it once, you can do it again.'

'What about papers?' said Johannes.

'You can always say you had to leave in a hurry and forgot them at the station. That way, if anyone tries to contact my station about you, I'll tell them that you're a new recruit with us and warn my colleagues at the station to say the same thing. You can send the uniform back to me from England. Meantime, it might even get you out of a scrape.'

'What'll I say if my case is searched while I'm in my civvies and they discover your uniform in it?'

'Just keep your head and say whatever comes to mind. If you feel it's too much of a burden, just chuck it away somewhere discreet.'

Kristina and the boys followed the signs to the rail station. The latter was teeming with Nazi soldiers and police officers. But there were also a lot of civilians milling about, so that their party seemed to go unnoticed.

Kristina, Heinrich, Johannes and Werner started to queue up to buy rail tickets for Cologne, taking their place at the back of a long line. Johannes suddenly spotted the mustachioed policeman who had been observing them so closely a few hours before. He was talking to some Nazi soldiers who were laughing in response to whatever he was saying. Two young women walked past them, and the whole group — soldiers and policeman — whistled, cheered and clapped. Ignoring the men as best they could, the young women sped up their pace. The men followed them with their eyes and only looked away once the women had started walking down the platform alongside which stood their train. Johannes tried to make himself smaller, bending his knees and hunching his shoulders to blend in more with the people behind and in front of him in the queue. He muttered to his mother under his breath to turn towards him: the policeman and soldiers were nearly level with them. The line crept forward, and at last, Johannes, his mother and Werner reached the ticket counter. The conversation the policeman was having with the soldiers simultaneously drew to an end. The soldiers seemed to have lost interest in him and were wandering off, doubtless in search of the two young women or other amusements. Kristina said to the ticket saleswoman: 'Three tickets for Cologne, please.' She kept her voice down so as not to attract the policeman's attention. But the ticket lady had not heard her amid the hubbub of the station, and she had to reiterate her request more loudly. Her accent identified her as Viennese. The policeman, who stood with his back to her several yards off, spun around and stared at Kristina, Heinrich, Johannes and Werner for a split second before striding over to them.

'Your papers!' The policeman pretended he had not seen the group before.

'You've already checked us once today. Why do you want to do so again?' said Kristina, lying for her group's and her own life, taking care not to remind him that he had not actually seen the papers she claimed he had. The policeman made as if to strike her but at the last second restrained his hand.

'Your insolence will not go unpunished.' He was evidently concerned with not losing face before the crowd slowly gathering around him and the group. He turned to Johannes, who was no longer wearing the policeman's uniform Schmidt had given him, and Werner: 'Your papers!'

'Show me your own papers!' Johannes spoke with all the bravado of youth.

What the policeman did not know was that the group of Nazi soldiers from whom he had separated a few minutes before had returned to the concourse and, seeing the policeman in discussion with a beautiful woman, had drifted over to him and stood behind him. They heard and saw Johannes telling the policeman to show his papers and seemed to admire his courage. One of them started to clap and stamp in slow rhythm while calling out, *'Zeig mir deins!* — Show me yours! Show me yours!'— a cry soon taken up by the other members of his group. His quick-witted and more voluble colleague at the roadblock had already overshadowed him a few hours before; the policeman's face reddened with shame at his second humiliation of the day. He saluted the Nazi soldiers and stormed off towards the station exit, turning around just before going outside and shouting, 'I know you're up to something! I'll find out soon enough!'

'Show me yours! Show me yours!' went the Nazi soldiers.

Johannes turned to the soldiers: 'He has found nothing to accuse us of. And now, if you'll excuse us, gentlemen, we have a train to catch. The Führer would be ashamed of you. Your brains are as small as your ambitions.'

Nineteen

'My name is Schmidt, and I'm a policeman in a small town in Southern Germany.'

Silence at the other end of the line.

'Can you hear me?'

'I'm listening.' Listening was Willy Schwartz, Lichtblau's printer friend.

The Resistance group to which Lichtblau belonged had gathered at Schwartz's printer's office. Lichtblau had felt highly nervous ever since his wife and children had left Vienna. He had still had no news of them. Schmidt told Schwartz he had seen Frau Lichtblau, one of her sons, and their friend, while they were in transit. They had been held up occasionally but were all right when he said goodbye to them. He hadn't held them back because he was working for the Kreisau Circle in Germany, with two of his colleagues.

'Tell Herr Lichtblau —'

'Herr Lichtblau is with me now,' said Schwartz.

'Tell him I gave his son Johannes my policeman's uniform. I thought it might come in useful. Many Nazis are stubborn and stupid. They are suspicious, but many of them are not discerning. They are content to follow orders and shut their eyes to anything beyond their orders unless it will bring them a promotion or financial gain or satisfy their sensuality.'

Lichtblau took the receiver from Schwartz. 'We're looking to put one or two of the Nazi hierarchy here in Vienna out of action, even if they have to die in the process.'

Schmidt told Lichtblau he and his two colleagues were trying to do the same in Germany, put a few of the Nazis out of action. 'By the way, Herr Lichtblau, you are a lucky fellow.'

'I know why. That wife of mine has brought me more compliments, more joy and —'

'More trouble,' interrupted Schmidt.

'More trouble than I could ever have imagined when I first met her.'

'We've done what we could to ease their passage. We must end our conversation: the phone lines in Germany are no longer safe.'

Lichtblau put the phone down. The members of the Resistance group waited for him to speak. 'You may be wondering whether we can rely on him. All I can say is he won Kristina's trust and helped her and the boys on their way. Where's Nubik? He should be here by now.'

Nubik did not appear for another hour. In the meantime, the group talked of how they might work with Schmidt and his colleagues in unsettling the regime, however slightly or temporarily.

One of the men broke down in tears: 'I feel weak.'

'Our position is fragile,' admitted Lichtblau, 'but we have determination.'

Clouds of tobacco smoke filled the room. The men had shut the shades and sat in darkness, where their cigarette ends shone like glowworms. In darkness but not in silence: they tried to support each other, devising schemes, however unlikely or crazy, for undermining the Reich and setting Vienna free of the Nazi plague. Whatever scheme or schemes they decided to put into action, they were all aware that, for the greater good, they would, if need be, both have to risk their lives, and kill. They unanimously agreed that they were prepared to do so — and they unanimously agreed that there were more important things in life than life.

They were starting to get ready to go home when a knock at the door told them Nubik had at last arrived. They recognized his signal, since they all had a different one and knew each other's signals by heart. When Schwartz opened the door, Nubik stumbled in, nearly falling over, breathless, blood streaming down his face.

'They tried to get me to squeal. They kept me at the Metropole for I don't know how many hours. They bashed me around. But I played the businessman to the end. They said I was debauching their officers and soldiers with drugs and drink. I told them they should take in their officers and men, my clients, rather than me, since they were the ones both buying the goods and fixing the rules. That was when one of them kicked me in the face and asked whether I denied supplying. It was the most hypocritical thing I had ever heard.

'Of course, I don't,' I replied. 'It isn't my problem if they want drugs, and whether I or anyone else supplies them is all the same to them.' They had no answer to that.

'I might even be useful to you some time. Some of them tell me things,' I said.

'Some of those present cast their eyes down momentarily at that since they were my clients and really had told me things.

'Some of my clients are already high when they stop me in the street,' I continued. 'They tell me what's going on in your hierarchy. High up in your hierarchy.'

'The chief interrogator said, 'We have no way of knowing if you're telling the truth or not.'

'Believe me or not, it's all the same to me. Some of the men in this room could nevertheless, I think, corroborate what I've told you.'

At that, the one who had punched me the first time did so again.

'I'm just a simple businessman,' I told them as soon as I'd recovered my wits.

'Give us an example of the kind of thing you say you know,' the chief interrogator said.

'I told them some stuff that was supposed to be inside information, including something about a niece who knew a lot more than I did — who, in fact, knew a lot more than most generals did. They smiled knowingly and let me go after that but told me I could expect to be brought in for questioning again.'

'You protected us all, Alfred,' said Lichtblau. He told Nubik about Schmidt's call, how Schmidt had seen and helped Kristina and the boys, and how he was a Resistance fighter in the guise of a member of the Gestapo. He had given Johannes one of his Gestapo uniforms.

'I've got one of those,' said Nubik, promptly fainting. They brought him round and cleaned him up before all taking leave of each other except for Lichtblau, Markus Jäger, Nubik, and Schwartz, the printer who lived upstairs. Nubik hid his Gestapo uniform in a special place only he knew about. He had never worn it.

'Will you wear it tomorrow?' as he was later getting ready to leave Schwartz's printing works, where Nubik was due to spend the night on the floor by the printing machines. For his part, Lichtblau would go and stay at a friend's flat. He now never stayed at the same place two nights running. He did not sleep much, though. He wrote poetry till morning, except for the moments when he simply thought or let his mind wander. A spell had fallen over the city, the continent, even the world. Did such a thing as forgiveness still exist for anyone except fools and children? To live meant to be always saying goodbye. All one could do — if that — was to stand in the eye of the storm and try to be good. And what did being good mean in a war like this? But he and Nubik had agreed to meet in front of St Stephen's Cathedral in the early afternoon.

Just as Lichtblau and Markus Jäger were about to put their coats on, a half-crumpled sheet of foolscap happened to fall out of an outside pocket of Lichtblau's coat. There were what looked like some lines of verse on it. Jäger picked it up and handed it to Lichtblau. As he did so, he saw the lines written on it.

'You know how I have always admired your writing.'

'This is nothing — just idle scribbling. In fact, Schwartz asked me for something that might help our cause. But this is a long way from ready. Not fit for anyone's eye or ear.'

'Do let's hear it.' Nubik, Schwartz and Jäger gazed expectantly at Lichtblau. Lichtblau himself studied his lines. They were a challenge to the Reich. Their violence surprised even him, he who was outwardly so gentle. Lichtblau read out the title: *The Ravens of Vienna*. Then he stared at the page but felt unwilling to recite the whole poem. In a loud voice his listeners had never heard from him before, he recited three of the verses:

They'll roam the streets till nightfall

And long after it gets dark

If only Noah'd had the wherewithal

To leave them out of his ark!

They croak and caw all over town

They goose-step tall and straight

They'll hunt you and they'll track you down

And burn you with their hate

They'll catch and grip you in their claws

And peck you to your graves

Cut down the plutocratic whores!

No longer be your Führer's slaves!

'Amazing! I must have a signed copy of the manuscript. I'll share it, one way or another.' Markus Jäger passed Lichtblau a clean sheet of paper and a pen. Lichtblau copied his poem onto it and signed his lines without a thought. He returned them both to Jäger.

In a dark suit, dark red tie and shiny black shoes, Lichtblau stood some yards away from the cathedral, on the edge of the forecourt, to the left of the main door. He could not see Nubik anywhere on the forecourt, but there was a stream of people exiting the cathedral, and he soon spotted Nubik among them, wearing his Gestapo uniform. Nubik put his hand up to his cheek to tell Lichtblau he had seen him, and Lichtblau responded by making the same gesture. A group of Nazi soldiers and Gestapo walked onto the forecourt from behind Lichtblau, who had a notebook in his hand, which he opened and peered into for just the purpose of shading his face in situations like this. But in any case, none of the men seemed to notice him and walked on in the direction of the cathedral. He watched Nubik stride over to them and engage them in conversation. He did most of the talking and kept pointing at the cathedral, the men nodding whenever he did so.

Nubik walked away from them in the general direction of Lichtblau, while the group of men disappeared inside the cathedral.

'See! It didn't occur to them I wasn't the real thing! I told them there was a suspicious-looking individual walking round in the cathedral muttering sentiments that sounded anti-Nazi. They all mechanically went off to collar this non-existent person. People with such a mentality should be easy to draw into a trap.'

While they were walking, they continued their conversation but only for a minute or two: an officer hailed them with the Nazi salute and a friendly manner and began asking Nubik questions. He soon told Nubik to take his cap off.

'I don't know you. I've never seen you before.'

'Naturally. I've only just been transferred from the Interior Ministry in Berlin.'

Out of the corner of his eye, Nubik now spotted the group of soldiers and policemen he had directed to the cathedral. He turned further toward the officer so that he had his back to the group. He kept his head down. The two groups saluted each other. Useless to try to keep a low profile: the officer asked them whether they knew Nubik. They at once said they did. Did they know to which unit he was attached? They replied that they had not tried to find out and that, in any case, it did not matter as he had tipped them off about an anti-Nazi suspect in the cathedral a few minutes before. Had they found the suspect? They had questioned a few people, but nothing conclusive had emerged. Nevertheless, they applauded the conscientiousness of their unfamiliar colleague. Why had they not asked the colleague to go into the cathedral with them and point out the individual he claimed to find suspicious? He had told them he had an urgent appointment at Gestapo headquarters and was late already.

'But he might have been setting a trap for you,' said the officer.

Suddenly a new voice joined the discussion. Lichtblau, who had been present but silent all the while, addressed the officer: 'Who are you, anyway?'

The officer had not yet taken in Lichtblau's presence. His eyes now swiveled in his direction. So struck was he by the nature and tone of the question that his hand went straight to his revolver in its holster.

Nubik grinned: 'Don't worry. He's like that with everyone.'

'That doesn't excuse him,' said the officer.

'He's a friend of Lucht's,' persisted Nubik.

'It so happens I've been a lieutenant in the SS for several years, though it's not for you to question me,' the officer retorted.

'Of course, if you like, we can take this up with Lucht,' said Lichtblau, playing along with Nubik's game.

'Then that's what we'll do, as soon as he gets back,' the lieutenant said.

'That's right,' said one of the group of soldiers who had just come out of the cathedral. 'As you know, Lucht has gone to Germany for a week or two on business of extreme importance to the Führer.'

'And who are you?' said the officer to Lichtblau, not to be put off by such distractions.

'My name is Hutt, Peter Hutt,' said Lichtblau, who was not used to lying and had hardly ever lied in his whole life, but who sensed that the moment was critical. Nubik was impersonating a member of the Gestapo, and he, Lichtblau, was supposed to be checking just how effective his impersonation was, rather than lying to save his own skin.

'Look,' said Lichtblau, raising the stakes, 'there's no need to wait till Lucht gets back. Why don't we just contact him today and sort this out once and for all?'

'That will not be necessary,' said the officer.

'Why not?' broke in the soldier who had said Lucht was on Reich business in Germany, 'What are you afraid of? I'm sure Lucht will be interested to learn from Herr Hutt that one of his officers has been bothering him.'

'I have not been bothering him,' said the officer, 'I merely want to know who he is.'

'If anyone wishes to report this incident to Lucht or anyone else, let him do so,' said Nubik. 'For my part, I consider the matter closed.'

'So do I,' called out the soldiers who had come from the cathedral.

'So do I,' said Lichtblau.

'So do I not,' said the officer.

Nubik said, 'You are free to file a report should you wish to do so. But I suggest everyone go about his business now. Time is getting on.'

They all gave the Nazi salute. However, Nubik and Lichtblau kept their left hands in their pockets where they clenched their fists to cancel symbolically the Nazi salute that circumstances were forcing them to make.

'Herr Hutt,' said the officer, 'I do not find your behavior has been quite appropriate.' The man stood square in front of Lichtblau as though to block his way. 'You and my colleague' — he indicated Nubik with his chin — 'should not be saluting the Führer with your hands in your pockets.'

Lichtblau feared the officer might have sensed their game by now. But the soldier who had intervened previously, either hot-headed or drunk or both, interposed himself between the officer and Lichtblau:

'Why shouldn't they keep their hands in their pockets? There's no law against it. And you're not the Führer.'

At this, the officer slapped the man across the face with his black leather glove. In return, the man head-butted the officer, who went down but got back on his feet almost at once, drawing his pistol as he did so.

'Drop it,' said a member of the group of soldiers from behind the officer, 'or I'll shoot.' By now, the whole group of soldiers was crowding around the officer, who was looking more and more shaken. By tacit agreement, Nubik and Lichtblau started backing away from the group, who were all simultaneously talking with or, rather, at the officer. They nodded to each other after a few steps, spun around and strode away from the scene, leaving the Nazis to their infighting.

A voice called out, 'Hey! Where are you going?' It was most likely the officer. But they ignored the voice and kept on walking faster and faster.

Behind them, footsteps were clattering on the cobblestones of Ruprechtplatz. They started running. The footsteps behind them accelerated.

Then a gunshot crashed in the air: 'Stop now, or I'll shoot you in the back.'

Lichtblau and Nubik turned round. They saw the soldier who had previously defended Lichtblau against the officer. He was smiling.

'I told them I'd come and bring you back. The officer is furious you got away. It only confirms his worst suspicions about you. Take my advice: leave Vienna as soon as possible. He's told headquarters and ordered reinforcements. They'll be closing in on you if you don't hurry. He cursed me for challenging him and so giving you time to slip away unnoticed. I told him I would prove my loyalty to the Reich by going after you and bringing you back in.'

'Why don't you, then?' said Nubik, 'we're unarmed, and you've got the gun.'

'Why do you think I'm smiling? I want to join you. I'm suffocating in the army. I'm dying.'

'So are a lot of people at this time. Too many. And it's not just an image,' said Nubik.

'How can we trust you?' said Lichtblau.

'You fool!' said the soldier. 'I could have killed you when you were running away. I could still do so now. I'm trying to help you.'

'How do you know who we are? Or, rather, why do you think you know who we are?' asked Lichtblau.

'I realize you want to resist the Wehrmacht. I do, too. You saw how I behaved a few minutes ago with the officer. He could have had me arrested or even shot me on the spot for my attitude.'

Lichtblau noticed an SS officer walking towards them. He told the soldier to train his gun on Nubik and himself and walk them away from there. The soldier obeyed, signaling to the two men to put their hands up. The three of them walked as fast as dignity would allow them without seeming to be fleeing the SS officer behind. He called out to them to stop, but they kept on walking. He threatened to shoot the three of them down. The soldier turned around: 'Can't you see these are my prisoners? They've been working against the Reich. They're taking me to their Resistance hide-out. Why are you bothering me? You may report me if you like. I'm certainly going to report you for holding me up and trying to prevent me from doing my duty to the Reich. Do you know who my commanding officer is? Colonel Hellroth.'

The SS officer shuddered: 'In that case, I think I can see my way to forgetting this encounter.' The SS officer turned back the way he had come, and the soldier, Nubik and Lichtblau, resumed the same configuration as before.

Nubik asked the soldier: 'Do you really know Hellroth?'

'I can't claim to —'

'Have the honor?' said Nubik.

'I can't claim to have the honor of knowing that gentleman personally. However, I've seen him at work at the Metropole —'

'At work,' Nubik said.

'He's sent many Viennese to their deaths.'

'He harassed my family and me. He... My wife...' Lichtblau's voice trailed off. As he thought about that episode, his mind reeled; he instantly felt as though he was faltering forward in a field wet with drizzle.

'I know,' said the soldier. 'He tried to seduce your wife, and when that didn't work, he tried to blackmail her into having illicit relations with him. But I gather that, fortunately for your wife and you, events were against him.'

'He has an enemy.'

'Lucht,' said the soldier.

'Is there anything you don't know?' said Nubik.

'What I know a lot of people know.'

'I have an idea,' said Lichtblau. 'To persuade Hellroth and Lucht that each one is plotting to kill the other.'

The soldier nodded and smiled in acquiescence. 'Could be a great contribution to the Resistance, especially if they do kill each other. At the very least, it should be a good cockfight, I'd have thought.'

Twenty

Kristina was thinking a thought she would not share with Johannes and Werner: she felt like turning back and returning to Vienna to be with her husband and, if it came to it, die with him, rather than die without him or leave him to die without her. The strain of the journey, and anxiety about the circumstances in which her husband and Nubik had chosen to go on living, were beginning to tell on her. To make Kristina's party less conspicuous, Thedel had got a message through to them and then taken Heinrich under his wing; the two of them were now traveling separately. Kristina hardly slept at all now and, when she did, nightmares filled her sleep. A boa constrictor would sometimes appear in them, seething, hissing, bloated. Total blackness suffused these dreams, except for the snake's red eyes, which seemed to grow ever wider the nearer it got to its prey — a man whom she could not at first identify — and coiled itself around the man's neck. Just as it was about to strangle the man to death, she would wake up screaming. By that point, she had recognized the man: it was her husband. The snake had cross-like markings on its skin. The crosses were swastikas.

Kristina, Werner, and Johannes sat in a compartment with wooden seats in a train running through France. She had heard from Dagmar about the French academic who had caused controversy at an Oxford college dinner but who had turned out to be — though how long he could keep it a secret from the Nazis and Vichy was uncertain — a member of the Résistance. He had confided in Dagmar, Ilse and Tom Oliver that he worked with two young ladies in the Résistance. One went by the name of Annie Rousseau. Her mixture of charm and innocence and her mastery of several languages, including German and English, had enabled her to win the trust of German officers in charge of the Occupation in France while working closely with General de Gaulle. The other was called Berg. Françoise Berg was an attractive and brilliant young English student at the Sorbonne. The academic, Soubrenie, was convinced that he or a member of his circle could help Kristina Lichtblau and the two boys and that they, in turn, might even be useful to them.

Kristina could not forgive the French for having given rise to a Pétain and letting a part of their population and some of their leaders collaborate with the most ruthless regime Europe had ever known. Françoise had apparently told Ilse she could help Kristina and the boys if they managed to reach Paris, though at that moment, the likelihood of their ever reaching Paris, let alone England, looked doubtful. Their train stopped every ten minutes. At least, that was how it seemed to Kristina, and every time it did so, she did not know whether or not they would be herded off and boarded onto another train to be taken to a death camp. Would they stop forever or move on again after a mysterious halt designed to show all passengers their lives were now in the hands of Vichy?

Kristina fell into a deep sleep as the train sped towards Paris. Hardly had she fallen asleep when she awoke to prods from Johannes. An SS officer stood over her, his leather boots creaking and his thumbs hooked into his belt. She did not want him to hear her accent and take the three of them into custody.

'What do you intend to do in Paris?' he asked.

She replied as quietly as possible: 'Stay with a friend, sir.'

Taking his right hand out of his belt and raising it as though he meant to strike her, the officer thundered: 'Speak up! And look an officer in the eye when you speak to him!'

The officer kept up the pressure: 'You realize we can check up on everything you tell us and everyone you mention. Your papers!'

She opened her handbag and, turning up her passport, tendered it to the officer.

He looked through it. 'Austrian?'

She nodded. He glanced quizzically at Johannes and Werner and then back at her. 'My son and a friend,' she explained.

The officer's probing was cut short as a fellow officer burst into the compartment, out of breath, and whispered in the first officer's ear, gesticulating with one hand and tugging at the officer's sleeve with the other, clearly wanting him to go with him elsewhere on the train. The officer standing over Kristina looked and sounded irritated as he whispered back to his fellow. Then he began stamping on the floor and looked as though he might strike the other man at any second. The man, in turn, whispered something in his ear — a threat? A useful piece of information? — and that seemed to calm him. He handed Kristina back her passport and left the compartment with the other officer. Then, just before his boot disappeared out of the compartment, he turned round to Kristina, Johannes and Werner: 'You'll see me again. You're up to something.'

At Gare de l'Est, Kristina, Johannes and Werner stepped off the train into the early morning grey. The trio walked down the boulevards and, as the day grew brighter, were surprised at how quiet the city was. Kristina overheard as much German as French spoken on the streets by the rare passers-by. Tanks rolled by, trucks carried soldiers laughing and joking. Kristina had Soubrenie's address and decided to head there with Johannes and Werner, despite vague misgivings as to whether she would be able to trust Soubrenie and the people around him. She rang the front doorbell, remembering the arrangement: the concierge would come and open it, at which point she was to say they had come to see Monsieur So-and-so. All this she did. As they walked upstairs, a cat was coming down. As it passed Kristina, it spread its claws and scratched her leg, laddering one of her Viennese sheer silk stockings and drawing blood. The gentleman's door was already open as they reached the fourth-floor landing. Kristina didn't need to knock since Soubrenie was standing on the threshold. He welcomed them in, holding a packet of new stockings in his hand.

'I apologize for the cat. Always happens with lady visitors. It's just his way of saying hello.' He handed Kristina the stockings.

'Please come to the bathroom, wash your wound and put those on. Then I have a surprise for you.'

He showed them into the flat, where they found Ilse. She and Kristina fell into each other's arms. Kristina shed an involuntary tear — involuntary because these troubled years had made her feel it necessary to hide her feelings, if not harden her heart.

Kristina realized that Soubrenie's flat represented the first non-hostile environment they had been in for weeks, if not longer, since Vienna had too long been antagonistic to them all. She could hardly have imagined seeing Ilse in Paris.

Soubrenie smiled. 'Whatever made her leave the shelter of Oxford and risk falling prey to the wolves' jaws in Paris, I don't know.'

'We didn't know about your connection with Ilse, nor that she would be here.'

'I haven't been here long,' said Ilse, 'but as a native German speaker, I'm able to get about and survive, despite occasional resentment from some of the locals.'

'What are we going to do now, Mother?' asked Johannes.

'I have a friend I have told about you. The two of us combined think we should be able to help you leave for England.' Soubrenie answered for Kristina. 'Her name is Françoise. Françoise Berg. She's a Jewish student. She helps everyone, Jewish or not. She loves everything about England and English culture. Her dream is to live there, at least for a time. You'll have to stay in hiding here until we find the means to get you to England. I'll arrange a meeting between you and Françoise.'

Ilse soon fell deep into conversation with Werner. They both had mixed feelings about being in Paris, hardly a less dangerous place than Vienna. Werner felt that, despite such feelings, his accompanying Kristina and Johannes as far as Paris and bringing them to Soubrenie meant he had accomplished a big part of his mission. They would have to explain about Heinrich and Thedel, about whom Dagmar felt anxious.

'As I am about Heinrich,' said Kristina. They had been out of touch for some time now. They had thought the five of them all traveling together was too likely to attract the Nazis' attention. Would Heinrich and Thedel be trying to join them in Paris? That wasn't part of the plan, according to Kristina. But they had Monsieur Soubrenie's address and would contact him if they found they needed to come to Paris.

'The first thing is to tell Tom we have arrived safely in Paris, are with Monsieur Soubrenie, and want to get to Oxford as soon as possible,' said Werner. Soubrenie had, he said, stopped using his own phone, and they would have to go to a friend's house if they wanted to phone. The friend, Soubrenie said, had 'done a little deal' with the Nazis so that they left him alone. Without being in the Résistance, or a collaborator, this friend helped Jews and refugees whenever he could. He had no ethical or political standpoint, said Soubrenie; he just wanted the war to end as soon as possible and, until then, to manage from day to day.

'And by the way,' Soubrenie continued, 'when you've seen this friend, don't tell Françoise Berg. She dislikes his relations with the Nazis and the way he takes their money.'

They walked from Soubrenie's flat on the right bank near Gare du Nord down to the river, crossing it just in front of Notre Dame, and then through the side-streets of the Latin Quarter, up Boulevard St Michel, past the Sorbonne and the English Institute library where Françoise Berg worked, and then to Rue Auguste Comte and an austere, tall grey building. All of them went: Soubrenie, Ilse, Johannes, Werner and Kristina. But for the same reason as Kristina's original party of five did not all travel together, the present group did not all walk close together. Ilse and Werner walked together, as did Johannes and Kristina, with Soubrenie walking a few steps ahead of them, pretending he was moving quite independently. None of the four spoke or looked around. Whenever a soldier walked in the opposite direction on the same pavement, they would carry on, looking straight ahead, above all avoiding eye contact.

Soubrenie's friend was likely in his fifties, with a mustache and a winning smile. He talked in smooth tones and spoke fluent German. He gladly, if not servilely, let them use his phone. Kristina saw Soubrenie slip his friend a few banknotes.

'Does the phone company take so much money from you for every call?' asked Johannes, who was becoming rather outspoken as he grew up. The others worried that his provocative manner would sooner or later attract the enemy's attention and arouse their suspicions. This time, Soubrenie turned on him:

'Be quiet, will you? This man is our friend. He can help us as long as you don't rub him up the wrong way.'

'Easy,' said the man with the mustache. 'That's all right. No, the phone company doesn't take so much money from me per call. But this is how I get by these days since the war started.'

Since the war started. The words rang in Kristina's head. The man might have said: since peace had ended. Ended almost as soon as it had begun. And peace which was hardly peace at all but more like a prelude to an even deadlier war. This was the second war she had lived through – she was almost surprised to find herself alive. Since this wild dash had started, it seemed never-ending. As a courting couple, she and her husband had been to Paris in the thirties: in no other city could she imagine feeling so free, she remembered thinking to herself back then. She ran her hand through her hair and glanced at her son, their son, who was growing up much faster than he should have done. He defended himself against the buffetings of circumstance with his arrogant attitude; his brow, though, was lined with care. He worried more about his brother and his father than he did about himself, and he took care of his mother, too, as best he could. He had wanted to study agriculture and then move to the Tyrol to farm. He had only ever envisaged that one kind of life for himself. His father had been setting aside money for the farm, with Johannes promising to work off the debt. Since the war had started, Kristina sensed, he lived with the shattered dream he had so lovingly nurtured. In despondent moments they each — mother and son — in their secret thoughts felt that the absence of a foreseeable future made the present hollow: what point was there in struggling to survive, in killing if it came to it, if there was to be no future at the end of it all, none except a living death under the heel of a soulless empire, after the blood of so many people had flowed out of their bodies and into the earth? But pessimism led nowhere; even realism, it seemed to her, had its limits. *Cherish whatever crumbs of hope, of good, life has to offer*, she told herself. Preserve your hope from getting sucked into the vortex of evil. Were the Allies gaining ground in certain parts of Europe? They were said to be. She had to press forward and trust the words and plans of this Englishman whom she had never met for, unlike the Cumaean Sybil upon whom Tom Oliver frequently lectured, Kristina Lichtblau wanted to live, and she knew it.

Her son roused her from her thoughts by shaking her arm and handing her the receiver of the friend's phone.

'We've got through to Oxford,' said Johannes, 'there's someone wanting to speak to you.'

'Hello?' she said, putting the receiver to her ear.

'Kristina?' said a woman's voice.

'Dagmar! You sound so close you could be in the next room!'

'Alas, I'm not. I wish I were or, rather, I wish you were not in the next room but in the same room as me!'

'Dagmar, Werner will have told you we've met up with Ilse in Paris. But you'll be wanting to know about Thedel. He and Heinrich are making their own way to Oxford. I have no idea where they are at present. We decided five of us traveling together would be too conspicuous, so we split up into three and two. Have you heard from Thedel?'

'I did hear from him a couple of days after he and Heinrich had left you. They were still in Germany and had joined a group of students who agreed to help them with their onward journey. I haven't heard from them since. They had not been called up or imprisoned by the Gestapo. But they constantly feared something of the sort. They belonged to the White Rose. Thedel and one of the girls, Heike, have taken a liking to each other. He has asked Tom and me to help her get to Oxford. Werner spoke to Tom just before our conversation, and Tom seems to be reassured. Tom's a man of strong feelings. He's been tense since Werner left for Vienna. Ilse did her best to help him after Werner left, and since she left, I have been —'

'Keeping Professor Oliver company?' By some miracle, Kristina had kept her sense of humor.

Dagmar laughed. 'Quite so. At least —'

Kristina laughed too. 'At least when the place is free.'

She looked out into the powder-blue evening light of Paris and remembered how clement she had found it when she and her husband had stayed in the city, drunk Moët before dinner, and wandered along the banks of the Seine without a care in the world, or almost.

Twenty-One

Lichtblau and Nubik were drinking Gemischter Satz in a *heurige* on Rauhensteingasse. It was one of the ways they reminded themselves that, despite the Gestapo's best efforts at appropriation through terror, they were neither strangers nor guests in their native city. Anybody seeing them from a few feet away would have thought they were two friends having a quiet drink and, if not exchanging pleasantries, at least able to smile and laugh at regular intervals. This was how they had learned to behave, or rather to act, in public. They had known for some time that they wanted to draw Hellroth and Lucht into a trap of their own devising. They wondered whether they could evacuate the prisoners from the Metropole and then blow it up with the two enemies arguing in it. Perhaps they could begin by sending a letter from Lucht to Hellroth accusing the latter of embezzling Nazi funds for his private purposes. Failing to report his dealings with the Jews? Being drunk on the job? Bringing ridicule and shame on the Reich and therefore on the Führer? The letter would notify him that the Führer was stripping him of his powers and rank and that henceforth Lucht would be replacing him, while he, Hellroth, would continue to serve the party as Lucht's valet. They would send it as from the Führer's secretary. They would also write Hellroth a second letter, as from Lucht, to say that the Führer had ordered him to take over all Hellroth's duties and that Hellroth was to report to him on a given date as his new valet.

'Hellroth will probably react unpredictably,' Nubik considered. 'He'll either lie low in order to think through his predicament, storm off to kill Lucht straight away, or contact the Führer's office to check that the information is real.'

'If he finds out it isn't, he'll be even more furious with Lucht.' Lichtblau sank into thought. It could just work. Their friends would help print the letter to make it look like the Führer's office stationery and writing style. What had they to lose, after all? *Only their lives*, thought Lichtblau, which were in constant danger every day anyway. He had chosen to stay in Vienna when he might have got away and found safety in England with his wife and children. So he could not complain about his life being in danger nor refuse to endanger it if obeying his conscience meant putting his life at risk. He was certain that to obey one's conscience was always the right thing to do. But was killing Hellroth and Lucht the right thing to do? And even if it was — for he was not so sure it was not — was it a useful thing to do? He could answer both these questions in the affirmative. But Nubik reminded him that the plan, at least at this stage, was not to kill the two Nazis but to maneuver them into killing each other. In any case, Nubik was right when he said that the time for reflection and scruples was past. Hellroth was away but would apparently be returning to Vienna in two or three days' time. They needed to have a letter from Lucht waiting for him when he returned to his office.

That evening Lichtblau and Nubik met up with Schwartz at his place along with the other members of their Resistance group. They had already told the group about their idea to draw Hellroth and Lucht into a trap in which they would accuse each other (of what, it did not matter) to the point of threatening to kill each other and going on to do so. Now they were able to tell them they had a definite plan for putting such an idea into action. They argued late into the night in the Memphis-smoke-filled room as to the wording of the letter. Nubik would take it to Hellroth's office. Schwartz forged headed note-paper, imitating the heading and paper from an actual letter sent out by the Führer's office, which Lichtblau had managed to steal a long time before when Hellroth had called him to his office to discuss his supposed financial needs. This theft had posed Lichtblau no difficulty since Hellroth rarely stayed sitting at his desk for more than a minute or two but would walk around the room as he talked, even turning his back on Lichtblau or peering out of the window as though looking for someone. On these occasions,

Lichtblau would stand in front of Hellroth's desk, resisting all attempts on Hellroth's part to cajole him into sitting down. Standing up as he was, Lichtblau took in with his gaze the whole of Hellroth's desk, examining the various papers on it. The framed photo of an elderly man struck him. He must have been Hellroth's father. The man had the same chubby red cheeks and contemptuous leer as his son. His son had probably acquired his alcohol habit from his father. He imagined Hellroth basking in his father's admiration of his only son. The better he served the Reich, the more evil he did, the more he would be worthy of his father's love.

Once when Hellroth had called Lichtblau into his office, an incident had occurred. An officer stormed into Hellroth's office, shouting at Hellroth, carrying a sheaf of papers under his arm. Hellroth stood up and saluted him. Lichtblau could not rise as he was already standing (and never sat down when in Hellroth's office). He ignored the officer. The latter thrust some of his papers under Hellroth's nose and complained about 'irregularities.' Hellroth tensed and blanched. His hand went instinctively not to his holster but to his hip-flask, which he kept in his trouser pocket.

The officer said, 'See what I mean?' and then shouted to him to follow him out of the room. Hellroth replied that he could not, as he was in the middle of negotiating a deal with the banker.

'To hell with bankers! We are our own bankers now! The Führer wills it! Now you come!'

With this, he spun on his heel and strode out of the room, giving every appearance of being sure Hellroth would follow him, which he did, though only after he had whipped his hip-flask out of his pocket, sucked down a swig of (Lichtblau presumed) schnapps and put it away again.

So, Lichtblau, alone in Hellroth's office, tried to think of a course of action. If he left now, when Hellroth came back and found him missing, Hellroth would likely hunt him down before he could make a proper getaway. On the other hand, if he stayed, he did not know how long he would have to wait for Hellroth to return. While he was wondering what to do, his eye was caught by a typed letter signed *Your Führer.*

The letter lay on top of a pile. Lichtblau realized he could read it if he wanted to. Hellroth had left his office door open on his way out. A secretary had her desk in the hallway outside Hellroth's office, but his desk was not visible from where she sat. Lichtblau blew onto the letter and saw that the one below it had exactly the same letterhead. He blew on both letters and, having displaced them, saw that the third letter from the top was also from the Führer's office. He took one of the letters from the middle of the pile and saw that it, too, had the same letterhead and bore the Führer's signature. He knew he could be searched on the way out (he was never sure he would actually get out), so he folded the sheet of paper until it was as tiny as it could be and turned around. He was now facing the door, holding the now-tiny square of paper in one hand. He put his hand behind his back and slipped the square of paper down between his buttocks, where he wedged it in tight, exulting in this daredevil feat: he could hardly think of a more deserving place for the letter. He walked to the door, opened it wide and asked the secretary if and when the officer would be coming back. He would be coming back shortly. Ten minutes later, Hellroth returned with another officer, not the one who had ordered him away. Hellroth looked worried and talked fast, even breathlessly, to the other officer. The latter listened to him but had his eyes to the ceiling as though he did not believe a word he was hearing. Neither Hellroth nor the officer paid much attention to Lichtblau. When Hellroth realized Lichtblau was still in his office, he waved him away:

'We'll finish our conversation another time. Don't go too far away or —'

He rubbed two fingers across his own throat. Hellroth seemed to Lichtblau to be trying to impress his fellow officer. Lichtblau prepared himself mentally to be searched on his way out by the guards at the front door. But just as he got there, a pretty secretary walked over to them, and they let Lichtblau go out without bothering him. Once at the flat of a Resistance friend of his, he went into the toilet and withdrew the letter from where he had placed it a couple of hours before. Now he was with Schwartz the printer, his wife and her two girlfriends, and his other

Resistance friends. He showed them the letter and explained how he had come by it. It could undoubtedly help their plan to cause conflict between Hellroth and Lucht. Schwartz had an idea: 'We must write the letter as if from the Führer to Hellroth. Lucht will be the very reason for the letter.'

They all agreed at once. Ada Schwartz took charge of drawing up the letter and making sure it reproduced in every respect the Führer's writing style. The letterhead and signature would remain; she would use erasing and printing techniques to replace the text of the letter. The final wording of the letter went as follows:

Hellroth:

The Reich has become increasingly dissatisfied with your performance and results over the past year. You have failed to meet the professional standards of officers privileged to serve the Führer and the Reich. I, therefore, have no alternative but to inform you that I am demoting you and stripping you of your powers. I have decided to transfer your responsibilities to Herr Lucht. Unlike you, he has proved to be a stalwart friend to the Wehrmacht. He already has considerable responsibility but has confirmed to my office that he would be willing and able to take on work that, as he has told me, 'other, less competent officers have shown themselves ill-equipped to handle.' He has furthermore asserted that he is 'thrilled' to be given this further proof of the Führer's trust in him. He deems this fair recognition, on the other hand, since he claims one or two officers who have, in his eyes, been 'slacking', should return to the ranks. He has been requested to name names. He replied that it would dishonor him to reveal the names of the particular officers he had in mind but that the service of the Reich was a higher honor than his own and that he could and would refuse nothing that the Führer asked of him. Yours was the only name Herr Lucht could bring himself to utter. Furthermore, Lucht's valet does not seem to have time to carry out all the tasks his function requires of him. Therefore, Lucht has asked us whether we could send him someone to second his valet. You, Hellroth, shall henceforth second Lucht's valet. Your duties will begin as of receipt of this letter, and you will report to Lucht bearing this letter on the day you receive it.

I am sending him a copy of this letter and keeping him abreast of events. If you serve Herr Lucht with all due conscientiousness and zeal, I may decide to restore you to a higher status after an appropriate period of time has elapsed.

Your Führer,

(signature)

This letter was the product of the combined imaginations of the whole Resistance group. Now it just remained to be printed and delivered. Schwartz spent the rest of the night working on the printed version, using the letter Lichtblau had taken from Hellroth's desk as a template. By the first light of dawn, he had managed to create a letter that looked in every respect as though it had been written by the Führer.

In the room where the permanent odor of Memphis mingled with the aroma of coffee and the smell of printer's ink, the group, who had all stayed in the room, asked Schwartz to read the letter back to them, which he did, caricaturing the Führer's voice and speech mannerisms, the shouted rising tone at the ends of sentences, the way certain vowels were drawn glottally back into the throat. Despite the horror surrounding them and the terror in their minds, the group, men and women alike, fell about laughing. They were not only laughing at this spoof on the Führer; they were imagining how Hellroth would react when he read the letter. But although none of the others noticed, one of them was not laughing: Markus Jäger. And once Schwartz had finished reading the letter aloud, Jäger stood up and left, saying he had to get home.

Nubik considered that they did not need to send the letter through the post, which hadn't been working well anyway since the start of the war. The Führer had his own courier service within the SS. Everyone knew what such delivery staff looked like. They always rode around Vienna on motorbikes with sidecars. Two of them rode, one on the bike, one in the sidecar, both in SS uniforms. The courier himself rode in the sidecar. The rider waited while the courier delivered his letters or parcels to the addressees. What they needed to do was to get hold of a couple of uniforms and a motorbike with a sidecar, and deliver the letter themselves to

Hellroth's desk. They would put the Führer's letterhead on the envelope. It would, they hoped, be their 'Open Sesame,' and they would flash it about if any guard or official wanted to know what they were doing. Nubik had observed the regular couriers: 'I know I can get away with it. I enjoy this kind of dare. And I know where to borrow a motorbike with a sidecar. And I've got the uniform. I just need someone to drive me.'

One of the men said, 'I can ride a motorbike. You can get me a Gestapo uniform, can you?' Nubik nodded.

Nubik knew the address and floor, and they stopped the bike outside the building where Hellroth had his office. They knew Hellroth was there because they had seen him go in. Fearing that a secretary or official who saw the Führer's letterhead on the envelope might try and pry it open to see what the missive said, Nubik wanted to make sure he handed it to Hellroth in person.

Nubik acted as though he did this kind of delivery routinely, both his manner and his uniform helping him nod his way through security and head straight up to the first floor with the envelope in his hand. When he saw the secretary sitting to the side behind her desk outside Hellroth's office, he smiled and uttered a word of greeting, showing her the letterhead on the envelope as he passed her and pointing its corner toward Hellroth's office.

The secretary, a naturally shy girl, looked up and smiled back at him but made a dubious kind of face as if to say, he's not in a great mood at the moment, he's got problems, watch out. Nubik winked in reply, and the girl, repressing a second smile, looked back down at the papers on the desk in front of her. He knocked on Hellroth's office door, walked in without waiting to be called to do so — he was the Führer's emissary, after all — and strode up to Hellroth, who was sitting at his desk. He was apparently poring over some documents. He paid no attention to Nubik; Hellroth seemed used to couriers entering his office with various messages to deliver. Nubik saluted and put the envelope uppermost on Hellroth's desk. When Hellroth saw it was from the Führer's office, he frowned and reached for the letter. That was all Nubik saw him do. Hellroth had not even noticed the courier was someone he knew or might have known.

On his way out, Nubik winked at the secretary, and she winked back and smiled at him. She was young but judging from the circles around her eyes and lined forehead, it occurred to Nubik she had suffered or was suffering. Her hands were wrinkled and looked older than her. He wrote something on a slip of paper, folded it and handed it to her. Nubik gestured with his chin toward Hellroth's office door. They nodded in unison, Nubik went back outside to his motorbike rider, and off they went.

The next day at five in the afternoon, she was waiting for him at the place he had written on the slip of paper. Her name was Gudrun. He told her he loved her name. She told him how Hellroth had acted since Nubik had delivered the letter. First, he had shouted down the telephone at Lucht. Then, after ten minutes or so of this, he had slammed the phone down and paced around his office like a caged jaguar. Finally, he rang Lucht back, but by then, Lucht had left his office. That drove Hellroth even more furious. He tried to get through to the Führer's office but was told no one was available to speak to him.

On the morning of that day, Michael Lucht had come to Hellroth's office, accompanied by a woman and his valet. They had greeted the secretary but not asked her to announce them or checked whether Hellroth was free to receive them. The woman wore a Nazi uniform, but Gudrun had no idea who she was or what she was doing with Lucht. She thought the woman might be Lucht's mistress and Lucht wanted to show her off to Hellroth. Lucht and his party pushed the door wide open as they went into Hellroth's office so that Gudrun could see everything going on.

Lucht preceded the other two, head held high. He walked all the way up to Hellroth's desk. Hellroth did not rise. In fact, he barely looked up. The woman and the valet stood flanking Lucht. Lucht gave the Nazi salute, with a sort of mock solemnity in his eyes. Hellroth saluted fleetingly, just brushing his hand against his temple, but still did not get up. Lucht smiled at Hellroth.

'Stand up, will you!' Lucht thundered. Hellroth did not move a muscle. Lucht signaled to the woman and the valet, who went around Hellroth's desk, one on each side of him. Together, as one, they hoisted him out of his chair. He tried to push them away, but they clung to him.

'Now salute, or I will have you shot instantly!' murmured Lucht with lethal calm. Lucht spotted the Führer's letter to Hellroth on his desk and picked it up.

'Put that letter down, you wretch!' Hellroth said through gritted teeth.

'Don't worry,' said Lucht, 'there's nothing private in it and, anyway, I've received a copy. Say goodbye to your office and secretary. Oh, and say goodbye to your officer's life, too, Hellroth. You will assist my valet and, on days when I don't need either of you, serve him as though he were your master. You will be working for the lady, too. She works with me. The Führer has told me in a separate letter that I may put you to work as I see fit. You have apparently disappointed him. He was thinking about firing you, but I —'

Hellroth fisted a hand to strike Lucht, but the valet held him back.

'Touchy, aren't we?' said Lucht. 'It is rather a come-down for you, isn't it? As I was saying, I persuaded the Führer not to fire you. It was his idea to appoint you to my service. And I intend to take full advantage of it.'

Hellroth said, 'I need to go home to sort out a few things first.'

Lucht replied, 'You'll go home when I tell you to, and not before. Now you're coming with us.'

While they were talking, the lady officer — or so she appeared — was settling in to Hellroth's chair behind his desk. Hellroth gave her a baleful look. Lucht called Gudrun into Hellroth's office or, rather, what was now his ex-office. He told her Hellroth was leaving his office, having been stripped of his rank and appointed to serve under his, Lucht's, direct orders. Her job was not threatened, and she would be performing the same tasks for the new officer as before. Lucht introduced Gudrun to her. The two women saluted each other. Lucht, Hellroth and Lucht's valet walked out of the room in single file. As they went downstairs, the valet, unbeknownst to Hellroth, had unsheathed his pistol and was pointing it at Hellroth's back. They walked out into the street, still in single file.

'By the way, Hellroth, don't try and attack me or give us the slip,' said Lucht without turning round. 'My valet has his pistol trained on you. No false moves.'

At one point, they passed a man wearing a suit, holding a briefcase. He turned his head to the side as the three went past him, looking as though he were distracted by something. Nubik waited till they were out of sight and then went to find Lichtblau. He told him that he had seen Lucht and his valet walking Hellroth through the streets as though he had been their prisoner. He wondered whether Hellroth would write to the Führer. He hoped he would.

Gudrun went back to her desk. But soon the woman officer went to see her:

'You must be asking yourself who I am. Lucht wanted me along. He said it would be easier to dislodge Hellroth if there was someone to replace him straight away. I don't expect to be here long. They will most likely want a man to replace Hellroth definitively. Either that or they'll close his office down, and you will be relocated. Sometimes there seems to be no method to what they decide. No method and no sense.'

Gudrun was astonished to meet someone, apparently a Nazi, who admitted to being skeptical of the whole Nazi plan. She wondered why she was telling her these things. She was secretly pleased that Hellroth had gone and found herself delighting in his humiliation. She had always found him hypocritical and deceitful, the perfect party apparatchik. He had rarely acknowledged even her existence; he had slapped her as the mood took him, which was more and more often recently.

'You realize that after this, Hellroth will try and kill your friend Lucht, and anyone associated with him, at the first opportunity.'

'What makes you think he's my friend?' asked the woman. Gudrun did not reply. 'Well, you're right. Lucht is…' Her voice tailed off, and she looked down.

'No one could stand to work with Hellroth,' said Gudrun. 'Good riddance.'

'Lucht may kill him first. Anything may happen. Lucht has behaved naïvely. He won't be able to leave Hellroth unwatched.'

'Lucht's valet will watch Hellroth for him. Unless he manages to kill the valet first.'

'I don't think Lucht is as naïve as you say,' said Gudrun. 'He's merely carrying out the Führer's wishes, which in this case suit him perfectly.'

'Hellroth is unlikely to see it that way,' said the woman officer.

Gudrun did not tell her what Nubik had told her a few days before: there was no letter from the Führer. However, she did say to the woman officer: 'I think they will both try and contact the Führer — Hellroth to express his indignation at the Reich's treatment of him, and Lucht —' Here the officer interrupted Gudrun: 'Lucht to tell the Führer that he's done exactly as the latter required him to do and that he remains at the Führer's disposal should he wish him to take up higher responsibilities or serve under his direct orders.'

Gudrun agreed. The woman continued: 'You seem to be well-up on all this for a secretary.'

'I keep my eyes and ears open. And Hellroth is a loudmouth. Besides, he never shut the door. He used to shout at everyone. At me. Down the phone. A real slob, too. And a woman-hater. They all are.'

'You realize you're talking to an officer about your boss,' said the woman, retreating into her role.

'My ex-boss, and no longer an officer, not even a common foot-soldier now, just a valet. In any case, I'm not officially an employee of the Reich. I just happened to be around a few months ago when a secretary was needed.' Gudrun lit a cigarette. 'Time for me to knock off,' she said. 'Shall I come back tomorrow, or will you do without me?'

'The job is yours as long as there's someone here.'

'I really couldn't care less about this silly *job*,' said Gudrun, puffing her cigarette smoke into the woman's face and then walking off.

'One more thing,' the officer said.

'Yes,' said Gudrun, turning round with a fake smile and a fake curtsey, as if to say, I'm not here to like you or, even less, respect you.

'Watch out, young woman, or you'll be going the same way as your ex-boss, and not because I confided in you a second ago —'

Gudrun feigned to ignore the threat. She left the building and walked a few streets away to where she had arranged to meet Nubik. He told her he had informants inside Lucht's offices who had observed the goings-on with the new man, Hellroth.

'He'll be working round the clock. He's forbidden to talk to other members of staff, including Lucht's first valet, whose orders he'll be under whenever Lucht decides. Some of the people in Lucht's department who had known Hellroth when he was an officer turned their backs on him as he passed by, clearly having found out about his demotion. Typical Nazi hypocrisy: they had previously pretended to be his friends. In fact, Lucht organized an impromptu meeting of all the staff in his building and told them, with Hellroth, in overalls and without his uniform, standing by his side, that Hellroth had now joined them as his new valet and would be working too hard to be able to converse with them. If ever Hellroth gets out of there alive, and if Lucht and his cronies haven't completely managed to crush him, he'll have lost all interest in fighting the Nazis' enemies. He'll just be looking for ways to get his revenge on Lucht. For this reason, Lucht will be able to argue that Hellroth has become useless to the Reich, as good as a traitor, in fact, and will suggest executing Hellroth for treachery.'

'I've got an idea for you and your friends,' Gudrun said to Nubik. 'I suggest you phone Lucht's office and say you're calling on behalf of the Führer, to tell Lucht that as from next month he is to work for Hellroth and obey his every order. You could say your call would be officially confirmed by a letter that would be arriving by courier.'

'If they weren't convinced someone was up to something before then, they would be if they received that kind of call. I'm not sure they'd be taken in even if we followed it up with a letter from the Führer. What we want to do is maneuver them into a conflict where they're accusing and attacking each other, thus deflecting their energy away from fighting the enemy and directing their hostility towards each other. At the moment, Hellroth's hostility towards Lucht has every reason to be at its most deadly.'

'But wouldn't appointing Lucht as Hellroth's valet have the same effect on Lucht?'

Gudrun decided to take the situation into her own hands. She felt her insolence toward the woman officer had in retrospect been near-suicidal and decided to adopt a more neutral attitude towards her. She had never been much of a strategist, but now she thought this woman officer could be useful to her. Over the days that followed, she went on working at her desk — pretending to work, that is — hardly doing anything except changing the addressee's name on written communications to Hellroth from the latter's name to Zimmermann, the woman officer's name.

One morning she spotted an envelope addressed to Hellroth with the Führer's name and office as sender marked on it. Gudrun opened it. It read: *I will shortly be sending you two prisoners suspected of betraying the Reich. You will interrogate them and find them guilty. Then do with them as you please. Once you have had them executed, make sure you send me their death certificates.*

Gudrun slipped the letter into her handbag and took it to Nubik. 'I thought this might be useful to our efforts.'

'Our efforts?'

'Yes, ours. I'm with you now. I'm on your side. I've always been on your side.'

'Do you realize you might get killed for this if they find out? Tortured and killed.'

'I want us to use this letter to cause more conflict between Hellroth and Lucht. And I want Lucht to be Hellroth's valet.'

Nubik replied: 'Are you sure you don't just want to have fun with a new friend?'

Twenty-Two

Thedel, Heinrich and Heike, Thedel's friend, were somewhere in the north of Germany: where exactly they were not sure. They had got talking in an inn with an understanding *Unteroffizier*, or sergeant, in the German army, who was fed up with the war and did not ask them any questions or ask to see their papers. He was on his way north and glad to give them a ride. He realized they were not all German but made light of this. He claimed not to care whether they were Aryans or Jews, Jews passing themselves off as Aryans or anyone else. He said that as a member of the army, it was his duty to make war if called upon to do so, but that he wanted no part in the persecution of Jews. He was driving north to deliver his van to an army company he had been told needed it. Someone from that company would drive him back to his regiment. But he thought he might desert. He spoke so candidly to them that they were disconcerted.

'Anybody who can still think, anybody who wants to think and not just obey orders, can see that what's going on is wrong.'

It was the first time Thedel had heard a German army officer speak with any sense of morality. He said, 'We want to get out of this hell, that's all. We're refugees. If we manage to get to England, we'll help other people get out of Germany and Austria.'

'We're all refugees now.'

'Why don't you join us?' said Heike. 'You can do what we're doing and start a new life in England. Even change sides. It sounds as though you'd like to.'

'I have a wife and children here in Germany, as well as my parents. If I desert or leave the country without them, they will likely be punished for it. My wife and children would come with me, but my parents would not. Apart from their age, they are not against the Führer and would rather stay in the country and live under a regime they are too stubborn, afraid or stupid to call into question. They also think Germany will win the war.'

'We already know Germany is losing the war,' said Thedel.

'The Reich will carry on till the end, striving to transform the whole of Europe into one big death camp. Every day I wake up expecting the Allies to arrive and save us. To arrive and defeat us. Our defeat will be the salvation of those of us who believe in a decent future. But I don't think I'll get far if I try to flee. You three will be better off without me. I'll drop you off in a city, where you'll be able to melt into the crowd. I cannot go with you, not only for the reasons I've told you but for others as well. I've killed since the war started. I must stand or fall where I am.'

'Thousands of people have killed since the start of the war,' Thedel said. 'You had no choice.'

'I could have shot my commanding officer. Or myself,' said the sergeant with a grin. 'But what good would that have done? I must make it through the war for my family. They're depending on me to do so.' The sergeant suddenly went quiet. Heike put her hand on his shoulder. 'On the contrary, your family will admire you for changing sides.'

'Don't touch me!' he shouted. 'I don't want to be touched. I don't deserve it. I'm untouchable. Unworthy. If it weren't for the drugs I take, I would have cracked up long ago. I'll let you out here.' He stopped his van. Even though they were not in a city, Thedel, Heinrich and Heike felt they had no choice but to get out of the van. Thedel and Heike exchanged glances as though to tell each other they both agreed it would be better for the three of them to move on alone without this sergeant, whose emotional ramblings and unpredictable behavior made him a liability to them. He had clearly managed to remain untainted by Nazism. But he did not seem to be quite of sound mind. As they were about to say goodbye, he grabbed a scrap of paper and a pen from the glove compartment and scribbled a number on it, then handed it to Thedel. He then wound his window up, reversed with a screech of brakes, and was gone. They had not discovered his name nor even asked what it was. Nor had he asked what theirs were. The number on the piece of paper seemed to be a phone number. His own? Someone's who would be helpful to them? Was he telling them to phone him if and when they reached England? Or would it be better to throw the scrap of paper away and forget all about the soldier?

The three walked in silence along the roadside. Cornfields spread out on one side of the road, scrubland and the outskirts of a wood on the other. The late afternoon sun dipped below the horizon. They felt hungry, Heinrich especially. They had seen road signs to Cologne but could not say how far they were. A tear ran down Heike's cheek. Thedel wiped her tear away and told her they would soon be in England. Heike wondered aloud what they would do if ever they did get to England. She should not have stayed with Thedel. Their money was running low. They had the boy to think of. She gestured in the direction of Heinrich. They did not even know where they were going. The sergeant had left them in the middle of nowhere. They were just tramping around in no particular direction. If the Nazis came upon them, they would shoot them all. She burst into tears. Thedel pressed her hand in both of his. They just had to keep going. Any backtracking now could be fatal.

So they kept on walking along the road. They walked through a hamlet. They could have stopped there but decided to keep walking. A little while later, they came to a village at around nine in the evening. The main street was deserted, as was the only road leading off it, even though a tavern and a phone box stood at the far end of the village just where the street became the main road again. There was a light on in the tavern, but no cars were parked outside it. They decided to go in. There was one man behind the counter whom they took to be the landlord, and another sitting on a bar-stool with a glass of Märzen on the counter in front of him. Though in plain clothes, his determined expression, clean-shaven face and short-cropped hair hinted at his being an off-duty army officer or member of the Gestapo. The three said good evening to the two men, who replied in kind. Despite this potentially threatening presence, Thedel decided to risk being brief and, above all, frank. 'Landlord, we're traveling across Europe, trying to get out of the war by going to a safer country. We're non-combatants. We don't have much money and what little we do have is mainly for when we get close to England. Can you give us a slice of bread and cheese each and a drop of something to drink?'

The landlord eyed them. 'Running away, are you? I don't want any trouble from people saying I've been aiding and abetting renegades or traitors to the Reich. Your destination is an enemy of the Reich.'

'We want to live, sir,' Thedel replied. 'We're just looking to be out of and away from the war if possible.'

'Why didn't you go to Switzerland?' the customer broke in.

'My mother's already in England,' said Thedel, 'she's waiting for my friends and me to join her there, sir. We have been invited by an Oxford professor.'

'Why aren't the three of you fighting for the Reich?' asked the customer.

Before they could answer and wanting to avoid trouble, the landlord asked them how much they could pay him. Thedel told him how much they had altogether and what they could spare. The landlord disappeared through a door behind his bar. The atmosphere between the customer and the three newcomers had grown uneasy. Thedel noticed the man had no control of his left eyeball: it ran around the white of his eye and undoubtedly meant his vision was defective. It gave him a crazy look. The man took a swig of his Märzen and then said, 'Why don't you answer?'

'You're an officer, aren't you?' said Thedel. 'You'd like to turn us in.'

With his one good eye, the man looked up from his beer. He was not wearing a gun, or at least he did not seem to have a pistol on, but his hand slipped down below his hip to where a gun would have been. 'If I took you in now and had you tortured, the Reich would make me a general overnight.' Thedel thought the Reich must be frail to be built on such self-mythologizing.

The landlord returned with three plates of cold sausage, bread and gherkins. He set them down on the bar and got out three gin-glasses which he filled brimful with schnapps. The customer raised a hand and glared at the glasses and plates as though he were about to sweep them off the bar. The landlord seized the man's arm. 'Business has been bad for years. There's trouble enough as it is. Why make more? You have no need to prove yourself. What's it to you whether these three die tonight or in seven or eight decades? I'm poor enough, and they don't look much richer than I am.'

'You're either for the Führer, or you're an enemy of the state. A traitor.'

'Do you think I'd be trying to run a small country inn, struggling to make ends meet, if I had any truck with politics?'

'Politics died in this country on January 30th, 1933, if not before,' said Heike, whose boldness amazed all those present. Again, the customer made as though to strike her, and again the landlord held him back.

'It so happens I'm off duty tonight,' said the man, chucking some loose change onto the bar, 'and you're right, I am an officer. And proud to be. I say again: you should be serving the Reich, as I am.' He looked at Thedel.

'I'm just an art student,' replied Thedel, 'I have no taste for warfare. Physical warfare, at any rate.'

The man appeared to take no notice of this remark, however seditious it was, pulled his coat about him, and started to walk towards the door. Just before he got to the door, he turned round:

'Don't let me see you anywhere in the area from tomorrow onwards. You also need to be aware I may come looking for you. That would be excellent sport. So, if I were you, I'd make myself scarce. I won't be so lenient if I run into you again. And may that one,' he pointed with his chin at Heike and leered at her, 'live to regret the day she was born.'

With that, he went out, slamming the inn door behind him. The landlord and his three customers did not speak. A moment later, the officer came back in and strode up to the bar:

'It's a cold night out. One more drink — a little schnapps, like your friends here — to warm up my soul, and then I'll be off.'

The landlord produced a gin-glass and filled it to the brim with Obstler. The officer downed it in one gulp — 'sweet fire' he called it, laughing — again tossed a few coins onto the bar, and walked back to the door. And again, he turned around as he was about to leave. But this time, his words were for the landlord:

'And as for you, don't think I can't see you're not quite as innocent as you seem. You don't seem as apolitical to me as you pretend. You're in cahoots with some of your customers. Don't think I haven't seen you winking and whispering. Don't start colluding with these people: they're traitors to the cause of the Reich. Or you'll be dying of gas just like the rest of them.' He again slammed the door on his way out. But this time, he did not come back, though the landlord and the three young customers waited for several minutes in silence to see whether he would.

'He's been in a few times,' said the landlord, 'I saw him a few days ago snooping around in the village. I don't know what he's doing here. He's not from the area.'

'If he's looking for people to torment,' Thedel said, 'he could have taken us in this evening. But he did not.'

'True. First of all, he may have other priorities and, second, it's still quite early. He may decide to come back yet again, alone or otherwise. Or he could be waiting somewhere out in the dark for you to go outside. Then he can ambush you as he said, just for the thrill of it.'

'Cheap thrill,' said Heike. She and Thedel could see that with all this threatening talk, Heinrich's eyes were filling with tears. As for Thedel, he was not an emotional young man, but he felt that just when they were starting to gain their freedom, it had been somewhat unlucky to come upon this off-duty army officer who had threatened them verbally but had held off from harming them, for reasons he alone knew.

The landlord said, 'I see at least three possibilities. You can walk out that door and be on your way. You could also leave by the back door and head out into the open countryside, then make your way out of Germany cross-country by night. But you may not be sure where you're really going. Or you can stay here tonight and review your options in the morning. Perhaps you have had enough excitement for one evening.'

'We've already had enough excitement if that's what you want to call it' — he saw the landlord smile — 'to last us for the rest of our lives. So, we accept your offer,' said Thedel, 'though you understand we can't pay you now. But if we get to England, I'll gladly repay you a hundredfold for your kindness.'

The landlord put the three of them in the same room and said good night. But his wish was not to be fulfilled. In the early hours, the trio was awakened by the revving of a car engine and a dazzle of headlights shining on their window. Footsteps crunched on gravel, and then they heard a banging on the front door of the inn. A voice they recognized shouted, 'Open up in the name of the Führer, or I'll blow the lock off this door!' The landlord had also heard the officer. He went to open the door.

'Where are they?'

'Upstairs, sir.'

'Out of my way!' The officer brushed past him and pounded up the wooden staircase.

To save the officer having to go from room to room — there were seven rooms altogether on the first floor — and thus getting even more worked up, Thedel opened the bedroom door and stood in the doorway. The officer, holding a gun, pointed it at Thedel.

'Go back inside!'

Thedel obeyed and joined Heike and Heinrich, who were standing by the one bed in the room, doing their best to hide their fear. Thedel could see at once that the officer had continued drinking since he had left the inn earlier in the evening.

'Put your hands behind your heads, all three of you! What am I going to do with you? Take you to Berlin and show the Reich what a good boy I've been? How well I've served Germany's forthcoming victory in the war by rounding up spies and traitors?'

'We are neither spies nor traitors,' said Thedel. 'We just want to live our lives in safety.'

The officer slapped him across the face with his leather glove. Thedel, Heike and Heinrich were facing the bedroom door; the officer was facing them with his back to the door.

Suddenly Heinrich said, 'Perhaps you would care for a glass of Obstler? I'll go and get it for you.'

'You will not.' He pointed his gun at him. 'You won't do a thing unless I've ordered you to do it.'

'The landlord can bring it up then,' Heinrich insisted.

'Well…well, you're right. He can,' the officer said, swaying on his feet. 'Landlord!'

Silence.

'Landlord!' he bellowed again, louder still. Silence once more, and then they heard the landlord's footsteps on the staircase. He stood just outside the bedroom, taking in the scene.

'You called, sir?'

'A bottle of Obstler.'

'I don't sell it by the bottle, sir. And, with all due respect, we're closed at this time of night.'

'A bottle of Obstler, I tell you, you peasant.'

'And four glasses?'

'No glasses. Just the schnapps. And be quick about it.'

'Yes, sir.'

The landlord glanced at the trio and looked at Thedel as though he had some-thing urgent to tell him. Thedel somehow picked up the tacit message that he had some kind of plan in mind. He did not know why, but he suddenly felt a strange sense of relief. They listened to the landlord's footsteps scurrying back down the staircase. Then they heard what sounded like rummaging and glass clinking against glass. At this sound, the officer mechanically licked his lips, keeping his gun trained on the trio all the while. But the landlord went quiet.

'Hurry up with it, man!' the officer shouted.

'Coming,' the landlord called back.

Again, there seemed to be a long wait.

'If you don't come up by the time I've counted to ten, I'll shoot one of your fresh and innocent young guests here. One or two of them.' He grinned with a show of dark yellow teeth. 'Or maybe all three.'

'I'm just opening the bottle for you. It's my best schnapps: not Obstler but rather Williamsbirne.'

Again, the officer involuntarily licked his lips.

'My oldest. I'd been saving it for a special occasion. But I'll be happy to let you have it. Your visit is quite an occasion.'

Thedel smirked to himself at the landlord's irony.

'Cut the chat,' said the officer, 'and just bring up the bottle.'

'I've told you how old it is. I'm having a bit of trouble opening it. I don't want to spill any of your Williamsbirne.'

'I'll open it up here if I have to smash the top off,' said the officer, getting more and more jittery for a drink.

'Come on,' shouted Heinrich to the landlord, 'the customer wants serving!'

'You'd make a good soldier in the Reich,' the officer said. Heinrich smiled and saluted.

'I'd like that.'

Thedel had noticed Heinrich's flair for acting when he had worn the policeman's uniform. He seemed to enjoy playing the game of being the enemy or the enemy's sympathizer.

'I might even be able to get you some kind of youth officer's job in the *Bund Deutscher Arbeiterjugend*. Something juicy, anyway.' The officer rolled his eyes lasciviously.

'I'd like that very much.' Heinrich led the officer on. 'And I'd like a cap like yours and a uniform like yours. And boots like yours. And a gun like yours. And I'd like you to be my commanding officer.'

'You are a most appealing young man,' said the officer.

Heinrich yelled, 'Will you get a move on down there! Otherwise, I'm going to come down, punch you till you drop, and bring the officer his drink myself. He's waited long enough.' The officer started at Heinrich's sudden vehemence but looked gratified at this future version of himself.

Generally taciturn and calm, Heinrich was taking Thedel and Heike quite by surprise. The landlord did not reply.

'I'll go down and see what he's up to,' Heinrich said. 'He shouldn't be keeping you waiting like this. It's outrageous.' He started walking towards the door.

'No one is to leave this room!' The officer, who was already barring the way with his body, pointed his gun at Heinrich.

'I am honored to be your most obedient servant, sir,' Heinrich said. 'But that Williamsbirne of yours must be getting warm downstairs, the time the landlord's taking over it. I wonder what's keeping him. He is behaving most disrespectfully towards his honored guest.'

'All right,' the officer said, 'you have my permission to go downstairs and beat him unconscious. Then bring me up my schnapps. Once I've had my schnapps,

I'll take these two prisoners' — he signaled to Thedel and Heike — 'and set about getting you a commission.'

'I hope I'll be working alongside you,' Heinrich replied, 'my one desire is to serve you.'

'Go on down, now that I've given you permission. Enough of this chatter.'

Heinrich's footsteps reverberated on the hollow wooden staircase as he walked down. Thedel marveled at how Heinrich had managed to win the officer's trust. These Nazi officers were decidedly simple-minded!

Heinrich's and the landlord's voices could be heard conferring downstairs. They sounded quite excited. Heinrich bawled several times in anger at the landlord for taking so long about bringing the officer's schnapps up to him. Heinrich was saying things like, 'Officer of the Reich…disgraceful… such a fine gentleman…must not be kept waiting like this…hurry up…getting impatient… shooting Heike, Thedel and you.'

'Why not you?' they heard the landlord asking Heinrich.

'Never you mind!' Heinrich shouted back at him. 'Just serve the officer's drink!'

'All right! All right!' the landlord said.

Then they heard the sound of a bottle being uncorked and the footsteps of the two of them on the stairs. The landlord walked into the room in front of Heinrich who, Thedel saw, was holding a revolver. The officer still had his back to the door and his gun pointed at Thedel and Heike.

'Get a move on, you dog, give him his drink!' Heinrich shouted as the landlord walked towards the officer, who did not turn round but nodded approvingly at Heinrich's use of language. Just as the landlord got to the officer, Heinrich pushed him so hard that he bumped his tray with the bottle on it against the officer's back and then crashed into the landlord, so that landlord and officer both went tumbling down, along with the bottle. As he fell, the officer shot himself in the thigh and then instinctively let go of his gun. Thedel at once grabbed it off the floor and pointed it at him. The officer was screwing up his eyes and contorting his face in pain. Heinrich also pointed the gun he was holding at the officer.

'Now, what do we do with him?' Heike said.

'Puppy-dogs!' the officer grinned.

'Say whatever you like,' Thedel said. 'Game over as far as you're concerned.'

The landlord said, 'We'll tie his arms behind his back and gag him to stop him from screaming. I'll watch him for a few hours while you all go and get some sleep. Then you can replace me. In the morning, we'll decide on our next move.'

'No,' Heike said, 'he will only try and pursue us.' She took the gun from Heinrich, pressed it to the man's heart, and fired. She felt in his trouser pockets for his car keys, and the three of them set out for England.

Twenty-Three

Kristina Lichtblau was sitting in the living room of a flat in Rue Mouffetard, while sitting opposite her, gesticulating as she spoke, was a young girl who looked twenty-one or twenty-two: this was Françoise Berg. She was reading English at the Sorbonne and was devoted to her studies; she was also learning the violin. She spent as much time as she could spare ministering to civilians whose lives the war imperiled, Jews and foreigners especially, helping them either to live underground or, more often than not, to get out of France. Although the Nazi occupiers had so far imprisoned just her father and were shortly to deport him, the rest of her family felt it could only be a matter of time before the Nazis dealt with them in the same way.

'I think I may be able to help you get to England. But you may have to risk your lives in the process. My friends tell me I read too many books and believe what I read too readily. But be prepared to make up stories about yourselves and how you came to be in Paris. You'll need to come up with something convincing.'

'Why don't you try and get away yourself?'

A fierce look came over the girl so that Kristina at once became aware of another side to her, charming and free as she was. 'You can see why. My mission consists of helping others here, including helping them escape.'

'A dangerous mission.'

'It's not only a mission; it's what I consider to be a vocation. I feel I have no choice in the matter. Nor would I want it any other way. It is my burden and my joy. If someone should betray me, or the occupiers arrest me, as most likely they will, I know I will have served a useful purpose, or tried to. That's all I ask. And someone else will take my place. So it will go on, until this war is over.'

Johannes, who so far had been listening to the conversation between his mother and the girl, said, 'You're a student of English and a lover of Shakespeare and Keats. We're trying to get to Oxford, where we have friends who could help you to enroll at the university.'

'That life is not for me at this time,' replied the girl, 'and I don't need to go to Oxford for that. I can be with Shakespeare and Keats any time I read a page they've written.'

'So, in practical terms, what do you suggest we do?' asked Johannes.

'I would advise you to keep as low a profile as possible. If you go out, do what you need to do without walking around aimlessly. Sooner or later, they'll stop you and take you for questioning. I'll need to talk to people who may have ideas about the best way for you to travel to Oxford. I'll try to see them over the next day or two. We can meet again in three days' time. I think we can meet in the Luxembourg. The Nazi soldiers knew *étudiantes* sometimes went there, and they used to try their luck with us. But they never seem to think we might be working against them or even that we were the least bit intelligent. But we mainly avoid the place now, and they rarely seem to go there now either. Never mind them. It is as good, or as bad, a place as any. Only, when we meet, you must speak as little as possible. They mustn't be able to hear you're not French, and nor must they know you're German-speaking. It would only cause trouble for us all. See you by the pond in the middle of the park at three in the afternoon next Friday.'

It was Tuesday.

So Kristina and Johannes lay low for the next three days. They told Monsieur Soubrenie everything. Like him, they considered Françoise Berg a remarkable young woman, fearlessly helping Jews and refugees escape from occupied France at daily risk to her own life. They were due to meet her again next Friday, by which time she hoped to have made arrangements for them to travel out of Paris and on to England. Ilse and Werner had been waiting anxiously to find out the outcome of Kristina and Johannes's meeting with the young girl.

'Will the four of us be able to travel together?' asked Johannes.

'Françoise will tell us on Friday what, if anything, she's been able to plan for us and how she thinks we may most safely travel.'

On Friday, Kristina and Johannes again left Ilse and Werner at Monsieur Soubrenie's flat and went to the Luxembourg Garden as arranged. Kristina had asked Soubrenie whether they should get there early. 'Absolutely not; otherwise, the police or the Nazis may suspect you of loitering. They'll arrest you and show you no mercy. The best thing to do is arrive on the stroke of three. Françoise is punctual to a fault and will not keep you waiting.'

Kristina and Johannes stood by the pond, watching the children sail their yachts on it. The children pushed their yachts with wooden poles. That, and the flow from the fountain in the middle of the pond, propelled them. Sometimes the yachts sped across the water, leaning over and tracing arabesques and curves; sometimes, they crashed into each other, or several of them would block each other and form a pile-up. When Kristina looked up from the yachts, it was five past three. Johannes wondered why Soubrenie had reported Françoise as being strictly punctual.

'I'm sure she is, but this is war, after all,' retorted his mother.

At half-past three, just as Kristina and Johannes were about to walk away from the pond and go back to Soubrenie's flat, a young girl about the same age as Françoise suddenly joined them. She had bad news for Kristina and Johannes: Françoise had been taken to Avenue Foch. She had been allowed to make one phone call. She had phoned home and spoken to her mother, whom she had told to phone the girl and tell her to go and meet them, to explain the situation. She was a fellow student of Françoise's and a friend of hers. 84, Avenue Foch. Kristina had heard of the address — the Gestapo headquarters in Paris. The girl thought they might have taken Françoise in at random. They sometimes did such things to scare the population. She might be released quite soon — today, even. The girl had no other information about Françoise's current state to offer: a police van had picked her up at about two in the afternoon at her home. Johannes had grown anxious listening to all this. What were they to do now? Only Françoise could answer that question, the girl thought. The girl suggested they wait a day or two to see whether Françoise came back. The Nazis would likely interrogate her. The girl advised them to go back to where they were staying and go out as little as possible. They could meet again in the same place in three days' time. Either Françoise would come herself if she were free by then, or her friend would come again.

Johannes said, 'As long as you haven't been arrested yourself.'

'Nothing is certain,' replied the girl, and told them if they found another opportunity to get out of France before their next meeting, of course, they must take advantage of it. The whole city was crawling with collaborators and spies. It was not safe for anyone. Jean-Luc, the little man with the pencil mustache, would sell his soul or anyone else's for the paltriest sum he could get.

Kristina wondered how well the girl knew him: she admitted he looked a bit shifty, but he said quite openly that he was motivated by money and seemed quite sincere towards her and Johannes, even helpful.

'Don't have anything to do with him,' replied the girl. 'Soubrenie has set up some kind of financial arrangement with him. I've always known Soubrenie himself to be trustworthy, but the little man is a real wheeler and dealer, out for anything he can get. He would sell even Soubrenie to the Nazis if he could, although he seems to need him for the moment and may be afraid that Soubrenie will sell him to the Nazis. Don't be fooled by his manner. He's nasty. A girlfriend of mine started to take an interest in him just before the war broke out. But as soon as the Occupation began, he grew deceitful. He stopped looking my friend in the eye.

'Then once, she was walking past Notre Dame when two men talking in the square in front of the cathedral caught her eye. She's rather short-sighted, but she could see that one of them was in Nazi uniform and the other in civvies. Once she was within a few feet away from them, she realized the one in civvies was Jean-Luc. She was both pleased to see him and worried at finding him conversing with the enemy. She hailed him by his name. He turned and looked at her, as did the Nazi.'

'I can't see you now. I can't talk now. Leave me alone, can't you see I'm busy?'

'He turned back to the Nazi, and they went on with their conversation.'

'A couple of days later, it was he who sought her out at her own place. He invited her out for lunch. She felt this to be a definite step forward in their relationship. At lunch, she tried to ask him about the Nazi she had seen him talking to, but he clammed up and refused to discuss it. My girlfriend stood up at this point, wanting to leave the restaurant. But Jean-Luc grabbed her by the arm and held it firmly, too firmly. He apologized for not answering, but he simply could not. He begged her to stay, though his grip told her she had no real choice. She still somehow felt attracted to him despite everything. She sat down again. A little while later, as they were talking at the table, she saw a Nazi uniform walk by the restaurant. So did her table companion. He got up at once and excused himself: he had to go outside and talk to someone but would be back straight away. After a few minutes, she got tired of waiting and went to the restaurant door to find out what her lunch companion was up to. She saw him talking to the same Nazi she had seen him with a few days before. The Nazi was slipping some banknotes into his hand. The girl went back to their table to get her coat. Just as she was putting it on, the man and the Nazi came walking towards her. Jean-Luc said he had to leave on urgent business, but the soldier would take care of her.'

'I don't need taking care of, especially by an enemy soldier.'

'Jean-Luc shrugged, said goodbye and left. The Nazi had been smiling all the while. He had been unable to get her out of his mind ever since he had seen her in front of Notre Dame. The girl replied that she was not interested. The Nazi protested he would at least be glad to pay for the lunch she'd had.'

'So your friend didn't even leave money for the bill. He left just like that. And I have no money on me.'

'Don't worry,' said the Nazi, 'I'll take care of it.'

'She hated the way they kept using the phrase 'take care of.' It was starting to sound sinister to her ears. She walked away and headed towards the door.'

'At least wait until I've paid,' said the soldier.

'Against her better judgment, she complied. They then walked out of the restaurant together. The soldier invited her to his lodgings. She excused herself, shaking inside but striving not to let it show. 'I have to get back to my studies.' She wanted to go home but did not want the Nazi to know where she lived, even though she knew Jean-Luc could have told him. 'I'm going to the library, and then I have a lecture.'

'I'll walk you to the library, then. You'll be safe with me. I'll take care of you.' Again, the phrase set her teeth on edge. She started walking away from him, but he kept pace with her, talking to her all the time in his broken French. At a deserted street corner, he took her arm, looked her in the eye, and said, 'You naturally resent our presence here. But I'm just doing the job I'm paid to do.'

'I didn't realize imposing on young women was part of your job.'

'I like a woman with spirit,' said the Nazi. The dreadful cliché made her even more determined to get away from him. But nothing seemed to put him off. Grabbing her arm, he maneuvered her so that she had her back against the front wall of a block of flats. He put his other hand on her shoulder.

'One kiss, and then I'll leave you in peace.'

'What do you mean? Let me go.'

'Just then, a policeman and a man in plain clothes walked out of the front door of the block of flats. As soon as the Nazi saw them, he stepped back from my friend, who shook herself free of him. The Nazi waited to see what the two men would do. He and the policeman sketched out a quick salute. There was a second's silence, and then it was my friend who spoke first:

'This German soldier was molesting me. If you hadn't appeared, he might have raped me.'

'Do you know this soldier?'

'Not at all,' said my friend, 'I have nothing to do with him. He forced his attention on me in a restaurant an hour ago or less.'

'You have no right to speak with this woman unless for professional purposes. When they get to hear about you at Foch —'

'All right,' said the soldier, giving a perfunctory salute and walking away. My friend thanked the two men and then, instead of going to the library, walked home to recover.

'That should have been the end of the matter, but it was not. A few days later, my friend saw Jean-Luc, the man with the pencil mustache. He accused her of betraying and impoverishing him. He admitted he had taken money from the Nazi in the hope my friend would comply with the Nazi's wishes. She said that that was outrageous and never again spoke to him after that. I'm telling you all this to warn you that the man with the pencil mustache cannot be trusted, however sincere he may seem.'

Johannes asked her: 'Did your friend ever see the Nazi soldier again?'

'She did,' she replied, 'only once, and fleetingly at that. I saw him on the same occasion. We were walking along one day after lectures. There was a group of Nazi soldiers passing by on the other side of the street. They didn't seem to be paying us any attention, but one of them broke away from the group, ran across the road, thrust a small piece of paper into my friend's hand, and nodded to her — she did not nod back but seemed much shaken. Then he went back to his group. She made sure that we went as far away as possible from the soldiers.'

'I looked at her inquiringly. 'That was the Nazi soldier I had that trouble with a while back,' she told me. She uncrumpled the paper she had stuffed into her pocket. There was a name written on it, and that was all: Gunter Lantz. 'We don't even know if it's his real name. We don't know whose name it is, if anybody's.

Well, at least he didn't harass me this time. He didn't even speak to me. As for the paper, I'll either keep it or throw it away. It's an easy enough name to remember, anyhow.'

'But the man with the pencil mustache is a thousand times worse than the soldier, so I'm just advising you to have as little to do with him as possible. Above all, don't change your attitude towards him outwardly or betray anything of the conversation we've had.'

'I promise we won't,' said Kristina, while Johannes nodded in approval.

There was nothing else for Kristina and Johannes to do now but wait for three days at Monsieur Soubrenie's flat, as Françoise Berg's friend had told them to do. Soubrenie was not often at home himself but clearly had every confidence in Jean-Luc, manifested, for example, in his having given him a key to his flat. Kristina felt they now had a double problem. Despite having found Soubrenie thanks to Tom Oliver — who clearly had every confidence in him despite their initial disagreement — she and Johannes actually saw very little of Soubrenie. He seemed to be present at his flat at irregular intervals and only for brief spells, sometimes twenty minutes or half an hour, day or night. She never found out where he was or what he did and refrained from asking him. The man with the pencil mustache came and went at will, too. He would hang about in the flat, or at least it looked that way to Kristina, drinking Pascal Combeau, smoking, staring into space. He did not appear to pay much attention to Kristina, Johannes, Ilse or Werner. However, he did once ask them why they did not want to go out and walk around the streets of Paris, especially when the weather was so pleasant.

'Our situation is difficult, as you know, and it must surely be obvious why we would rather avoid arrest or expulsion by going out more than we need to.'

'Maybe I could make your situation a little less difficult,' the man said, not without a certain ribaldry as it seemed to Kristina, almost winking at her and giving her a leer as she spoke. Besides, he was gap-toothed, which made him look even more vulgarly ingratiating whenever he smiled.

'Thank you, but we don't need your help, as far as I know.' Kristina was starting to feel imprisoned in the stranger's flat, and doubly so because of the invasive presence of the owner's friend.

'Quite. That's as far as you know,' retorted the man. 'But some circumstances are unforeseen. You may be grateful for a helping hand, either now or if and when circumstances should take a turn for the worse.'

'You are not our friend,' Kristina replied. Nevertheless, she had no wish to antagonize her host's friend and one who had enabled her to speak on the phone to Tom Oliver.

Not seeming to be discouraged, the man said, 'You might like to make a phone call.'

'I'm grateful to you for lending us your phone, but we don't need it again for the moment.'

'But what about when the moment is over?'

The more he persisted in trying to offer his help, the more suspicious she felt his offers were. If she were not careful, the man might end up blackmailing her despite being their benefactor's friend. She turned away from him, hoping he would drink up his Pascal Combeau and leave. But he seemed to sense her impatience, even to enjoy it. The more impatient she felt herself becoming, the more time he seemed to take, even, to Kristina's dismay, pouring himself another cognac, a large one. However, it soon dawned on her that what he expected was either money or favors or both. Traveling without a man, elegantly dressed, she must seem an easy prey to a certain kind of man — or a man simply made desperate by the circumstances of wartime.

'Listen, *fiston*, here's ten francs' — he held out a note to Johannes — 'there's a bakery called Chez Renée a short walk away from here: why don't you go and try it? The outside is decorated in red and gold. Buy yourself a couple of cakes. You can walk back through the Luxembourg and have one of your cakes there. You might even see a girl you like. You can offer her a cake.'

Johannes took the note and stared at it. 'Where exactly is this bakery of yours?'

With a look of weariness, the man poured himself yet another glass of cognac, as though it would give him the strength to answer Johannes's question.

'You go out of the building and turn right. Go to the end of the road and turn right again. Then you'll be in Rue des Ecoles. Go to the far end of the street, and walk on till you get to the Gobelins crossroads. Then you turn left and walk till you're facing Saint-Médard Church. There you start walking up Rue Mouffetard —' Johannes suddenly opened his fingers, letting the banknote fall to the floor. The man with the pencil mustache rose and gave Johannes, who was standing, a push backward.

Kristina got up and stood face to face with the man. 'Come and sit back down,' she said softly, 'and finish your drink. My son and I are not keen on cakes. As you may understand, we have other things on our minds. And I don't think my husband — Johannes's father — would quite approve of us accepting cakes from a man whom we did not know.'

'Damn your husband,' said the man.

Johannes picked the note up and handed it back to the man. 'There's something I'm not clear about,' he said to the man, looking him straight in the eye, 'I've seen enough of the area to know that your bakery — Chez Renée as you call it — is much further away from here than several others. I wonder what your friend Monsieur Soubrenie will think — or do — when he learns you have been making advances to my mother. And in front of her son, too. And insulting her husband to her and her son's faces.'

The man smiled. 'Damn Soubrenie, too. Don't worry, Soubrenie isn't as clean as he seems, you know. He's only doing this for you because he and Tom Oliver struck up an understanding in Oxford, if you see what I mean. Apart from helping you, his morals are no better than mine. In his own way, he's as much of a profiteer as I am, and there are many others around.'

Kristina again spoke quietly. 'You may say what you like. We've been advised to stay here until Friday, and that's what we'll do. As for Monsieur Soubrenie's morals, the faithful friendship he bears Professor Oliver and the help he's giving us are enough morals for us. The rest is no concern of ours, or of yours. We would appreciate it if you would leave us in peace now.'

The man again leered at Kristina and drew a pistol from his inside jacket pocket. 'Now you'll appreciate doing what I say.'

'My mother and I will now go together and get a baguette and your cakes,' Johannes said, 'I'll get our coats.'

'You'll do no such thing, sonny.'

Kristina was starting to wonder whether this man was afraid of something or someone. She thought she could take advantage of his fear to get the upper hand. She walked up to him. He was just about to light a Gitane and was struggling with the match, matchbox and the gun in his hand. She gently took all four items from him, put his Gitane in her mouth, lit it, sucked on it, took it out of her mouth, and placed it between the man's mustachioed lips. At the same time, she returned his gun. Shocked and pleased at the same time, judging from the expression on his face, the man thanked Kristina and sat down. She gave a flicker of a smile. Then, apparently troubled, the man dropped his gun; it slid on the wooden floor just out of his reach. Kristina, Johannes and the man all stared at the gun for a moment, wondering who was going to be the one to pick it up. The man's afternoon's drinking seemed to have slowed his reflexes down. He would have had to get up out of his chair, take a step or two, bend down and pick up the gun: a set of coordinated actions which, Kristina thought to herself, the man looked unlikely to be able to pull off. She picked the gun up and turned to face the man. All this happened instantly. She did not point the gun at him, but he nevertheless shrank back.

She removed the bullets from the pistol. 'After all, you wouldn't want to do yourself a mischief with it, would you? Shoot yourself in the leg? Or shoot one of us by mistake? That would be a shame, wouldn't it?' Kristina shook the bullets from the pistol, went over to the window, opened it and threw them out into the street, where they rattled on the pavement. Then she handed the man back his gun.

A key turned in the front-door lock. It was Soubrenie. He was smiling as he walked in, but when he took in the scene in the living room, his features froze. He looked at Jean-Luc.

'I was just keeping them company till you got back.'

'They don't need keeping company. I don't know what you're doing here.'

'You gave me a spare set of keys.'

'I made it clear that was only for emergencies. What are you doing with that gun? How dare you behave like this towards my guests?' Soubrenie took the man's gun from him — he did not resist. 'And the keys.' He handed Soubrenie his keys.

'Wait till they hear up at Avenue Foch about this little band and all your doings.'

'I admit I was wrong to trust you. Not to trust you, but to use your services, at least. I should never have lent you my keys. I expect you've had a copy made. Now I'll have to change the lock. You would report your own mother to Foch if they paid you enough. I should have realized you'd use the key for your own purposes.'

'I've removed the bullets from the gun. He's had a lot of cognac.' Kristina felt Soubrenie needed to know this.

'If you're still alive when *Libération* comes, as it surely will, justice will be done, and that will be the end of you. Get out, and don't come back.'

'Spare me your crystal-gazing and your moralizing. I'll go, but I'm warning you, I may be back. Sooner than you think. And not alone.'

The man left the flat.

'I hope to have good news for you shortly,' Soubrenie said to Kristina and Johannes once the man had left, 'You may be able to get away quite swiftly now. However, you must be ready to leave at any minute.'

Soubrenie knew about what had happened to Françoise and her appointment with Kristina, Werner and Johannes that Friday. Her friend would come again if Françoise had not been freed by then. He assured them that, whoever came to the appointment, they could look forward to leaving France soon. Soubrenie now disclaimed any friendship, past or present, with Jean-Luc. They had at one time helped each other out, but he was not to be trusted. Soubrenie should not have asked Jean-Luc to help them with phone contact to Tom Oliver, but it was too late now for regrets.

When Friday came, Kristina, Werner and Johannes again went to the pond in the Luxembourg, watched the children sailing their yachts, and waited for Françoise or her friend to show up. It was again Françoise's friend who came to meet them and, again, she brought bad news. Françoise had been released from Avenue Foch three days before. But on the following afternoon, the Gestapo had gone to her family's flat and taken her and her father away. She and her father had this time been betrayed to the Gestapo by Jean-Luc, apparently. He had been seen drunk on Tuesday evening a few yards from her building. As the Gestapo were walking away after delivering Françoise back to her place, Jean-Luc had been seen stopping them in the street and talking to them. He may have told them something to make them suspicious about Françoise and her father and mother. When they came back the next day and took Françoise and her parents away, Jean-Luc was still hanging around. As the group walked past him, one of the Gestapo slipped some banknotes into his hand and winked at him.

'O dread! Panic! Funk!' shrieked Jean-Luc — he seemed to find the sound of the English words amusing.

Twenty-Four

Michael Lucht was finding it hard to concentrate on his work these days. It had now been a fortnight since Hellroth had become his valet, on the Führer's orders, or so they both thought. He was heading across town to his office in his chauffeur-driven Daimler — Hellroth was the chauffeur. Although army command insisted on staff punctuality, since Hellroth had become his valet, Lucht had got into the habit of arriving late for work or various professional functions. For one thing, it made him feel more important than he was; for another, he wanted to show Hellroth that he, Lucht, was not only in charge of him but of himself and that he could also put himself above his own hierarchy's orders and requirements; and for still another, he also wanted to show Hellroth that, even though Lucht knew he was only relatively important, no meeting could start until he had arrived. Arriving at his office on this particular day at about half-past ten in the morning, Lucht greeted the staff and secretaries, sat down behind his desk and had Hellroth light him a cigar. Hellroth then went to sit down on a chair provided for him in the corner of the room. His job required him to sit there all the time unless ordered to do otherwise and, like a dog, hang on his master's every word.

While Lucht was savoring his cigar, as usual beaming to himself on the ascendant he now had over Hellroth, a secretary knocked.

'Come in if you must.'

'I'm sorry to bother you, sir. A letter has come for you, and there's also one for Herr Hellroth.'

'I've told you before,' yelled Lucht, 'you're not to call him Herr! In fact, you'd do better to omit his name altogether, as well.' The secretary nodded and curtsied and walked out of the room.

'Ah,' said Lucht as soon as she'd gone, 'a letter from the Führer.'

He seemed not to have taken in the fact that Hellroth had also been handed a letter by the secretary. Lucht was convinced that he was about to be promoted to the inner circle of the Führer's advisers. He again sat back in his chair and basked in the thought of his new-found glory; and if you could not be the sun, you could still be a satellite, near enough to give off a reflection of its glow; the sun was declining even as it burned, consuming itself into nothingness; perhaps he, Michael Lucht, would one day replace the dying sun.

A thought was all it was to remain. He opened his letter, not noticing that Hellroth was opening his own. He checked the signature and saw it was from the Führer. He took a puff of his cigar and breathed in. This must be it, he thought: my promotion. He started reading:

It has come to my attention that your work is not all that a servant of the Reich's is expected to be. I am henceforth stripping you of Hellroth, your assistant valet. Your sloth and tepidity shame our Empire. You systematically turn up late for meetings. You spend much of your time idling and drinking. I wish to inform you that as of receipt of this letter, you are to be Hellroth's valet. I am reinstating him in his previous position. He has shown himself more eager than you to serve the Reich. This new disposition will thus take place with immediate effect, as the separate letter I have sent Hellroth confirms.

Lucht took another puff of his cigar. He put down the letter on his desk and stared at it. After a minute or so, he looked over at Hellroth, who was smiling. Then he picked up his letter and walked over to Hellroth, who was clutching his own letter. They instinctively exchanged letters.

'Who has been telling on me to the Führer?'

'The letters could hardly be clearer,' said Hellroth. 'If you respect the Führer and the Reich as much as you claim, you will obey their orders. Of course, if you're in any doubt, we can always check with his office. As you can imagine, this would be even further proof that you do not trust the Führer or the Reich. Then you'd be likely to get called —'

'Absolute rot!' barked Lucht. 'Either this valet business is serious, or someone is trying to make fools of us.'

'You seem to have been taking it seriously enough yourself so far, especially when it's to your advantage and you're the one to call the shots while I have to obey. But now we're about to find out how it feels to have the boot on the other foot.'

'I still say we should phone the Führer's office for confirmation.'

'As you will,' said Hellroth, yawning, 'not that you wanted to phone his office when you were the master and I the slave. Anyway, you haven't read my letter properly.'

'I won't let you speak to me like that. You're still my valet as far as I'm concerned.'

'Not as far as I'm concerned.' Hellroth remained cool.

Lucht grudgingly perused Hellroth's letter. The part he had skipped, towards the end of the letter, read: *You and Lucht will shortly be getting a visit — the date and time will not be made known to you in advance — from a high-ranking Reich official. The latter will check that all is in order and that Lucht is fulfilling his duties as valet to the Reich's satisfaction.* Lucht looked up from the letter. 'Looking forward to the visit?' Hellroth said. 'I know I am.'

'The wheel may yet turn again. Don't be too sure too soon.'

'So do you want to phone the Führer's office or not?' Hellroth said. 'If not, I consider that you are now officially my valet and that I have been reinstated in my previous position.'

Lucht said, 'I'll play your valet for now, and we shall wait for this visit. We'll sort things out when the official comes.'

'You're my valet, as good as forever, not only 'for now.' It is not for you to decide how long. You are no longer in charge, Lucht. And another thing: there will be nothing to 'sort out' when the official comes. He'll check that all is in order, and then he will go. If all is not in order, he will report you to the Führer, and that will be the end of you, if the end of you does not come before.'

Hellroth asked Lucht what 'if your end does not come before' meant. Lucht told him not to be naïve: he had used the two Jewesses and then all but raped Kristina Lichtblau. And then he let her get away. He was the laughing stock of the whole Nazi army in Vienna.

'I will play your valet for a few days or weeks until the official has been and gone. Then we will have it out between us. Plus, Kristina Lichtblau's one aim has always been to save her husband and family. And that she seems to have succeeded in doing.'

'Kristina and I love each other,' Hellroth said.

Lucht snorted: Hellroth was either lying or naïve to the point of stupidity. 'She has never loved you. You wanted her to love you, but she never did. It is pure fantasy on your part. Your plan to get Kristina into your bed was just a means of attacking her and her husband. But even with a Gestapo presence on every street, she still got away from you. You have dragged your personal feelings into the war, Hellroth. The Reich won't forgive you for that.'

'We'll see what the Reich will do. That is not your concern. You are now my valet, and your only duty is to obey me in all things.'

'Not to obey you, but to obey the Reich,' replied Lucht.

'The official will hear of your insolence.'

'You don't get it, do you, Hellroth? The official will examine the whole situation impartially. He will not simply be checking up on whether I'm serving you properly as your valet: he'll also want to find out whether you're treating me properly as my master. You have the important part now. You're the one they're going to be interested in. Watch out. Your career's on the line and not for the first time, as everyone knows.' This allusion to the drunken incident in which Hellroth paraded — or was paraded — in the street with his trousers down resolved Hellroth to kill Lucht even if it cost him his own life. Lucht knew how proud Hellroth was and was well aware of the risk he was taking. He was trying to kill Hellroth with words.

Lucht nevertheless decided against phoning the Führer's office. His own failures, his moments of cowardice, his boot-licking when it suited him — these were not things he wanted the Reich to probe into, even though they were common enough in the Führer's army. Yet he also sensed that, but for some drastic reversal, it would not be the Reich looking into his past but the Allies, since the war, he thought, would be over before long, and the victory would not be the Reich's.

A few days later, the official did arrive. Though neither man was looking forward to the official's visit, both tried to hide their apprehension, pretending to each other, as well as to the official, that his visit was the most desirable thing in the world. The official had clearly done his homework, and if his intention was to discomfort the two men as much as possible, he succeeded. His very presence was an accusation and a threat.

He strode into what was now Hellroth's office, accompanied by two other soldiers. All three were heavily armed. The official at once noted that the men had switched roles, as required by the letters, and that Lucht was at Hellroth's command. The official did not greet the men but clapped his hands and shouted, 'A bottle of schnapps and four glasses! Steins, not gin glasses!' Lucht headed for the door to do the official's bidding. But this was not what the official had in mind. 'Stop! Not you! Hellroth, you shall do it!' Lucht could not help smiling as the latter walked past him and out of the room. 'And be quick about it!'

While Hellroth was out of the room, the official turned to Lucht, 'Where were you on the night of 8th February 1944?'

For the first time, Lucht looked closely at the official — looked him in the eye, in fact. He could not tell whether the official was mocking him. He only noticed his sharp gaze and the spotlessness and sheen of his clothes and shoes. He had his cap pulled down low so that its peak shaded his eyes.

'Well?' said the official.

'I was doing a job for the Führer, as you seem to know,' Lucht replied.

'Seem to, perhaps. But I have testimony to the contrary. You reported that you had done the job. But in fact, you messed it up, didn't you?'

Lucht remained silent.

'The Führer's office told you to go after someone, but you got the wrong person. You tried to make out that the person you got was the person you'd been told to get. But it was not. You try to pretend you're more efficient, harder-working for the Reich than Hellroth. And you are. But you're good at keeping secrets, when they're about you, at least. You didn't do what you were supposed to do; you weren't where you should have been.'

In the guise of the SS official, Nubik had done his homework.

Nubik and the group at Schwartz the printer's had been working on this plan for several months now, ever since they had been sure that Hellroth had become Lucht's valet. Nubik's facility for acting and caricature was legendary among his friends, and he was the natural choice to play the part of the official. Having succeeded once in forging the Führer's stationery and epistolary style, they were confident they could carry on doing so indefinitely, or at least until someone realized what was going on. Nubik poured himself a glass of schnapps and left the other three empty. Hellroth and Lucht drooled, especially Hellroth. The two soldiers accompanying Nubik were members of the group who met at Schwartz the printer's, who had been brave – or foolhardy – enough to take part in the plan. They gave each other approving nods at the way in which Nubik had taken on the mannerisms of a Nazi officer and was able to manipulate these two officers as though they were puppets and he the puppet-master, using their lust for dominance and alcohol to lead them on, as well as their fear of degradation or worse. Nubik split the rest of the bottle into two tall glasses and told Hellroth and Lucht to down them. 'It's what you wanted, isn't it?'

'To answer your question, Lucht, not only does the Führer know about your blunder, but his whole cabinet does, and most of the SS hierarchy. If you carry on like that, you'll end up in Mauthausen. Besides, I think your friend here knows more about you than you realize.'

'He isn't my friend.' Lucht was looking more and more worried.

'I'm sure it would not take the Metropole for your friend to reveal all he knows about you.'

'Lucht,' said Hellroth, who had not spoken since the arrival of the 'official', 'do you not have some American friends?'

Nubik had been bluffing and had certainly not gathered that Hellroth knew anything compromising about Lucht.

'What if I have?' replied Lucht. 'Since when has it been a crime to have friends?'

'There are no friends in war,' said Hellroth, 'only two enemy sides, and then one the victor, the other the vanquished. What have you told your Yankee friends?'

'You understand the Allies are getting closer and closer?' Nubik said.

'I have nothing to do with that,' Lucht replied. Nubik turned to his two companions and then nodded towards the door. They marched Lucht out of the room, leaving Nubik and Hellroth on their own. Lucht and the two 'soldiers' went into an office two rooms away. They could then hear Nubik start to shout. They could only make out a few words here and there, but these were shouted by Hellroth: women... Americans... not enough... losing... irresponsible... bastard....

After half an hour, the two 'soldiers', as agreed beforehand with Nubik, marched Lucht back into what was now supposed to be Hellroth's office. They then marched Hellroth out and left Nubik alone with Lucht.

'Hellroth has brought to my attention certain irregularities in your behavior. Therefore, I have no alternative but to have you taken to the Metropole and interrogated.'

Lucht, at this point, saw himself as good as dead. But he made one vow to himself, which was that if he were to die before his time, he would take Hellroth with him. The Führer, according to Nubik, blamed both him and Hellroth for bringing the German army into disrepute in Vienna and even for creating the difficulties it currently faced with the Allies. He had given Nubik leave to dispose of their fates as he wished. Neither of them was to be trusted: they seemed intent on betraying each other.

'I have not betrayed Hellroth. I believe he has been in trouble with the Reich. I don't need to betray him, to you or anyone else. He may have betrayed me to you.'

He called to the two 'soldiers' to bring Hellroth back in. One of these 'soldiers' was Lichtblau. He wanted to see again the man who had threatened his family and would have raped his wife if he could. The five of them stood in the room: Nubik, Lichtblau and the other 'soldier,' Hellroth and Lucht.

'You are disgusting,' Nubik told the two officers, 'you have not hesitated to betray each other.' But Hellroth had forgotten about Nubik and Lucht: he was looking hard at Lichtblau. 'You!' He pointed at Lichtblau. Lucht took advantage of the situation to grab the pistol the other 'soldier' was holding. Lucht pointed it alternately at Hellroth and Lichtblau, who were anyway standing almost side by side. Hellroth had recognized Lichtblau. Lucht asked him who the latter was:

'I know him. He is no Nazi.'

'If he is no Nazi, he deserves to die. I will shoot him now.' He lifted the pistol to the level of Lichtblau's temple, took aim, and fired. The body fell to the ground — but that body was not Lichtblau's. Just as Lucht pulled back the trigger and pressed it, Hellroth leaped in front of Lichtblau while at the same time pushing him out of the way. He cushioned Lucht's bullet. His dying words were: 'For her.'

Lichtblau and Nubik understood these words, as did Lucht. Hellroth had finally not wanted the woman who had always spurned him to be bereft of her husband. His death was the only good thing he had ever done in his life.

'Now lay your gun down,' Nubik said to Lucht, who seemed to be at a loss after killing his arch-rival. 'I will not,' Lucht said, 'Hellroth is dead, but this man' — he nodded towards Lichtblau — 'is still alive, and if he is no Nazi, he still deserves to die.'

'We are all Nazis here. Hellroth lived and died a fool and a coward to the end. You realize your career is over, don't you? At the Führer's office they will all want to see you. You probably won't get out alive. I can pick up the phone and tell them now.'

Nubik dialed a number. 'Hello Sabine, it's Hermann. We are holding Lucht in Hellroth's office. Hellroth is dead. Killed by Lucht. Yes, I'll hold on.'

A minute later: 'Yes, I can. When shall I bring him to you?' Pause. 'Tomorrow is fine.' Lucht looked at Nubik.

'You're clever, but you won't get the better of me. When I tell the Führer all about today —'

'I'll tell the Führer all about today.' Nubik looked determined. 'You've killed a member of your own army. Our own army. And I know some of the shameful things you've done.'

'What shameful things?'

'Lotte told me.'

Lucht lunged at Nubik at the sound of the woman's name. Nubik stepped aside a bit and pointed his gun at Lucht.

'What do you want?' Lucht said. 'I can help.'

'You're right,' Nubik said, 'we're not Nazis. Your people are holding two friends of ours at the Metropole. We want them out. We want a chauffeur-driven SS car. You'll be our chauffeur. We want travel passes and documents. We want safe conduct and protection. We want money.'

Lucht spat. 'You want too much.'

'Walk ahead of us till we get to a Mercedes-Benz 770,' Nubik told Lucht. 'There will be a gun trained at your back in case you try a false move. You will drive wherever we direct you.'

Lichtblau had seen it as his role on this mission not only to confound Lucht and Hellroth and prompt them into killing each other — only half of the mission had been fulfilled — but to watch over Nubik, who was younger than him and whose life he valued as though he had been a brother. Both he and Nubik — Nubik, too, he knew — valued their own lives hardly at all. In peacetime, one's own life seems precious. But in wartime, death is common, and it becomes easier to sacrifice one's own life when so many around one are dying. Nubik's gift for acting and mimicry had served them well so far. Lichtblau wondered what they were to do with Lucht.

The latter could not decide whether the so-called 'official' and his henchmen were really Nazis or not. If not, they must be Resistance. He might do best by joining them and working for the overthrow of the Reich from the inside just as they were doing from the outside (if that was what they were doing). He did not know that Nubik considered him as impossibly corrupt. Nubik knew no Nazi, not even Hellroth, who had bought so many drugs or liquor as Lucht. Nubik assumed Lucht fed at least some of these products back into the black market at a high profit. He also seemed to run a ring of escorts — all part of the Nazi machinery.

Lichtblau was haunted by qualms and scruples. But Nubik was not. Things had gone too far — so far that language could not convey it. He remembered a piece of film he had seen a year or so before. A man — a Jew — was leaping out of the seventh-story window of a building that the SS had set on fire in a Jewish ghetto — he only had to think of it, and the blood rushed to his face and he began to sweat. Both man and building were on fire. The camera panned to the ground where some Nazis were watching, laughing.

When they were on the street, Lucht asked where they were heading.

'To the Metropole,' Nubik said.

They walked with Lucht in front, Nubik slightly behind, Lichtblau on one side of Lucht and the other member of their Resistance group on the other. They all wore Nazi uniforms. They met a group of Nazis walking towards them. The two groups saluted each other. Nubik tried to press Lucht to carry on walking, but he told the other group at once that they must arrest the others he was with as impostors.

'Forgive me, gentlemen, but I must see your papers,' said the officer leading the group of newcomers.

'And I yours,' replied Nubik, whose instinct lay in playing his part to the full and never revealing his feelings in any kind of crisis.

'This man says you're bluffing,' the officer said, pointing out Lucht. But then he did something that was to cost him his life. As Nubik and the officer were talking, Lucht slipped through to the back of the other group and started walking away from them all. Nubik called out: 'He's our prisoner! He's trying to get away! Stop him!'

One of the men in the other group shouted in Lucht's direction, 'Come back at once, or I'll shoot!'

Lucht did not turn round but broke into a run. The man who had just shouted to him shot him at once in the back. He crumbled to the ground. 'Firmiangasse,' he muttered, and died. Firmiangasse? A long street. It might have been his favorite street in Vienna. It might have meant anything. Nubik could not inform the officer as to why Lucht had said this. But Nubik refrained from telling him that Schwartz the printer's home and office, where the Resistance group met, lay in Firmiangasse.

The officer wanted to go to Firmiangasse to see what they could find. Lucht's behavior had distracted the Nazis from wanting to check Nubik's own group's papers, Nubik noted with relief. Still, Nubik, Lichtblau and their friend had no choice but to go with the Nazi group to Firmiangasse, hope they spotted nothing suspicious, and that they left forthwith. It turned out to be less straightforward than Nubik had hoped. The officer marshaled them all to the first houses along Firmiangasse. They would all walk down it together, in two parallel groups. The officer would take one side with Lichtblau and the friend, while Nubik would go with the officer's three soldiers on the other.

As they were walking, Nubik caught sight of a woman he knew, some way off, coming in their direction. He could either turn his head away and hope she did not see him or wait till they were close enough to see each other's features and tell her with his eyes not to acknowledge him in any way. She was Anna's sister, Beata, and though they had not known each other well, they had always been on first-name terms. She would be astonished to see him dressed as a Nazi, walking with Nazi soldiers and with friends of his she also knew vaguely, also dressed as Nazis. Or would she? She looked from a distance as though she were lost in thought and unlikely to take much notice of groups of soldiers in the streets, a common enough sight in the city for several years now. Yet Firmiangasse lay on the outskirts of Vienna in a neighborhood where soldiers rarely went. Nubik felt she would be bound to wonder what they were doing there and so look at them closely, and, when she did so, she would see him among them.

The encounter with the woman did not go the way Nubik had foreseen. As she and the soldiers — she walked on Nubik's side of the road — came towards each other, the woman's gaze never alighted on Nubik at all but rather on one of the real soldiers with whom he was walking. They seemed to know each other. She took in the fact that another group was walking on the other side of the street. He noticed that her dress was shorter than average for Vienna. His group stopped as the woman and the soldier she seemed to know greeted one another. He asked her for a cigarette, and she obliged. Nubik looked placidly on at their exchange — the war had changed some people's relationships and loyalties. He kept his head turned away from her while continuing to watch them out of the corner of his eye. As he was smoking, the soldier beckoned to the group on the other side to come over to him and his group. He motioned to the woman to offer her packet of cigarettes round to any of them who wanted one. They all accepted — Lichtblau, Nubik knew, reluctantly, since he did not smoke, though he did not show it. The three Resistants all shared the idea that they must not stand out in any way.

The woman took aside her friend, if that's what he was, saying she wanted a private word with him. The soldier said she was a friend of his and had a place nearby. It turned out she was inviting them all back to this place where she had food, drink and things to smoke. She thought she could even persuade some of her girlfriends to join them. *Vienna!* thought Nubik. *You would sell your soul for a thimbleful of dust if you thought it would bring you a few moments' thrills. Or what soul you have left among all the traitors, profiteers, collaborators, and bootlickers.* Nubik's thoughts ran on: *the soul of the city has been all but sucked out of her since the terrible years began.*

The place the woman wanted to take the group was not on Firmiangasse. The real soldiers soon forgot why they had even come there. Nubik, Lichtblau and their friend would not have gone near Firmiangasse in such circumstances but for the fact that they had been trapped into going by what had happened to Lucht. Though they avoided speaking, each of them knew the other two were thinking the same thing as himself — how to get out of this situation before someone found them out. If the woman were to look closely at Nubik at any time, she would, he thought, cry out in astonishment, and that would put paid to their lives.

'You wear your skirt too short,' the officer said to the woman.

'I enjoy dancing,' she said to him with a smile, 'dancing in a shorter skirt is easier. I'm sure you like dancing, too.'

The woman came to a halt and turned to the men: 'Gentlemen, would you like to eat, drink, smoke, and make merry with some of my beautiful girlfriends?'

She went ahead and up three steps to the porch of an eighteenth-century baroque house. Without waiting for the soldiers to catch up with her, she rang the bell. An elderly man, clearly a domestic servant, came to the door. He and the woman nodded to each other, then the man let the whole party in, leading them to a ground-floor room right at the back. The man opened the door of the room to let them in and stood aside. They all walked into the room, the group of real soldiers first. As Nubik passed the woman, who was standing next to the servant, she tugged at his jacket sleeve. He did not turn to look at her or speak to her but realized from this gesture that she had recognized him from the start and that all this was some kind of plan of hers. When they were all in the room, the girl said to the assembled company:

'I need three volunteers to come with me. We'll buy some extra bottles and go and get the girls. I wasn't expecting so many of you.'

'My two colleagues and I will be delighted to come and assist you,' Nubik said to the woman.

'I'll come, too,' the officer said.

'Darling,' the woman said, walking up to the officer and standing just in front of him, almost touching him, 'don't worry. These men are not going to run away. They want the same things as you.'

With one hand, she caressed his cheek. The blood rushed to the officer's face.

One of the real soldiers said to the woman, 'Do you know an officer by the name of Michael Lucht?'

'I do,' the woman said, 'he used to come to this area sometimes.'

'He's dead,' the third real soldier said. The woman did not show any reaction. 'His last word as he lay dying was Firmiangasse. You say he used to come to this area. We've been to Firmiangasse and haven't found anything unusual. Why was it so important to him? What could he have meant by it?'

'Firmiangasse is a code word; it's a code word for —'

'For what?' said the soldier.

'For the same things you're here for now. Eating, drinking, smoking, the girls I'm about to bring back for you. Your colleague was trying to tell you to come to this area, even though where we are now is not actually in Firmiangasse.'

The officer and his two henchmen seemed satisfied with this answer, especially as the promise of food, drink and women made the area itself and their original reasons for coming there unimportant. Beata left them in the room, came back in a few minutes with drinks for the three real soldiers, and then she walked out again, Nubik, Lichtblau and their friend accompanying her. The other three stared after them.

Then the officer called out, 'How long will you be? We're getting impatient.'

'Don't worry, darling; I'll be as quick as I can. These men will help carry the food and drink. A feast awaits you. Ring for the butler if you want more drinks. This will take a while. I wasn't expecting guests, and I'll need time to round up my girlfriends.'

When they had been walking in the street for two or three minutes, Nubik said to the woman: 'Beata, there are no girlfriends, are there? Nor any food or drink, either.'

'I'll have something to show you in a second.'

They came to a street several blocks away. The woman headed for a five-story building, the façade of which was a dirty brown color. She had a key to the front door. As they went inside, their footsteps rattled on the stone floor of the hallway. The whole of the building was empty, the woman told them.

Nubik's and Lichtblau's friend said, 'I'll do it if anybody has to.'

The four of them — Nubik, Lichtblau, their friend, and Beata — all nodded in agreement. The friend's words needed no explanation. The three men realized what the woman had in mind and why she had brought them to that house. She led them up to the top floor and into a bedroom where some wicker laundry chests were piled one on top of the other. She motioned to the men to help her lift the top chests off the bottom one. She opened the bottom chest and pulled off a blanket from the top of several heavy-duty machine guns.

'How will we get these to the house without arousing suspicion?' the friend asked.

'We're in uniform, after all,' said Nubik, 'we'll just sling them over our shoulders and walk back pretending we're so used to it we hardly even know we're wearing guns.'

'What about the lady?' the friend said. 'The lady will play the —' Nubik replied. Beata smiled and puckered her lips.

'See what I mean?' said Nubik. 'Three soldiers walking along with a loose woman in the streets of Vienna. Nobody will bat an eyelid.'

'How come the guns are loaded?' the friend asked.

'They were waiting for you to come along and use them,' said Beata. 'My Life had stood - a Loaded Gun ….'

'My life, their death,' he replied. 'Or vice versa. You never know, these days.'

Lichtblau said, 'Why do all three of us need to take guns if he's going to be the one to fire?'

'These plans might not work out,' Nubik said, understated as usual, 'we need to be able to protect ourselves and each other in case anything goes wrong.'

Lichtblau said, 'This is too dangerous for me.'

'Just bear with us for this operation.'

Lichtblau's anxiousness was a side to him Nubik had hardly ever seen before. Since his wife had left Vienna, never being sure of her whereabouts had made him jumpy.

The four of them were drawing near the mansion. Their faces were set grim against the imminent night and whatever the next few hours held in store for them. The soldiers in the house had guns, too, though not as effective as machine guns. Lichtblau looked straight ahead, but his thoughts lay elsewhere. The next hour or two would be decisive. Beata unlocked the front door, and they all headed upstairs where the soldiers were awaiting the entertainment they had been promised. When Beata and the three Resistants got to the landing, Beata signaled to them to stay there. Then, through gesture and whisper, she told them that when they heard her cough, they were to come into the room with their machine guns aimed and ready to fire, though they were to avoid firing if possible.

Beata went into the room. Voices were soon raised. 'Where are the girls? Where is the feast?' Beata sounded as though she were reassuring them. 'And where have the other soldiers who went out with you got to?' Beata told them they were carrying the food and drink and would not be long arriving. The girls would be along soon, too.

'Enough! You've led us here under false pretenses!' Beata then began to cough. Nubik, Lichtblau and their friend burst into the room, their machine guns aimed. The officer did not look surprised to see they had been deceived.

'It was too good to be true.'

'Let's tie them up and get out,' Nubik said.

Beata went to an adjoining room and returned with several sheets. While the friend kept guard, Nubik and Lichtblau tore the sheets into strips, made the soldiers sit down on chairs, and tied the soldiers up.

The friend said, 'I thought the plan was to kill them. Let's do it.'

'You're too soft to kill us,' the officer broke in, 'it would go against your consciences to kill us while we were defenseless.'

'You're one to talk about defenseless victims,' Nubik muttered. Beata motioned to them it was high time to stop talking and leave. But one of the other soldiers, looking at Lichtblau, suddenly sniggered, 'With your guns and us tied up, you have the upper hand. But wasn't Hellroth involved with your wife?' The officer and the other soldier began to laugh.

'What did you say?' Nubik said.

'You heard. This man's wife and Hellroth had a rel —'

A shot rang out. The man fell backward in his chair, crashing to the floor.

'Enough!'

The whole room went suddenly quiet. No one knew whether Lichtblau was giving an order to stop the shooting or the conversation, or both. It was the Resistance friend who had shot the man. 'I couldn't bear to hear him speak of your wife in that way.' The man was alive and had his eyes open. The friend had shot him in the thigh, taking care not to kill him, though his desire to do so had been nigh-irresistible. Lichtblau walked over to the man, took a look at his wound, and told the friend to go and get something with which to staunch the flow of blood. Lichtblau waited for the friend to come back, and then Lichtblau tied a bandage around the man's thigh. Far from manifesting any sign of gratefulness, the man retained the same disdainful, haughty demeanor as before; if anything, his attitude had become even more arrogant.

Lichtblau said to the man, 'Now you listen. What you said about my wife is a lie. This whole Reich is a vast death machine, all built on lies. And this is one of those lies. Lies never win in the war between truth and lies, nor do those who fabricate them.' The man closed his eyes.

Twenty-Five

Tom Oliver opened his eyes at the stroke of six in the morning. He tried to re-member how long it had been since he had last seen Werner. His companion shifted in the bed. Oliver got up and went to open the window. As requested, they had been given a room with a view of the sea. He breathed in the sea air and listened to the waves crashing and the sea-gulls' cries. White spume flew up. Oliver peered at the horizon. The hotel was perched on a cliff-top, and Oliver could make out breakers gathering size and momentum a long way off, drawing closer and disintegrating when they hit the rocks below the hotel. Daylight. He spotted a black fleck in the distance.

Oliver left his companion to sleep on, got dressed, and went downstairs and out of the hotel, heading towards the beach. As a boy, he enjoyed slipping away from his parents on their summer holidays in Wales to be alone with the sea. It seemed to call to him and fill his senses as nothing else could. He thought then that a fisherman's or sailor's life was best. He had been teased at school. No: not teased, bullied. He could hold back the tears on the way to school, but not the vomit induced by the fear of another day at school. He had grown up overweight and remained so. Nobody minded but him. He had shown exceptional scholarly promise early, had left behind the mockers and scorners. His love of the sea and admiration for the open-air life had never changed or diminished. But he had never been an Ahab or a Silver. His adventurous spirit had had to find other spaces to play and grow in. Though he had taken part honorably in the First War, his real adventures had lain in the realm of the mind, art and poetry. But working to bring Jewish refugees to safety, a task in which secrecy and diplomacy were of the essence

— for diplomacy, too, is an art — and in the accomplishment of which the slightest mistake could cost innocent lives: this, too, was an adventure, doubtless the greatest of his life.

The black speck he had seen from his hotel window had disappeared from view or, from his vantage point on the beach, seemed to have disappeared. But when he walked back up the path to his hotel and looked out again over the sea, he noticed that the speck had grown but was now further to his left than it had been before. And there were two smaller specks behind it. Whatever was in the boat he had come to that seaside town to meet — whoever was in that boat — was what, he felt, contained the meaning of his whole life and of all the work he had ever done. Though he was Master of an Oxford college, had published many books and was a world-renowned academic, these were meager achievements compared to this other work he had been doing since the mid-thirties. He had not found academic life demanding: it coincided with his deepest intellectual passions, he was not accountable to anyone, he could keep his rooms in college on into his retirement and the rest of his life. But if his ship foundered — if *that* ship foundered — he felt he would consider his whole life to have been worthless.

The three ships now eluding his view, he went back inside his hotel and up to his room. He at once saw that his companion had gone, leaving no trace of having been there. He went down to the hotel lobby and asked the receptionist whether she had seen anyone walking out of the hotel in the past hour. To her knowledge, nobody had left during that time, but she had only intermittently been at her desk. There, in that cliff-top hotel, Oliver felt the ground sinking beneath his feet. His ship had disappeared, his companion, too. How long had he been in the habit of trusting anyone who agreed to sleep with him for a night or two? Trusting them and sometimes giving them his heart, only to have it flung back at him sooner or later with a snigger or contemptuous silence? War dwelt here, too. He hid this heartbreak and struggle behind a bluff exterior — English upper-middle-class impassiveness.

He went back down to the beach, sat on a rock and lost himself in thought as he looked out to sea. He had heard from Françoise three weeks before. She had entrusted his friends to her friend Sarah since she had an inkling the Nazis would be taking her in quite soon. Tom Oliver and Françoise's father had become friends when they were both students at Oxford shortly after the First World War. Françoise's father had returned to France, while Oliver had stayed on in Oxford. Françoise had told him to be in that town on that day when his friends' ship would be putting into harbor, if all went according to plan. According to plan... His gaze blurred as he stared out to sea; he felt as though he were dissolving into the green water, into the blue light, the light blue....

His eyes shifted focus as he made out the ship he believed was bringing his friends to England. Three other vessels were now pursuing 'his' ship — unless they were escorting it. He took a pair of binoculars out of his inside jacket pocket and started scanning the sea with them. A few seconds later, a metallic object jolted him in the back, and a voice said: 'You're making trouble, Jew-lover. I have a si-lencer on this gun and will shoot you now unless you come with us.'

Oliver lowered the binoculars from his eyes and took in the two shadows thrown out beside him. One, he ascribed to the man with the gun, the other to his companion. How could such a brilliant mind be such a naïve judge of character? Or, perhaps, when it came to physical attraction, character had nothing to do with it. And was he mistaken, or had the man holding the gun to his back not spoken with a Germanic accent? But, for now, Oliver had no choice but to walk as the voice and gun directed him.

'Where are you taking me? You can't do this. My land is a land of freedom.'

'Just keep walking,' said the Germanic accent.

His companion's shadow was striding alongside the Germanic man's. How did the man come to be in England? Why had he not been arrested by the Home Guard or the police? There were, to his knowledge, no Germans in England except those few who had been interned since the start of the war. Then the man and Oliver's companion began whispering to each other. The man gradually got very excited, raising his voice. Oliver's companion told him to keep his voice down if he did not want to be identified and shot. But if he were shot, he said, he would first do his utmost to shoot Oliver and the latter's companion. Oliver now realized that the man's accent was Austrian — Viennese, in fact. Perhaps he had some connection with the Lichtblau family and their friends. In recent months Oliver had taken to confiding his activities and plans, hopes and fears to his companion who, more than sympathetic, he now felt, had seemed positively curious about them. His companion might have relayed Oliver's confidences to this Austrian and perhaps others, and now he was handing him over to him. Tom Oliver wanted to turn round a hundred and eighty degrees in order to see the sea. Perhaps these two people were responsible for the ships chasing the one he had been looking out for, on that sea-shore and that cliff-top, if they really were chasing it.

The man with the gun agreed to Oliver turning around. The ships were now apparently heading for the English shoreline. He felt he could do nothing outwardly to resist his two abductors. He had done his part for the Lichtblaus and their group, as he had done for many other refugees.

'All right, that's enough dawdling. Let's be off.'

With his gun, he coaxed Oliver into turning back around; the three of them started walking inland again. Just then, the sound of an ear-splitting explosion came from the sea. The three on the shore all turned around again to face the sea. One of the ships had disappeared, leaving only flotsam strewn over the surface of the waves.

'A submarine,' said Oliver's companion. Oliver wondered whether the submarine knew what it was doing: would it spare his friends' ship or blow both remaining ships up?

'Let's hurry,' said the Austrian, again prodding Oliver with his gun. Another deafening racket came from the sea, and another straight afterward. Again, all three turned around.

The submarine had left one of the three ships intact. The sea was quieter now.

'I don't know how you come to be here,' Oliver said to the Austrian, 'but I think you should give yourself up. You'll be treated as a prisoner of war. If you leave me unharmed, you may get off lightly. Even more lightly if you decide to change sides and work for the British war effort.'

The man was lessening the pressure of his gun against Oliver's back. His step faltered.

'I've been promised a reward if I bring you to Germany.'

'I'm nobody,' replied Oliver. 'I help Jews and others escape death. But I'm no soldier. I'm no threat to anyone. You're wasting your time.' Tom Oliver, who had spent his whole life looking for what he saw as truth, was lying. He was not nobody.

'How much is the reward? You never told me there was a reward waiting for you,' said Tom Oliver's companion to the Austrian. 'How much of the reward do you intend to give me for turning the prisoner over to you?'

Oliver was baffled. His companion knew Oliver was not nobody; knew he was in touch with a certain Anglican clergyman who was trying to make Europe safer for everyone; knew he had counted among his contacts a German Protestant theologian who had been working underground for the overthrow of the Führer — for his death — but had been executed after being arrested by the Gestapo in 1943, though the theologian had friends who were working in the same spirit as he had. How much of this did the Austrian know, though? And was he trying to get himself killed by walking around England so freely? Oliver had an idea.

'The ship,' he muttered.

'Be quiet about the ship. Don't you realize we could kill you any second? Then where would you and your ships be?' his companion said.

They were now at a blind angle to the sea.

A new tone crept into the Austrian's voice: 'No. Maybe he's right. What about the ships? What about the one the prisoner came here to meet? If I can get to the people he's expecting, the Reich may pay me an even bigger reward.'

'Have the Reich told you to bring in more prisoners than this one?' Oliver's companion said.

'Don't you worry what the Reich have or have not told me to do.'

'They might divulge useful information.'

'I'm not here for information. I'm here to capture this Jew-lover. But all right, we'll see the ship.'

Tom Oliver himself felt in no hurry to see the ship in such circumstances. Either his friends were on it, or they were not. If they were, they would be as safe as they could be once they had set foot on dry land, though there were still this Austrian aggressor and the companion to contend with. They would meet up in Oxford if they happened to miss each other on the coast. That was what they had agreed. Oliver wanted to try a ploy, one the Austrian would fall for, he thought. As they turned round and began heading toward the shore, he mumbled:

'How about a drink at the hotel?'

The Austrian looked inquiringly at Oliver's companion, who nodded.

'A drink before our next move won't hurt,' said the Austrian. The prospect of a drink seemed to have a softening effect on him. He put his gun in his inside jacket pocket, and the three of them walked into the hotel.

At the bar, the barman said, 'What'll it be?'

Tom Oliver spoke first. 'Glenlivet.'

'Same for me,' said the Austrian.

'Wonderful,' said Oliver's companion.

Once they had been served their drinks, Tom Oliver looked over at his companion and nodded. His companion nodded back imperceptibly and then said, 'We could go and sit on the terrace. It's warm enough. We might catch some movement out at sea, too.'

They sat beneath the clear blue sky.

'Another?' Oliver's companion said to the Austrian.

'Make it a double.'

'I'll get you a triple to thank you for bringing us here.'

The Austrian licked his lips. Oliver's companion gave Oliver the hint of a wink.

They could not see the shoreline below, so they could not know whether or not a ship had come in. The Austrian did not want to go back to the beach since he was afraid that if there were British or French sailors or soldiers, he would stand no chance against them even if he tried to tell them that he had taken Tom Oliver hostage. That in itself would be one more reason for killing him. They might take him in for questioning, torture him, and end up killing him anyway. He knew his own side's methods only too well — had practiced them himself — to be at all optimistic about what the enemy might do to him. Oliver's companion suggested they walk along the cliff-top in order to scour the sea and beach from different vantage points.

As they walked along the cliff-top, Oliver's companion, jocularly pretending absent-mindedness, went over to the edge and almost straddled it, one foot on it, the other in mid-air. Tom Oliver followed after, and so did the Austrian. The Austrian was lost in contemplation of his own vainglory. The Nazis would thank him for this: risking his skin in enemy territory, bringing in one prisoner, maybe more. They would love him for it. It would be his apotheosis. Oliver stopped walking and, hearing he had done so, so did his companion. The Austrian and Oliver looked each other in the eye. Just then, they heard voices coming from the shore below. At the sound of the voices, the Austrian looked away from Oliver, to his right and down. While they were intent on the shore below, from somewhere behind the three of them on the cliff-top came the report of a gun. The Austrian swiveled round to his left. As he did so, the ledge he was walking on crumbled beneath his feet. He let out a long, piercing cry that faded as he neared the shore below. The voices rising from the beach grew louder.

Oliver and his companion ran down the winding cliff path to the beach.

'What was that all about?' Oliver asked his companion.

'He came into the bedroom while you were out. He threatened to kill me if I did not take him to you.'

A breeze slapped them in the face as they ran. When they reached the bottom, they saw a small crowd huddled over the corpse. Only Oliver and his companion knew who the man was, or even that he was foreign. The crowd shifted uneasily, not knowing what to make of the situation. They seemed to be wondering whether or not Oliver and his companion had pushed the man, especially as they did not look troubled by the man's death — if anything, rather the contrary. But if they had pushed him, they would surely have run away and not gone down to the beach. The crowd appeared to be waiting for Oliver or his companion to speak. Oliver breathed in and sniffed the tang of sea salt on the wind. The glint of a knife among the crowd caught his eye. Whoever was brandishing it might try and use it against him if he did not quickly say something. The knife seemed to be edging closer to him.

'This man was an Austrian Nazi. He came to England to this place to capture me and take me to Germany. He would have handed me over to the SS for torture and certain death and taken all the credit and a great deal of money for it. The Nazis mandated him to do this because I try to help refugees to get to safety in England. I am not a soldier. I might have killed the man, but I did not, in any literal sense. My companion and I drew him to the edge of the cliff. He was walking along it and, surprised by the sound of a gunshot behind us, fell off. But this is no time for debate. We must get this corpse out of the way. This man was as evil as the regime whose aims he served.'

People in the crowd started wondering aloud what to do with the body or where to put it. A policeman and two soldiers soon arrived on the scene. Oliver told them all that happened to him regarding the dead man. They noticed the tiny scar beneath the man's right ear. Had he had it before he fell? Oliver replied that he had.

A woman stepped forward from the crowd. Tom Oliver observed her. Her beauty struck him at once. Her face was pale and gaunt, her eyes sharp blue. When she spoke, it was, like the dead man, with a Viennese accent.

'I recognize this man. But first, I must thank Professor Oliver. You are the reason I am, for the present at least, a free woman, standing on this English beach.' Oliver realized this woman was Kristina Lichtblau. 'This man is Josef Jäger. He was one of the vilest servants of the Reich. As a member of the SS, he was supposed to wear a swastika armband. But he never showed his. Someone once told me Jäger wore his under his left sock so that if ever the Nazis mistook him for an ordinary civilian, he could prove he was not.' Kristina stepped toward the corpse, pulled the man's left trouser leg up and the sock down, revealing the swastika armband. 'I must now explain my presence here to this police officer and his two colleagues, and hope to join Professor Oliver later.'

Twenty-Six

Nubik had gagged and bound two of the soldiers, who sat at opposite ends of the room, with a large chest that Nubik had heaved into the middle of the room so that the soldiers could not see or communicate with each other. He tied one to a massive oak desk: he would not be able to move. The other he attached to the legs of a massive wardrobe. The wounded man lay with his eyes still closed.

They heard running boot-steps and voices shouting coming from Firmiangasse. The shot had likely been heard by soldiers patrolling the streets. Nubik and his friends had to make a lightning decision. If they decided to take the Nazi soldiers hostage, they would probably be shot down by the invaders, whether they killed the hostages first or not. These Nazis did not care for or stand by each other. The soldiers outside sounded close to the house now; they seemed to be trying to decide which house the shot had come from. If they went into the wrong house, Nubik and his group would have a little more time to think and act; they held their breath. Then they heard: 'The front door of this house is unlocked. Let's try it.' The voices and shuffling withdrew to the neighboring house.

'I'm going to see if there's a back way out of here,' Beata said.

The man with the wounded thigh opened his eyes and smiled. 'Hey Lichtblau,' he said, expectorating bloodily onto the floor, 'your pretty little wife is just a flirt, and you know it. She will toy with any man, civilian, Nazi, Jew; it's all the same to her.' At this, the other two Nazis guffawed behind their gags.

The girl came back in. 'There is a back way out. We'll have to hurry.' The Nazi who had just mentioned Kristina Lichtblau said, 'I expect all three of you enjoy this girl.'

The girl said, 'I heard what you said before about Frau Lichtblau. You can say what you like about me. Frau Lichtblau would not want me to do what I'm about to do. But you have sent enough people to Mauthausen. You won't be sending any more.'

She grabbed an old rag of a towel that was lying on top of a dresser, turned into a corner of the room and faced inward and away from the people in it so that what she was doing could not be seen. Then she turned round to face outward and walked over to one of the gagged and bound soldiers.

'How funny is this?' She pressed her pistol to his chest and fired. The rag towel muffled the shot. She crossed the room diagonally to his comrade and did the same. At last, she went up to the leader of the three, the one who had spoken obscenely about Kristina Lichtblau and herself. Tears were streaming down his cheeks.

'No, please, no. Have mercy.'

'I knew you had a big mouth,' said Beata, 'I didn't realize you were a coward, though I should have guessed. How many innocent people have you killed? How many innocent people have you had put to death?'

'I'm really an uncircumcised Jew. I've always behaved that way with the Nazis. It was the only way I could find to survive,' said the man.

Nubik said, 'I'm taking your papers off you.' He briskly scanned them. 'There's nothing here to prove or disprove what you say.'

'The Nazis forced me to join them. Otherwise, they were going to kill my parents, my wife and children. They let them go. They are in America now. I was playing the Nazi a second ago. I didn't mean any of it.'

'So you'll help us get out of here?' Nubik said.

They heard the front door opening and the boots and voices ringing in the hallway. The soldier said, 'Put your guns down and pretend to be my prisoners. It's your only hope. You've left it too late to get away. Either trust me or die. Herr Lichtblau, you do want to see your wife and children again, don't you?'

Now the boot-steps were clomping up the wooden stairs, and the voices echoing. Then they were on the landing. The Jew called out, 'In here!' Lichtblau's and Nubik's friend handed the machine gun he was holding to the Jewish soldier; Lichtblau, Nubik and the girl all dropped their weapons. A group of Nazi soldiers, five or six of them, charged into the room.

'Sieg Heil!' the Jew said. 'I have taken these three people prisoner. They managed to kill these two comrades of ours.' He pointed to his colleagues lying dead on the floor.

'Then they must die instantly.'

'Not so,' replied the Jew. 'When they were cornered by these three people, our comrades renounced their allegiance to the Führer, or so these people say, and promised to combat him to the death, him and all the members of his regime. However, one of them had a gun hidden inside his jacket and suddenly turned on these three people. So they shot him and his colleague. They were right to do so. I am now taking them away for interrogation. And don't worry, gentlemen, I shall not go easy on them.' He gave the Nazi soldiers a knowing smile.

'But how have you managed to take them prisoner? And why did they kill the others but not you?'

'They were about to kill me,' the Jew said with perfect poise, 'but they got scared when they heard your voices and footsteps in the street and then in the house. They grew frightened for their lives. They could have taken me hostage and used me as a bargaining chip but decided I would not be worth much as a hostage. So they downed weapons in the hope that I, and you, would spare them. I told them that if they surrendered, I would guarantee they would not be executed summarily. I shall keep my word' — the soldiers as though by reflex stepped forward, glaring at the Jew and his three so-called prisoners — 'but shall naturally be happy to turn them over for execution later on if the interrogations should prove… convincing.' He held his pistol to Nubik's temple. The Nazi soldiers grinned.

'So, I'm taking them to the Metropole. We'll see how they like it there. Turn and face the door,' he said to his prisoners, 'and get one behind the other.' They did as ordered. 'Now put your hands on your heads and start walking.'

He turned to the group of soldiers: 'I suggest you deal with the bodies of your comrades.'

'Our comrades,' retorted one of the soldiers.

'Our comrades,' parroted the Jew.

'Wait,' said the soldier who had corrected him. 'We have no idea whether you are telling the truth. We don't even know who you are. We aren't gravediggers or undertakers. We'll send for someone to dispose of these bodies.'

All of a sudden, the blast of a gunshot filled the air. A bullet hit one of the soldiers in the arm. He poured forth a stream of obscenities. They all looked to see where the shot had come from. One of the soldiers lying on the floor was not dead after all, though whether he had intended to shoot the soldier remained unclear. The group of Nazi soldiers sprang towards the soldier on the floor, who was, in fact, still gripping his pistol. They seemed at a loss to know what to do. Nubik thought to himself, *we can either make a dash for it while they are distracted or stay and kill them all.* The Nazi soldiers ignored the two sub-machine guns where they lay. Nubik and his friend glanced at each other and then moved stealthily for the sub-machine guns. The soldiers were now crouching around the soldier who had just fired. Nubik and his friend grabbed the sub-machine guns and shot all the soldiers in the back at close range. They pumped both soldiers lying on the floor with a round of bullets to make sure they were really dead this time. Nubik thought, *if necessary, we must do more than resist; we must be warriors.* But they did not kill the one who called himself an uncircumcised Jew.

The latter said, 'You four' — he meant Lichtblau, Nubik, their friend, and Beata — 'will have to keep pretending you are my prisoners.' He picked up one of the sub-machine guns. They stepped outside the house and into the street. They had left all the other guns in the bedroom with the dead soldiers.

'What do you intend to do?' asked Nubik.

The girl was sullen.

'Just a little while longer,' said the Jew.

'What do you mean?' said the girl.

'What he means is that the Nazis are losing the war. Have all but lost it now.'

'A little while longer, and we'll be free again.'

'How will we ever be free again,' the girl said, 'when so many of our loved ones, and so many of our countrymen, are dead?'

'Vienna is still under the Nazi heel. Much of Europe is, too,' said the Jew. 'If we want to survive, we must go carefully.'

A car stopped alongside them, and three SS officers got out.

They gave the Nazi salute, and the Jew did the same in return.

'Where are you taking these people?'

'To the Metropole, for questioning. I have reason to believe they are traitors to the Reich. I'll get the truth out of them fast enough.'

'No,' said one of the SS officers. 'I will take them to my office for questioning myself. It's just around the corner from here.'

'They are highly dangerous enemies of the Reich. These three managed to get uniforms and have been impersonating members of our military.'

'If that is so, they deserve to die as soon as possible,' the officer said. 'I will take care of it.'

'For the moment,' the Jew said, 'there is only the interrogation to take care of. These people may have information to give us. It might even help us turn things around.'

'Turn things around?' The officer feigned surprise.

'You know exactly what I mean.'

'Another word along the same lines, and I will report you at once to Herr Goebbels.'

'First, with all due respect, these prisoners are no concern of yours. Second, since you mention Herr Goebbels, I was just on my way with these prisoners to see him now.'

'But…Herr Goebbels is in Bonn with the Führer.'

'Herr Goebbels was until very recently in Bonn,' said the Jew, 'but today he is overseeing operations at the Metropole. He's expecting me there. I'll be delighted to tell him you held me up on my way to my appointment with him and tried to prevent me from doing my duty to the Reich.'

'You wouldn't dare,' the officer said.

'Don't you understand?' said the Jew. 'This war is nearly over for us. Such arguments are futile. You would be more useful in combat than in the city of *Wienerschnitzel* and decadence.'

One of the other officers said, 'I told you we shouldn't have stopped the car.'

'That's enough lip from you,' replied the chief officer. 'Let's get back into the car. And as for you,' he looked at the Jew, 'I shall see you in a few minutes at the Metropole.'

'Fine,' the Jew said, 'Herr Goebbels is a friend of mine. I'll be delighted to introduce you to him personally.'

The four officers climbed back into their car and drove off.

'You didn't tell us you knew Goebbels,' Nubik said. 'If I'd known that, I'd have —'

'I don't,' said the Jew. 'I was bluffing. We're not going to the Metropole. What we need is a car.'

'I haven't got a car, and I can't drive,' the girl said. 'But my sister Anna can drive and has a car. Let me walk in front. I'll show you the way. The car is about five minutes' walk from here.'

'We'll have to hurry. When the others find out Goebbels is not at the Metropole and nor are we, they'll be coming back for us soon enough, and they won't be so keen to listen to us next time around.'

Anna greeted Nubik as though she were expecting him.

With Anna at the wheel, they took the Ringstrasse and then exited north out of Vienna. They stopped at one checkpoint on the way out of the city: the two guards on duty looked weary and discouraged, just waving them through without so much as a glance. It seemed as though people sensed that the Reich had as good as lost the war, and there was little point in keeping up appearances. However, when they were about a mile beyond the checkpoint, Nubik said:

'Stop the car; I need to get out.' Nubik could no longer stand the idea of leaving Vienna.

'We can't,' said the Jew, 'we have to keep going now till we reach some Allied-occupied territory, wherever it may be.'

'Stop the car, I tell you! I'm getting out. I need to stay here. I'll fight my own war till the end.'

'He doesn't have to come if he doesn't want to,' Lichtblau said

The Jew did as he was requested and stopped the car.

'Good luck for the rest of the trip. Give my love to Kristina and the boys, and don't forget to think of me once in a while. Let me know when you get safely to England.' With that, Nubik started walking back towards Vienna.

And death, perhaps, Lichtblau thought.

'Come into the park they said was dead,' Lichtblau said. 'But despite appearances, it wasn't quite dead. It was only said to be dead. As long as there is a spark of life, even a single blade of grass there to defend, he has little or no choice in the matter. It is hardly a decision at all. It is a question of —'

'Conscience,' his friend said.

'Of conscience, yes. Some people understand that, even though it is hard for them to accept. Still, tomorrow, next week, or next month, we'll be able to come and go freely again, in our cities, our country, between our country and the others. Ah, our democratic freedom, that the Germans squandered. The creation of the ghettoes. Then all the ghettoes were emptied and laid to fire and the gun. People on fire leaping out of windows to certain death. So many millions of innocent people murdered.'

'Do you know why I've never been circumcised?'

The Jew was trembling. On the day of the *brit milah*, I was taken to synagogue as arranged. But when we got there, the door was locked. My whole family, uncles, aunts and cousins, were there. The *mohel* had been removed from the synagogue by the new regime two days before. He had no time to warn us he would not be able to perform the circumcision. Nobody referred to the matter again, and I was never circumcised. I later found myself being dragooned into the Führer's army. I just played along, a stick insect on a stick.'

'So you've been working for the Führer and carrying out his orders and schemes ever since.'

'Working for the Führer? No. Even though I've nominally been a member of his army since before the war. Carrying out his orders and schemes? Never when I could avoid doing so. I did anything I could to get out of it: played sick, sabotaged military efforts whenever I felt I could get away with it — and I did get away with it; also helped a few people escape the country, though not as many as I would have liked. And I've often given my salary to workers' groups. I'm guilty, guilty, guilty. I should have laid down my life for my fellow Jews. Perhaps I've risked it once or twice. But I'm no Stauffenberg. Kill me if you want. I know I could have done better. But I could have done worse, too.'

Lichtblau looked thoughtful. 'You've saved our lives, and we've saved yours. There's been enough killing in this war. We have contacts in England, and we just want to get there.'

'Count me in,' said the Jew. 'I have nothing and no one to keep me in Vienna.'

'Why weren't you ever found out?' asked Anna. 'Circumcision is not everything.'

'I changed my name. I had false papers made. I was drafted into the army under my false name. I tried to desert. They brought me back and tortured me. They were going to kill me but decided to keep me on because they were afraid of running short of employees. I came into contact with a member of the Abwehr. He told me a lot about a Lutheran pastor and an English bishop. I'm not religious, but from what he told me, I instinctively felt some kind of kinship with those people. I felt attracted by their goodness. The Abwehr man talked about them in a way that commanded my respect — that moved me. I can't fathom why he should have trusted me.'

'It seems you have found the right people,' Lichtblau said, 'our friend in England has ties with the sort of people. And my friend here and I are Vienna Resistance members.'

The girl wiped away a tear from her cheek. 'I'm a friend of Nubik's, the man who left us to return to Vienna. We haven't seen each other for some time. He used to supply Nazis with fake drugs. He managed to stay out of harm's way, and out of the Abwehr, by keeping the officers happy with his goods. They never suspected he was against them all along. Part of me wanted to stay with him when he got out of the car, but part of me felt I couldn't come so far only to turn back. He should not have come in the car. He should have stayed in Vienna if that was his strongest conviction. Alfred has his own inner compass. He never imitates anyone, or kowtows, or blames anyone else if his plans go wrong.'

'He got by like that right up to the end,' Lichtblau said. 'I mean, right up until now. He hampered them as he could. And I know he has many friends in Vienna.'

'I know what you're thinking,' the girl said. 'I saw how close he is to you. You think we may never see him again. But he's —'

'Unpredictable,' Lichtblau's friend said.

The girl and Lichtblau both nodded.

They now drove in silence. The Gestapo could still catch them. If they did, certain death awaited Lichtblau and the others, and no one might ever know what happened to them. Anna's parents were in Vienna. The thought that if the authorities discovered she was missing, they would take it out on her family tormented her. She hoped Nubik would tell them she had grasped the opportunity to leave Vienna. He could reassure them she was in good hands and had not disappeared. But his wanting to go back suddenly to Vienna she found understandable and foreseeable. Had he not behaved similarly at least once before? Was he feeling the weight of killings his countrymen and the Germans had committed? Or that he himself had committed? Was there any point in undertaking such a perilous journey when all the signs were that the war would soon be over? Perhaps the city simply exerted some sort of magnetic hold over Nubik? Or does he have a sweetheart, Anna thought, from whom he could not, when push came to shove, finally bear to be parted from? That must be the most likely reason. Her family and Nubik knew each other. Just as he might be able to inform them about what she was doing, they, too, could give her news of Nubik.

The Jew gave her a quizzical glance. She turned her head away.

Twenty-Seven

Nubik was at that very moment heading towards Vienna through the long grass of a field several miles from the city. Just as Anna had been thinking of him, so had he been thinking of her and her family. They had been students together and sweethearts in the thirties. He had been too wayward for her, and she had withdrawn from their relationship. Nubik had never held it against her — he was not the kind to bear grudges — and they had occasionally seen each other over the years. Once again, they had slipped into their old empathy at once. He knew her family — her parents and sister — and guessed she would want him to make contact with them to tell them how Anna was and what her plans and whereabouts were. They would be sure to wonder — even if they would probably not dare ask him to his face — why he had not stayed with Anna, or she with him. As long as the war lasted, he could be more useful in Vienna than anywhere else.

Now he could see car headlights on the Ringstrasse. He would not go back to his old haunt under the bridge in Döbling. The authorities must anyway have demolished the site. A chilly breeze swept up, and he thrust his hands into his trouser pockets. In one, he could feel a small piece of paper that had not been there before, or at least he had been unaware of it. It said: 'STARS 412'. Nubik knew what it meant: it was Anna's family's current address in a code the two of them had worked out between them years before. Thus, Anna hoped Nubik would look for them there.

He was now approaching the street that in their code they called STARS, not far from the Ringstrasse on the north side. He took the slip of paper out of his pocket, kissed it — for he was in love with Anna — then hunted for something to burn it with. He felt it might be suspicious, incriminating even, for him, Anna or her family. A couple of soldiers came out of a house a few yards along from where Nubik was. Their eyes met.

'What are you doing?'

Nubik noticed one of them was smoking:

'I was looking for someone to give me a cigarette.'

From the house the two soldiers had left came the sound of laughter and clinking glasses. The soldier who was smoking took a cigarette packet from his pocket and handed it to Nubik. He waited for the two of them to go. But they seemed to linger for a second. Nubik opened the packet and discovered the soldier had left him several cigarettes.

'I'll save them for later.'

The two soldiers shrugged and started walking off, although one of them turned around and looked back at Nubik, perhaps sensing that there was something out of the ordinary about him. But they did not go back to him. He took a cigarette from the pack but had no means of lighting it. He did not, in fact, smoke, but felt the need to destroy Anna's note. He had not seen, and could not see, anywhere he felt he could safely throw the paper away. Coming from the house the two soldiers had just left, he could hear the sounds of a party in full swing. He hesitated: he could either carry on walking, though he still felt the piece of paper was a liability, or go and knock at the house and ask for a light. He decided to risk it. Some kind of foot-soldier or private opened the door, but when Nubik told him what he wanted, he started to close the door on him. Just before it shut, a woman who had followed the foot-soldier to the door opened it again, asking him what the stranger wanted. A light for his cigarette. She opened the door wide, and the light from inside shone full on Nubik's face, though the young woman did not seem to take any interest in him, except for telling the private to go and get what the gentleman required. The young woman also vanished.

She returned in a minute, carrying a glass of wine which she offered Nubik. He took the glass but did not put it to his lips, the years and the war having made him suspicious.

'You know Anna and Beata. I have been told to look out for you. I'm glad you're here. But I must get back to the party. I'm entertaining,' she said.

'I can tell you about Anna —'

'Tomorrow, at this address.'

She whispered an address for a meeting the following afternoon and dissolved into the lights and sounds of drinking and revelry, leaving Nubik to slip away into the night. He turned around, only to see the private peering out from the gap between the door and the frame until it closed.

Was this how this girl was getting through the war, he wondered, serving Nazi officers who, if they were anything like the two soldiers, seemed to be waiting for the end after channeling all their energy into doing as much evil as possible without caring whether their lives or afterlives, if they had one, would be anything different from the hell and death they had put millions of people through? First Beata, and now this friend of Anna's?

Nubik first forgot to burn the shred of paper and, when he did remember it some days later, he decided not to destroy it. It was some kind of keepsake.

'Anna never forgot you,' said the young woman.

'Nor I her,' replied Nubik. 'We have been back in touch, most recently a week ago. We fell in together again at once. We both nearly got killed but managed to get away. Anna and I were driving north with Lichtblau, a friend of ours and a Nazi deserter. Lichtblau's family is, we hope, in England by now. All of us were trying to join them in England. The opportunity was too good for Anna to pass up. She gave me a slip of paper with her parents' address on it in our own private code. I found the piece of paper in my pocket. She must have put it there. I don't know why, or at least she did not tell me why. It's in her handwriting, and it wasn't there before we were in the car together, so I'm as sure as I can be that it was she who put it there. I must have been asleep at the time.'

He continued, 'The further we got from Vienna, the more uneasy I felt. I finally could not go on. I asked them to stop the car so I could turn round and return to Vienna. Felix Lichtblau quite understood, he who for so long had felt unable to leave Vienna. I was not surprised to find Anna's note, though. She seems to want me to find out how her family and friends all are, as she'll naturally be worried about them and knows they will be about her. She's well aware her disappearance may get them into trouble with the Nazis.'

'The Nazis,' said Elfriede, the young woman, 'have apparently stopped checking up on them since Beata began to be useful to them, and I in this house. If there is a choice between being sent to a camp to die and doing what I do, I'll do what I do, for a little longer at least. It may not be resistance, but it doesn't help the Reich. Anna's father works as a clerk in a Nazi office — don't worry, he is not and has never been, a Nazi. He resists them secretly, as he can, as you do. The problem is some of his colleagues go to Anna's parents' place from time to time.'

Nubik raised his eyebrows.

'He does not invite them. He hates them. So does Anna's mother, who has to put up with their jokes and drunkenness. But they are used to seeing Anna there. They will soon be wondering where she's got to.'

'The parents will have to leave,' said Nubik.

'They would have got away a long time ago if they could.'

'Anna would never forgive me if I did not do all I could to help them. To help them flee before they are taken away by force.'

There was a pause. Then Nubik said:

'Do you know how I've survived in this war?'

Elfriede laughed. 'I've heard. You've been keeping the Nazis supplied with their favorite substances.'

'That's been my way of doing whatever I can to do the Nazis as much harm as possible. None of the substances I sold them was ever what I claimed it was. Most of them were poisonous. My clients thought they were getting high-quality Pervitin specially made for them. But they weren't. I was selling them rubbish. Some of my clients died after ingesting those substances, and no one realized why they had died.

'It's not my fault they're so gullible. But how can we help the parents get away? We could tell the Nazis Anna's gone ahead to prepare her wedding, which is due to take place some way away from Vienna in an obscure country village. We'll say she's marrying a Nazi soldier. Her father will tell his colleagues he has to take a week off for his daughter's wedding.'

'You certainly have imagination. You can be the chauffeur driving Anna's parents, Beata and me to the wedding.'

'A small private wedding, almost no guests, only very close family and you. The Nazis shouldn't balk at that.'

'The Mayers are attached to Vienna,' said Nubik. 'But then again, that's a reason for leaving. Vienna grows less like Vienna by the day.'

Early next morning, Nubik went straight to the address Anna had encoded for him on the slip of paper. He hoped to catch Anna's father on his way out to work. Elfriede had told him she would try and tell Beata and Anna's parents about Nubik's intended visit but was unsure because she was afraid the parents' phone was being tapped. He knocked at the door. Silence. He knocked again. The door opened suddenly into the inside; two hands grabbed him around the throat and dragged him into the flat. He heard the front door shut behind him. The hands around his neck dragged him into the living room and thrust him to the floor before he could work out what was going on or in whose presence he was. Then someone held a gun barrel to his back while someone else blindfolded his eyes.

'What is your business here?' said a man's voice.

'Who are you?' Nubik said.

Someone slapped him across the mouth, and he tasted the blood flow from a split lip.

'Just answer.'

'I'm a friend of the family.'

Anna's parents were tied to chairs with their hands behind their backs but not blindfolded or gagged. In the room were two Nazi officers, who now looked to the parents for confirmation: they nodded.

'You know that Anna, the eldest Mayer daughter, has disappeared?' said one of the officers. 'We're here to find out her whereabouts.'

'I may be able to say a word or two about that. Please remove the blindfold, give me a handkerchief to swab my lip, and set me free. I don't believe I'm under arrest or even under suspicion.'

He fell silent and let his head slump forward onto his chest. He could hear the wail of sirens and, though a common sound in the city, wondered whether they signaled the approaching end of the war. Or was it just wishful thinking? One of the soldiers removed Nubik's blindfold. He blinked, and Anna's parents came into view. They were shaking, and their faces had lost all color.

'I understand Anna has not disappeared, but she cannot be reached at the moment.'

'Go on,' the officer said.

'I've already told you. If you want to know more, you'll have to untie me.'

The two officers seemed to find Nubik's calm stubbornness convincing and irritating in equal measure. They decided to untie him, 'but don't move a muscle.'

'She's getting married,' Nubik said.

The two officers looked at each other and at Anna's parents, who nodded. Around two in the morning of the previous night, Elfriede had managed to get through to the Mayer parents by phone. Anna had left Vienna to get married, and they would learn more later. She had then cut off. No phone tapper, she thought, would have been astonished to hear what she had told her parents, even though they might have been taken aback by such a sudden announcement.

'You never told us about this, Gunther,' one of the soldiers said to Anna's father, 'I thought we were friends.'

Anna's father replied, 'We're no longer friends, if we ever were.'

'When we asked you where your elder daughter was, you replied you didn't know.'

'I don't.'

Someone knocked at the front door of the flat. One of the soldiers went to open it.

'Who is it?'

'Beata. And I've got something nice for you.'

He opened the door. She put one arm around him and held a bottle in her other hand. She kissed him on the mouth and then poured some liquid from the bottle down his throat.

'Mmm... Delicious.'

'What? Me, darling? Or the drink?'

'Both.'

She was wearing a scarf and wrapped it around the soldier's neck. Now she began to caress him, feeling awkward about using her act in front of her parents.

'Does it feel good?' she asked. She was edging him gently, imperceptibly, out of the door, half-blinding him with the scarf, trickling the liquid into his mouth.

The poison started to take effect. He found himself choking.

'I need air.'

She opened the door at the end of the corridor that led off from the flat. It gave onto a fire escape. Still caressing him, she put the bottle down on top of the fire escape, where they were both standing. She edged him towards the fire escape railing so that he was leaning with his back against it.

'Feeling better now?'

She pressed up to him. His eyes were closed. 'I'm spinning, spinning....'

'Spinning into space?' she asked.

'Spinning into —'

She pushed him over the top of the railing with her left hand. He grunted, falling into the back courtyard amid the trashcans and rats.

'Beata?' She heard her father's voice and walked back down the corridor to her parent's flat. In the living room, she found her mother and father, Nubik and the other Nazi soldier. 'Where's my colleague?'

'He got a little excited, and when I gave him some of this' — she held her bottle up — 'he got a little overheated, too. He's gone out to the fire escape to cool down —'

'And throw up?' the soldier said.

'Quite,' Beata said.

The soldier said, 'I'll wait till he comes back. None of you move.'

'Be careful with guns around my mummy and daddy. What are you holding them hostage for? Can't you see my father's infirm? He already spends much of his waking day in a wheelchair. His legs gave out years ago.' She gave her father a reassuring look to tell him she knew what she was doing and not to respond.

'Your sister has disappeared. Maybe she's working for the enemies of the Reich. We haven't been able to learn much from your parents or this man.'

Beata ignored this, saying: 'You look tired, darling. Are they working you too hard?'

The soldier was lusting after the bottle Beata was holding — or perhaps not the bottle but her.

'Want a drop?'

'Where's my colleague?' the soldier said again.

'Taking the air, darling, I told you. Have a drink. You're wasting your time. You can do whatever you like with us: we don't know where Anna is any more than you do. We wish we did.'

She walked over to the soldier. This was their only chance of getting out of the situation. Her father was refusing to meet anyone's gaze and stared into the middle distance. Her mother looked suddenly old and frail. Perhaps she would die, exhausted by the heartbreak and evil of the war, in the next few hours.

The Nazi seemed at a loss as to what to do. If he went out to look for his colleague, he would be leaving the people he was supposed to be interrogating to their own devices. Beata noticed from the look in his eye that he wanted her and wanted her bottle. She fleetingly glanced at Nubik to let him know she was going to try something. She forced a smile into her eyes and drew the soldier's gaze to hers. She put the bottle down on a table next to her. The sound of a man groaning reached them. Beata still held the soldier's gaze.

'Who, or what, was that?'

'Don't you like me? It was nothing, darling. Just an elderly neighbor of ours. He's a bit mad.'

She looked away from the soldier and towards the bottle. She glanced all the while from the soldier's eyes to the bottle and back again. Beata was now facing Nubik, while the soldier had his back to Nubik.

'Where is my colleague?' the soldier shouted, as though coming abruptly to his senses. Again, the sound of a man groaning.

'That was him, wasn't it? What have you done to him, you little slut?'

Beata's father appeared to be paying little or no attention to the soldier. But hearing his daughter being called a slut was too much for him. He dived for the soldier's calves and brought him to the floor with a rugby tackle.

The soldier was so astonished he could barely struggle against the old man. Nubik held him down. Beata decided to try and pour the liquid down his throat.

Nubik held the man's jaws open while Beata thrust the neck of the bottle into his mouth and poured in the liquid. He sputtered and choked so that some of the liquid flew back into Beata's face. She took her eye off the Nazi to wipe the foul stuff out of her eyes. The Nazi took advantage of this brief lull to whip the revolver out of his pocket and fire several bullets. The retort from the gun was so loud, and the reaction of the man's body so convulsive that Beata's mother screamed; Beata and Nubik were thrown backward. The man turned round to face into the room and fired at the first person he saw — Beata's mother. Nubik threw himself in front of the latter and was shot in the calf, while Beata's father, in another fit of superhuman strength that his frail frame belied, leaped at the man and brought him to the floor once again. The man tried to fire again, but Nubik kicked the gun out of his hand. Beata grabbed it and shot him dead.

'I'll dispose of the body,' said Beata, as cool as though she had been disposing of bodies all her life.

Beata's mother was unhurt but crying, while her father had reverted to the impassive expression he had worn on his face a few minutes before. Beata tied up Nubik's wound with a piece of rag. He felt the tiniest motion of joy run through his heart.

Without changing his expression or looking at anyone in particular, Beata's father said: 'The address book. Dr. Riegler.'

Beata went at once to her father's writing desk and took his address book out of the top drawer. She turned to R and phoned Dr. Riegler.

'I'll come straight away.'

When she arrived, Dr. Riegler said, 'I have no nurse to assist me.'

'Just tell me what to do,' Beata said.

They turned Nubik over onto his back — he had been lying on his side groaning, clutching his leg.

'Help me get him onto the sofa.'

Along with the doctor, Beata and her mother and father carried Nubik over to the sofa and laid him on it. When they had shifted him, they saw a pool of blood on the floor. The doctor took off the bandage, examined Nubik's calf and felt it.

'There's a bullet lodged in here. I'll have to gouge it out with a scalpel. But I've used all my painkiller up, what with the war.'

'Water,' Nubik coughed. Beata's mother brought him a glass of water and held it to his lips so he could sip from it.

'I have something that might help me,' Nubik said after a silence. 'My stock in trade,' flickering a smile at the doctor.

'Where is it?' she said.

'Untie my belt. Undo my trousers.'

Inside them, the doctor discovered a pouch with dozens of drugs — pills, capsules, syringes, vials with droppers.

'Take out the blue ones. I'll take one of those.'

'Better take two or three,' the doctor said, 'this is likely going to hurt.'

She disinfected the wound, pushed back the hairs surrounding it, and peered into it.

'The bullet seems to have gone in rather far. It might start to work itself loose and dislodge itself over the next week or so, especially if you are able to get up and walk around a little. In that case, it would be much easier for me to take out and less painful for you. Or I could try and take it out now. Without an anesthetic, you'd have to grit your teeth.'

'The painkiller seems to be working,' Nubik said, 'and the longer the bullet stays in my calf, the greater the risk of infection. Also, if we delay the extraction of the bullet, I'll just be a burden to Herr and Frau Mayer.'

'You won't be a —,' Beata's mother started to say. But she was interrupted by a scream coming from Nubik. The doctor had driven her scalpel deep into Nubik's wound and scooped the bullet out with it.

'More pills!' Nubik shrieked.

'One will suffice,' the doctor said. 'Any more, and you'll be in danger of dying from an overdose.'

'This is already worse than death.'

'Here's one,' the doctor said.

Nubik, lying on the sofa on his back, writhed in pain.

He soon calmed down. The doctor showed him the bullet. He turned away from it in disgust. He was not the kind of person who cared what happened to him, for better or worse. He had no interest in his wounds, whatever kind they might be. He was just glad he had been able to save Beata's mother from certain death. He thought: *That is why I could not leave Vienna when I had the chance to. This is the only place where I feel I can be of any real use.*

Then he heard another voice telling him: *Nonsense! Anyone can be of any use anywhere. You just wanted to indulge yourself again in this sty of decadence. Who are you? Where are you?'*

He called out; looked around. The sea sparkled and frothed. Waves pushed toward the shore. Gulls circled in the sky. They swooped, grey-white darts of noise. He could tell from their swooping down to the sea that the sun had shone warm on the sea, and its afterglow could still be felt in the early evening in the water itself. Fish only came to the surface if the day had been warm. Strange that evolution had not taught the fish to stay below the water's surface; that if they rose to the top, they were likely to be swiped up into the air and eaten by a gull. The attraction of the sun's warmth was too strong for them; it drove them crazy. He drew his gaze from the gulls back to the beach. He wanted to see whose voice it was addressing him a moment before. A small ship lay immobile on the water, not far from the shore. People were disembarking, carrying cases, walking knee-high in the water till they reached the sand. A rotund, smiling middle-aged man was greeting a small group, three young men and a woman.

Someone was shaking him. He woke up, reassured by the dream, even though he felt it had not yet finished and had more to say to him. Beata had brought him warm milk.

'You haven't eaten or drunk for two days. But you seemed to be having a good dream.'

'My dream was safe enough,' Nubik said, 'it is only we who are not.'

He looked out of the window at the expanse of blue sky.

'Perhaps I dreamed I was a seagull, hovering over sea and shore. I was a seagull who could read human beings.'

'Enough talking,' Beata said, 'or you'll start to lose your strength again.'

'I have lost everything else.'

'So have we all,' Beata replied.

Anna had known that her leaving Vienna would make her family even more vulnerable than before. And that had proved to be true. And yet, Nubik thought, here they were, helping and protecting him. He had survived the early years of the war by selling fake drugs to the Nazis in the guise of a businessman. His friendship with the Lichtblaus had enabled him to join Lichtblau's Resistance circle and — along with the poisonous substances he sold the Nazis — had enabled him to do some slight but real harm to the Nazi war machine. But the bullet in his calf, though it had weakened nothing of his resolve, if not strengthened it, had weakened him in body. *The war will soon be over,* he thought. He could try and organize the departure of Beata, her parents and himself, and make a break for it. He could try and move them all to another flat in Vienna, where with luck, they would not be quickly identified and could hope to tough it out till the end of the war. He could look for Schwartz the printer and other members of Lichtblau's Resistance group.

Nubik now walked with a limp. He could walk fast but could not run. He was able to drive a car, but riding a bike would be hard. He barely gave himself a thought, however. His thoughts were constantly drawn back to Anna. He had always idealized Kristina Lichtblau; she had always been remote; but Anna was a woman he felt he could be close to, whom he had been close to, whom he still felt close to, but who had somehow eluded him, or whom he had somehow let slip through his fingers. He had never tried to hold her back, and when she had wanted to flee, he had helped her. He loved Beata in a brotherly fashion and loved her all the more for what she had done for him. Her parents were intelligent, bewildered by the war, not understanding how, after the humiliation of the First War, so many people had so easily favored entry into the Second. For the satisfaction of revenge? What satisfaction? Their heart and home were in Vienna. But one daughter had left, and another, they sensed, longed to leave. There again, Vienna was hardly home to anyone anymore — many of those who remained felt almost as though they had become exiles in their own city.

Nubik decided he would try and find Schwartz the printer. Because of his complicated business dealings with the Nazis, while managing to remain apart from them, they had always reluctantly tolerated Nubik. Some thought he might well be conspiring with the enemy, though nothing had ever been proved on this score. Similarly, some who would have nothing to do with the Nazis and whose one desire was to be rid of them forever, did not trust Nubik, although the Lichtblaus, Schwartz and the others had never doubted him and knew his commerce with the Nazis was designed to harm them.

Nubik nevertheless felt he was in a quandary. He wanted to go and find Anna, who was on her way to England. He wanted to save her family and did not see how he could do so except by taking them away from Vienna, and it was unlikely her parents would go. He had been unable to face going far from Vienna, or at least being forced out of the city by the pressure of war, and was loath to leave again. But if he did, it would not be to save his own skin — by which he set so little store — but to save and be with people he knew and loved.

He found Schwartz the printer's door locked. He knocked on it in the cryptic way he and his Resistance comrades had agreed. But no one came. He tried to peer through the window. He could not make out whether the place, especially the printing machines, looked abandoned or not. He waited a couple of minutes and then gave the coded knock again. No answer again. He started walking away. As he was doing so, a head popped out of a third-story window of the building next door to Schwartz's.

'If you're looking for Schwartz, I haven't seen him for a while. A week, maybe ten days.'

'Ah,' Nubik said. 'Thank you.'

'Are you Alfred Nubik?'

'Who are you?' Nubik had never heard Schwartz mention a neighbor.

'Come up if you like. Schwartz has left something for you. If you want it, you can come straight through the front door. You won't need a key.'

Nubik walked in but hesitated in the hallway: what if he were walking into a trap? Whatever Schwartz had left for him, for all he knew, it might save his own life and those of Beata and her parents. If this was an ambush, and this neighbor intended to turn him over to the Gestapo — well, what of it?

Never one to shirk a challenge, he walked up the three flights of stairs. The neighbor was standing in her open doorway as he reached the third-floor landing. She was a woman who looked about thirty — a couple of years younger than Nubik.

'Come in. You look tired after your walk up the stairs.'

Nubik's face did show the strain on his left leg and hip. She led him into her studio flat.

'Your name is?'

'Ingeborg Shroder. Schwartz has left you a message. He told me more or less what was in it.'

Nubik opened the envelope the woman handed him. The message read:

We gather the Russians are not far away now. They look almost certain to free Vienna, and the war will be over. But between now and then, word has reached us that the Nazis intend to batten down on the city one last time and round up anyone who looks even remotely suspicious to them. If you are reading this, it means you and Ingeborg are still in Vienna. I tried to persuade her to leave, but she wouldn't. You must leave as soon as you read this and try to persuade Ingeborg to do the same. I am trying to make my way to Switzerland. By the time you read this, I may be dead or alive. I will send word to Vienna and Oxford if I manage to get to Switzerland. I know Ingeborg will help you, just as she always helped me when we were neighbors. If you can see any use for my printing press while you are nearby, you are welcome to go in and treat the place as your own. Ingeborg has the key.

The note closed with a friendly greeting, and that was all. Nubik, dazed as though he had just suddenly awoken from a dream, looked up from the message. It even took him a second to remember where he was and who Ingeborg was.

'You read it,' he said, 'it's for you as much as it is for me.'

'I know what he says. He thinks it's foolish for either of us to stay in Vienna, and he may be right. But...'

'Will you come with me to Schwartz's? I feel like looking one last time at the place where we held our meetings and tried to look to a future for Vienna.'

Ingeborg nodded. 'But your leg and hip don't look good to me. Stay here, at least for tonight. If they haven't arrested us, we'll go next door to the printing press.'

She took him by the hand: 'Come.'

In the early morning light, they heard rumbling on the roads and the rattle of occasional gunfire as they walked out of Ingeborg's building and went to Schwartz's flat next door. The place was in perfect order. Doubtless, Schwartz had tried to make it look as nondescript as possible and, above all, that it had not been abandoned. In the middle of the room stood the compositor's equipment and printing machine. At the back of the room was a closed door which Nubik knew led to Schwartz's spare room. Nubik flopped into an armchair and laughed, almost with relief.

'Why're you laughing?' Ingeborg said.

'We're still here and still alive. Why shouldn't it last?'

That closed door suddenly slammed open. A man in a dark suit and peaked cap walked towards them, pointing a machine gun. Was this the trap Nubik had feared? And had Ingeborg knowingly led him into it?

'Because,' said the man, 'the lives of enemies of the Reich never last.'

'How did you get in?' Nubik said.

'You don't mean to tell me this is not a meeting-room for Resistance plotters?'

'What plotters? What plot?' Nubik said. 'Whether by hemlock or decapitation, anyway, the plot is always the same.'

'Look,' Ingeborg said, 'why prolong the usual comedy? You've got the gun. If you think we've done wrong — or whatever you think — why not shoot us now? After all, those are your methods, aren't they? Otherwise,' she said, walking up to him and looking him straight in the eye, 'get out of here. You know you've as good as lost the war. You have nothing more to gain from it.'

The man made as though to strike Ingeborg over the head with the butt of his machine-gun when Nubik said softly to him:

'What about your colleague? Why is he waiting? Wouldn't he like to kill us now, just like you?'

'What colleague?'

'What do you mean, what colleague? The one standing behind you, of course.'

The man turned around. Nubik shouted to Ingeborg, 'Run!' and hurled himself on the man, pinning him to the floor. Ingeborg did not run, though. She rushed to the two men and wrested the machine-gun away from under the soldier. She pressed it to his temple as Nubik pushed the man away and stood up.

'Hands above your head, now!' Ingeborg pressed the barrel harder against his temple. 'What are we going to do with him? Shoot him dead and have done with it?' The man seemed to be crying. 'Don't kill me! Please don't!'

'Why do they always start out so virile and mighty with a gun in their hands, yet as soon as you reverse the situation and threaten them with their own methods, they lose all dignity and end up so pitiful? You were quite prepared to kill us a few minutes ago. You can hardly be surprised if we wish to return the compliment.'

'I can help you get out of the city if that's what you want to do.'

Ingeborg pressed the barrel mouth still harder against the man's temple, saying:

'Don't try to bribe us. Just tell us how you think you can help us.'

'But first, tell us how you come to be here,' Nubik said.

'We've been keeping an eye on this place for some time. We've been taking it in turns to stay here on twenty-four-hour shifts. It's been empty and quiet, but yesterday someone was knocking — maybe it was you. I thought whoever it was would probably be back.'

The man's jacket fell open level with his belt. Ingeborg saw at once that he had a revolver in a holster. His hand was a few inches from it, and he clearly intended to use it if he could.

Ingeborg used the gun barrel to remove the man's hand from his belt and then pressed it against his temple again while taking the revolver out of its holster and throwing it to Nubik.

'You say you want to help us, but you were just about to use your pistol on us.'

Someone knocked at the door.

'Get up,' Nubik said to the man. Ingeborg positioned herself to the side of the door. Nubik now held the barrel of the machine gun to the man's back.

'Keep your hands on your head and walk to the door. The slightest false move, and I'll shoot.'

'Come in,' Nubik called when they got to the door. Ingeborg opened it. He said it loud and imperious, hoping the soldier at the door would think the words had come from his colleague. The soldier at the door seemed a little distracted or drunk, and as he walked in, Ingeborg had no trouble threatening him from behind and neutralizing him.

'As you like,' the soldier said, 'for us, the war's over, or as good as over.' He was slurring his words. He had likely tried to drink himself into a state of oblivion in which he could forget his probable defeat.

'You'll both have to leave this place with us. We'll drop this man off —'

'My brother,' the man said to Nubik.

'Your brother, if you say so. We'll drop him off in a side street.'

So the Nazis themselves realized they were about to lose the war. Nubik thought it best to gather up Beata and her parents and get them out of the city as soon as possible since the battle for ultimate control of the city and country threatened to be vicious. If he wanted to do so, he would have to turn his back, perhaps forever, on Vienna. If he started to leave, he felt he would not return. But for now, he and Ingeborg had to maneuver their way out of Schwartz's printing office and through the Vienna streets with these two Nazi brothers, not letting anyone suspect that the latter were their prisoners. But how would this be possible?

Nubik told Ingeborg to keep her gun trained on the two men while he went to Schwartz's spare room and got some of the printer's clothes out of his wardrobe. He returned, told the younger brother to take off his uniform and put Schwartz's clothes on. He put the soldier's uniform on over his own clothes and donned his cap. Ingeborg smiled at him. Unbeknownst to her, this, Nubik felt, was the first ray of sunshine that had fallen on him for some time. Why did he always think his place was with the Lichtblaus? Couldn't he settle down somewhere with a wife and start over? If, that is, he made it to the end of the war. His mind was wandering; he drew it back to the present. He told Ingeborg she had to play the prisoner; she nodded. This was real *Burgtheater*. City of theatre, masks, acting.

Out in the street, the air felt thick with expectation (or was he only imagining it?), and there seemed to be silence everywhere. Nubik walked behind the other three. Ingeborg and the younger Nazi walked in front, the other Nazi between them and Nubik. They were passing an alleyway to the right when Ingeborg turned round to Nubik, signaling to him that they could leave the younger man in that alleyway. Nubik could feel something heavy and metallic inside the pocket of the soldier's jacket he was wearing. He pulled out what was a pair of handcuffs. Just what he needed. He handed them to the older Nazi and ordered him to put them on his 'brother's' wrists behind his back. Then as he looked down the alley, Nubik spotted some railings running along the front garden of a house. They handcuffed him to the railings and used Ingeborg's scarf to gag him. Nubik forced him at gunpoint to swallow a pill, and then the three of them — Nubik, Ingeborg and the elder Nazi brother — walked back to the street. Nubik turned around just before they moved away from the entrance to the alley and saw what he expected to see: the man's hands were still cuffed to the railings behind him, and he had slumped forward so that his forehead was almost touching the ground and he was down on his knees. The drug would take a few hours to wear off, and Nubik counted on being far away by then.

Nevertheless, Nubik started to wonder whether he should not have killed the younger Nazi rather than immobilizing him and giving him a soporific. That might have lent him more leverage over the older one, though it might have de-moralized the latter so much that he would have begged to be killed along with his brother. As it was, he could not tell whether the Nazi took him seriously or whether he, Nubik, could take the other seriously. This game of second-guessing was getting too much for Nubik.

The man said, 'We'll get a car from a Nazi garage and then go and pick up this family you've been talking about. Then you can get away from this city, with or without me. If I get you the car, the least you can do is do me a favor. It is only a minor one: I would like the key to unlock my brother's handcuffs.'

'How dare you ask a favor of us?' Ingeborg said, almost slapping the Nazi. 'We would have been out of here long ago but for you and your brother. We would never have had this war but for you.'

'How far to your garage?'

'We're nearly there now.'

When they reached the garage, which looked like a hangar, it was locked up. The Nazi banged on the iron front door. No one came to open it. He led them round to the back of the structure, to a wooden door. The man pushed it open. He turned on the lights. Some of the cars had military markings on them; others looked like civilian vehicles. As they walked down the aisle of the hangar with rows of cars on each side of them, Nubik spotted a dark red saloon car which he felt was big enough for five or six people without being especially conspicuous. He chose that one.

'I'll need to go and get the key from the booth over there in the corner,' the Nazi said.

'Not without us.' Ingeborg and Nubik kept their guns trained on the man as the three of them walked over to the booth. Keys hung on hooks; the man seemed to know which keys to take down for the car in question. The Nazi drove them out into the street, and then Nubik guided him to where Beata's parents lived. Beata was there with them, ready to go. They had one suitcase packed for the three of them.

'This man is our prisoner. We found him lurking where he had no business to be. He and his brother have caused us much trouble. We did not kill his brother but ditched him. If he alerts the authorities, they will be after us in a short while.'

'What do you intend to do about this man?' Beata's father said.

'You need me,' broke in the man.

'We don't,' Nubik said.

'With me, you're sure to be able to leave Vienna, even Austria.'

Beata's father spoke again: 'None of them can be trusted. They'll say anything to save their own skins. They'd spit in their mothers' faces if it got them the slightest advantage. If I had my way and the guns you're holding, I'd shoot him dead on the spot.'

'I never wanted this war. I've taken no part in exterminating Jews. I always managed to find an excuse to skive off whenever round-ups were being organized.'

This time, Ingeborg slapped the man around the face.

'You've taken no part in the exterminations? But what did you ever do to stop them? You've spent your life asking no questions, playing the yes-man, and look where it's got you and all of us.'

'Let me live. I'll look after my brother. He's weak. He can't survive alone; he only got conscripted instead of being removed to a camp for weakness.'

'You will drive us,' Nubik said, 'but I won't guarantee your safety or your future once you have served our purpose.'

The man gave the faintest nod. Then the seven of them — Beata and Anna's parents, Beata, Nubik, Ingeborg and the soldier — walked out of the house to the red saloon car. Nubik wondered if he would ever see Vienna again — wondered if he would ever want to see Vienna again.

They stopped at a red light. Before they realized what was happening, a man in a black peaked cap and black Nazi uniform, with long leather boots, stepped out in front of the car, which was at once surrounded by four or five soldiers. The gaze of the man standing just in front of the car met that of the one driving it.

'My brother.'

The driver made as if to get out of the car.

'You can't get out of the car,' Nubik said. 'We have our guns trained on you all the time. We need to be moving on, whether this man is your brother or not. Especially if he is your brother.'

The man replied, 'My brother only has to give them the word, and the soldiers surrounding the car will shoot you all.'

'You wanted to come with us. If your brother and these others find out about that, you'll be taken in as a traitor and if, that is, they don't kill you straight away.'

Not for the first time, Nubik felt he had drawn Beata and her parents into a trap that might prove to be the death of them. Why hadn't he killed this Nazi's brother when he had the chance to, instead of drugging him and chaining him up? If he shot the driver of the car now, it would mean certain death for them all. The brother walked round to the car window next to the driver's seat. He motioned to his brother to wind it down. But just then, a line of tanks came rolling towards the car from behind. The tank in front boomed out a signal to the dark red saloon car to get off its path.

Although most of the tanks simply overtook the red car, two stayed behind it, wanting to make sure the driver knew who was in charge. But one of the soldiers the younger Nazi brother had with him was standing in front of the car, and there seemed to be nothing Nubik and his companions could do. The rumble of the tanks rolling by made it hard for the two brothers to hear each other, and they began to shout. Some soldiers from the tanks soon joined them in an effort to try and dislodge the car. The younger brother was brandishing a gun. One of the tank men was arguing with the soldier standing in front of the car, telling him to move to the side so that the car would stop obstructing the traffic. That soldier was gesticulating wildly. Tears streamed down Beata's father's face. His wife gripped his hand to try and help him control his emotions. Sitting in the passenger seat, Ingeborg had her gun pointed at the driver from under a scarf on her lap. The soldier standing in front was telling the tank man that he was at the orders of the officer talking to the driver of the red car. That officer had told him not to move. The tank man abruptly screamed that he would get back in his tank and roll straight down on the car and those standing around it if they did not get out of the way. Much chaos and shouting ensued.

The soldier standing in front of the car, getting fidgety, kept waiting for his superior, the younger Nazi brother, to give him a new order, either to stay where he was or move. A line of tanks and cars rolled along the road in the distance: they were coming towards the car and seemed to be headed for the city. The younger Nazi brother at last called to the soldier standing in front of the car to come to him. Nubik tried to catch Ingeborg's eye, but she had her gaze fixed on the car's driver. Nubik coughed. She turned around for a split second and glanced at him. With his eyes and chin, he indicated the accelerator. She gave an imperceptible nod.

The two brothers were still deep in discussion, the conversation having got even more involved with the addition of the soldier previously standing in front of the car. All three were shouting to each other to make themselves heard, all the more as Ingeborg had forbidden the driver to wind his window down. The younger brother had begun to suspect his brother of voluntarily being the prisoner of the others in the car and of deserting the Führer and the party. Ingeborg shifted her left foot over to the accelerator and pressed it down to the floor. The car shot forward so fast that no tank could have kept up with it. The younger brother fired his pistol at the car but did not hit it. Ingeborg had taken the wheel with her left hand and steered the car for a minute while the driver gained control of his senses. Beata and her parents had their eyes shut and were bracing themselves, their shoulders hunched and tense.

'I only hope the Allies are going to let us be,' said the soldier.

Nubik scoffed. 'Better them than fall into the hands of the Führer's men again.'

Lichtblau and his friend, Dieter, had managed to get through a number of checkpoints. These were rarer anyway than they had feared. They were now close to the Austrian border with Switzerland. They breathed a sigh of relief. They were almost in safety. Occasional trucks and cars, which did not look German, passed them going the other way. They had one more checkpoint to pass through before the border and freedom. Hailed by an officer, they automatically showed their papers, expecting that it would be the usual formality. Instead, the officer took the documents away, returned five minutes later with Dieter's alone, told the latter not only that he could, but that he must, leave the checkpoint and not wait for

Lichtblau, and told the latter to get out of the car and come with him to the office. As he walked to the office, Lichtblau saw a man he knew only too well: Markus Jäger.

'Plutocratic whores? Isn't that what the poem said?'

'If the cap fits. But very clever of you, Jäger, to ask me to autograph my manuscript. I'm sure your new friends — or perhaps they are not so new — will reward you and your brother handsomely for your services.'

'My brother's doings are no concern of mine.'

'You're lying. You're two peas in a pod.'

'Enough talk,' said the soldier. 'Felix Lichtblau, for your betrayal of the Reich, for writing and publishing this work, you will be summarily executed tomorrow as an enemy of the Reich and the Führer. The bill for your execution will be sent to your wife.'

'My widow,' smiled Lichtblau.

One way or another…

Twenty-Eight

Tom Oliver was wining and dining his guests, who were now, as for them, out of the Führer's clutches, on the first floor of a Cornmarket restaurant — one he was particularly fond of, as his parents had told him they had had their wedding lunch there. He derived no egotistical satisfaction from his guests' now being ensconced in the refuge that was Oxford in the early spring of 1945. He was just glad that, as far as he knew, no one had died because of his initiatives. He longed for the rhythms of university life, the peacetime ones, skinny-dipping in the Cherwell, traveling freely across Europe in the summers, indulging his appetites. His work with the Lichtblaus was not over, though. Werner and Johannes had not sent word for some time now. Kristina, Thedel and Heinrich smiled and appeared to delight in Tom Oliver's endless monologue – he only ever stopped talking when he was alone, reading or writing. Apart from that, he kept up an uninterrupted flow of speech. But — and this was something about him that was not easy to guess — he was also observant, even sensitive. He realized that Kristina Lichtblau and Heinrich would never be at rest until they were reunited with Johannes. But he and Werner were on the move, as far as they knew, and their silence was due to the necessity for being discreet. That is what they told themselves. They smiled at Tom Oliver, but the latter knew they were only half-listening to him. He knew, too, that their anxiety for Johannes made it hard for them to make small-talk.

'If I hear the slightest word, I'll let you know at once, I promise,' said Tom Oliver, refilling their glasses as though to clinch his promise. He would have winked at them reassuringly if the circumstances had not been so grave. Instead, they drank a hopeful toast to the safe arrival of Johannes and Werner. Just as they did so, a waiter came over to their table and murmured in Tom Oliver's ear. 'I'm told there's someone on the phone for me. I'll be back shortly. Do excuse me.' He wiped his lips with his white serviette, bowed to Kristina, and followed the waiter downstairs to the phone.

As soon as Tom Oliver was out of sight, Heinrich said to his mother, 'What good is our life here to anybody, in the midst of all this comfort and learning?'

'Where we are and what good our life is doesn't matter. What matters is the safety of our family and our hope that we will soon be reunited.'

'Our delightful host takes care of our every need, and I have nothing to do all day except wait for news of my brother. And that's no occupation.'

'But waiting is an occupation,' replied Kristina, 'how we wait, what we do while waiting, how patient we can be: all these things are active. They're a measure of our character. And you'll soon be going to university.'

'Hundreds of thousands of lives, maybe more, whole families, wiped out by that foul regime, and you talk of patience and character.'

'Complaining won't bring those people back to life.'

'If Johannes isn't here within the next ten days,' said Heinrich, 'I'm going back to the Continent to look for him.'

'And I'll go with you,' Thedel said to Heinrich.

'You can't do anything more for him than Werner's doing for him at this moment.'

'Maybe he and Werner are no longer traveling together. Maybe Werner's dead —'

'Maybe they're both dead,' retorted Kristina, 'but we have to go on hoping and praying they're alive and well and on their way to us right this minute.'

Heinrich fell silent. Although he knew such bickering did no good and only upset both his mother and himself — though she kept it hidden — he felt it was the only way he could let out some of the anxiety that was constantly eating away at him. He felt ashamed that when this mood overtook him, he was unable to support his mother and that she managed to be strong enough, rather, to support him.

Tom Oliver returned to the table. His face was grim. He smiled in greeting, sat down and took a swig from his glass of wine. His gaze traveled from Heinrich to Frau Lichtblau to Thedel, and he looked them all in the eye.

'That was Werner on the phone. He's currently in the South of England, on his way to Oxford. He has found some people who believe his story and have taken him under their wing. They're on their way to the Midlands and will drop Werner off in Oxford or near it. He says he got separated from Johannes somewhere in Normandy. They were trying to get to the coast. They got shot at by some Germans as they were walking along a road. Neither of them got hit. Both ran into the undergrowth by the roadside. Werner crouched down and kept still till the soldiers who had fired at them were well away. But Johannes kept on running. Werner saw him emerge from the undergrowth into an open field. He ran across the field until he was no longer even a dot in the landscape. Werner decided that it was unwise to risk getting lost in the Normandy countryside and that he would do better to press on to Dieppe, where they were both supposed to be going. He felt Johannes would try and make his way there if he was not caught by the enemy. Once there, Werner waited two days, sleeping rough and living off any scraps he could find. Better live like a dog for a couple of days than get killed as a man with his whole life ahead of him.

'On the third day, at his wits' end, he trudged all the way back to the patch of country where he and Johannes had got separated. He came across a farmer and asked him whether he'd seen a stranger, a teenage boy, anywhere. He had trouble, though, convincing the farmer he was not a German spy. He had trouble convincing him he was not German but Austrian, though this, quite evidently, was no better a recommendation. He took leave of the farmer, feeling he had failed to win his trust. He might even report Johannes to the police or the armed forces. However, something happened as he and the farmer were walking away from each other. The farmer began whistling a tune but then broke off. Werner knew the tune: he whistled it from the note at which the farmer had stopped. The farmer turned around, smiled, and carried on whistling when Werner stopped. Then Werner picked up the tune. Finally, the farmer called out to Werner and asked him if he would care to have a meal at his place. The two walked off together.

Over a glass of Calva in the farmer's kitchen, the farmer told Werner he'd glimpsed an unfamiliar young boy on his land a short while ago. How long ago? Three days? Werner asked. Right. He had shouted he was trespassing and fired his shotgun into the air to scare the boy. But then the farmer had had a change of heart and decided to go after the boy to see exactly what he was about. He walked back to his farmstead, got into his van and started scouring the local roads. He tracked Johannes down and, even though they had no common language, managed to discover that he was trying to get to England.

'The farmer said he had fishermen friends who could help him cross the Channel. So he drove Johannes to a fishing port, gave him a meal at a café, and then took him to meet some fishermen who agreed to take Johannes out in their boat and link up with the first Royal Navy vessel they came across. Two days later, the farmer learned from the same fishermen that they had transferred the boy to a Royal Navy ship. That was the last the farmer heard of the boy.'

'How do we find out where he is now? Whom can we appeal to for information?' Heinrich asked Tom Oliver.

'I'll see what I can do. I'm expecting Werner to be here in a day or two. If Johannes is with the British armed forces, they will naturally have a lot of questions to ask him. Get info out of him on the one hand, and check he is not a spy on the other. Perhaps you would like a schnapps as a nightcap to calm you both down.'

Kristina nodded, surprising her son since he had always known her as teetotal. Tom Oliver hailed the waiter and asked for a bottle — rather than four glasses — of schnapps.

'Your Johannes is getting us drinking a lot tonight,' said Oliver to Kristina.

The waiter soon returned to their table and again whispered in Tom Oliver's ear. As he was doing so, three men appeared at the top of the stairs at the entrance to the room where they were dining. One of them came up to their table and asked for a word in private with Tom Oliver. Standing on the landing, Tom Oliver listened as the stranger spoke, from time to time knitting his brows. Then he came back to their table:

'Frau Lichtblau, the gentlemen request you go with them.'

She got up and joined the three men.

'You'll need your coat. We can't talk here.'

They showed Kristina their police identification papers — they were in plain clothes — and told her they were going to the police station. There they explained why they wanted to talk to her:

'We gather you know your son boarded a British Navy vessel. He was brought to England. After the ship had docked, the ship's captain decided to take him to the local police station, where he was to register as you have done in Oxford. So the captain turned the boy over to our colleagues in Southampton. He cooperated with them and told them he was hoping to join you. The colleagues offered to arrange transport for him up here to Oxford, and he accepted. The man who was due to drive him walked with him out of the police station and pointed out to him the car they'd be taking him in.'

'Kind of your colleagues,' said Kristina.

'The bad news is still to come. The driver told him he had forgotten something or other in the station and went back to get it. When he came back out a minute later, your son was gone.'

'How long ago was this?'

'Three days ago,' replied the policeman. 'You will understand that because of the war, our police departments are undermanned, at least on the civil level. But we cannot be sure your son is not a spy or an infiltrator until we manage to track him down. Why did he give our Southampton colleagues the slip if he had nothing to hide?'

'How do you know he was giving them the slip?' Kristina replied. 'You seem to be saying no one you know saw him leave. Maybe he was kidnapped. Maybe one of your colleagues kidnapped him. Maybe once he was spotted as a native German speaker, he was either taken away to be forced into being useful to the war effort or used as a pawn either by or against the enemy.'

'Our Southampton colleagues are unlikely to have kidnapped him. We can speculate till the cows come home.'

'You could conduct an inquiry into your own forces.'

'We're short of staff at the moment, as I've just explained. We just want to concentrate on catching —'

'You mean finding,' Kristina broke in.

'We want to find and question him.'

'Just find him. Then there'll be plenty of time for questioning him. First things first.'

'Does he know anyone in England apart from you and your son?'

'Not that I know of. As you know, we're here thanks to the good offices of Professor Oliver.'

'Professor Oliver is a good man, but he leads a life that is rather —'

'Risqué?' ventured Kristina.

'Just the word.'

'I don't care how he leads his life. He's saved our lives.'

'But your son is missing.'

'That has nothing to do with Tom Oliver.'

'Tom Oliver has a broad network of contacts in all kinds of places and countries. I do not suspect him personally, far from it. But can he be sure that all his contacts are honest and discreet?'

'As I say, he got us through to England. My son may be on his way to Oxford this minute. He may just have wanted to get away from officialdom, authority and police questioning and make his own way to Oxford in freedom.'

The best plan was to drive down to Southampton and scour the area around the police station and further afield. Kristina set off in the early morning and arrived at noon. She met up with the Southampton colleagues and talked with the two who had questioned Johannes, as well as the one who had been due to drive him to Oxford. The latter was still unable to comprehend how the young man had been able to disappear so fast and so utterly. If he had got away of his own volition, he must have been looking out for an opportunity to do so. The Southampton police did not believe the young man was a spy or malevolent. But they could not rule out his being an excellent actor. Yet he had appeared grateful for the offer of a lift to Oxford and had shown no animosity towards the police — if anything, quite the contrary. The whole thing did not add up.

'I suggest we spend the rest of the day scouting around, maybe asking the locals a few questions. With his Germanic accent, the boy will not have gone unnoticed if he's tried to talk to anyone. But you say no one has come forward to report speaking to a teenager with such an accent?'

The Southampton colleagues shook their heads. One of them said, 'You'd better hurry. You'll have to stop looking once the curfew falls.'

After a fruitless afternoon's search, they checked into a hotel. The next day they returned to the police station, but there was nothing further anyone could say or do for them there. Just this: 'We'll look for him as and when we can.' Kristina had sunk into silence. It was ironic that having crossed Europe in one of the most dangerous periods in the continent's history, her son should vanish in what was supposed to be a safe country: at the very least, the army or police would have noticed him, heard his Germanic accent and taken him in for questioning. But apparently, this had just not happened. Had nobody in the town spoken to a foreign-sounding teenager? He might be being held prisoner, and if that was the case, how could they find him? Every house in and around town would have to be searched, and even then, there was no guarantee of finding him.

Neither Kristina nor the Oxford policeman knew where to continue their search for the boy. The sea air stung them with its coldness. Soldiers, sailors and a few civilians were walking around the streets. Suddenly a voice called out to Kristina from behind, but quietly, whispering in German: *Erinnerst du dich nicht an mich?* 'Don't you remember me?' She turned around. The Oxford policeman did not seem to have heard the voice and carried on walking. But he soon stopped, only to see Kristina in conversation with a tall, bearded man. Seagulls wheeled above their heads. Kristina glanced at the face and recognized the man at once, despite the beard, which was new to her.

'Markus Jäger.' Kristina looked unimpressed. 'How long have you been working for the Reich? You and your brother. And all the time, you were trying to make out how much better you were than him, how much more moral. Haven't the Nazis realized you're no good to them?'

'If I were no good to them, I wouldn't be here now.'

'What do you want?'

'We'll see what I want in a minute. It's what you want that interests me.'

By this time, the Oxford policeman had joined them. 'Who is this man?'

'I'd be much obliged,' Kristina replied, 'if you'd leave us alone for a few minutes.'

'That I cannot do, Ma'am. This man may be able to help us with our inquiries.'

'Quite. But this man may have information to impart to me which he might be loath to give unless he were alone with me.'

Markus Jäger again spoke to Kristina in German: 'If you want to continue our discussion, you'll have to lose your friend here.'

Kristina nodded. She said to the policeman: 'Just as I thought. He refuses to speak to me in your presence. He claims to know where Johannes is but won't reveal anything while you're here. If you would just for a few minutes be kind enough to move about ten yards down the road, he and I will be able to talk, and you to keep an eye on him.'

Markus Jäger said to Kristina in German, 'Anything I may be able to tell you will depend on absolute assurances from this man that I will go free as soon as our conversation is over.'

Meanwhile, Jäger refused to look the policeman in the eye or even look at him at all. Kristina noticed a tic that Jäger had always had ever since she knew him in Vienna, which was that whenever he was under strain, his hands would start to shake. She could make out this tic even when, as now, Markus Jäger had his hands in his pockets. She said to the policeman, who had by now walked some yards away: 'Look, sir, you've been very good to my family and me. But this man has led me to believe he has information about my son. He will only pass on that information to me on the condition you let him go free.'

'What sort of assurance does he want?' the policeman replied.

Kristina returned to Jäger.

'He asks what kind of assurance you want.'

'That if I tell you about your son, I will be entirely left to my own devices, free to go about my business and not followed or made the object of a police hunt.'

She went back to the policeman. 'He'll tell me about my son if you agree to leave him alone. Just bear with me, please, and nod your head.' The policeman did so.

She returned to Jäger. 'He agrees to your demand as long as what you tell me helps us get my son back safe and sound.'

'What do you think?' said Jäger.

'I think that at this point, there are no guarantees on either side. I think it's up to you to show me you know where Johannes is. I just want my son restored to me. What goes on between the police and you is no concern of mine.'

'Yes. But I'll only tell you about your son as long as I can be sure the police won't worry me. If they do, you and your family may regret it.'

'That's enough,' replied Kristina, 'I won't be threatened in this way by you or anyone else. You seem to know something about my son; otherwise, you wouldn't have mentioned him to me first. If you intend to be helpful, be so now and come to the point. Otherwise, I withdraw from any further discussion with you and leave you to the mercy of the police.'

'Come with me, but your friend must stay here. He is to stay where he is until we are out of eyeshot. And if I see him or any of his colleagues coming after us, I'll shoot you and your son instantly.'

Kristina walked back to the policeman. 'He says if I go with him now, he'll be helpful to me. He says you are to stay where you are. He says he'll shoot my son and me if he sees you or your colleagues coming after us. I suggest you and your colleagues keep as far away from us as possible.'

'I give you my word we will carry out the most discreet possible search for you that you can imagine. Nevertheless, you must realize my hands are not going to be tied by this German,' the policeman replied.

'He is not German but Austrian.'

'Tied by this Austrian whose presence in this country is dubious, to say the least, and who claims to know your son's whereabouts if he isn't holding him hostage, perhaps with accomplices. How he got here and what he's doing here are questions I am naturally keen for him to answer.'

Kristina nodded and hurried back to Jäger: 'He agrees to stay away from you as long as I get my son back.'

'Come with me, then. If I see he's moved an inch from the spot where he is now, I'll kill him, you and your son.'

Jäger turned round so that he now had his back to the policeman. Then he started walking away. Kristina followed him just slightly behind. She had one hand behind her back as she walked and shook her hand up and down to tell the policeman not to budge. Once or twice Jäger turned round to make sure the policeman had not moved. He and Kristina inevitably came to a bend in the road, and the policeman lost sight of them.

'Start running,' said Jäger, 'Run alongside me and don't stop till I do.'

But Jäger did not stop.

'You know Josef is dead. He died here in England,' he said to Kristina as they ran. She did not respond. She tried not to listen to him but to keep all her strength for running and for concentrating on the thought of finding her son. But Jäger would not let her think her own thoughts. He started running jerkily, zigzagging from one pavement to the other, alternately slowing down and speeding up, shouting to Kristina as they ran how needless his brother's death had been. They had by this time reached the northern outskirts of Southampton. Shadows stretched out from chestnut and lime trees. Kristina wondered whether she would ever see her son again.

'It was because of you my brother died,' said Jäger, still running. 'You turned him over to the Gestapo. You told them lies about him.'

'Nonsense,' said Kristina, 'I have never turned anyone over to the Gestapo.'

'I'm here because you're responsible for my brother's death.'

'I'm not responsible for your brother's death. True, I have never been your friend or your brother's. I have never approved of you. But I'm no informer. And you are a hypocrite. You and your brother used to be enemies. Then you went over to the Nazis, the side your brother was on, the side Hellroth was on. Hellroth and your brother fighting on the ground over a woman. It was ridiculous. They deserved each other. Suddenly you started feeling some kind of perverse loyalty to your brother. But in any case, he's dead now. Perverse or not, your loyalty comes too late. You'd do better to turn yourself over to the English.'

What else can I say to stall him? thought Kristina.

'If the English knew who you were — and most likely they do, by now — if they knew about your past, you wouldn't be alive speaking to me now,' she said.

'You'd like to turn me over to the English, wouldn't you?' he snarled.

'The English will get you sooner or later. Your brother's dead, Jäger. Nothing either of us does or says can bring him back to life. As for me, all I want is my son back. That's why you wanted me to come with you, isn't it? Or was it to get revenge on me for your brother? You can kill my son before my eyes and then kill me. But it won't bring your brother back to life. It won't change the past. Think of the future. How do you expect to get out of England alive? The war's as good as over now. Your position's untenable. Whatever you do now, try to flee back to the Continent, stay in England, set me free, keep me prisoner – you'll be treated as exactly what you are: a Nazi or Nazi collaborator. Give yourself up. If you know where my son is, say so. Tell the English what you know. So far, you're only making things worse for yourself and me.'

'Your husband's poetry did him no good, did it?' Jäger said. He hated the Lichtblaus for being everything he wanted to be but had not tried hard enough to be.

'So it was you who betrayed him to the Nazis. First, my husband. And now you want my son's life, and perhaps mine, too.'

Kristina tried to slow down her step imperceptibly to give the police as long as possible to find her, Jäger and, above all, her son. When she slowed down, Jäger did so too, so that, she concluded, he must be getting tired. They had left behind the main roads and were slow running over scrubland where sparse heather grew, and here and there stood occasional beech copses. Did Jäger really know where her son was? Had he, in fact, already killed him? Kristina felt that, like his brother, Jäger was the kind of man who was quite capable of playing games of deceit, especially when he was under pressure. All she knew was that, if his story were true, he had somehow gone after Johannes, entrapped him, and was now trying to blackmail her. Why had the authorities not spotted and arrested Jäger before he had accosted her in the street? She wondered how to stall their progress even more. If her son was still alive, he could surely wait a little while longer. After that, there would be enough time for the police to set up a cordon and close in on Jäger.

'If you try and involve the police in our business, I will do my utmost to kill you and as many of your family and friends as I can,' said Jäger as though reading Kristina's mind. 'And don't walk so hesitantly. If you try to get me to lag, I'll make you pay for it, and your son will suffer all the more. He has not eaten for two days.'

'Show me my son, and then we'll see what there is to do.'

'You are in no position to bargain,' said Jäger, 'Your son's life matters to you, doubtless more than your own does. But mine doesn't matter to me or anyone else.'

'It matters to me,' replied Kristina, 'especially for my son's sake.'

By now, they had come away from the scrubland, running in what seemed to Kristina like a suburban street, with detached houses behind fences and high iron front gates. Jäger pushed Kristina in front of him and held her arm, guiding her through a half-open gate. The front door was at the top of three steps. Lights were on in the porch and inside the house. A man stood at the top of the three steps. Kristina noticed that the man's features were creased and sere; he was frowning. He did not acknowledge her presence. The three of them went inside. Jäger and the other man jostled Kristina into the living room, locked the door and pocketed the key.

'He's gone.'

'What do you mean, 'gone'?' Jäger replied.

'I got called out on urgent business yesterday evening. I was away an hour at most. When I came back, he had vanished.'

'How could he have escaped?'

'The padlock on the cellar box where we put him had been broken off, and the door to the cellar had been unlocked and locked up again, even though I had the only key in my pocket all the time, and still have it in my pocket.'

Jäger flopped into an armchair and covered his face in his hands.

'If he was under lock and key, behind two locks, three if you count the front door, how could he get away?'

'Someone may have come and freed him while I was out, unless he let himself out somehow.' Then the man turned on Jäger:

'You should not have left me alone here with the boy.'

'You should not have gone out and left him in the house on his own. You were supposed to keep guard every second of the day. Your business must have been truly urgent.'

'No good going into that now.'

'The police will be looking for us as we speak. If we stay here, they'll find us, and fast. We need to get away now.'

'And forget about the boy?'

'We can use this woman' — he indicated Kristina — 'as a hostage and human shield.'

'How little you value your own lives,' Kristina said. 'You can't hope to win. The war is all but over. Give yourselves up, and face judgment, but stop persisting on this ruinous path that can't do you or anyone else any good.'

'I'll get my gun,' the man said, ignoring her words, 'and we'll drive off out of here.'

Jäger said: 'What's the plan once we're out of Southampton?'

'We'll deal with that later. We agree it would be suicide to stay here any longer.' The man went over to a desk and unlocked a drawer, but after a second turned to Jäger: 'My gun's not here.'

Jäger said nothing.

'You've taken my gun, haven't you?'

'Don't be ridiculous,' Jäger said.

'You saw me put it in here the other day. No one else did, as you know.'

'The boy must have taken it on his way out.'

Kristina tried to make her presence as inconspicuous as possible. The longer these two went on arguing, the more chance there was of the police tracking them down, if they weren't already in the vicinity. She started slowing her breathing down. She thought of either feigning some kind of epileptic fit or pretending to faint. Such behavior, she thought, would serve to confuse them even further, although they might conceivably decide to kill her on the spot. But just then, all three of them heard a muffled noise coming from outside, and then another.

'You stay with her,' the man said to Jäger, 'I'll go and see what the noise was.'

When he was out of the room, Kristina said to Jäger, 'What if we do leave this place? How far are we going to get? Come clean, I say again. The game's up. If the English take you prisoner by force, they're not likely to treat you delicately.'

'Such a prospect doesn't scare me. I have fought nobly for —'

'You have fought ignobly for a deadly, hollow regime. Deadly because hollow. You have, in fact, not fought for anything except yourself. You are a profiteer. Change your ways.'

Jäger was about to reply, not realizing Kristina was playing games with him, when the man came back into the room:

'My car. Someone has punctured two of my tires with bullets. We can't leave, not by car at least.'

Kristina kept a fleeting smirk to herself. 'Don't you think it's time you gave yourselves up? Pretty soon now, they're going to find you anyway.'

The man was about to slap Kristina across the face, but Jäger stopped him. 'We have nothing to gain by striking the woman.'

'For now,' the man said.

'Didn't you see anyone prowling around?' Jäger said.

'No one.'

Suddenly the window of the living room smashed inward, and the door burst open. Jäger and the man were so surprised that they could only submit to the masked armed men who had invaded the room, two through the window and two through the door. As they did so, they shouted obscenities and let out cries like animal shrieks. Two of them held Jäger down, two the other man. They did not touch Kristina, and one of them addressed her by name, telling her that her son was safe and sound. The policeman who had spoken with her in the street must have described her and Jäger to his colleagues. She decided they had told her about her son in order to let Jäger and his friend know that all their plans had come to nothing.

'We will take these men to local army headquarters. Then we will escort you to where your son is.'

All seven of them — Kristina, the four masked men, Jäger and his accomplice — went out of the house and walked to the police van parked a few streets away. When they got there, Kristina saw a whole line of police cars and army trucks parked one behind the other. Some sirens flashed, though soundless. Some soldiers came up to them and, after a brief word with the man in charge of the masked men, led Jäger and his friend away, blindfolding them at once.

Jäger called out in German, 'Blast you and your son, Kristina. You're the real reason I'm here, damn you!' He *even has a wife*, Kristina thought. *Or had*. One of the masked men asked Kristina what Jäger had said, but she merely replied, 'He's bitter he's been caught, that's all, and Johannes and I are free.'

Twenty-Nine

In the heart of the Home Counties countryside, they at length turned off the main road and down a side road, but he had no idea where he was going. Road signs seemed to have vanished a half-hour before. The car turned off the side road into a leafy lane, then a dirt track with patches where gravel chippings had been put down to smooth the surface and fill pot-holes. Still, the car bumped and had to slow down as it rolled over stones or dips in the road. Along the road, it pulled out of the cover of a wooded area and into open country. It went straight on and at the top of a hill, on the other side of an expanse of bracken which the car skirted, stood a brick-red mansion and a smaller white house on the side of the hill.

'Your son is here,' said the driver as the car pulled up in the car park at the top of the hill where many civilian and army vehicles were parked. Two men came out of the mansion, one dressed in military uniform, the other — Kristina saw at once — her son, Johannes. Kristina rushed to greet him.

'I've been here for three days. The food is great. So are the people.'

'What have you been doing?' she asked.

'Answering their questions about how I got here and about conditions in Europe and Vienna. Anything of interest I saw on the way to England. They told me you were with the Southampton police and would soon be coming to see me.'

'To see you? I've come to take you to Oxford.'

'I want to stay here for a while, Mother.'

Kristina noticed that her son, despite mentioning food before people, had matured since she last saw him in Vienna. He was turning into an adult, as though the war and the journey together had made him so.

'They've asked me to stay on. They say they'll pay for my education as soon as the new academic year begins. They have few native German speakers to draw on. I want to be part of the war effort, even if the war is almost over. And of the peace effort. They do indispensable work here. And I've met two gentlemen, Alan and David, who are working on a computer program they've got me playing chess with.'

'What happened with Jäger, and how did you get away from him?' Kristina asked.

'I found myself in the streets of Southampton. Jäger was there and spotted me, unless he somehow already knew I was there. He accosted me, seemed friendly and made out he wanted to help me. He took me to this house where there was a friend of his. His friend pointed a gun at me, which he put away in a drawer once I had convinced him I was harmless. They locked me in the cellar but otherwise did not mistreat me. Jäger wanted to know where you were. I told him you were somewhere on the continent. He said you must be in England because his brother had died in England because of you. I told him I didn't know anything about that. He said that when we had stayed with him in Vienna, he had taken us in in good faith but had started to become wary of us after we had snooped around in his flat.

'His friend started to get excited and kept asking Jäger why he had brought me back to the house. He seemed to mean he and Jäger had better things to do — what, they didn't say in front of me — and that I was a liability which could only attract the attention of anyone: the police or the authorities, neighbors or passers-by.

'On the second day, they agreed that Jäger would go out all day and the friend stay in to make sure I didn't move, even though I was already shut up in a large cage-like box in the cellar. They gave me food and water, but I didn't know why they were holding me or what they intended to do with me. I heard the friend moving about on the ground floor above me till mid-afternoon it must have been. Then the front door opened and shut, and the house fell silent. By the sound of it, the friend had had a heated phone conversation; his leaving the house most likely had something to do with that. After maybe twenty minutes, I heard feet shuffling above me and a dog barking. I began knocking on the cellar ceiling with a broom handle that had been lying about in the cellar. There was a sudden silence above me. Again, I banged on the ceiling. Then, in a flash, the cellar door opened, and a group of men rushed down the cellar stairs. They were British army, and I was now in safe hands. They rushed me up the cellar stairs, locked the cellar door and took me out of the house. They told me that I would be protected from now on and that you were safe in Oxford. They wanted to take me to a certain secret service house but only if I agreed to go; otherwise, they would drive me straight to Oxford. I was happy to go to this house they were talking about as long as they would explain to me why they wanted to take me there. Their Intelligence Service colleagues could give me some work that would help put the finishing touches to the Allies' war effort. So here I am. I'm useful here. I like it, and I want to stay. I'll come to Oxford later, when the war's over.'

Kristina glanced away from her son and looked around. To the right of the house, she could see angelica-green fields, some with cows grazing in them, stretching away as far as the eye could see. Her gaze traveled to behind the house where the forest they had passed through on the way also lay. Her son seemed happy where he was. He did not need his mother as he had done only a few months before. She laid her hand momentarily on her son's shoulder and then turned and walked away. There would be time enough to tell him the news of his father's death.

Thirty

Tom Oliver had just been speaking on the phone to Southampton Police. Kristina had gone to a British Intelligence office to meet up with her son, who had expressed his desire to stay on there for a while. He now phoned that office.

'Kristina Lichtblau has seen her son and is satisfied all is well with him. She is now heading back to Oxford.'

'Has she left yet?' asked Oliver.

'Her car is just pulling out of the car park.'

'I have something urgent to tell her. Please try and call her back and get her to come to the phone.'

'Hold on a minute. But I can't guarantee anything.'

After three or four minutes Kristina, panting, came on the line. 'It's Heinrich,' said Tom Oliver. 'He said this morning he was feeling weak. Then he fainted. We managed to revive him, but he's still weak and is lying in bed.'

'Has a doctor seen him?' she asked, concerned.

'The doctor is with him now. He says Heinrich will have to be hospitalized. The doctor will be calling an ambulance as soon as we finish our conversation. Come back without delay. It would be better if Johannes came with you.'

Kristina relayed all this to one of the Intelligence office secretaries, who went to look for Johannes.

Nobody spoke in the police car as, sirens blaring, they sped north towards Oxford. They went to Tom Oliver's lodgings first, but there was no one in. As they were on their way out of the college, the porter was standing outside his lodge:

'You looking for Professor Oliver?'

When Kristina replied that they were, the porter, an off-hand, bad-tempered young man, asked which one of them went by the name of Lichtblau.

'I am Kristina Lichtblau and this is my son.'

'I don't care who he is. If that's your name, Professor Oliver' – here he coughed and spat on the ground – 'has left you a message.'

He handed Kristina an envelope with her name on it. It was burnt on one edge. 'Why is it burnt?' asked Kristina.

'I smoke, don't I?' said the porter, as though that were sufficient explanation.

When Kristina laid her fingers on the envelope, the porter clung onto it, looking her in the eye. She let go of the envelope and fished in her bag for a coin. When she tended it to the man, he took it, spat on it and, with an oath, threw it on the ground. Kristina then took her wallet from her bag, opened it, withdrew a note and held it out to the man. The latter snatched it and, still staring Kristina insolently in the eye, grabbed a wad of banknotes from the wallet, at the same time handing over the envelope for good this time.

'These two gentlemen are policemen,' Kristina told him, gesturing to the two who had accompanied her and Johannes.

'I don't care who they are,' muttered the porter, spitting on the ground again, 'I deserve this.' He sauntered back into his lodge.

Kristina tore open the charred envelope. 'Urgent. Come to Radcliffe. Am going now with Heinrich. Tom.'

When they went to reception at the Radcliffe, they were directed to the fourth floor. They found Tom Oliver and Heinrich, along with Thedel, Heike, Werner, Dagmar, and Ilse, who had gone back to Oxford for now thanks to Soubrenie's connections and with his blessing, standing outside the door of a private room.

'The doctor is with him now,' said Tom Oliver.

The doctor in his white coat soon came out of the room.

'He seems to be falling into a coma. Don't disturb him for a while. He needs to rest.'

'This is the first I've heard of his illness,' said Kristina, 'I saw him only three days ago, and he was perfectly fine.'

'He seems to have some kind of illness which went previously undetected.'

'I must see him,' said Kristina.

'As you wish,' replied the doctor, 'though you must realize how frail he is. I'll bring you some masks to put over your mouths. You wouldn't want him to catch an infection. Please wait here.'

The doctor disappeared. He came back a few moments later carrying a bundle of masks. However, he did not give them the masks straight away. Instead, he looked at Kristina.

'I thought you might like to know there is a man at the reception desk on this floor asking to see you.'

'What's his name?' asked Kristina.

'I don't know and didn't ask. I told him to wait where he was.'

Johannes said what his mother was already thinking: 'What are we to do if this is Jäger?'

Kristina did not flinch. 'Please give us our masks, and we will look in on my son. This man will have to wait, whoever he is. If you decide to throw him out, you'll get no complaints from me.'

'He seemed quite peaceable,' said the doctor. 'He has a Germanic accent.'

Tom Oliver said, 'I'll go and see who he is if you like, Frau Lichtblau.'

'I just want to see my son,' said Kristina. 'Whoever this man is, he is not wanted at this time.'

The whole party except Tom Oliver put on their masks and filed into Heinrich Lichtblau's room. He lay pale and lifeless-looking, his eyes open and staring up toward the ceiling. He showed no response when Kristina kissed his cheek and took his hand, nor when she tried to talk to him. Ilse and Dagmar tried in turn but were equally unsuccessful. Johannes was too overwhelmed with emotion to approach his brother. A nurse went back and forth, bringing chairs for the visitors.

Tom Oliver came back. All the visitors turned to look at him as he walked into the room. 'The visitor with the German accent is Austrian. We spoke in German. He tells me he does not wish to impose. He says he knows you and your family well.'

'How dare Jäger behave like this, following us around and pretending to be a friend?' Johannes cried out, 'How did he escape from the police? Why isn't he in custody? He deserves to be. He ended up giving in to his attraction to the Nazis. And anyway, after the way he imprisoned me —'

'Johannes is right. He's a distraction,' Kristina said. 'He should be in prison. Why is he stalking us?'

'He wants an answer,' said Tom Oliver. 'He says if you don't want him here, he'll go.' Heinrich's breathing grew perceptibly louder. Kristina held his hand tighter.

'The hospital authorities must deal with him before he kills us all,' said Johannes.

'What makes you think his intentions are malevolent?' said Tom Oliver.

'He's a good actor,' said Johannes. 'That's how he lured me to the house where he imprisoned me. We knew him in Vienna. He used to be better than this.'

'We can't go on arguing like this all day,' Kristina said. 'We must find out who he is. Tom, kindly show the man in.'

Tom Oliver did as requested. All eyes turned to see Alfred Nubik walk into the room.

Nubik's face told them what had happened. He said, 'He was going to kill you. All of you.'

'Then why didn't he kill me?' asked Johannes.

'For two reasons. He reasoned that if he killed you, he would not be able to kill the rest of you as the police would have nabbed him all the quicker. Second, he hoped you would take him to your family. Then he would have had the satisfaction of killing you all together.'

'How do you know all this?' asked Heinrich.

The doctor exclaimed, 'That's the first time he's spoken in days!'

Nubik continued, 'I kept watch on him in Vienna. I saw him on several occasions by the Pestsäule, always at the same time of day, conferring with a group of shady-looking men. I saw them exchange money and documents. Then I followed him to England. I lost track of him for a while but found him again last night. He had managed to escape from the police. He was in a murderous mood. He was planning to come to Oxford to kill you all.'

Kristina kissed her son's forehead. 'You must sleep now.'

Heinrich smiled and closed his eyes.

Nubik was the first to leave the room. The others filed out as quietly as possible. Heinrich followed them with his eyes. They felt like celebrating. It was May 8th, 1945, and the war was over that very day. Churchill had announced it.

Kristina, Johannes and their friends were trooping downstairs, making for the hospital exit. They all walked out into the early evening red Oxford sunlight. Kristina could just hear someone whistling a Strauss waltz somewhere. She smiled to herself.

The shadows of night were falling. They were not invasive here.

A few days earlier, when Kristina had been in Southampton, Tom Oliver had picked up two letters for her at the porter's lodge. Although he had always believed in the inviolable privacy of any mail, he had, for the first time in his life, decided to open someone else's letters. The envelope of one was blank except for the addressee's name and address. He took it upon himself to open it, thinking it might be some kind of threat to Kristina that he wanted to intercept. But it was not a threat. It was postmarked January 1945. It read:

Dear Frau Lichtblau,

You never paid me much attention, but I want to tell you how sorry I am about your husband.

I recently decided to leave my husband and want nothing more to do with him ever again. He is dead to me. If I survive the war, I will go to America, where I have relatives. However, my ex-husband and his brother have decided to go to England separately and without telling each other. They seem to think they have ways and means of getting into the country. Josef has heard about the Oxford professor and wants to kill him. Markus will harm your family any way he can. If you receive this letter in time, you will be able to tell the British authorities before these brothers can carry out their evil plans. By the way, Frau Lichtblau may have heard the name of Gunter Lantz while she was in Paris. He turned traitor to the Nazis, who dealt with him as they saw fit. He had time to get some sad news through to me: despite his best efforts to save them, Françoise Berg, her family and her best girlfriend were sent to the chambers.

Ursula Muller (ex-Jäger)

Tom Oliver decided that he would keep the letter and give it to Kristina when things had settled down.

The envelope of the other one carried a December 1944 postmark and bore a swastika. It was a bill. Since opening it, he had carried it around in his pocket. He would not give it to Felix Lichtblau's widow. He took the bill out of his pocket, lit a match and watched it flare up in the darkness. When the flames started to burn his fingers, he dropped the paper. It flew up into the air.

'Where's Nubik?' Kristina asked suddenly.

But amid the shadows of night, Nubik was nowhere to be seen. Nevertheless, Kristina was confident: 'He will not be far away.'

Even though the threat of ravens was gone, he would not be returning to their old city, for now at least. Vienna was bombed out. The old life had turned to dust and ashes.

She little thought that Nubik was heading for Munich, for the house at 9, Friedrichstrasse. He had found an old rifle in a disused barn in the countryside around Munich, as well as a box of matches and a canister of fuel. When he got to the house, it was so rundown Nubik wondered how anyone could still live in it. He opened the gate, walked to the house and looked through the window. He made out an old man slouched in a shabby armchair, surrounded by tins of food and photos everywhere of a soldier in uniform whom Nubik recognized.

The old man was poring over a letter. Perhaps he was weeping: the room was dark, and the old man was standing in shadows so that Nubik could not see clearly. Nubik loaded the rifle with bullets he had in his pocket, took the cap off the fuel canister and took a match from the box.

He could sense that something was tugging him back to the English university town where starlings nested in the college eaves and ravens — which Noah, he delighted to think, had not left out his ark — perched in the tulip tree of a certain Master's garden. Nubik was about to bash the window in, but he abruptly changed his mind. He turned around and went back to the street, poured the fuel into the gutter, put the match back in the box, emptied the bullets out of the rifle, snapped it in two across his knee, tossed the pieces away. He withdrew from his coat pocket a crumpled piece of paper which someone – he did not know who – had shoved into it while he had been in Oxford, and which he had not yet read. He uncrumpled it. All that was written on it was: 'STARS 412 over. STARS amid dreaming spires now.' He folded up the message, put it back in his coat pocket, and began making plans.

Acknowledgements

I would like to thank the following:

My wife Natacha and children Julia, Dylan, John, Mary-Carolyn and James, my mother-in-law Elisabeth and all my in-laws, my cousins, friends, neighbors, students, and colleagues everywhere, Zéline Guena for her expert literary advice and unfailing support for this book and, of course, my editors at Histria.

My family would never forgive me if I omitted to mention our wonderful chocolate labrador, Bobby. He likes to chase the wild birds of Paris when he gets the chance but has, fortunately, not caught any – so far!

 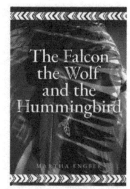 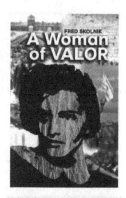
 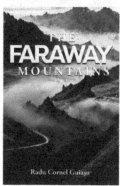